Praise for Suzette Hollingsworth's novels

"The Great Detective in Love" series is a finalist in the Chanticleer Mystery & Mayhem awards, Goethe Awards for Historical Fiction, International Book Awards, and Readers' Choice Book Awards.

"A Sherlock tale with Hepburn and Tracy flair . . . It had the feel of a classic old Hollywood mismatched romantic comedy to me.... Hepburn and Tracy. It was charming and would really appeal to people who love the idea of a kind of Jane Austen meets Conan Doyle mash-up." - RaynaRed, Audible reviewer

"Cumberbatch/Sherlock meets his match!" - Jan, Audible reviewer

"Sherlock in Mr. Darcy mode . . . " - PandaRS, Audible reviewer

"Irene Adler has competition" - Mary, Audible reviewer

"A GREAT ROMP FOR A FUN TIME OUT!" – Amazon reviewer

"Very well done watch out Johnny Lee Miller and J. Brett and B. Cumberbatch and Robert Downey Jr., this is the real deal" – Byron, Amazon reviewer

"A delightful female counter view to Sir Conan Doyle. An intelligent and fun read with just the right amount of Victorian sexual tension." – Geof, Amazon reviewer

"Suzette has certainly captured Sir Arthur Conan Doyle's style. This is a very good read and would certainly make a very good movie! It was a real 'page turner'." – Charles, Amazon reviewer

"Loved the book and its premise! I enjoy the banter and charged atmosphere between Sherlock and his 'detective in training'! There is a difference in their relationship that cannot be in any way compared to that with Watson. It is actually fun watching Holmes the instructor/trainer, fight his inner awakening more human feelings starting to develop from interest, to admiration to ? Please write on. I am thoroughly enjoying this series!" – Amazon reviewer

"I'm truly enjoying Suzette Hollingsworth's The Great Detective In Love series. I love the actor for the audiobooks as well. . . She keeps the integrity of Sir Conan Doyle's original characterization of Detective Sherlock Holmes and Dr. John H. Watson, while shaping a strong, confident, feminine, and loveable character in Miss Mirabella Hudson. The cases are dark and suspenseful enough without being stab-you-in-the-face scary, while providing scenes of well rounded characters. I hope she continues writing more, as they add a layer and depth to Sherlock Holmes that I've always wanted and hoped for with him. As a massive Sherlock Holmes fan, this series warms my heart, gets it racing, and makes it sing."
– KF, Amazon reviewer

Also by Suzette Hollingsworth

"The Great Detective in Love" mystery series:
Sherlock Holmes and the Case of the Sword Princess
Sherlock Holmes and the Dance of the Tiger
Sherlock Holmes and the Chocolate Menace
Sherlock Holmes and the Vampire Invasion

"Daughters of the Empire" historical romance series:
THE PARADOX: The Soldier and the Mystic
THE SERENADE: The Prince and the Siren
THE CONSPIRACY: The Cartoonist and the Contessa

To be released in 2018:
Sherlock Holmes and the Confirmed Bachelor

Acknowledgements

I must thank, first and foremost, Kris Wilder, who brainstormed the idea for this book over lunch at the 59'er Diner in Cashmere, WA in a 5-minute interval. Yep, he's that good. Kris is a plot wizard, not to mention a creative genius, as well as a bestselling martial arts Amazon author.

I am indebted to the master, Arthur Conan Doyle, who created the captivating characters of Sherlock Holmes and Dr. John Watson, who are so real in our minds that many consider them to be historical figures rather than fictional characters. I have drawn upon "The Sign of Four", chapter 8, by A.C. Doyle, in describing the introduction of the Baker Street Irregulars.

This book would not be possible without my editor/writer/artist husband, Clint Hollingsworth, an award-winning author. I wish to thank all my editors: May Peterson, Kate Richards, and Peter Senftleben.

A special thanks to the following awesome beta readers: Renee Arthur, Lisa Millett, Susan Cambra, and Heather Chargualaf who so generously gave of their time, input, and encouragement. The feedback from these readers is invaluable.

I'm so fortunate to have found the voice actor who produces my audiobooks, Joel Leslie Froomkin, four-time winner of the prestigious earphones award. Joel is a phenomenal talent who brings my books to life and truly turns all books into theatre. He is an amazing actor and has directed Molly Ringwold and Charles Shaughnessy, (of "The Nanny" fame).

To my BFF Charlsie Sterry, D.D.S., who has been to Nicaragua FIVE TIMES to offer her services for free, and who also donates her expertise to Wycliffe in Dallas, TX, all insults to dentistry are for former time periods only. Today, your dentist is as valuable as your doctor. Dentistry is so important to heart health and to all aspects of the body's functioning. There is no longer anything to be afraid of and everything to gain.

Please, do not be afraid of the dentist: there have been enormous strides in pain management in the last ten years alone. My dentist in Washington state, Dr. Aaron Kelly, is state-of-the-art and an expert at pain management as well. You can ask for laughing gas or whatever you need. You might not get it, but you can ask. Dr. Kelly does not supply margaritas however, but it's in the suggestion box. It's the healers who are among our angels in this life: for me, Amy Brazil, Diane Garris, and Dr. Butruille.

To be a writer is a magical journey, to be in a place of creativity and openness to the whispers of the universe. At times it feels like one is in the presence of God, and at other times it feels like one has been punched in the gut. Like all endeavors in life, one can be debilitated and frozen by self-doubt and criticism and nurtured by centeredness, connection, friendship, and listening to the muse.

This has been a difficult time for me, and I am indebted to my friend Moria Gebhard (named from J.R.R. Tolkein's "the mines of Moria"), the sunshine in my life for the past year. I thank Moria for the positive energy, the down-to-earth perspectives, the joy in every day events, the willingness to go to new places and see new things, and, last but not least, the lemon drops. I love Moria's entire family, Luka, Ivan, Kyan, & James "Papa" (the myth, the legend). They are all like art and music: they put the "life" in living.

This book has enabled me to re-visit my friend, Johnny Hooks, who put a smile on my face EVERY time. Johnny was one of the most interesting, fun, lively, amusing people I ever met. I miss him. I have a vivid memory of Johnny in an after-death visit at the Seattle Opera House and stranded on the I-405 corridor. Johnny was one of those people: every encounter with him was brilliantly memorable.

So to all true friends everywhere who keep our dreams alive when they falter in our hearts: Charlsie & Clint Sterry, Susan Bartroff (also a great editor!), Harvey Gover (who was the rock of my childhood and in my heart forever), Virginia Hashii, Amy Brazil, my mother Mary Denison, my grandparents Omah Lock & Marvin Hewitt and readers and friends Michelle Masuda Berry, Valerie Spurlock Bolton, Jilly-Bob Delabano, SueAnn Green, Rena Kohr, Kem Chambers, AnaMaree Ordway, Denae Lancaster, Rex Gordon, Patsy Cantrell, Julie & Zack Hubert. I cherish the SHS class of '75 and the Beach Girls.

"Dreams, unspoken or not, are living whispers inside our hearts. Our whole life's potential lies in the spaces between these whispers. Our dreams want us to say 'yes', to speak their truth." – Kelly Rae Roberts

Sherlock Holmes
and
the Vampire Invasion

Copyright © 2018 by Suzette Hollingsworth

ISBN: 978-0-9975-170-9-5

Cover Design by Fiona Jayde Media
Inside artwork by Clint Hollingsworth
Cameo of Sherlock Holmes and Mirabella Hudson by Clint Hollingsworth

First publication January 20, 2018
Happy Birthday, Shelly Tyler

Imprint: Historical Fiction/Mystery with romantic elements

Printed in U.S.A.

PUBLISHER: Icicle Ridge Graphics

Sherlock Holmes
and the Vampire Invasion

by Suzette Hollingsworth

The Great Detective In Love, Book 4

Sherlock Holmes solves the most perplexing mystery of his life —
unlocking the human heart

To Clint

The light of my life and my everything

Sherlock Holmes and the Vampire Invasion

Chapter One
Without a Case
221B Baker Street

"Mr. Holmes, what has happened to the ice that was in the ice box? Our food will spoil without it." Mirabella Hudson, chief bottle washer and female operative for the Great Detective, closed the metal chest so no more heat would enter into the food storage. The only thing keeping the contents cold was the ice, delivered twice per week, now strangely missing.

Mirabella sighed heavily, miffed at her own frustration. Not that long ago she had been locked in a tiger's cage by a Russian spy. Now she was in search of missing ice. How mundane had her life become in such a short time?

Mirabella had long grown weary of her domestic duties. Even though there was invariably terror and risk where Sherlock's cases were concerned, she found she became bored in their absence. She might not miss the threats on her life, but she, like her employer, did miss the mental stimulation. It was frightening how much she had in common with Sherlock.

"What? The ice? Hmmm. It's in my bedroom," Sherlock replied.

Isn't it cold enough in there? Sherlock's bedroom was a foreboding place she tended to avoid due to the pictures of criminals lining the walls.

Perplexed, she glanced around the galley kitchen corner to face her esteemed employer, his raven black hair framing his face in loose curls, his expression composed but relentless even as his eyes remained focused on the *Police Gazette*.

"Why on earth is the ice in your bedroom?" she asked, moving into the living room in a state of confusion. No day with Sherlock Holmes was ever the same or without surprises, but, honestly, she couldn't imagine what possible reason he would have to take the ice—or to move it into his boudoir.

"I needed it," he said simply, not looking at her.

And Sherlock did not seem predisposed to tell her. He clearly thought this was all the information she required.

Mirabella had a different view of things. She planted herself before him. While she waited for an audience she surveyed her formidable employer. He wore a white silk ascot tie and a purple-blue velvet embossed vest on his muscular frame.

Quite handsome really. As opposed to his frightening intensity and unforeseeable, unstable behavior.

Sherlock's lack of concern for the fact that absconding the kitchen supplies affected her duties was a touch annoying, to say the least. Mirabella appreciated her circumstances, to be sure, but working for Sherlock Holmes was, at best, disorienting, and, at worst, suicidal.

Looking past Sherlock to the wingback chair opposite his, she observed Dr. Watson napping in his chair. Prinnie, his bulldog, sat at the good doctor's feet. Even sleeping, John Watson was immaculately dressed in a three-piece wool suit, his blonde streaked hair perfectly styled. He was dreamy awake—and certainly asleep.

Sleeping in the middle of the day. Everyone was blasé, it seemed to Mirabella. John Watson was the best-tempered of men and not one to require either stimulation or peace; in general, he was pleased with whatever came his way as long as his friends were with him. But even John needed something to do with a patient load of some twelve patients per week. Ambition was not among his many fine qualities.

The Afghanistan war had done that to him. And yet, John Watson had survived and thrived. That must speak to his character.

But back to her immediate problem of locating the ice. "For heaven's sake, there isn't another delivery until Thursday, and I don't know how I'll be able to preserve our groceries at this point."

"Groceries are of little to no concern to me," Sherlock muttered. "And I guarantee heaven has little to do with it."

Mirabella sighed heavily. Honestly, what was she supposed to do? It was enough to attempt to find something to stimulate Sherlock's appetite without his causing the spoilage of the food.

"Yes, I am quite aware of that, no one more so than myself," she said. "But even a machine must have fuel. And if you don't care about your own health, at least think of Dr. Watson."

"Is it time for dinner?" John Watson stirred from his nap with the talk of food. Ever since his army days which had left him emaciated, attached to the Fifth Northumberland Fusiliers as an assistant surgeon, John's appetite had been commendable. It was not clear if a Jezail bullet from enemy lines, enteric fever, or the army food had almost killed him—certainly all had made an attempt. His orderly, Murray, had thrown the doctor across a pack horse in enemy fire and saved him from the first of these assaults, but John thereafter dined on hospital food at the Peshawar Hospital, reversing his orderly's efforts.

"This evening will be your last meal for a few days, Dr. Watson, unless I am able to locate the ice." She returned her gaze to Sherlock. "May I have the ice back, Mr. Holmes?"

"I wouldn't advise it," Sherlock scanned the *Gazette*, still not meeting her eyes.

"Oh, and why is that?"

He glanced up at her, his expression one of indifference. "Go then, and get the ice from my bedroom, if that is what you wish, Miss Hudson."

John momentarily closed his eyes again, clearly unconcerned with the insanity that was Sherlock Holmes.

"Grrrrr! ZZZ-Zzzz." Prinnie, a Bulldog quite obviously bred from a Mastiff, continued snoring, but intermittently there was now growling, probably as he detected Sherlock's voice, even in his slumber.

Believe me, I share your viewpoint, Prinnie. Mirabella moved from Sherlock's laboratory and past the sitting room to Sherlock's sleeping quarters—on those rare occasions when he slept. How anyone could find the images of one's enemies conducive to sleep was a mystery to her. Clearly Sherlock didn't, as evidenced by his playing the violin at 3:00 a.m.

There were many challenges to working for Sherlock Holmes. For one thing, he only utilized her on the cases so dangerous no one else was stupid enough to take them. The Great Detective was a master of disguise, but even he could not play every female role.

And where would he find someone else so lacking in intelligence and self-preservation instincts that she would throw herself into every manner of danger? As well as cook his meals and keep his laboratory organized?

Enter one Mirabella Hudson, who had already lost one position when she came to the Great Detective. Her employment was precarious at best.

And it means the world to me. She was working for the world's finest detective. Sherlock Holmes was a young detective, true, but quickly making a name for himself. If he could only hold his tongue and cease making enemies with the powers that be at Scotland Yard. But Sherlock was not one to feign admiration where none existed nor to alter his course in the pursuit of truth.

As she opened the door to Sherlock's room, she encountered an odd smell. He had obviously been burning incense in here, a practice he had picked up on a recent trip to the Orient, but that didn't account for the essence of pungence meeting her nose.

"AEEeeee!" she screamed, as she beheld the contents of the room. Quickly she exited and slammed the door shut.

"What? Hello?" Dr. Watson exclaimed, fully coming out of his nap.

"Miss Hudson, if you could manage your histrionics, we would all be more comfortable," Sherlock said.

"*I* would be more comfortable if there weren't a corpse in your bedroom."

"First you interrupted my reading of the paper, and now you have awoken Watson." Sherlock shook his head gravely as if she were the one to have committed an uncivilized *faux pas* when he had a corpse in his bedroom.

"Why is there a dead body in your room, Mr. Holmes?"

"Where else should I put it, Miss Belle? You don't suppose I would put a cadaver in the sitting room or the kitchen, do you?"

"Yes I do. I can very well imagine you would."

"Then I've proved you wrong, Miss Hudson." Sherlock muttered under his breath, "We are not barbarians here."

Dr. John Watson and I aren't. "And why is there ice on the body?"

Sherlock stared at her in disbelief, as if he had overestimated her intelligence. "The ice is keeping the body cold."

"Obviously." She placed her hands on her waist as she re-entered the sitting room.

"Then why did you ask?" He raised one eyebrow at her. "Please go about your business and do not waste my time further."

"Mr. Holmes," she repeated. "Why is our ice—all the ice—on the dead body in your room?"

He shook his head in annoyance. "I can see I must spell this out for the unscientific and lazy of mind." He knew very well the pursuit of science was her dream and that he had called both her competence and devotion into question. Sherlock was not one to soften his remarks where he might offend.

I wish to keep this job. I must hold my tongue.

Where else could a young lady find employment which was not factory work, changing the chamber pot, or being a scullery maid? All of which involved twelve hour shifts, six days a week, for very little pay? As well as having one's every waking hour and behavior monitored?

She glanced at the bedroom door. *Surely this position is better?*

"Please do so, sir."

"If it concerns your duties, Miss Hudson—which it does not, recall that I do not answer to you but the other way around—I intend to determine the degree to which ice slows the decaying process." He returned her stare, disappointment apparent in his eyes. "Surely that must be evident. I do not believe in speculation but in science. Speculation only serves to produce theories that must then be tested."

"Hello! There's a dead body in your bedroom, Holmes?" Dr. Watson asked.

"Naturally there is," said Mirabella. "I wondered where the missing table had gone. I don't know why I troubled myself."

"Nor do I." Sherlock shrugged.

"Why is there a cadaver in your bedroom, Holmes?" asked Dr. Watson.

"I only just explained that, Watson." Sherlock replied, snapping his newspaper, clearly exasperated with having to explain that which he presumed to be evident. "To further the study of forensic science."

"Ah, yes. To determine the time of the murder." Watson nodded his head in understanding, even as his expression remained disturbed.

"Precisely. If we can accurately know the time of death, we can eliminate the suspects who have alibis and could not have performed the murder—as well as point directly to the murderer. There can be no conclusions without a concise timetable."

"Who would have thought the study of forensics would provide so much information?" Watson added.

"And that it would be so close to one's kitchen?" Mirabella shuddered.

"As you are well aware, Watson, Scotland Yard has little to no interest in the subject of forensics, and so I must undertake it myself."

"Not perfectly fair, Holmes," Dr. Watson countered. "The Yard has actually begun performing autopsies."

"At my insistence," Sherlock objected. "Prior to my involvement, a murder investigation consisted of attempting to locate eye witness reports rather than investigating the clues at the murder scene."

"Unless the murderer was stupid enough to perform the murder in front of witnesses, there would not be any eye witnesses," Mirabella said.

"Precisely. Whereas clues are always present." Sherlock looked at her with the slightest glimmer of hope in his eyes.

Very slight.

"And, in the absence of an eyewitness, the Yard's second and final method of finding the killer was torturing suspects into a confession," Dr. Watson added.

"Since there was no analysis of the murder scene, the probability of having the actual murderer in custody rather than some unfortunate passer-by was fairly low. At my direction, the police force now attempts to analyze the murder scene for clues." Sherlock sighed heavily. "Astonishing. Perhaps someday we shall even, God forbid, utilize the *fingerprints* at the scene of the crime."

"That would require that the Yard took fingerprints," Dr. Watson said.

"They're still measuring the skulls of all the suspects," Mirabella observed.

"Yes, yes, the Bertillon method," Sherlock muttered impatiently. "A grand waste of time."

Mirabella cleared her throat. "And the body in your bedroom? How long will it remain there?" Mirabella shuddered. "On the table next to your bed?"

"Until I have concluded my experiment, naturally."

"And when will that be?" Mirabella attempted to return the conversation to the pertinent points.

"If I knew that, I would not need to run the experiment, would I?"

"Please hazard a guess." She knew very well that Sherlock's guesses were more accurate than most people's facts.

"Very well. Under ordinary circumstances, I would expect to see discoloration on the skin of the abdomen in two to three days, spreading to the veins in three to four days. On the fifth and sixth days, the abdomen will appear bloated, with internal gas pressure. In three weeks the tissues will have softened, organs and cavities bursting, and the nails falling out."

"Three weeks?" Mirabella exclaimed. "You intend to have a cadaver in your bedroom for three weeks?"

"Oh, no," Sherlock objected. "That would be under normal circumstances. I would expect it to be longer with the ice." A smile of anticipation and delight graced Sherlock's expression. "To be in the center of scientific discovery is glorious, is it not? The *first to know* that which was previously unknown to the entire world."

"Really, Holmes, I don't think . . ." Watson protested, shaking his head. "I can't really fathom having our after dinner sherry in this room with the odor . . ."

Sherlock's disbelief was evident. "The odor will give us information. All of this is data that I will mentally catalogue and utilize to solve future crimes."

Mirabella never thought of Sherlock as childlike. Rather, she imagined he had never been a baby. Surely he had come out of the womb spouting theories and refusing to cry, finding it to be unnecessary and serving no purpose. But at this moment Sherlock did not look to be his eight and twenty years but rather an exuberant boy in the throes of discovery.

The dinner that evening was more solemn than usual, followed by the sherry in the sitting room. After Mirabella had cleaned up the dishes, she sat quietly reading Sherlock's scientific periodicals for some time before deciding to retire to her room below in Aunt Martha's first floor flat.

She was having some difficulty with her conscience over the decaying body in the flat. Was her loyalty to her employer? Or to her Aunt Martha, who owned the building and who housed her?

Mirabella had been with Sherlock over a year, but if anyone interfered with his work, or did not bow down to the god which was Sherlock's vocation, they were out on their ear. On this he was clear.

In the midst of her conflicting reflections, she heard a strange sound.

Oh, no! The corpse has come alive! It no doubt wished to leave. Even a zombie could not bear Sherlock's bedroom.

Terror filled her being as a frantic knock on the door interrupted Mirabella's disturbed thoughts and fueled her guilt.

"Miss Hudson, are you going to answer the door or shall I?" Sherlock asked, his eyes moving to the door.

Her heart did nothing to slow down as Mirabella realized the sound was coming from the entry to the flat.

At this late hour? Mirabella moved to open the door. Standing there before her was the more charming of the Holmes brothers, noticeably shaken. Did Mycroft know about the body in the bedroom as well?

"Miss Hudson," Mycroft Holmes bowed in a distracted fashion. "Is Shirley at home?"

"Yes, sir," she replied. "Are you feeling quite well, Mr. Holmes?" She stood frozen in place studying him. This was the only time she had ever seen Mycroft looking less than polished.

There was nothing unattended to in his dress, but his complexion was almost ashen, in contrast to his ordinarily dashing, unaffected, and stylishly disinterested persona. Even with his being fully four inches taller than Sherlock, who was not lacking in height, and sharing the same mesmerizing grey eyes, Mycroft looked decidedly bedraggled.

Sherlock set his sherry down on the end table abruptly. "What is it Mycroft?"

"It's Percy." Mycroft was breathing heavily. "He's been found dead in his home."

"Lord Percival. Murdered?" Sherlock asked.

"It appears so," Mycroft replied. "But it is quite a peculiar murder scene."

"Oh, and how so?" Sherlock rose from his chair.

"There are marks on his neck. Teeth marks."

Dr. Watson shuddered. "It is not entirely without precedent."

"Perhaps not, but these are different. They look quite like . . . *fangs*."

"Fangs," Dr. Watson repeated, jumping up from his chair. "How on earth?"

"And . . ." Mycroft added, "the body has been drained of all blood."

Chapter Two
The Archway of Tears
Saint Pancras Workhouse

*"We have very little bread, sir. It's an exceedingly
small quantity of bread."*
– Charles Dickens, firsthand account, Marylebone

"Please let me care for my baby. She's only two, and you can see
what she is sick."

Evie had only that day entered the workhouse through a red
brick archway, marking the distinct end of one life and the beginning
of another. She could have turned around and not gone through the
gateway, but she knew that there was no turning back. Much like hell,
she supposed.

Living on the streets was a different kind of hell: no food, no
shelter, and attempting to sleep under the bridges in the rain while
the police moved one along every hour.

Her children cold, wet, and hungry.

She had thought the workhouse would be different. The masters
might despise her—but who could be unkind to children? Rosie was
only a baby, after all.

"The baby will be under the care of the nurse, along with the other
children," Woodhead, the workhouse overseer commanded. "Did you
think we'd give you special attention?" He let her know she was to be
despised for being poor.

Evie certainly felt the shame of being required to live off the charity
of others, but she protested for her baby's sake. "Rosie needs to be with
her mother."

"How dare you question me? You'll learn who is boss here."
Woodhead barred his teeth, reminding Evie of a mad dog.

"Ouch!" Evie had persisted and the next thing she knew, she was
stripped naked and beaten.

She endured for the sake of her children. She had heard the law
allowed a child to accompany her mother, but now she knew it was up to
the discretion of the guardians and the particular workhouse.

I should have known not to believe anything good. Always those in power did as they wished.

"Only save my baby. Please." And why did she not run? At least her five children had a roof over their heads and would not starve or freeze to death here. There would even be school.

The workhouse split up the men and the women upon entry, but she had thought her children might stay with her.

Life in St. Pancras was intended to be harsh, to deter the able-bodied poor, ensuring that only the truly destitute would apply. She understood that. Her husband had lost his arm in an accident on the docks and could no longer find work. So why did she feel guilty?

Crack! Evie bore the pain and humiliation that her children might live. She cried, thinking of her infant. Should she take the baby and run? And where would they stay? And how would she protect both herself and her baby?

***

Rosie died. But Evie's four other children still lived, faring much better here than they had on the streets.

Still, she had never recovered from the grief of losing her baby. She had known in her heart it hadn't needed to end that way, whatever the nurse might say.

Evie was hungry for actual food, having dined on pork water for lunch, the pudding made from the fat skimmed off the surface of the water used to boil the pork.

But the workhouse guardians' luncheon following their monthly meetings was far different. Evie worked the meal for the guardians, so she knew the truth. For once, the truth was worse than the rumors.

Each meal started with bread, cheese, and beer. After the meeting, which lasted about an hour, there was fish, beef, roast mutton, various birds, puddings, and sweets. That was followed by a series of toasts with champagne and fine wines. Copious amounts of spirits were consumed as the men toasted everyone from the queen to the youngest member of the board.

"Here's your wine, sir." Gwyneth poured the wine. Gwyneth was young and pretty, so the guardians liked her.

Fully half of the residents in the workhouse were children; most of the rest were the sick, infirm, and elderly. That was why this position in the dining room had been open: Evie was able-bodied and hard-working—and not too hard on the eyes. The guardians would rather look upon the attractive ones and maybe sneak a slap on the ass. She didn't complain: this position allowed her to get food to her children.

Evie was allowed to see her children when she minded her tongue, which was the reason she stayed. There was an hour's visitation time every day. And today would be a fine visit, as she would sneak scraps from the feast to her children.

"The best slice of pork for you, sir. And would you like the gravy?"

There was a great shame attached to being here, but Evie didn't care about that. She didn't care about anything except her children.

And it was better than mopping the floors on her hands and knees, which Evie also did.

It is my best hope.

When she had first seen St. Pancras, the sight of the magnificent four-story building had filled her with hope. It had once been a gentleman's mansion—with a lovely chapel, all surrounded by a six-foot high wall. Only when she entered did she experience the hunger, the exhaustion, the betrayal, and, above all, the broken heart.

Evie knew now why the brick archway of Saint Pancras was called "The Archway of Tears". She had shed more than a few tears herself.

She felt the slices of bread and cheese in her pocket.

I might cry, but my children will live.

Chapter Three
Piccadilly, Mayfair
The Feast of Blood

"Of all ghosts the ghosts of our old loves are the worst"
— Voltaire

Despite the late hour, in the end Sherlock had allowed Belle to accompany them to Lord Percival's mansion on Green Street in Mayfair. In spite of her illogical protests regarding the body in the flat at Baker Street, his female operative had a strong stomach. At least her curiosity generally trumped her distaste, which he had to admire.

And Miss Belle had proven to be useful.

She had excelled at everything he had taught her: shooting, fencing, boxing, knife-throwing, and even *Jiu-jitsu*. She was an admirable whipster. She was coming along with disguises.

In one area she needed work: Belle talked too much and gave too much away. She had to learn to blend in the background and to observe.

It could mean the difference between life and death.

Even so, if anyone else had shown Miss Hudson's promise, he would have thrown her headfirst into every case that came his way—as he did with Watson. Sherlock would never think of leaving Watson behind, no matter the danger.

So why did he protect Mirabella Hudson as would only be the privilege of her father? *Or her husband?*

Sherlock immediately pushed the question to the back of his mind, even though he knew that wasn't where the problem originated. He didn't like dealing with anything outside the exercise of his logic.

The Great Detective found it difficult to leave any question unanswered. *But this is one answer I wish to avoid.*

All four arrived at Lord Percival's mansion, resplendent with blue velvet, gold, and coral. Ivory and crystal chandeliers, oriental rugs and white marble columns gave the mansion's interior a decidedly exotic ambiance. The former possessions of the maharajas, sultans and emperors of India from the 1600's onwards somehow complemented the romantic paintings lining the walls inspired by Shelley, Keats, and Lord Byron. One could almost hear the music of Strauss and Donizetti in the air, so romantic was the poetry of the décor.

Watson hurried past the priceless vases to examine the body without delay, almost knocking over a vibrant blue elephant statuette in the process. "Who found Percy?"

"I did." The tall, slim man who had answered the door, initially presumed to be an off-duty policeman, moved forward. He wore a voluminous tie and a long, dark frock coat, pinched to the waist to form a skirt of sorts.

"And you are?" Mycroft asked.

"I am the gentleman's butler."

Mycroft raised his eyebrows in both surprise and disapproval. "And your name?"

"Longstaff."

"And your first name?"

Longstaff cleared his throat, as if not wishing to give his name, an odd bit of arrogance, even for the butler. "Mr. Nathan Longstaff, if you please."

His appearance was abruptly remarkable in two ways: he was unusually handsome, and he was inappropriately dressed. Sherlock knew immediately the reason for Mycroft's disapproval: even though Longstaff's suit was well made and fashionable, to say that he was not wearing the typical butler's attire was an understatement of vast proportions. Mycroft was the most congenial of men, but on matters of deportment and manners he was uncompromising.

"I see." But he didn't. And he never would. "Mr. Longstaff." Slowly Mycroft repeated the name of the head of staff and the highest ranking household employee. In general, the female staff outnumbered the male staff by twenty to one, and the butler sat at the head of the household, both male and female, below stairs.

Undisturbed by his debonair brother's disapproval, Sherlock was in fact relieved to see the color return to Mycroft's complexion, even if disdain was the vehicle to his recovery.

Joining Mycroft in his scrutiny of the house butler, Sherlock considered the matter. In the evening hours a butler might have been mistaken for a gentleman attending the opera: the accepted attire was an all-black tuxedo with tails, a low cut waistcoat, and a white tie.

The one exception to a butler's accepted attire was that oft times a butler would wear something mismatched or slightly inferior in quality—a waistcoat of clashing colors, for example—so he was not mistaken for a gentleman. In other words, so it was clear to the guests he was a servant. Not one of *them*. In every other way—address and deportment—a butler might very well blend in with his distinguished guests.

Longstaff's morning suit went well beyond the deviating accessory. Either it was the butler's night off or this household was run in an extremely lax manner. And if it was Mr. Longstaff's night off, then why had he returned to the home early?

Even so, more than his dress, Mycroft's objection was as much to the butler's manner, lacking the airs, confidence, and condescension one would generally attribute to a butler. True, his large, heavily lashed dark eyes seemed to find everyone distasteful, but in all the wrong ways, with airs of disdain and repulsion rather than insider smugness. Much like a drunken sailor would find his captain objectionable.

Finding one's master dead was likely to disturb anyone however, Sherlock considered. He glanced sideways to see his brother's frown lingering. Clearly Mycroft didn't think there was any excuse for a lapse in style or polish.

Longstaff's attire supplied information to Sherlock and was of great interest, without any of the judgment accompanying Mycroft's assessment. Personally, Sherlock could have cared less except as his observations affected the capture of the murderer. Also of interest was a slight northern brogue.

"Is it your night off, Mr. Longstaff?" Mycroft asked pointedly.

"It is," Mr. Longstaff said, his hands still shaking.

"And why did you return early?" Sherlock glanced at the clock, now at half past nine.

"See here, Mr. Holmes," Athelney Jones protested entering the room from the stairwell. "This is my investigation. This is not for amateurs."

"I am here at the foreign secretary's request," Sherlock replied simply.

Police Constable Jones turned to scrutinize Mycroft. "So we have the foreign secretary with us do we? This is nothing to do with foreign affairs. This is a domestic issue, and you have naught to say to it, Mr. Mycroft Holmes."

The steel returned to Mycroft's eyes. "Perhaps not, but I presume that you still answer to the Queen, Constable."

"So her royal highness takes an interest in this case, does she?" Constable Jones' manner was both suspicious and flashy. This would have been the case even without his red hair and green eyes. He was slightly pudgy and jovial in appearance, though he was anything but jovial this evening.

"I suggest that you ask her yourself."

The constable swallowed hard, knowing very well he did not warrant an audience with Queen Victoria. Just as Sherlock knew that Mycroft had not consulted her. *But he likely could.* Still, it was a bit of a bluff. Mycroft was here because Percy was his friend.

"And what can Sherlock Holmes bring to this? He solved a jewel robbery, to be sure, his methods are interesting, parlor tricks as it were, but they have no place here." It was obvious the police constable thought Mycroft did little actual real work—and that Sherlock's contributions were overrated as well.

In truth, Sherlock was painfully aware that he was a young detective on precarious ground with very few cases under his belt, some of them on foreign soil, top secret and not known to the general public.

"Actually my esteemed brother recently solved a case of international significance in Paris, but I am not at liberty to discuss it with the city police," Mycroft retorted haughtily.

"Let's all see what we can come up with, shall we?" Sherlock said. "This is a difficult case and we might be of some assistance."

Athelney's expression was disturbed. "It is that."

"I am sure Her Majesty would be grateful," Mycroft added.

"I suppose there's no harm," Athelney muttered.

"And what have you learned, Police Constable?" Mycroft asked politely.

"Mr. Longstaff came back early from his night out," Constable Jones interjected. "He had intended to return to his room upstairs unseen when he suspected something was not right."

"And why did you return early?" Sherlock repeated the question.

"Why? Oh, I . . . I made a ridiculous mistake and forgot my handkerchief."

Mycroft raised his eyebrows, his opinion clearly not improved. He would sooner have forgotten his purse than his handkerchief.

"What struck you as untowards upon your return, Mr. Longstaff, that you looked in upon your master?" Sherlock asked.

The gentleman's butler patted his forehead with a cloth he pulled out of his pocket, noticeably sweating even though it was a cool evening. "I didn't hear any sounds. No talking, no laughing . . . *nothing.*"

"And that struck you as odd?" Dr. Watson asked.

"Yes, for this household." Mr. Longstaff colored slightly. "So I tip-toed around the corner, merely to insure the master was all right, mind you, when I saw the body lying on the floor."

"And yet you didn't send for the police," Athelney pronounced with suspicion. "It was one of your neighbors what did so, seeing strange comings and goings."

"I had barely returned from the theatre when the police arrived."
Suddenly emotion overtook Mr. Longstaff, as if he were attempting not to
cry.

"Control yourself, my good man," Mycroft said. In truth, only a
substandard butler would exhibit such an unprofessional demeanor.

Perhaps Mr. Longstaff was particularly attached to his master.
Interesting.

Or he was attempting to divert attention from himself as a suspect.

Mycroft motioned to one of his underlings. "Procure a sherry for Mr.
Longstaff."

Athelney motioned with his head to the couch, indicating the butler
was to be seated for now.

Once Longstaff had his sherry, Sherlock approached him. "I notice
you have a touch of the northern brogue—almost undetectable." *As I
expect is your intent.*

Longstaff's eyes opened wide, as if the discovery surprised him.
"I've spent some time in the north country."

"In manual labor?"

Longstaff almost dropped his sherry. He downed it in one gulp. "For
a short time."

Sherlock expected Longstaff's stint as a butler was of the shorter
duration.

"How did you know, sir?" Longstaff asked, shaken.

"You have a slight limp. As if you're recovering from an injury."

"I've found being a gentleman's butler I'm less inclined to injury."

"The same is not true for your master unfortunately." Sherlock made
the attempt to appear sympathetic. "And you've been in a workhouse, Mr.
Longstaff."

"Have you been checking up on me?" The butler was suddenly
alarmed.

Sherlock wasn't sure the gentleman could handle anymore shock.
"Certainly not. No more than I have observed since meeting you."

"Holmes, this is most alarming," Dr. Watson exclaimed as he looked
up from studying the body, his voice shaken.

"What is it, Watson?" Sherlock moved towards Lord Percival.

"The body has indeed been drained of blood."

"As I told you at the flat, my good doctor," Mycroft reiterated,
surprisingly dispassionate. Mycroft was socially engaging, but he was
not lacking in sentiment nor in animation. One might call his brother lazy
but never unemotional. Mycroft had the unique distinction of being both
slothful and radiant.

"*Deuce it all*," muttered Constable Jones. "I've never seen anything to match it."

Turning to glance in Mr. Longstaff's direction, Sherlock saw something else that gave him pause: Longstaff was wearing red plaid gaiters under his trousers, an odd clothing choice. Was this the article of clothing he typically wore to differentiate himself from gentlemen?

Or was it to protect his shoes and clothing from blood? He also noticed the butler had unusually narrow feet. Sherlock was in the habit of observing all details, many of which he discarded, some of which he later recalled.

"And that is not all," Watson's expression was disturbed. Having served in the battlefields of Afghanistan, he was not one to be queasy. "His neck has the marks of . . . *fangs*."

Sherlock bent down to observe the neck. "They appear to be the teeth of a wolf."

"Large, sharp teeth is all I might have observed," Watson said.

"Smaller than a tiger or a lion—you will recall I have seen both marks in the Parisian Circus—and larger than a dog."

"We must determine the cause of death. What killed his lordship?" Dr. Watson muttered to himself, as if he was at a loss to know where to begin.

"It is obvious what killed Lord Percival," Athelney Jones exclaimed. "He has no blood."

Cough! The constable turned to the butler, now seated, who looked as if his complexion had been drained of all color as well.

"Who was the last person to see your master, Longstaff?" Athelney asked.

"It was . . ." Longstaff cleared his throat.

"Spit it out man," Athelney commanded.

"His lordship's dinner guest was quite unusual, even for this establishment."

"Who was it, Longstaff?" The constable spoke through barred teeth.

"I haven't the faintest, sir."

"Now look here, if you think you're going to mess about with me, you have another thing coming."

"I wouldn't dream of messing with you or with anyone, Constable."

"Did you meet the guest at the door?"

"I did," Mr. Longstaff said.

"But you can't identify him?"

"I cannot."

"Excuse me, Constable. Perhaps I can help." Sherlock interjected, turning to the butler. "Was the guest dressed in a costume?"

"He was."

"And what was the costume?" Sherlock pressed.

Longstaff waved his hands as if this would help the words escape his mouth. "He was dressed as a . . ."

"Get on with it, Longstaff," Constable Jones commanded.

"Lord Percival's visitor was dressed as a *vampire*."

A collective gasp filled the room.

"A vampire? As in the penny dreadfuls?" The words escaped from Belle's mouth, followed by covering her mouth with her hands. She had been instructed not to interfere with the investigation upon threat of being banned from the case. Sherlock glanced at Mycroft. One diva was enough.

Sherlock forced himself not to smile, something he never had the slightest difficulty with except in Mirabella Hudson's presence.

Subterfuge was necessary, however. He didn't wish Belle to think he approved of her outburst, although it secretly amused him. Despite her being raised by a curate, he could always count on Belle to speak when other young misses of the day would either contain their tongues or faint, following the expectation for both their gender and their ages.

Belle was refreshingly unpretentious: remarkably mature in many ways, but she managed to maintain a youthful genuineness, curiosity, and straightforwardness he found appealing.

Even her dress did not match the style of the day. She wore a simple wool suit—a skirt and jacket—somewhat masculine in cut, which Miss Belle could never be with her shapely hourglass figure. Her shiny chestnut brown hair and her light brown eyes, almost golden in appearance, gave her both a professional and a softly feminine demeanor.

Sherlock stopped his train of thought abruptly, his private thoughts disturbing to him. It wasn't the thing for a career man. *This cannot be.*

"Varney the Vampire, *The Feast of Blood*," Mycroft repeated, his eyebrows knitting together as he glanced at the remains of the dinner table. A melancholy crossed over his expression as he added, "A vampire who despises his condition but is nonetheless a slave to it."

"There was no vampire," Sherlock said.

"There was something," Athelney countered, motioning his head to the lifeless body on the floor.

Dr. Watson shook his head in perplexity, his voice subdued. "These are not human teeth."

"And the only man to have entered the building, as described by Mr. Longstaff, was a vampire," repeated Athelney.

"Shall we say 'A person *dressed* as a vampire'?" Sherlock posed. "Please be so good as to recall Mr. Longstaff's exact words, Police Constable."

"Dammit, Holmes! How do you explain those teeth marks?" the constable said as he focused his attention as Dr. Watson directed.

"I don't. Not yet. The question is, how was the blood drained, and was Lord Percy already dead when the draining of the blood was initiated?"

"Not a vampire?" Mr. Athelney Jones of Scotland Yard cleared his throat, his face ashen white. "Naturally it wasn't." The constable answered his own question, talking to himself as he was wont to do. "But, as Dr. Watson said, those marks were not made with human teeth."

"You don't suppose it to be a vampire who sucked the blood from our deceased do you, Constable?" Sherlock focused his full attention on Jones.

"Why, no, I . . . of course, I . . . What has drained the blood, then?" Jones sputtered.

"Ah, that is the question isn't it?" Sherlock asked. "And no marks to the head, are there Watson?"

"No other injuries of any kind that I can see. No blows to the body, no major bruising, nothing. Except the teeth marks on the neck."

"No wounds. No place for the body to lose the blood." Athelney shook his head.

Sherlock returned to his knees to examine the body and, in particular, the mangled neck. "Did you notice this, Watson?"

"Well, of course I did, I just said—"

"I'm not referring to the animal teeth, which could certainly distract from that which I now draw your attention to—no doubt the intent of the fangs."

"The *intent*. What madness are you spouting, Mr. 'Olmes?" Police Constable Jones exclaimed. "So a werewolf was commissioned to distract from other marks on the body?"

"Not a werewolf, a vampire," Mycroft corrected. "According to our only witness."

Mr. Longstaff protested. "I wasn't here when the murder took place, I can't even say with a certainty who the murderer was. I can only report on the last guest I admitted: a man dressed as a vampire." He shuddered, glancing towards the body. "That is to say, I thought it was merely a costume, until I came across this scene."

The constable turned his attention to the butler. He drawled, "Didn't it surprise you to see a vampire come to the door, Mr. Longstaff?"

"To be quite honest . . . No."

"And why not?" Athelney demanded.

"I suppose I . . . given Lord Percival's predilections . . ."

"His predilections? What do you mean?" Athelney demanded.

Longstaff cleared his throat. "Lord Percival had any number of *interesting* visitors."

"For God's sake, man, stop speaking in vague generalizations! What do you mean by 'interesting'?"

"Men dressed in costumes came to the door on various occasions."

"Male prostitutes, then," Constable Jones pronounced.

"I couldn't say, sir." But it was obvious this was precisely the meaning intended.

"Let me direct your attention to the actual evidence, Constable, and away from speculation," Sherlock said, his eyes narrowing.

"What are you talking about then, Mr. 'Olmes?" Athelney's manner was a combination of impatience and apprehension. "What do you see?"

"Ah, I see it now," Watson murmured, still crouched over the body. "There is a circle inside the fang marks, in the shape of a human mouth. Perhaps it is . . ." he cleared his throat "the result of love-making."

"That's a strange type of love making," Constable Jones muttered.

"Agreed. I don't believe love has anything to do with it," Mycroft said from his seat on the couch, feeling no need to study the evidence for himself, which he left to his capable brother. His was to analyze the data once collected.

"And there's more, Watson. The circle interests me—a little too perfect for a human mouth—but there is something of even greater interest." He motioned to Mirabella, curious to learn if she would see what he saw. "Miss Belle, come see if you can discern this. Sometimes the young with their sharp eyesight are more observant."

Mirabella moved closer, dropping to her knees almost instantly as Dr. Watson made room for her. "Heavens!"

"Do you see it, Miss Belle?" Sherlock looked up. The girl was ordinarily quite perceptive and he wished to learn if she could look past the horror of the scene and *observe*.

"Are you speaking of the tiny prick in the center of the circle?"

"I am."

"I don't fathom how you can see anything amidst all these wounds and blood," Athelney muttered.

"We amateurs are particularly interested in the details," Sherlock explained. "Having nothing of any real importance to do."

"That's a fact," Athelney muttered. His failures in no way diminished his high opinion of himself. Likewise, the successes of others did nothing to increase his opinion of them. "You can't see the forest for the trees, and that what's wrong with you, Mr. 'Olmes. All the time missing the point. Yes, yes, I admit it was very clever how you solved that jewelry heist, but this is serious business."

"I assure you, Constable Jones, the solution is always in the fine points." Sherlock took care not to reveal his amusement even though Athelney was a constant source, even in these grim circumstances. He waved to the mangled corpse below them, blood still evident on the neck. "As for the injuries, in the absence of a physical blow to the body, that only leaves poison."

"There have been cases of a victim being frightened into a heart attack," Dr. Watson said. "Certainly a vampire could fill that bill."

"A widow's curse upon you both." Athelney Jones looked as if steam might come out of his ears at any minute. "That makes no sense. Frightened to death? Maybe, but Lordy, we have fangs! This is the most gruesome murder scene I've seen in some time." He pulled on his navy jacket. "Poison indeed."

"Precisely the point, my good man. Someone went to a great deal of trouble to create a macabre scene here." Sherlock shook his head.

"Your theories are all well and good when there ain't no skilled personnel about, Mr. 'Olmes, but let us deal with the facts here, if you would be so good. You're saying this is all staged?" the constable demanded.

"To a degree," Sherlock said. "Not entirely."

"Let me remind you that our plan is to become less obtuse instead of more." Athelney huffed.

"Only consider, Constable. What if the killer wished to make it look like a vampire murder, thus putting us off the scent?" Mycroft asked.

"If that were his intent, he did a fine job," Athelney grumbled.

"Indeed. If it were a poisoning, where would we naturally look?" Sherlock asked.

"To the cook," Mirabella suggested.

"Then why drain the blood?" Athelney demanded.

"Perhaps the killer wanted the blood." Sherlock began to pace the room.

"Poppycock!" Police Constable Jones exclaimed.

"I must consider all the possibilities."

Constable Jones shuddered. "Wanted the blood? What kind of idiocy are you sputtering Mr. 'Olmes? Why?"

"My dear constable, this is far from idiocy," Dr. Watson said. "There is an enormous amount of money in cadavers, did you not know? I believe we will someday look at this era as the dawn of medicine. Medical schools are so desirous of bodies that there are those unscrupulous fellows who cut out the middle man, so to speak, and murder someone in order to sell the body."

"Egad, man. The body is still here. It's the blood we are missing," Constable Jones said.

"He has a point," Mycroft agreed, adding "It has the feel of the Old Testament: the blood of one who is pure might redeem the impure. As in communion."

"We all know there ain't nothing pure in this room," Athelney objected.

"Communion is based on a supreme act of love and the forgiveness of sins," Mirabella said softly.

"There's a lot to forgive here," Athelney muttered.

Sherlock appeared deep in thought. "The reference to religion and the concept of purity may be relevant."

Mirabella cleared her throat. "The talk of communion sparks a new idea. Perhaps the draining of the blood had nothing to do with the blood."

"What do you mean, Miss Belle?"

"Could it have been part of a ritual? As revolting as the thought is."

"Indeed, an interesting possibility," Sherlock considered.

"This is a police investigation." Athelney shook his head. "You people are wasting my time with your philosophy and foolish speculating."

"To the contrary." Mycroft's height towered over Athelney as he rose, standing close to him. "*If* a vampire did not do this—which any thinking person must assume—and *if* the body was drained of blood, it is quite obvious someone wanted the blood. To not know 'why' at this point does not change the facts."

"And how was it done with no other marks to the body?" Athelney cleared this throat.

"Outside of the animal attack, you mean," Watson interjected.

"I don't believe that is what killed Percy," Sherlock said.

"Certainly not. What man would die from a wolf attack to the neck?" Athelney posed with an admirable degree of sarcasm.

"As we discussed earlier, I believe the teeth marks and the gruesome nature of the murder are meant to be a diversion," Sherlock said.

"A diversion from what?" Athelney demanded.

"It is the small circular mark which is the most revealing," Sherlock said.

Police Constable Jones cleared his throat. "We'll look into that. But the idea of poison is still harebrained."

Mycroft motioned to his underling. "Do see if you can procure a sherry for me as well."

"Only consider," Sherlock said. "As Dr. Watson described, there are large puncture marks on the left side the neck, appearing indeed to be the incisors of a wolf. Within the fang marks, there is also circular bruising, possibly created by a human mouth. But the truly interesting component is a small mark within the circle, almost like the entry of a dart."

"How can that be of any importance when we've got the teeth of a monster as well as the draining of the blood?" Jones demanded.

"It does pale by comparison, does it not?" Mycroft asked. "Perhaps that was the thinking."

"Ha! ha!" Athelney appeared to be momentarily enjoying himself. "You keep forgettin' what we've got here: A dead body without blood and the marks of fangs on his neck." He motioned to Longstaff seated in a powder blue Louie XIV chair in a comatose state. "And an eyewitness what saw a vampire. Two actually, counting the neighbor what called in. I'm not one to ignore the facts as you are used to do. And I'm not sayin' it was—o'course it *wasn't*—but how do you account for the absence of the blood if it wasn't a vampire?" Athelney added under his breath, "I'll tell you how. I didn't want to say with ladies present."

"By all means, you must treat Miss Hudson as indifferently and with as much disregard as you do Watson and myself, Jones."

"Oh, I couldn't possibly," Athelney protested.

"It does present a challenge, but you must try, Police Constable."

"Very well." Athelney nodded distractedly. "Lord Percival. Don't you recall that young man . . . the rumors was . . ."

"A failed love affair with Percy?" Mycroft completed Athelney's sentence, while taking a sip from his newly acquired sherry, looking most comfortable on a beige silk settee situated in front of a white marble fireplace.

Jones nodded, grimacing.

"Indeed," Sherlock said. "He committed suicide. A Mr. Bristow, I believe."

"Mr. Overton Bristow." Athelney Jones frowned. "A pharmacist."

"And the point you are making, Constable?" Mycroft raised his eyebrows.

"I'm sayin' that Lord Percival was a man . . . well, you know . . ." Athelney cleared his throat and added in a whisper, ". . . Who had sexual relations with *men*."

"Very likely, but we are most interested in knowing if Percy had intimate relations on this particular evening only—on the night of his murder—and with whom. As we would with any murder victim. That will have to be determined in the autopsy," Sherlock said with a certain detachment. "That is not for us to theorize utilizing idle gossip."

"Oh, so that's how it is now, is it? I don't think our young lord was that idle," Athelney Jones motioned in the direction of the body.

"We are only interested in the facts. The results of the autopsy will give us more information about the murderer and his purpose for being here." Sherlock turned to Athelney. "One thing I am certain of, Constable, is that this is not the scene of a love affair gone wrong, or a lovers' spat, as you seem to suggest, but an act of pre-meditated murder."

Mr. Longstaff gasped, as if it were the first time it had occurred to him.

Jones shook his head, his eyes fixated on the body. "It's a rotten business."

Dr. Watson leaned close to Sherlock and muttered in his ear, "But you have an idea what has happened here, don't you Holmes?"

"I do," Sherlock said in low tones. "But we must illustrate method and order at this point. I might hypothesize and hit the mark, but I fear that is very unlikely in the case of the Yard. We must not encourage speculation on their part."

"Indeed. Give them a fighting chance to solve this murder before you do."

Sherlock had his own strong reasons for not wishing to be the one to solve this case, not least of which was anonymity.

He glanced at Mycroft. Much depended upon it. Certainly the case must be solved, but he hoped it did not require that he step in and resolve it.

"Let us be clear on one point, Constable. If there is a deranged person here, it was the murderer and not the murdered man." Mycroft lowered his glass, looking at Jones with a hard stare which had faced the British Prime Minister—and even the Queen—head on.

"That's a matter of opinion, Mr. Holmes. In my way of thinking, it is both." Characteristically confident to the point of haughtiness, Jones raised his chin.

Sherlock shook his head. "This is going to be a difficult case, Watson."

***

It seemed to Mirabella the police constable wasn't the only one who was discomposed. Sherlock and Mycroft might look self-assured to the rest of the party—but she knew they were unsettled—a rare occurrence for the Great Detective. Nothing unnerved Sherlock.

They know something they aren't telling the police.

It is unthinkable.

She had never witnessed Sherlock Holmes wishing to conceal evidence. He had an utter and complete devotion to truth and justice, and anyone who got in the way be damned.

Sherlock's expression was characteristically unrevealing. Emotionless. His silver grey eyes were harsh, as if to foreshadow a thunderstorm. His raven black hair was combed away from his face, revealing long sideburns accenting strong facial features. The Great Detective's velvet waistcoat and black trousers were form fitted, revealing the muscles of a middleweight boxer.

He moved with confidence and his manner was unrelenting. It was far from obvious he was hiding something.

Mirabella glanced at Watson. *He knows as well.* She had no idea if John shared the secret, but he knew Sherlock well enough to know one was being kept.

She turned her attention to Mycroft, whom she had never seen distressed before this evening. Mycroft Holmes was the most composed, worldly wise person she knew; he never had his feathers ruffled.

True, this was the gruesome murder of one of his acquaintances, perhaps a friend, but she thought there was something more to it. Mycroft Holmes practically ran the government without the slightest degree of distress. What could be more shocking than the government? He could have faced a foreign invasion with more composure.

For the first time in their acquaintance Mirabella realized that Mycroft Holmes had his own secrets.

For all his faults, Mirabella preferred Sherlock's crisp, direct manner: there was never any wondering what Sherlock thought, so straight forward was he.

Except tonight.

Mirabella very carefully maintained an expression of professionalism.

She didn't want to be left behind at the flat with the corpse. Better here with the corpse than there with the corpse.

"Lord Percival was a member of the Diogenes Club, was he not?" Constable Jones continued, his eyes narrowing. He wore a blue uniform with gold buttons consisting of a belted long wool jacket and an oil-skin cape. A red baton hung from the wide belt. On his Helmet was "B-538", "B" for Chelsea, one of the seventeen divisions of London, and "538" his number of identification.

Constable Jones was quite the colorful figure with his red hair and green eyes, in his navy blue uniform. It seemed to Mirabella the constable enjoyed his life—and his station in life. Beyond a doubt he was confident.

"He was," Mycroft answered with unveiled disapproval. "Do you believe that has any bearing on the case, Constable?"

"Lord Percival didn't seem like the studious type."

"And what is the studious type?" Mycroft asked politely, taking a sip of his sherry.

"Not the type what has male prostitutes come to their house dressed as vampires."

"In the first place, we have only Mr. Longstaff's word for that." Mycroft glanced in the direction of the butler, who was gazing straight ahead. "Do give that poor man something for his nerves. In the second place, if it's true, it is no less interesting than female prostitutes dressed as vampires, I should think."

Sherlock frowned at his brother in a disquieting manner.

"Oh, for heaven's sake, Shirley. I'm simply attempting to discern the direction of the police constable's remarks, which sound more like accusations than revelations of fact. Sexuality does not exclude intellectualism. Nor would you presume that a man with a reputation with the ladies is not an intellectual."

"Certainly one does not preclude the other," Sherlock agreed.

"Consequently, I'm not sure how Percy's membership in the Diogenes is relevant. It is my club, and I have the right to be concerned with the reputation of a respectable and revered academic club," Mycroft continued. "Undoubtedly, it must be pertinent that Percy had relations with men instead of with women, but not in the manner Jones infers: in reference to finding the murderer only." Mycroft motioned to the body on the floor. "Percy was murdered in a particularly brutal fashion, which, to my way of thinking, is the most relevant fact here."

"Pardon me, but I'm not sure why we are assuming the vampire was a prostitute, we can't be sure at this point," Mirabella posed. "It appears to be an assumption based on Lord Percival's love affair with Bristow."

Sherlock turned to stare at her, a slow smile forming on his lips, accenting his strong facial features. "An excellent point, Miss Hudson." He turned to the butler. "The vampire was your height, Mr. Longstaff, was he not?"

"Yes, but I don't see—" Longstaff replied indignantly.

"—And he wore a size nine shoe. Which is the same size as yours."

Athelney's head turned like a spinning top to face Sherlock. "How do you know those weren't Longstaff's footprints then? And why do you assume them to be the vampire's?"

"We can't be certain. But, in the first place, Longstaff, as a servant, would have gone in the back door, where I likewise found his footprints. In the second place, Longstaff's shoes are not dirty or muddy. He said he went to the theatre. Why aren't his shoes dirty if he went to the theatre?"

"Maybe he cleaned them."

"He was caught by surprise when he returned home from his night out and was met by the police straight away by his own admission," Sherlock objected. "Either the prints in the front of the house are Longstaff's—why did he enter through the front door?—or they are the vampire's or . . . the vampire and Longstaff are one and the same."

"No! no! It wasn't me!" Longstaff objected.

"I don't believe Mr. Longstaff has the nerve to have pulled off this crime," Mycroft said.

Police Constable Jones tapped his chin. "I have at least one witness who saw both the vampire and Longstaff at the door."

"A reliable witness?" Sherlock asked.

"I should think so. In this upper class neighborhood."

"Indeed the rich would never lie," Mycroft murmured.

"A Mrs. Gage stepped forward—most respectable and quite hysterical. I assure you, Mr. Holmes, no one in this neighborhood wants a vampire running about," Athelney interjected.

"I should think they would be used to it. There are a number of bankers living on this street." Sherlock tapped his chin "So, those prints are the vampire's according to you, Constable. As I initially said. In addition, there are also two sets of women's prints outside, presumably the cook's assistants or the maid's."

"Where are they?" Mycroft asked.

"One in the front and one in the back." Sherlock was deep in thought before turning to Longstaff again. "Why are there women's prints in the front?"

"Sometimes it was necessary for a servant to enter in the front door. Lord Percival ran an unusual household.."

"That's an understatement," Athelney muttered.

"Percy was far too trusting," Mycroft said under his breath.

It is imperative to collect all the details at the scene of a crime, Constable," Sherlock said. "You don't know which facts will later prove to be useful."

"That doesn't address the matter of whether or not our vampire was a prostitute," Constable Jones said.

"I think it highly unlikely," Mycroft said.

"Oh, and why is that?" asked Jones.

"It cuts down on repeat business to kill one's clients." Mycroft took a sip of sherry. "Indeed, because someone is selling his or her body does not make him a murderer."

"Perhaps our vampire needed food to eat," Athelney said. "Or blood."

Mirabella looked away. Goodness, these people all had vulgar and dirty minds. Being the daughter of a curate, she had never quite gotten used to the idea of always assuming the worst about people.

Sherlock invariably concluded her conservatism was close-minded, but sometimes she gave leeway where he did not. Wasn't being inflexible in one's interpretation of persons and events the definition of being close-minded? Sherlock tended to see aberrance as a matter of course where there might be nothing but terror.

"And was Percy in the habit of having male prostitutes as his visitors?" Sherlock asked.

"As I said, I couldn't say," Mr. Longstaff was clearly embarrassed to be speaking of such things.

"I command you to say," Athelney roared.

"In my opinion . . . *yes*."

"Percy didn't have to resort to such things," Mycroft objected. "He was handsome, charming—and he had money."

And yet he retained Longstaff as his butler. *Or so it would seem.*

"I wouldn't say it was out of the question however. Prostitutes, that is." Mr. Longstaff cleared his throat. "He was extremely private about his goings-on."

"Indeed." Mycroft contained his condescension with some difficulty. "These are not isolated events in London."

"Some will say he had it coming," Athelney muttered. "Perhaps the demons came for him. It would seem so."

"We will be seeing that rendering in the newspaper, I have no doubt, the *Sunday Bull* or *Punch*," Mycroft muttered. "One of the gossip-mongers who would destroy the reputation of another simply to put a groat in their own pockets."

Mirabella had to agree; she detested idle gossip. And right now she was disgusted with the police, who seemed more interested in judging the victim than in finding the murderer. Honestly, she didn't approve of a man having relations with another man—how could she, given her upbringing? But it was not really the point here, and it was not her place to judge.

And if God loved all sinners, who were they to place themselves above God?

Sherlock would say that consensual relations between men was not sin. But Sherlock was too close to sin to know much about it. He socialized with prostitutes and ex-convicts, he gambled, he drank, he boxed in the ring, he used cocaine—heavens, he had even spent the night with Fantine Moriarty.

Which irked Mirabella to no end, she wasn't sure why, ordinarily she didn't concern herself too much with the souls of others. It wasn't for her to judge another's soul.

Because Fantine doesn't deserve Sherlock, of course. Fantine is a criminal, an evil, manipulative, scheming witch.

It infuriated her to think of Sherlock with that . . . that *woman.* And that was putting it nicely.

Sherlock didn't fit any mold: he worked tirelessly to uphold the law, and yet he had a disregard for the moral law. He had no sense of sin except anything that imposed on the personal freedom of another. Fantine, on the other hand, didn't care who she hurt as long as it benefitted her.

Sherlock might be corrupt, but he would never wish to hurt anyone. He had a benevolent soul underneath his formidable persona. And formidable he was: if she were in trouble, there was no one else she would rather have on her side.

"Mr. Overton Bristow was a member of the Diogenes, too, was he not?" Athelney Jones pressed. "The lover who committed suicide?"

"So we're back to that again, are we?" Mycroft sighed heavily, motioning to his assistant for another sherry.

"I'm surprised you would allow known sodomites in your club, being as it's illegal."

"Mine is an academic club, with no other requirements. Although necessarily all of its members are educated. Many men avail themselves of our periodicals and books. I have a singularly astonishing collection. My collection of Russian literature is second to none."

"I'll remember that in the event I've ever an evening to spare," muttered Jones.

"Let us return to the visitor dressed as a vampire." Sherlock interjected. "Are any of your men out attempting to capture him? Capturing the prime suspect would seem to be of a greater usefulness than Lord Percival's various affiliations for the time being."

"Granted if I were a murderer, it appears the best way to allude capture would be to choose as my victims those of whom the police have a low opinion," Mycroft said.

"We ain't found him yet. *But we will*." Constable Jones twirled his handlebar mustache in an unembarrassed fashion. "The vampire was cited both arriving—and leaving—by neighbors, but no one could give much description, outside of his unusual appearance. Even Mr. Longstaff, who was dismissed by Lord Percival after the vampire's arrival, did not give a useable description beyond the fact that the visitor was tall and slim, with dark hair. He wore a cape and considerable stage make-up—as well as the fangs."

"And there was no other staff present, Mr. Longstaff?" Mycroft's voice held disbelief, apparently unable to conceive that a household could function with less than a dozen attendants.

"All the staff were sent out for the evening."

"Only the cook, it would seem," Sherlock said, examining the remains of the dinner. "There must have been a scullery maid in attendance?"

"Mr. Denzil is the cook. He had one assistant, the scullery maid, a Mrs. Kitchens, and they delivered all the food via a dumb waiter," Athelney explained, seeming to appreciate being the one in the know. "Denzil and his assistant were threatened by pain of death to stay off the main floor."

"That's right," Longstaff said. "They always stay in the galley."

"Steak and mushrooms, along with an almost empty bottle of wine, and various accompaniments of potatoes, carrots, turnips, and aspic, it appears," Sherlock said aloud as he studied the remains of the dinner. He took a particular interest in the wine glasses.

"How long had the cook been with Percy?" asked Mycroft.

"Funny you should ask. Only about three months," Jones said. "But this wasn't the first assignation according to the cook."

"We'd like to speak with the cook," Mycroft said.

"It could prove interesting." Sherlock bowed to the constable. "I do have another question for Mr. Longstaff before he retires, if I may?"

Constable Jones nodded his approval.

Sherlock turned to the butler. "Mr. Longstaff, I notice you have used your handkerchief several times over the course of the inquiry?"

"Naturally."

"I had understood you forgot your handkerchief, which was the reason you returned to the house. According to your rendition, you were stopped by the murder scene before you had time to proceed to your room to retrieve it."

"*Blind me!* I must have had it all along."

Chapter four
The Cook

*"Those who find ugly meanings in beautiful things are corrupt
without being charming."*
- Oscar Wilde, "The Picture of Dorian Gray"

"Ah, Mr. Denzil, I understand," Mycroft acknowledged the addition
to their group as Sherlock continued to examine the remains of the dinner.
Longstaff had been escorted to the parlor with the possibility that he
might be called again.

"There were two plates and very little food left on either plate."
Sherlock directed his remarks to the chef.

"Not surprising. I'm as fine a cook as you'll find, and so it is." Mr.
Denzil was a sour-faced man of inspiring girth who appeared to resent
being summoned.

"It is a fair assumption these plates have not been tampered with,"
Sherlock posed.

"Har! har!" Mr. Denzil laughed. "Right you are. We was not allowed
upstairs and it'd be a cold day in Hell before Quality would lift a finger in
this house. The plates were not returned to the dumb waiter because there
was no staff upstairs."

"I don't believe the vampire in question was Quality," Mycroft
considered.

"Did you tamper with these dishes in any way?" Police Constable
Jones growled. "Answer the question, Mr. Denzil."

"I jus' did."

"I can sees why you were dismissed from your last job, Mr. Denzil."
Athelney tapped his baton on the wooden flooring several times. "Would
you like me to look into that for me investigation? There's a good number
'o high rollers interested in this report, bein' that Lord Percival was a
peer. Now as you'll be lookin' for work."

Denzil frowned, but it occurred to Sherlock that the cook was not
much concerned with his income—or with anything, for that matter—
which an unemployable man who had only just lost his position should
care about. True, the man had no great instinct for self-preservation, but
Sherlock would bet there was more to it.

And I usually win my bets.

"I do have a question," Mycroft considered. "If you didn't anticipate that Lord Percy would put his own dishes in the dumbwaiter, why are you still here, Mr. Denzil?"

Denzil turned to stare at Mycroft in disbelief. "There was still a sore sight to clean up. A fine meal such as this ain't delivered by the fairies."

Sherlock felt a twinge of amusement, sympathizing with the cook's frustration. Mycroft had never done a moment's physical labor in his life.

"Did you serve up mushrooms on both plates, Mr. Denzil?" Sherlock asked.

"I did."

"So both men ate the mushrooms?" Constable Jones asked.

"As you see."

"One plate shows a small amount of mushrooms left, and the other is clean," Dr. Watson noted.

"Precisely," Sherlock said. "Since one of the plates is clean, we can't be certain there were ever mushrooms on it."

"I tell you they was. I put 'em on both plates," Mr. Denzil objected. "An' both ate the 'shrooms from the looks o' this."

"Even if both plates contained mushrooms," Mycroft considered, "perhaps Mr. Denzil signaled to the vampire which plate was his by way of a pre-arrangement, perhaps with the addition of a sprig of parsley."

"I did no such thing," Mr. Denzil protested.

"No one has been up here but the police, so the plates have not been touched," Athelney objected.

"The police and the murderer obviously," Dr. Watson considered. "Maybe the murderer cleaned one of the plates off."

"The good doctor has a point, Shirley."

"Then where are the mushrooms?" asked Denzil, looking about.

"Why are you so damn concerned about the mushrooms?" Athelney shook his head in frustration. "What do they have to say to anything?"

"Both men appeared to have eaten the mushrooms, which I believe were the source of the poison. We must do an autopsy to confirm, of course."

"Nah, it can't have been the mushrooms!" Denzil objected. "I didn't poison nuthin'. And why would I poison him what pays me?"

"What better way to conceal the murder weapon than something consumed by both parties," Sherlock murmured.

"Or appeared to have been consumed by both parties," Mycroft added.

"If both men ate the mushrooms," Dr. Watson considered, "and one left in fine fettle, then the mushrooms couldn't be poisoned."

"That's right," Mr. Denzil chimed in.

Athelney suddenly appeared cheerful, if not insightful. "Are you sayin' the cook is the murderer? Did he poison Lord Percival? I'd love to take 'im in. The only thing I hate worse than a posy is a wanker."

"I find your sudden confidence in my brother's conclusions refreshing, Constable." Mycroft lowered his head in a gentlemanly fashion.

"Did you hear anything unusual during the dinner, Mr. Denzil?" Sherlock asked.

The cook loosened his collar, showing signs of becoming uncomfortable with the questioning. He might not be worried about his continued employment, which he didn't seem must distressed or surprised about any more than the demise of his employer, but he certainly didn't wish to go to prison—or, worse yet, hang. "If you mean by unusual, out of the ordinary for this household, no."

"What did you hear, Mr. Denzil?" Athelney Jones demanded.

"A few loud noises, as if a body were hitting the floor," Mr. Denzil replied, now tapping his foot.

"And you didn't come to investigate?" Police Constable Jones pressed.

"As I already said, it was not unusual for this household." He cleared his throat. "I had been threatened with dismissal if I were to set foot on this floor." He raised his nose towards the constable. "Lord Percival paid well—and he stayed outta' my hair, which I liked about 'im. He mighta' been a sodomite, he mighta' danced on moonbeams, it weren't none 'o my business long's he paid me." Mr. Denzil shrugged.

Sherlock would have thought Denzil would be growing on Mycroft, but he glanced at his elder brother's calculating expression to see that it was nothing of the sort.

For an unemployable man such as Denzil, Percy would have been a godsend. Percy certainly had a soft heart when it came to his employees.

And how did you repay him, I wonder? Was Mr. Denzil the type to do anything for money? Or was he a relatively decent man in desperate circumstances?

Sherlock thought it was probably the former.

"Ah. And where was your home before you came to London, Mr. Denzil?" From the skeptical look on Mycroft's face, he shared the same opinion.

"I was born and raised in Birmingham."

"A Brummie, eh?"

"I hope we have convinced you of the need to analyze the remains of the food, Constable?" Sherlock turned to Athelney. "Both below stairs and above?"

"I've landed in the mad house, and that's a fact. It's a fool's errand to test for poison—of all things—when we have this ghastly murder here. I never saw a murder what looked less like a poisoning."

"Precisely what the murderer wants you to overlook." Sherlock sighed heavily. "You're like putty in the criminal's hands, Jones. It's imperative we collect the data in order to confirm or deny our hypotheses."

"First we must test for poison to match the contents of the food to the contents of the bodies when the autopsies are performed," Dr. Watson agreed. "If there is poison in the food, we must confirm if it was actually ingested."

"Ah, yes. Well these are all new procedures to me. I've always been able to get me man with the old-fashioned methods," Athelney grumbled.

"In the absence of both suspects and eye witnesses, it would seem advisable to test the evidence left at the scene of the murder," Sherlock said.

"To the contrary, I've got two eye witnesses what saw this vampire— possibly more, as we make our rounds."

At least one of whom is a suspect.

"I beg to differ, Constable. The vampire was in disguise." Mycroft displayed his usual politeness. "A fairly effective disguise, it seems. Unless the vampire chooses to turn himself in, you have no idea who he was, do you Police Constable?"

Sherlock moved to look at the wine glasses, sniffing both. He took samples to consider under his microscope at a later time. "It appears only one glass had wine in it. This one would appear to be water."

"I weren't above stair. I couldn't say, sir," said Mr. Denzil. His unusual display of courtesy indicated that he liked the detective better than the others. On a rare occasion, Sherlock's lack of emotion had that effect.

Or perhaps the cook feared him more. That would indicate a greater degree of intelligence than Sherlock had previously assigned to Denzil.

"Oh, for God's sake. Enough with the meal already. I can't see how who drank wine would matter." Athelney rolled his eyes. "One man didn't drink wine, so what?"

"I assure you the entire murder revolves around this one point," Sherlock said.

"Which man drank the wine though?" Dr. Watson considered.

"It weren't Lord Percival who abstained, I can tell you that. Har! har!" Mr. Denzil exclaimed.

"Indeed, Percy liked his wine," Mycroft agreed.

"How much did his lordship ordinarily drink with dinner?" Sherlock pressed.

"About one bottle," Mr. Denzil said.

Mycroft coughed. "I should say more."

"And was this the only bottle you sent up in the dumb waiter?" Sherlock asked.

"Yes," Mr. Denzil said.

"The contents of the wine bottle will need to be analyzed," Sherlock turned to Athelney. "Shall I do the honors?"

"Be my guest, Mr. 'Olmes."

"Something else, Mr. Denzil," Sherlock said. "How many scullery maids do you have in the kitchen?"

"Only the one. I don't like anyone gettin' in me way."

"A Mrs. Kitchens, I believe," Mycroft said. "We shall need to speak to her."

"I should too. She came late and left early," Mr. Denzil growled. "She returned to her room before the work was done."

Athelney motioned to his partner to go to her quarters and fetch her.

Dr. Watson, now crouched over the body, seemed to suddenly go pale. "Holmes, there's something you should see here."

"Yes, Watson, what is it?"

"Oh, my," Mirabella murmured as her eyes followed Dr. Watson's gaze.

Watson moved his finger along the victim's mouth, parting the lips. "All of Lord Percival's teeth are missing."

At this moment, Constable Cockburn returned. "Jones, Mrs. Kitchens is gone. Her bags is packed and there is no one in her room."

Chapter five
What else shall go missing?

"No blood, no teeth, and now no scullery maid," Mycroft fanned himself. "What else shall go missing? I hope we may all leave this house with our limbs."

"So what if Percival wore dentures?" Athelney asked. "This attention to insignificant details is what separates the professionals from the amateurs. It is a common enough practice among the rich to have all of their teeth removed and opt for a finer set of pearly whites."

"To be sure, many a well-to-do groom has had all his young bride's teeth removed as a wedding present," Dr. Watson agreed. "It is the practice of those who can afford to do so—and a status symbol."

"Dentists have been known to convince their patients the misery experienced with one toothache will soon spread to their entire mouths," Mycroft lowered his fan. "The dentist will insist that it is better to simply remove all the teeth now and spare oneself the discomfort at a later date."

"There's some justification for it. There are cases of a person dying from an abscessed tooth," Dr. Watson argued. "However, the question is irrelevant. Lord Percival's teeth have been pulled recently. This is not a question of dentures; it is a question of a mouth without teeth."

"As I said," Athelney sputtered. "Lord Percival has no teeth. Common among the wealthy."

"No, Jones," Sherlock said calmly. "Percy had teeth before the murder. *Now* he has no teeth. There are no dentures in his mouth."

"Maybe the murderer took the dentures. He seems to have taken everything else."

"You can see for yourself, Constable. His mouth still contains blood." Dr. Watson added somberly, "It appears to be the only blood remaining in his body. These teeth were recently removed."

"And do we have a description of the missing Mrs. Kitchens?" Sherlock addressed Denzil.

"She was about thirty years of age, with dark hair and dark eyes. She was above average height—seemed rather muscular for a woman. Not fat mind you, but not frail either."

"Similar to Miss Hudson?" Sherlock offered.

Mr. Denzil considered Mirabella who stood firm under his gaze, which Sherlock appreciated. "Heavier. Older. About the same height. Darker. Less shapely but more ladylike if you knows what I mean."

Mirabella opened her eyes wide but said nothing.

"No, we don't," Mycroft said. "Miss Hudson certainly fits our definition of elegance."

"I don't need no hoighty-toity in the kitchen, but that weren't it. Mrs. Kitchen sort of cowered, no confidence. It were just a kitchen, for God's sake, no need to shake like a leaf. She was nervous. And flighty. She took off before all the work was done." Denzil shook his head. "I can't abide one what don't finish the job."

"Did you like her, Mr. Denzil?"

Denzil shook his head. "'Course not. I don't need no fainting princesses in the kitchen what couldn't say 'boo' to a goose. I'd rather have this 'ere debutante, elegance and all." He motioned to Mirabella with his head."

Sherlock cleared his throat. "What was Mrs. Kitchens' job?"

"She washed and cut all the vegetables and potatoes."

"Did she prepare the mushrooms?"

"She washed, selected, and sliced 'em."

"But you prepared them?" Sherlock pressed.

Denzil hmm-ed and hah-ed, obviously embarrassed. "She did. I didn't see no harm. I was busy with the meat, potatoes, gravy, bread, vegetables and dessert." He bit his lip. "I damn well can't do everthin'."

"It would ordinarily be the chef's job to cook all the food," Mycroft said simply.

"It were only cooking some 'shrooms in butter with a touch 'o sherry. Believe me, I kept an eye on her."

"We can see that," Sherlock murmured.

"Did Mrs. Kitchens send the wine up the dumb waiter?" Mycroft asked.

"She did."

Sherlock turned to the constable. "I am finished with this man for now. I strongly suggest you keep him in your custody. He is your only witness to Mrs. Kitchens. Even Longstaff did not appear to be acquainted, not knowing her name."

"Understandably. It is such a difficult name to recall for the kitchen help," Mycroft muttered, tapping his fingers on the arm of the settee.

Athelney laughed, his amusement soon turning to an objection, his *modus operandi*. "But Mrs. Kitchens weren't even at the scene of the murder."

"So far as you believe," Mycroft said.

"I think Denzil would have noticed if his scullery maid had gone missing," Athelney countered.

"Speaking of missing, as for whether or not Percival wore dentures, I suggest that you speak to his dentist, Police Constable, to verify our observations." Dr. Watson returned to the earlier discussion as Mr. Denzil was escorted out of the room. "I believe you shall find that there is no record of dentures."

"The case gets more and more perplexing," Mycroft's usually confident demeanor was noticeably diminished.

"It's as if someone was going to make dentures with Lord Percival's teeth—" Mirabella peered over Dr. Watson's shoulder.

"Aha! You may have it, miss. Teeth are extremely valuable." Athelney Jones was a working man who knew the value of things. "It doesn't surprise me someone took Percival's teeth now as I consider the matter."

"Naturally teeth are valuable," Dr. Watson said. "It's not unheard of for a girl of eighteen dying of consumption or one of the other diseases common to poverty to sell her teeth and hair for a meager sum in order to care for a family member, even a child." He added softly, "And done without any form of pain deadeners, which would only add to the cost, reducing her proceeds."

"Why not wait for the extractions until she passed on that she might not feel any pain?" Mirabella asked.

"She would wish to have the procedure performed while she was still alive to insure her earnings went to the intended."

Mirabella shuddered. It was indeed a harsh—but ultimately unselfish—ending to one's life.

"Your speculation is all very well, but it has nothing to do with this murder," the constable suggested. "I know your habits, Sherlock Holmes, but this is a matter where some common sense and true detective work is needed."

"I have been patiently awaiting its appearance." Sherlock shook his head. "And yet, it all speaks to motive. I wouldn't say that the removal of all of our victim's teeth is speculation, but rather a fact in evidence. What do you make of that fact, Constable?"

"Well, I . . ." he sputtered. I'd say we have a monster on our hands. A greedy bastard. And a *pervert*." He motioned to the body. "They're both perverts if you ask me."

"I'm gratified to know that we're only dealing with the facts," Sherlock murmured.

"The evidence does not support your theory, Constable," Mycroft said. "The removal of the teeth for a little extra blunt—as you yourself acknowledged—is not consistent with the scene before us."

"What do you mean, Mr. Secretary?" Athelney asked. One could say what he would, but the constable did wish to solve the case, as annoyed as he was.

Mycroft had been deep in thought most of the evening, but he was never mentally idle. Physically, yes, mentally, no. "You have presumed we have a male lover who killed Percy. Why? Was it part of an erotic interplay? And our murderer thought to make a few extra dollars after killing his lordship in a fit of passion. 'Mustn't forget the teeth,' he thought to himself."

"Along with draining all the blood from the body," Sherlock added.

"Most romantic." Mycroft shook his head. "And if it were for money, why are all these valuable paintings left lining the walls?"

"Hmmm . . . " Jones studied the walls. "I'd have to be convinced those paintings are valuable. Dreadful. Disgustingly risqué."

"That is unquestionably an Alma-Tadema over the fireplace," Mycroft said. "A particular favorite of mine: *The Roses of Heliogabalus.*"

It would be, for a hedonist such as yourself, Sherlock thought to himself without any intention of insult as he glanced at the ridiculously romanticized painting. "I acknowledge the painter's talent in technique and execution, but the subject matter is idealized poppycock."

"I have to agree with Mr. 'Olmes." The constable added under his breath, "Looks like an orgy to me."

"I think it's quite beautiful," Mirabella murmured so quietly it was almost a whisper.

Sherlock glanced at Miss Belle. Her curious golden brown eyes were glistening with excitement, which had likewise cast roses into her cheeks. If there was a young lady who could make one believe in romance . . .

Bloody Hell! He cursed himself. The only thing that mattered was justice—and the resolution of the case. Anything else was a waste of time.

And, worse, an illusion.

Mycroft raised his chin with a sudden idea, clearly unaffected by the slights to his taste in art. "Perhaps our murderer was paid by someone else to perform the murder."

"A possibility." Sherlock's eyes locked with his brother's. "Which would infer a much grander plot."

"And that there will be more murders," Mycroft said with a soft foreboding.

"Do have a care, brother dear."

Sherlock motioned for his coat. "Now that we have solved the murder, Constable, we must be off. There is much yet to do."

"Solved the murder? What in the blazes are you talking about, Mr. 'Olmes?"

"Really, you don't know, Constable?" Sherlock said matter-of-factly. "Mrs. Kitchens poisoned Percy."

"My esteemed brother is quite right," Mycroft muttered as he rose from the settee. "In a manner of speaking. Mrs. Kitchens—that, of course, is not her real name—at the very least made Lord Percival's murder possible. Maybe she didn't realize what she was doing, but she cast the deciding vote. The fact that she bolted certainly points the finger in her direction."

"Are you mad too, Mr. Secretary?" Athelney exclaimed. "It must run in the family."

"I do hope so."

"You will have to run all the tests and verify our conclusions, of course," Sherlock said. "Forensics is no place for guesswork. But I don't have to remind you of that, Constable, as I know unfounded speculation is anathema to you."

"Most certainly," Athelney agreed. "But . . . the vampire? The draining of the blood? The missing teeth? Surely it was the vampire?"

"Certainly the vampire had a role. But we need to start with the missing cook."

"Even if you're right and it was poisoning what killed him—and I don't say you are—you don't think it was Mr. Denzil what did it?" Athelney asked hopefully.

"No." Mycroft shook his head. "Mr. Denzil is not exactly what one would call employable with his attitude; it would not have been to his advantage to kill his employer. Moreover, he doesn't have the brains, the temperament, or the finesse to orchestrate it. His demeanor is not one of guilt. Believe me, I've learned to recognize guilt, I work in the government."

"And if he is telling the truth, Mrs. Kitchens made the selection of the mushrooms, the deciding factor." Sherlock added solemnly, "Denzil didn't handle the wine. Mrs. Kitchens did."

"And she ran," Mycroft said.

"Generally a sign of culpability, wouldn't you say, Jones?" Sherlock asked.

"I sees." Police Constable Jones tapped his plump forefinger to his chin. But it was quite clear that he didn't see. "And how did she do it?"

"The mushrooms introduced the poison into the body," Mycroft said.

"But there are still some significant points to tie up. As well as who was in cahoots with Mrs. Kitchens." Sherlock turned to Constable Jones. "Please, if you will obtain Longstaff's red spats for me. I should like to test for blood."

"And there's something else," Mycroft added. "Did you notice that Longstaff had a slight limp?"

"What of it?" Athelney asked.

"Despite his youth, he's recovering from an injury," Sherlock said. "And you noted that he is tanned?"

"I'm not in the habit of ogling young men, as you seem to be."

"Nathan Longstaff has not been a butler of very long duration. He's recently come here from the workhouse. There's no crime in that, but you need to check it out."

"How would you know that, 'Olmes?"

"Though he took great effort to manicure and soften his hands—there was scent on him from lotion—his hands displayed rope burns. No doubt used to pick Oakum."

Chapter Six
Saint Pancras Workhouse
A few weeks earlier

*"A sullen or lethargic indifference to what was asked, a blunted
sensibility to everything but warmth and food, a moody absence of
complaint as being of no use, a dogged silence and resentful desire to be
left alone again . ."*
– Charles Dickens, firsthand account, Marylebone workhouse

"She will do," said Mr. Fairclough, owner of The Madame's
Apothecary, so named due to its proximity to Madame Tussaud's. Before
him a row of young women lined up, most with hollow expressions
devoid of hope. His eyes alit on one: there remained a light in her eyes,
not yet extinguished. She lived for something—or someone.

"Evie works hard," the overseer muttered, seeing where Fairclough's
eyes went.

"She is strong." Franklin Fairclough studied the brunette. "Not a slip
of a girl."

"But she *steals*."

"Food for her children I expect. Does she have children?"

"Five." Woodhead spit on the floor. "No four."

"As I suspected."

"And does she have a husband in the workhouse?"

"Yeah. Fit to be tied. But we manage. He ain't that hard to
overpower; he's missing one arm."

Fairclough grew impatient. "Mrs. Travers. Does she have a temper?"

"It shows some times, but I 'ave 'bout beat it out of her."

"Bring her here," Franklin commanded. "I'd like to speak to her."

Woodhead shook his head. "Why do you always want the ones what
has too much spirit?"

"I believe you've answered your own question, Mr. Woodhead."

"I guarantees, she'll steal drugs from your store. Don't say I didn't
warns youse." Woodhead motioned to the woman to approach them.
"Evie! Get over 'ere."

"Mrs. Travers," Franklin maintained a polite distance. "Would you
like to come and work at my pharmacy? You'd have to do the cleaning to
begin with until I see how you perform."

"No, no sir," Evie shook her head adamantly. She looked fearful, pleading with the overseer. "Please, please, don't make me go. I want to be near me children. And me husband. I get to see him on Sunday." She lowered her head. "Thank you for your kindness, but at least here we has a roof over our heads and food."

"They may all come with you," Franklin said. "I have a commune of sorts on my land. You would have a small cottage and food for your children, as well as medical care."

"A *home*? Just for cleaning?" She looked astonished, as if the idea of having a home for her family was something that never entered her mind.

Franklin was well aware that even one room for the six of them in a tenement slum would be a mansion to Evie. They would be together, and no one telling them what to do and when they could see each other. A wood stove to cook on and to keep them warm—when they had wood and food—was a bit of heaven.

The cottage was his trump card.

He knew what Evie's life had been before entering the workhouse: one room for the entire family, dirty rags stuffing the broken spots in the windows, every day having to come up with the rent or be kicked out— many days leaving nothing for food—but it was a roof over their heads.

She teared up. "Four walls we don' share wif' others an not to 'ave to be on the streets—but our own room?"

Franklin chuckled to himself. "A bit more than one room. A *cottage*. It's small, mind you, but there would be two bedrooms and a kitchen living area."

"*Three* rooms?" Suddenly she began shaking, a wave of fear washing over her expression. "We couldn't afford to heat it."

"I will provide the fuel."

She glanced at Woodhouse. Clearly she didn't believe the pharmacist and thought he was up to something. "A cottage. Just for me family?"

"And food. In exchange, you'd have to work hard and to do things that are new to you."

She wiped her eyes. "I'm no stranger to work."

"There, there, I'm not here to hurt you, Mrs. Travers. I own the Willow Cottages on Willow Road in Hampstead bordering the Hampstead Heath. There are twelve little cottages on the property. Nothing fancy, mind you, but quite scenic. Before I bought it they used to be the homes for the workers who harvested the watercress from the ponds on Hampstead Heath. So you see, the park being so nearby is a lovely playground for your children."

"Me children get an education here as it were," she said in a whisper.

Franklin knew she didn't believe him, but she was fearful of losing this chance in the unlikely event he was telling the truth.

"Naturally I have a teacher for the children of my little community." He liked to keep his workers close-knit and isolated from outsiders. It was safer that way.

Fairclough neglected to inform Evie that there was a local parish school and a ragged school within walking distance of the cottages. Since 1880, some two years prior, it was the law that all children go to primary school, both boys and girls, and all communities were required to provide a school.

If she thought education an advantage of the workhouse, she was mistaken. Clearly Mrs. Travers had learned not to trust to anyone. She had also not learned to read or she would know there were already schools available to her children.

She looked as if she might cry, such an idyllic image he was creating in her mind's eye. Distrust was the only obstacle to overcome with these people.

And as long as they had spirit, they fulfilled his needs.

"What would I 'ave to do?"

He could already tell she would do just about anything for her family. *Perfect.*

"I myself live above the apothecary in Westminster with my daughter, Florence, who works alongside me in the pharmacy. She's a very bright girl, as smart as any man." He liked to bring up Florence as it tended to calm his female recruits, giving the appearance of a chaperone.

Franklin paused for a moment as he wrestled with his emotions. Florence had never been the same since her broken engagement to Overton Bristow and subsequent disgrace. Bristow had ruined her in more ways than one. She was now distant, quiet, reserved. She never wanted to socialize; and no wonder, from all the stares and whisperings.

He was furious that this had happened to his intelligent daughter. He would have gladly carried all the humiliation for her.

Franklin knew he had not been an attentive husband to his wife—he had worked all the time attempting to make a life for his family—and now he attempted to make up for it with Florence. His deceased wife had not been close to Florence, who had not been a particularly pretty child, which was no fault of Florence's. When she met Overton, Florence thought her life had taken a turn for the better.

Nothing could be further from the truth. Franklin cursed the day he hired Bristow.

Franklin regained his composure. "You would have to take the train from the Hampstead Station every morning and evening to work at the Apothecary, Mrs. Travers. It's a twelve-minute train ride. I would insist upon punctuality as a condition of employment."

"O'course."

"And you must never steal from me." His expression grew stern.

"Oh, no sir. All the poor ever want is fair work. Most of us, we don't want hand-outs, whatever anyone may say."

"Very good, Mrs. Travers."

"And my husband? What would he do? He has lost an arm." She looked as if she knew this would be the deal breaker. As it always was.

"We'll find something I am sure." He added softly, "*Everyone has their skills.*"

He liked to employ the desperate who had reached the bottom of the barrel. They appreciated their situation and were willing to do anything. Much like the loyalty of a stray dog.

Evie eyed him with disbelief. "But why? Why would you do this for me?"

"I've been informed you are a hard worker, Mrs. Travers. You have spunk. I like that. There are those who, through no fault of their own, have been dealt a hard blow in life."

Her eyes opened wide, as if unaccustomed to feeling understood.

"I carry my own pain. I understand the love of one's children and the sacrifices one would make for them." He cleared his throat. "If you can work with discipline and purpose, I will take care of you and give you a new beginning." He murmured, "God has blessed me with certain gifts and given me a purpose in life. This is what I was meant to do."

She looked down, attempting to not show too much emotion in the event it would be off-putting. "Oh, thank you sir, thank you. I will work hard for you. You will see. Please let me be with my children."

Chapter Seven
A Vampire Army

"You see, but you do not observe." - Sherlock Holmes,
"A Scandal in Bohemia" by Sir Arthur Conan Doyle

"Miss Belle, I'm glad you're here. You and I need to hail a cab."
Sherlock was still breakfasting when she entered the flat the next
morning.

"But Dr. Watson isn't even awake yet."

"Watson is still recuperating from the events of last evening. He
won't be joining us." Sherlock took his handkerchief and dabbed his
mouth.

"I thought you said the case was solved." She set down the scientific
periodicals she had borrowed.

"The case is far from solved. I merely identified the murderer."

"Mrs. Kitchens?"

"I'm relieved to learn that you were listening, Miss Belle. That may
have been overstating her role in one of the most heinous murders I've
ever encountered, but it was necessary to emphasize to Jones that the
scullery maid must be found. To be sure, she was the poisoner, whether or
not she knew it."

"If she didn't know, then why would she run?"

"It is still a possibility someone else is the mastermind." He studied
Belle's simple outfit favorably: a cameo at the neck of her white cotton
blouse embellished in lace, tucked into a serviceable cornflower blue skirt
with no bustle, simply gathered at the waist. *Most becoming.*

"What is wrong, Mr. Holmes? My outfit is just as you requested, is it
not?"

"It's a bit too fitted." He looked away momentarily.

"Too fitted? What do you mean, Mr. Holmes? Because it *fits* me?"
She tapped her toe, her frustration obviously increasing.

He really should have Watson examine her: Belle could be perfectly
calm and then escalate to volcanic proportions within a few seconds of
entering the flat. There was no accounting for it.

As if to prove his point, she continued on her tirade. "Honestly, you
won't allow me to wear anything even slightly stylish to work. And you
are so detailed in your requirements, Mr. Holmes, even specifying that I

can't wear a bustle."

"I am nothing if not specific." *A bustle would accentuate your hourglass figure. That will never do.* "You may wear whatever you like when you are not working for me."

"When would that be? Two hours on Sunday morning?"

"Give or take an hour," he agreed.

"And why should you design my clothing for me? Most unreasonable—and intrusive. Besides which, I need every fashion advantage as I am not frail or thin as is the style."

"True, Miss Belle. You are not." *You are much more attractive.*

"Then … why?"

I must allow nothing to distract me from my work.

"Do not waste my time, Miss Hudson. It is not your place to question me or to make demands. You know very well that I desire you to be simply dressed while in my employ, wearing nothing that might restrict your movement. At the top of that list is a bustle. Furthermore, as your employer, I have the right to require you to wear a uniform. If you continue to disrupt my progress, I shall do so."

It's all in vain. Sherlock sighed heavily. The lack of a bustle did nothing to hide Belle's alarmingly attractive figure. He cleared his throat.

"I am sorry, sir." She sighed heavily. "I merely asked. I suppose your request—actually, your edict—is understandable as I must be ready to run for my life at any time while in the employ of one Mr. Sherlock Holmes."

He stifled a smile. Above all, he must not appear to be amused when she was insubordinate. Which was most of the time.

"I accept your apology, Miss Belle. But might I add that I wish you were in my employ? Particularly since I pay you. If you were, we would be focused on the case instead of discussing ladies fashions, re-visiting a subject I have already concluded."

"So you've identified the murderer for the Yard, but you're still looking for the mastermind?" Belle's manner was decidedly apologetic as she put away the teapot. She truly did wish to assist, but sometimes her enthusiasm for the women's suffragette movement got the better of her.

"Was Mrs. Kitchens a pawn, working for someone else?" Sherlock moved to get his coat as Belle put on her hat. "This was not an isolated murder. There are much darker forces at work here—with bigger plans. And there are still many unanswered questions."

"Why was the blood taken?" She shuddered, fitting her hat atop her head. "And the teeth?"

"Precisely. And was this a hate crime—or something far different?" Sherlock placed his pipe in his pocket. "And when will our culprit strike again?"

"Heaven help us, I wish we might stop the killer before there is another murder." She looked to his laboratory table as was her habit, since she was responsible for keeping it neat, and her eyes stopped at a pair of red spats on the table. "Is that the pair Mr. Longstaff was wearing?"

"Very good, Miss Belle. And why do you think I have them?"

"To test for the presence of blood I would wager, as the red color might conceal the fact."

"Correct again."

"And did you find blood?" She asked eagerly.

"I did."

"This is the result you expected then?"

"No, it isn't. I found only minuscule amounts of blood, which could likewise be from a personal injury. It is not conclusive. Perhaps great care was taken—or perhaps Longstaff was not involved."

She stopped in her tracks, curiosity alight in her golden brown eyes. Of all her expressions, this was his favorite, curiosity combined with extreme intelligence. "But you're not disappointed in the results, Mr. Holmes? You appear to take it all in stride."

"It is mere information. I attach no emotion to the results. To desire a particular outcome might contaminate the conclusions."

"Particularly in a scientific experiment." She glanced sideways at him. "I understand your reasoning, Mr. Holmes, but given the importance of the results, I am frustrated, myself. Don't you attach emotion to *anything*?"

His eyes returned to her hair. Belle's nod to fashion was her chestnut brown hair parted in a V-shape in the front, the remaining hair forming a braid on each side and pulled up to meet her hair atop her head. A quite unnecessary concoction of her beautiful hair.

I long to see it loose and falling around her shoulders.

"Certainly not." He feigned disinterest.

She placed her hands on her hips. "What is wrong now, Mr. Holmes?"

"Your hair is too ornate."

"Too ornate? Whatever do you mean ...?"

"Never mind." He rose from his chair. "Let us be on our way."

She glanced at the laboratory table. "I suppose the lack of blood in the spats supports your conclusion that Mrs. Kitchens killed Lord Percival."

"As the purveyor of the poison, Mrs. Kitchens is certainly culpable, but she was downstairs." He shook his head. "It would appear that the vampire drained the blood from the body. Otherwise, why the vampire? Unless he was only a diversion."

"Do you still suspect Mr. Longstaff?"

"I must consider all possibilities."

***

And yet . . ." He shook his head. "I must admit it was perplexing not to find substantial blood on the spats. This is certainly not a neat crime." He smiled, a sudden joy alight in his eyes. "Precisely what I like."

There is the emotion. Give Sherlock Holmes blood and one might observe it.

Honestly she was delighted to be included in this outing, but she wished he might glance upon her with an expression of approval now and again. She worked so hard and truly wished to do a good job.

He was quick to criticize but not much else. She glanced at him sideways, neatly dressed this morning in black pressed pants and jacket, a white cotton shirt which did nothing to hide his muscular frame, and a grey and white striped silk ascot tie which made his smoky eyes look particularly thunderous.

Sherlock looked best in the gothic colors which were a match to his raven black hair and melancholy expressions. A look which had once been so frightening to her was now somehow dear.

The Great Detective was still intimidating, make no mistake, but it suited him.

"But there was a vampire," she objected. "At least three of the neighbors saw him."

"Probably. Most convenient, is it not? They believe they saw him. Is it that, or is it the romantic mind playing tricks?"

"But we know he was there, Mr. Holmes."

"And yet you never saw him. Still you are certain."

"Because I saw the mutilated body."

"That is not the same as seeing the vampire. Perhaps the neighbors were given the evidence by the police and told what they saw as well."

"But if there was no vampire, if he was only planted in the neighbor's minds, that would mean the story originated with the police."

"It wouldn't be the first time. Or perhaps it was not the vampire who was imagined—but Longstaff. After all, they expected to see the butler, who would have been uninteresting by comparison. Possibly they saw someone resembling Longstaff or dressed as Longstaff." Having procured his cane and hat he reached for the doorknob. "At any rate, our departure is overdue."

In no time at all, they were at the Great Peter Street Post Office sending a telegraph. She did her best to look over her Sherlock's shoulder in an effort to determine the intended recipient. The best she could make out was –"Urgent."— and –"Come at once."— and that the recipient's name began with a "W". She couldn't see the name.

Once Sherlock had dispatched his wire, it was not long before they were back in the cab.

"Who was the telegraph to, Mr. Holmes?"

"Only the most effective investigative force in the city of London."

"But the Metropolitan Police is already on the case, Mr. Holmes."

Sherlock laughed with a rare light-heartedness. It was unusual to see him jovial. He could be in a tortured state between cases, and it was at those times that melancholy and despondency overtook him. "I assure you, Miss Belle, those in my employ are more effective than the police force or they would not long be in my employ."

She found herself enjoying the unusual camaraderie she was sharing with her employer, as if they were partners. *I'd best not become accustomed to it.*

Partners. She liked the sound of that.

Mirabella had always thought science was her first love, but now she wondered. She loved the exhilarating feeling of solving the murder and putting the criminal behind bars.

In this, she and Sherlock were alike.

Glancing sideways at Sherlock, she wondered why she had never cast her cap after him, particularly as the thought of him with Fantine made her so angry.

Because it is ridiculous to imagine that Sherlock could be interested in me. He is extraordinary, amazing—a force of nature—and I am just . . . me.

Perfect Sherlock was *not*. His terrible mood swings were almost beyond endurance. Sherlock was just as incorrigible as he was brilliant.

It was his complexity that made him who he was, the other side of the coin. One didn't exist without the other.

And a world without Sherlock Holmes was, well, not a world for her anymore.

"Who is this remarkable crime-fighting group you seek to hire, Mr.

Holmes?"

"The same force I employed in the Jefferson Hope case."

"But who . . . ?"

He looked out the window for a moment, the determination in his silver eyes evident. His visit to the telegraph office had definitely left him more exuberant, as he always was when he had hit upon a new idea.

Upon returning to the flat, before Sherlock and Watson had finished their toast and eggs, there was a ruckus on the street to compete with the Queen's fortieth jubilee.

"Hmmm, are we expecting company?" Dr. Watson asked as he spread fig preserves on his toast. "Or is it the organ grinders convention right outside our window?"

"Heaven help me, it's Satan and the end times!" Mrs. Hudson screamed in the hallway. "I won't open this door, and so it is. I'll not let you hooligans in this building over me dead body!"

Mirabella looked out the window to see a dirty, smudge-faced boy with hair the color of wheat flapping his telegraph about.

"I've been summoned, I ain't no vagabond. I'm here on official business with Mr. Holmes hisself. And here's the paper to prove it."

Mirabella ran to the door of the flat and called down the hallway where her aunt was standing. "It's alright, Aunt Martha. I helped to send the telegraph myself."

"O' course you did, Missy. Why am I not surprised you had something to do with this tom-foolery?" Mrs. Hudson sighed. "And you used to be such a sensible girl before you fell in with Mr. Sherlock 'Olmes."

Mirabella couldn't argue with that; it was absolutely true. "You introduced us, Aunt Martha." Also true.

Mrs. Hudson made the sign of the cross on her chest. "May our heavenly Father and all the saints above forgive me for creating that tear in the firmament which has since rained purgatory upon us."

"Are you going to get the door, Aunt Martha, or should I come down the stairs?"

"Let me have a moment of peace before I expire, girl." Martha Hudson peered around the door to look out the street window. "Auch now, it's only an army of vagabonds here to kill us all and take our life's savings," she continued, regaining her composure. Slowly she opened the door and yelled through the crack, "You're not too old to paddle, and so it is. Mind your manners."

Mirabella turned on her heel to face Sherlock. "You can't mean that you telegraphed . . ."

"The Baker Street Irregulars, naturally."

"But *children*, Mr. Holmes? Don't you think this case is far too dangerous?"

"If there is anything the Baker Street Irregulars excel in, it is in not getting caught. That is their particular area of expertise in fact: to see things others miss, to remain hidden and unnoticed, and to move amongst a crowd and take what they wish without anyone being the wiser."

"Invisibility, do you mean?" Dr. Watson asked.

"That is their survival." Sherlock grew somber for an instant.

"Did you know, Miss Mirabella, that fully one-third of London is comprised of children? Those who are not among the gifted, do not survive at all." Dr. Watson buttered another piece of toast, completely unmoved by the chaos formerly outside the window and now heading for their rooms, his and Holmes' haven away from the shadowy and darker side of London, their retreat where pipes were smoked, clients entertained, books read, sherry sipped, fires burned late into the night, clues examined, scientific experiments performed and published, and the most perplexing criminal cases discussed and solved. Perhaps John thought there was a protective bubble over this Baker Street flat due to the transforming power it had enacted on him.

Hearing footsteps trampling up the stairs, Mirabella wondered if that bubble was about to burst.

"Or, as in the case of *Lady Graham's Orphan Asylum* where I volunteer, they survive but do not actually live." Mirabella smiled; nothing seemed to discompose the good doctor. He gave everything an air of calm, one of his endearing qualities.

He had been in Afghanistan, after all, which had made every attempt to claim his life, exhausting every angle when one method proved futile. She sometimes wondered if John Watson lived under a lucky star, spreading some of that light on all of them. There was nothing this earthly plane could do to John Watson that hadn't already been done.

She turned to Sherlock. "So . . who was the wire to, Mr. Holmes?"

"To Wiggins, of course." His eyes captured hers for a moment, challenging her in some way she didn't understand.

"The leader of this children's detective force?"

"The very same: the lieutenant of the Baker Street Irregulars as well as their fearless leader." He frowned. "I wish you will offer the proper respect, Miss Belle. This is not an amateur group. Wiggins is a twelve-year-old of remarkable talent, ingenuity, and leadership skills. And punctual as well. We have not yet concluded our breakfast and here they are. I'll wager you would not see a response to match it from the Yard."

The clomping of feet on the stairs was getting closer.

"Perhaps this is a bit more response than is to be desired."

"I begin to wonder that myself, Miss Mirabella," Dr. Watson murmured.

"Glory be, who did you steal this from?" Mrs. Hudson could be heard in the hallway with the boys, apparently examining the telegraph. "You ain't no 'Mr. Wiggins'. You can't be more than thirteen years old."

"I'll 'ave you know I'm twelve, and big for me age," Wiggins said proudly.

"You need to watch your mouth, and that's a fact, Mr. Big."

Even before the long-suffering landlady had finished her sentence, the air was filled with the slap of bare feet reaching the top of the stairs, accented with the whooping and hollering young boys tended to—along with a mixture of unpleasant odors. Mirabella opened the door to the flat, only to be hammered against the wall by the influx of a dozen street-urchins in rags, their faces covered in soot.

The toast from their breakfast table disappeared in a matter of seconds, with the exception of the piece in Dr. Watson's hand remaining so.

"Give back the toast," Wiggins commanded, at which point three grubby hands revealed half-eaten pieces of toast, even as the three culprits continued licking the jam off their dirty fingers.

"You may keep them at this point," Sherlock said with disapproval, lighting his pipe and examining the boys before him. "Stand at attention."

Two of the pieces of toast fell to the carpet, jam side down. Instantaneously the boys formed a straight line, or as straight a line as could be obtained in the not over-large flat.

"Here we are, sir!" Wiggins announced.

"As if that could be missed," Sherlock said. "Henceforth, you shall come alone, Wiggins, and impart my directions to your troops. I cannot have the house invaded in this way."

"Yes, guv'nor!" cried Wiggins.

"Yes, sir!" they all squealed.

"And prior to your leaving you shall all return anything you have picked up while on the premises," Sherlock continued, taking a puff on his pipe.

"Yes, guv'nor!" yelled Wiggins, his voice growing even louder.

"Yes, sir!" the boys all howled.

"However, it's just as well you are all here. This is a particularly dangerous villain we are after. Under no circumstances are you to approach him, do you understand?"

"Yes, sir!"

"You may now listen to my directions and cease to say 'yes, sir' after every sentence."

"Yes, sir!"

Sherlock sighed heavily. "I am looking for a vampire."

There was a collective gasp. Wiggins asked, "Like Varney the vampire?"

"Yes," Sherlock explained. "He is a person dressed as a vampire—but every bit as evil as if he were a creature of the night. He would kill you all given the chance. *Or worse*."

"How will we know him, guv'nor?" Wiggins' asked shakily, his voice noticeably softened.

"How many vampires have you seen, Wiggins?" Sherlock inquired with interest.

"Well . . . *none*." Wiggins looked at the other boys, who nodded their agreement.

"So, if you see a vampire, that is in all probability him, do you not agree?" Sherlock posed.

Wiggins shook his head, swallowing hard.

Sherlock lit his pipe. "I am also looking for a woman, about thirty years of age, with dark hair and dark eyes. Slightly above average height, not a feather."

"There be many women who fit that description," Wiggins said, puzzled.

"Indeed there are. But if you see such a woman in the company of the vampire, she would be of great interest to me."

"So we can approach the woman but not the vampire?" Wiggins inquired, always one to insure that he understood his directions, one of many reasons he was so valuable.

"Neither at this time. You report back to me. Do *not*—I repeat—do *not* approach either. If, at no peril to yourselves, you can find out where the vampire is going, that would be invaluable to me. You must travel in pairs. You are not to go out alone. And do not get too close, it may be a trap. Am I understood?"

"Yes, sir!"

"It's your usual pay rate of one schilling, and a guinea to the boy or boys who finds the vampire." There was a sudden outburst of chatter, as if they had been offered a palace in Monte Cristo rather than a guinea.

"Quiet. Now line up," Sherlock commanded. They all lined up and he handed them each a shilling as they passed to the door, checking their pockets as they went and retrieving a figurine, a silver spoon, and a lemon drop, the last of which Sherlock returned to its most recent owner.

"Miss Belle, take a note, please," Sherlock instructed when the boys had all exited through the front door.

She procured her notepad and fountain pen.

"Eight, Seven, nine, six, twelve," Sherlock began, reciting quickly as he tapped his pipe on the table, his eyes scanning the ceiling. He paused, as if recollecting. "Seven, five, eight, nine, five, eleven, six."

He held his hand out that he might review the scribblings. "Yes, it is correct. Please take it to James Taylor & Company without further delay."

Sherlock returned to smoking his pipe as if she were no longer in the room. "Miss Belle, why haven't you left?"

"What am I supposed to do with this list of numbers?" She was utterly mystified.

He looked at her as if he had thought better of her, his eyebrows raised. "As I said, take it to James Taylor & Company."

"And what will they do with it?" she asked, still no closer to understanding his directions.

"Who is James Taylor, Miss Hudson?"

"He is your cobbler."

"What would I have you do at the cobbler's? Buy bread? Send a telegraph? Purchase ice?"

"Make shoes, I suppose."

"Precisely. You are to instruct Mr. Taylor to make twelve pairs of boys shoes, of course. Those are the sizes. An early Christmas present, if you will. They should be working boots, comfortable but serviceable. You may then take the measurements and purchase twenty-four pairs of socks. London's damp and cold can be quite a health hazard." He sniffed disdainfully. "And when you have returned, I beg that you will clean the floor. It smells like a stable in here."

Chapter Eight
Resurrection Men.
And Women.

"That'll do, guv'nor." The Highgate Cemetery guardian pocketed the coin and allowed the intruders to start digging.

Rather than shedding light on Highgate, the full moon increased the sense of darkness. Highgate was a fearsome place in the daytime, but more so at night: the thirty-seven acres of wild and un-manicured woodlands incorporating winding paths, trees, ivy, and moss draped over every manner of mausoleum, statue and stone tribute to the dead. The lack of uniformity—even tombs and vaults dug into the hillsides—made the sculptures come alive.

These were not small statues but massive structures: the Egyptian Avenue entryway bordered by fifty-foot monuments was a majestic semicircle composed of sixteen vaults on each side of the arch. From there one entered the Circle of Lebanon, thirty-six vaults in a circle around an ancient Cedar of Lebanon tree. The effect was an imposing and ominous greeting to the west cemetery.

John Watson could never come into a cemetery without being reminded of how close he came to finding a permanent home amidst the moss and decay.

How did I let Holmes talk me into this venture? John sighed. Just as he allowed Holmes to talk him into everything: with the greatest of ease.

These past fifteen months had been nonstop stimulation and thrills—precisely what John needed. He had been emaciated and lethargic when he met Holmes. His flat mate had taken his mind off his troubles and switched John's focus to medicine, chemistry, and bringing criminals to justice. And staying alive, but that was nothing new.

In the shadows angels' wings were seen emerging from the cemetery, aimed towards the sky. The elevated cemetery had a view of London, rising as it did 375 feet above sea level.

If and when the ghosts were to rise from Highgate, there would be a lively meeting of personalities. Karl Marx was buried in Highgate. George Eliot—Mary Anne Evans—a radical woman in a repressive age, could be found. Here was bare-knuckle fighter Tom Sayers' marble tomb over which a life-size sculpture of Sayers' loyal and beloved dog Lion kept guard.

Mirabella shuddered. "There are some places a lady should never go."

John smiled to himself, one could always count on Miss Mirabella to say what everyone was thinking. She was a delight to be sure, as well as an insightful and capable young lady.

He had thought at one time they would be an item . . . but being lonely did not a match make.

If any woman is a match for me. He with his ghosts and demons, as well as his injured leg. *I am half a man.* Holmes helped to keep John's mind off his memories and on staying alive. There was some strange advantage to continuously being in mortal danger.

"Where is me cut for the clergyman?" the watchman pressed, greed apparent in his eyes. He knew how much these grave robbers were making. Why shouldn't he get his fair share?

"A clergyman didn't send me." Holmes dropped another coin into the guardian's hand anyway.

"Thanks, guv'nor."

"It's a pleasure doing business with you, Riley."

Riley tipped his hat. "And you as well, Mr. Holmes."

"Highgate is a surprisingly busy place," John murmured.

"Even without all the statues and shadows coming alive in one's imagination," Mirabella said.

There, she voiced his thoughts again. John smiled to himself.

"Dead bodies are necessary to understanding the workings of the human body," Sherlock said, adding, "We stand on the precipice of medicine my friends."

"And if a body has gone to its final resting place and thereafter is removed from the coffin, who is going to be the wiser?" John proposed with no small degree of sarcasm. Being a medical man, he was interested. Being a human being, he was repulsed by the ease with which Holmes crossed the line.

Sherlock shrugged. "Dealing in corpses is a lucrative business. The teeth in particular are a true goldmine, beginning with the Battle of Waterloo in 1815 when fifty thousand men died on the battlefield."

"The devil take them all," John cursed under his breath. "The earth was still shaking from the cannons fired and the air still ringing when the grave robbers flooded the battlefield to pull out the teeth of the dead and dying. A fine thanks to those soldiers willing to die for the freedom of all." If there was a hell, those grave robbers pulling the teeth of a soldier not yet dead were worthy candidates.

"As a result of the sacrifices made at Waterloo, the middle class can now afford teeth," Mirabella said.

"And a few grave robbers were made into rich men." Being a military man, the idea sickened him. He was one who was always short of the blunt, but money was not worth one's soul.

"Ah, but a beautiful smile completes the outfit. Surely a man of fashion knows this." Holmes continued digging while offering his commentary. Holmes was perfectly capable of withholding his opinion if it suited him, but it rarely did.

"I could not be induced to wear a dead soldier's teeth, no matter how straight and white." John muttered as he continued digging. "Speaking of which, we could have acquired a body through normal channels. Why are we doing this, Holmes?"

John was outraged at the disrespect and abuse shown to dying soldiers at Waterloo, but he would be a fool not to realize that he lived in fascinating times. No one actually understood how the human body worked. All those alive today were living on the brink of discovery, and he was part of it.

All because of a chance meeting with his old friend Stamford at the Criterion Bar—who subsequently took him to Barts hospital where he met Holmes.

His life changed at that moment. It was a strange truth that Holmes, a detective, had advanced John in his career of medicine.

In addition to bringing him back to life.

"Normal channels? Ah, yes, the workhouses, when no one comes to claim the bodies," Sherlock said. "I am a regular customer at Saint Pancras."

Mirabella shuddered, though she continued digging. "Are you any closer to finding the crime ring that murdered Lord Percival, Mr. Holmes? It seemed to me that you and Mycroft knew more than you disclosed."

John thought so too, but he had no expectation of Holmes explaining himself. There was something uniquely different about Holmes when it came to this case: an increased secrecy John hadn't previously seen.

But then, Mycroft had a great deal to be secret about.

***

"Did it seem so, Miss Belle?" Sherlock glanced her way and she could see the glimmer of a smile even in the darkness. The upturn of his lips almost never became a smile where Sherlock Holmes was concerned, but any foray into amusement was a decided departure from his usual serious existence.

Sometimes it saddened her that such a gifted and remarkable person did not enjoy his life more. She watched Sherlock tirelessly digging. Driven, yes. Enjoyment? She wasn't sure.

"Perhaps I shall allow you to solve this one since you have a greater understanding of the case, Miss Belle."

Oh, so we're going to play that game, are we? Very well.

"You said Mrs. Kitchens administered the poison that killed Percival—though I don't know how she could have accomplished that since both men ate the mushrooms. It seems fraught with uncertainty to me." She stopped to lean on her shovel momentarily.

Am I mistaken? Or did the Lion statue move?

"That which appears to be an inconceivable notion, a great mystery and an impossibility always presents itself as the only possible path once it is understood how the deed was done."

"The vampire must be the guiltier party as Mrs. Kitchens actually never touched the body."

"By that definition Moriarty is less guilty because he never performs the crime himself. When, in fact, he is the mastermind, the spider at the center of the web, without whom none of those vile acts would occur." A certain razor sharp quality tinged his voice. "The truth it that Moriarty is the most guilty of all concerned—and the most dangerous man in London."

Mirabella grew silent, having a guilty conscience as it were.

"Do you not agree, Miss Hudson?" Sherlock asked pointedly.

"Not entirely." She returned to her digging.

"You don't agree that Moriarty is dangerous?" he persisted.

"I'd have to be a fool to think that," she murmured.

"Precisely."

Oh for goodness sake. She sometimes felt even her private thoughts belonged to Sherlock Holmes. She had to fight to insure that she maintained her own being as distinctly her own.

"It is possible the vampire is a much more despicable—and dangerous—person who gave the orders," Sherlock considered. "It is also possible there is yet another person behind it all."

"Behind both Mrs. Kitchens and the vampire?" Mirabella asked.

"Yes. In fact, I think it highly likely."

"Why is that, Holmes?' Dr. Watson asked.

"Because of the complexity of the case. And how well orchestrated it was, every detail being considered. This was not a spur of the moment crime, there was a great deal of showmanship to it."

"Yes," Dr. Watson considered. "Almost as if it were theatre."

"Precisely, Watson. And add to that the disappearing blood and teeth. There are layers of motivations here."

"So you're saying it is not a crime of passion?" Mirabella asked.

"I didn't say that, Miss Belle."

"But what was the motive? I still have no idea why he did it. Or how to find him."

"That is the issue, is it not?"

"It's a very strange case," Dr. Watson paused to lean on his shovel.

"Beyond a doubt."

Mirabella glanced at the moon. "What if the man dressed as a vampire really *is* a vampire?"

"I'm sure he is," Sherlock replied without hesitation. "For some members of the human race, there is a thin line between the human and the monster. And definitely it was a monster who drained Lord Percival's blood."

Chapter Nine
Autopsy Results

"I may not agree with you, but I will defend to the death your right to make an ass of yourself."- Oscar Wilde

"We haven't been able to confirm that Longstaff was at the theatre," Athelney said, frowning. "We can't find anyone who saw him."

"So Longstaff could have been the vampire." Dr. Watson joined them, having only finished seeing a patient. He seated himself on the eggplant-colored velour couch next to the constable as Mycroft had already taken Watson's usual chair in front of the fireplace across from Sherlock.

"There's something else," Athelney added smugly, speaking in as soft a voice as he was capable of. Which wasn't very quiet. Constable Jones was not a soft-spoken man, try as he might.

Mirabella moved closer, her back to them but her ears open as she poured the sherry for the two new arrivals. The more invisible she was, the more freely they spoke in her vicinity. She had always thought Sherlock unkind to "shush" her or to complain about her talking, but now she wondered if the Great Detective hadn't cautioned her for her own benefit.

"What is it, Constable?" Sherlock took a sip of sherry, his expression less than eager.

"I can see you are gloating about something you perceive to be of significance, Constable." As usual Mycroft was impeccably dressed. It seemed to Mirabella, though, that the color had drained from Mycroft's complexion on the day of Percival's murder and never quite returned. His skin tone now matched his grey eyes.

"Even you will find it of interest, I am sure. We have the autopsy."

Sherlock raised one eyebrow, and it did seem to Mirabella her employer was curious, in spite of his nonchalance. A woman could wear a neglige in a burlesque show and he wouldn't bat an eyelash, nor would it hold his interest, but offer up scientific data and his expression would radiate with a sudden glow.

Underneath the papers he retrieved a Persian slipper, filled with his favorite tobacco, which he proceeded to place into his pipe. He lit the pipe and languidly indulged in a long puff before indicating with a tilt of the chin that he wished the constable to continue.

"There, that's the way of it. I know how you like them little details, 'Olmes." Athelney lowered his voice. "We learned from the autopsy that Lord Percival did *not* have *relations* with another man—or with anyone, for that matter—on the night in question."

"This gives you pause to question your theory, Police Constable, does it not?" Mycroft asked politely. His world had come crashing down around him over the past few days and terror gripped his heart, but that was apparently no reason to forego good manners.

"And what theory is that?" Athelney took a sherry from Miss Hudson.

"Oh where do we begin?" Mycroft murmured. "That Percy was depraved and corrupt. That the vampire was both a sodomite and a prostitute. That the real purpose of the dinner was to have an orgy. That Percy's evil ways are what did him in."

"In short, that Percy was the guilty party and in some way responsible for his own gruesome murder." Sherlock tapped the fingers of his free hand on the mahogany arm of his wingback chair.

"Hmph! But it was obvious from the autopsy that Lord Percival had . . . er . . . relations with men in the past. Even *those people* can't be engaged in sexual acts all the time."

"Ah, yes." Mycroft's eyes turned stormy. "So, you were wrong, Jones, but that has somehow made you feel justified in your false assumptions and—dare I say?—even more offensive in your bigotry."

"I wouldn't have thought it possible," Sherlock muttered, swirling his glass of sherry. "Indeed shouldn't being in error have the opposite effect from causing one to stick to one's initial theory?"

"It never does for you, 'Olmes." Athelney turned towards Sherlock. "There ain't nothin' to reduce your arrogance when you're wrong about something."

"How would we know?" Sherlock took a puff on his pipe.

Diverted, Mirabella turned her back, straightening Sherlock's stacks of papers on his desk next to his chemistry lab on the opposite wall. Sherlock was right of course, but she couldn't help liking Athelney in spite of his arrogance. She was steeped in arrogance after all, spending most of her waking hours at 221B Baker Street. At least Athelney was jovial. He certainly enjoyed his station in life. There was even a certain lightheartedness to his insults.

"Look here, Mr. Sherlock 'Olmes, this is a case that requires police work, not the speculation and theorizing of which you are so fond. I'm only dealing in facts here. And the facts is that Percival was a pansy. And he was getting a bit 'o action." He rubbed his chin. "Just not on the night of the murder."

"It is crucial information, to be sure. And have you been able to find the man dressed in the vampire costume, Constable?" Sherlock's sarcastic amusement was written across his face as he set down his pipe and picked up his Stradivarius, plucking on the strings.

"Naturally we have not. If we had, we would have the murderer."

"Technically Mrs. Kitchens was the person who poisoned Percy, allowing for his murder," Sherlock said.

"Now I know you're bonkers. Not so, Mr. Holmes! Ha ha! The body showed signs of asphyxia. There was no poison in Percival's system and no poison in the food." He smiled broadly. "Now who has the false assumptions?"

"Asphyxia?" Dr. Watson considered these words with interest. He appeared to be deep in thought as he inadvertently stroked his dark blonde mustache where it met his long sideburns.

"What are you thinking, Watson?" Sherlock raised his eyebrows.

"Lord Percival's blood was drained, and yet his body reacted in death as if he were strangled—which the marks on his neck did not indicate."

***

Recalling Percy's body, a young man taken in his prime—a *friend*—Mycroft felt his gut clenching.

True, he encountered murder and terror everyday, but to have his club and his friends targeted was devastation.

For Mycroft's own reputation and position, he was concerned, but those concerns paled before other considerations. To personally face the hatred in the world in such a beastly manner was sickening, taking him out of his usual joy and pleasure in life, to say the least. One had to take care not to let the hatred of others turn one dark.

The only solution was to hold onto the love, joy, and kindness in one's heart.

While taking solace in opera, art, and fine dining, of course.

Sherlock studied Athelney. "And what did the autopsy show was in the body? Only the dinner? Did it match up to the cook's description?"

"The dinner and the wine, yes."

"And the mushrooms?"

"Oh, the blasted 'shrooms. Yes, yes, they were there. Along with the beef and the vegetables." Athelney sneered. "Poison indeed."

"What type of mushrooms?" Sherlock set his violin beside his chair.

"You thought you had me there, didn't you, 'Olmes? Not the

poisonous type. It was . . ." He took a piece of paper out of his pocket which he subsequently read. "It was the Coprinus mushroom."

"Ah ha! As I suspected," Sherlock exclaimed, standing from his chair and punching his fist in the air. "The Coprinus mushroom was the instigator of Percy's death, administered by Mrs. Kitchens."

Mycroft yawned, motioning to Miss Hudson for another sherry. She was a dear girl. And curious, which a person of intelligence should seek to be. Curiosity was at the root of most pleasure and all achievement in life.

"But I just told you the Coprinus mushroom is not poisonous and there was no poisons in Lord Percival's body. What the devil are you spouting off about, 'Olmes?"

"The wine is where you should be focusing, Police Constable," Mycroft said languidly, accepting the sherry.

"*The saints preserve us.* What are you talking about, Mr. Secretary?" Athelney demanded. "We tested the remains of the wine bottle—it weren't poisoned."

"In a manner of speaking," Mycroft brushed the sleeves of his super fine tuxedo jacket.

"What in the blazes are you blathering on about? You're as bad as your brother."

"I should hope so. Perhaps something will be accomplished." *I do hope Shirley doesn't over-exert himself in the attempt.* His younger brother had been a person of unusually high energy even in the womb; he had almost driven their dear mother crazy. Shirley's brain *never* stopped, and rarely did his body.

He himself at least had the good sense to know when to rest.

"I tested the wine myself," Sherlock agreed, beginning to pace the room.

Of course you did, brother dear. Mycroft took another sip of sherry. *But I know what you found without asking.* Shirley was always one to do things by the book.

"I know very well the wine wasn't poisoned," Sherlock concluded. *Naturally.*

"How would the wine 'ave killed Lord Percival then? You're spouting nonsense as usual. Only I'm hearin' it in duplicate."

"I assure you there is nothing nonsensical about this murder," Mycroft said. "It was expertly planned."

"I know your great disdain for theorizing, Constable. Therefore, I withheld my opinion until I was certain. Which I am, now that you furnished the final clue," Sherlock proclaimed.

"Me? Furnished . . . And what clue was that?"

The relations of course, Mycroft thought.

"The relations of course." Sherlock looked about the room, appearing to lose interest in his conversation with the constable—quite understandable, it would bore a turnip—as the specifics of the case revealed itself to him.

"Do you remember the recent murder of the female prostitute, Constable? A particularly gruesome murder," Sherlock asked.

"Of course I do. I weren't put on the police force yesterday."

"This murder is along those lines: a crime of passion," Mycroft said. "Whoever performed this murder has a great hatred of men of a certain persuasion. You share that in common, Constable."

"Now see here. Because I don't think it is godly or natural, don't mean I support murder." Athelney cleared his throat.

"That's a relief, Constable. There was some question in my mind on the subject," Mycroft added.

"I assure you Police Constable Jones will proceed with the same degree of professionalism he advances to every case," Sherlock's countenance was expressionless.

"That is my precise fear," Mycroft murmured.

"Naturally I will. But the evidence shows that the vampire did not have relations with Percival. Or, rather, no one did on the night in question."

"And what does the lack of relations prove, Constable?" Mycroft asked. "That the vampire wasn't a male prostitute? That he wasn't Percy's lover? Not necessarily."

"But you told me earlier the lack of relations did prove that. And chided me right rough over it."

"True. But you can't expect me to pass up an opportunity to inflame your sensibilities, my dear Athelney." Mycroft leaned back into the settee, stretching his legs out before him. "It forces you to confront the disparity between your logic and your prejudices, as well as providing amusement for me."

"Deuce it all, Mycroft Holmes. We've a murder to solve and don't need foolish antics on top of it."

"There, there, dear Constable. The mental exercise is good for you."

Pointless, probably, but one must try.

"Perhaps the vampire loathes persons of this persuasion and has set a trap for them. Murdered them in fact," Dr. Watson posed. The good doctor generally had a handle on things.

Mycroft nodded absently. "Unless I miss my guess, the murderer wishes to send a message."

"Mere speculation," Athelney pronounced.

"It isn't speculation that we have a dead body. Or that Mrs. Kitchens has vanished. As the vampire has," Sherlock said.

"Both temporary employees, in a manner of speaking." Mycroft added somberly, "And yet, Mrs. Kitchens might be under our very noses—who Denzil will identify. I'm surprised you haven't rounded up some possible suspects for Denzil to identify, Constable."

"Damn it to hell," Athelney muttered. "I've no reason to be interested in Mrs. Kitchens at this point. Why do you keep saying Percival was poisoned? The autopsy proves it weren't so."

"To the contrary. The Coprinus mushroom causes illness when consumed with alcohol," Sherlock said "The Coprinus aren't deadly—necessarily. However, if combined with wine, they would result in sickness and weakness, enough to make the murder easier. *Much easier.*"

"Reducing a man's ability to fight back is often the difference between life and death," Dr. Watson said.

"They both ate the mushrooms. Then why didn't the vampire get sick?" Athelney asked.

"Aha!" Dr. Watson exclaimed. "Because he didn't drink the wine. Both ate the mushrooms, but only one of the party drank the wine, and we know it to be Lord Percival."

"Recollect that only one of the glasses had wine in it," Sherlock said. "As Watson pointed out, we already know that Percy was a wine drinker."

"Then how was Lord Percival actually killed if the mushrooms only made him sick enough to overtake?" Athelney asked.

Chapter Ten
An Unusual Murder

"There is nothing more deceptive than an obvious fact."
- Sherlock Holmes in "The Boscombe Valley Mystery"
by Sir Arthur Conan Doyle

"Watson, I know you can answer this question. But may I pose it to my assistant?"

Dr. Watson nodded graciously, his turquoise eyes alight with understanding.

Mirabella moved nervously towards Sherlock, hoping she didn't miss the question. Inadvertently she touched the cameo at her neckline.

"Miss Hudson, what plant when consumed does not reveal itself in an autopsy, the only evidence being asphyxia, which could be rooted in any number of causes?"

She released her breath. "Aconite. Sometimes called monkshood or wolfsbane."

Whew! With four men staring at her, she was relieved to know the answer.

"Precisely." A slight smile formed on his lips.

"I thought of that," Athelney said.

"Did you, Constable?" Sherlock ceased his pacing to return to his seat.

"But we found none in the food which was left on the plate." Athelney said smugly.

"Do you recall the small dart mark on the Percy's neck? Almost hidden by the fang marks, as was no doubt intended?"

Dr. Watson whistled to himself. "A tincture."

"The monkshood was put into a tincture, used to coat the needle, which was inserted into Lord Percival's neck," Mirabella said, feeling excitement as confusion moved to comprehension.

Sherlock nodded. "Then it was only a matter of time before he died of the loss of blood—or asphyxiation—whichever came first."

"Dreadful." She shivered. "What a horrid thing to do."

"Essentially both are caused by lack of oxygen," Dr. Watson added.

"Certainly not the dinner guest I would care for." Mycroft frowned.

"Would you say our murderer is a chemist?" Sherlock posed.

"That or a Shakespearean actor. There is quite a bit of unnecessary drama to the murder," Mycroft said.

Sherlock leaned against the window, looking out onto Baker street. "I wouldn't say the drama is unnecessary. It served its purpose."

"Indeed, the element of revenge is strong in this unholy assault," Mycroft added somberly. "It was not an immediate death. I expect that our murderer had a conversation with his victim."

"He genuinely hated the deceased," Mirabella said.

"I can't disregard the theatrical aspects," Mycroft said somberly. "The general public is all agog over 'Varney the Vampire'. The serial publication is somewhat humorous, but also terrifying in its implications of the supernatural."

Athelney shook his head. "The tincture doesn't make sense. Too much trouble. Why not kill Percival with the wolfsbane in the food?"

"Because the poison would have to be in both dinners," Dr. Watson explained. "It would have aroused Percival's suspicions if his vampire guest had abstained."

"Not the thing at all." Mycroft nodded somberly. "That's why this is so ingenious: Percy was just debilitated enough to be unable to fight back."

"And no poisons were found in the food," Dr. Watson added. "Creating confusion about the murder weapon and pointing to a supernatural being."

"The method threw suspicion away from the kitchen," With his prominent chin and piercing gaze, Mycroft's strong masculine features were never more evident. "Quite effectively, it appears."

"If indeed Mrs. Kitchens assisted in this heinous murder, what then was her motive?" asked Athelney.

"I should say that you find her and question her," said Mycroft.

Sherlock warned, "This case is confused by motive, knowledge, and means. If I give you poison telling you it is medicine, and you give it to someone who dies, who is the guilty party?"

"You, of course, Holmes," Athelney grumbled. "I've thought so all along."

"We only just learned that Lord Percival died of asphyxiation, leading us to the monkshood, which could not have been administered by Mrs. Kitchens. All clues point to the vampire as dealing the final blow," Sherlock concluded.

"That's what I said from the beginning," Athelney objected. "And you lead me on this wild goose chase. I was right all along."

Mycroft chuckled. "Collecting the facts is never a wild goose chase."

"Granted you were right, Constable," Sherlock conceded. "But for the wrong reasons."

"Faith and begorrah." Athelney looked up to the heavens, as if praying for patience. "Cooking up mushrooms could be done without intent to kill. But sticking a needle in someone's neck and pumping in poison is a bit more deliberate."

"Combining the wine and the Coprinus mushroom was both cold-hearted and deliberate," Mycroft said.

"As well as necessary to the crime," Sherlock said. "Nothing will hold up in a court of law without evidence. You must find your suspects, Constable. That will lead you to the motive."

"True. Simply taking a stab in the dark and hitting upon the answer will not do," Mycroft agreed.

"Perhaps it was a religious conviction," Mirabella suggested. "Because Lord Percival was *different*, you know."

There was no amusement in Mycroft's expression. "You speak of 'religious conviction' as if it were the murderer's relationship with God. This heinous act had nothing to do with God."

"If the victim's sexuality is a motivator, I suggest we look at the family of the man who had the love affair with Percival," Sherlock suggested.

"Overton Bristow?" Athelney rubbed his chin.

"Indeed."

"I wonder. Do you think there is the possibility Overton Bristow didn't commit suicide—but was murdered as well?" Mirabella asked softly.

"Ah ha! You're sounding like a detective now, Miss Belle." Sherlock turned away from Athelney to look at her. She would have been elated at the rare praise from her employer if it weren't for the somber nature of the topic.

"We already looked at that," Athelney said. "There was a suicide note indicating Overton's despair over his affair with Lord Percival, confessing that a love affair between men was wrong."

"I question the authenticity of that note. Overton and Percy got along famously," Mycroft said quietly. "And were *not* riddled with guilt."

"The obvious suspect would be the betrayed fiancé," Dr. Watson suggested. "She has been utterly humiliated."

"Overton was too heavy for a woman to carry," Athelney said.

"Remember, he was hung."

Sherlock rubbed his chin, "I believe it is something that we should consider. There is too much at stake."

"Do what you will, 'Olmes. While you are sitting in your warm parlor drinking your brandy and discussing the cases, we policeman will be out on the streets finding the answers." Athelney added under his breath, "Proving what we knew to be right from the beginning."

"We shall need every bit of brain power we can muster on this case." Sherlock picked up his hat as he headed for the door. His parting words were mere mutterings to himself.

"Data. I must have data."

Chapter Eleven
Whitechapel: The Body Tells All

"There was something awesome in the thought of the solitary mortal
standing by the open window and summoning in from the gloom outside
the spirits of the nether world."
- *"Selecting a Ghost" by Sir Arthur Conan Doyle*

"Shouldn't we be looking for the vampire and the scullery maid?"
Mirabella went to the wash basin to wash her hands.

"We haven't been given leave by the Yard to do so. We provide
the clues and it is the Constable's job to find the suspects." Sherlock
frowned, indicating that he was not entirely confident in the collaboration.
"Patience, my dear girl. Give the police a little more time. We mustn't
save them every time or they never learn."

From Sherlock's attire, it wasn't evident if he was about to engage
in a boxing match or if he was ready to work. He had foregone his usual
ascot tie and wore a loose shirt open at the neck revealing his muscular
chest. For warmth he wore a casual corduroy jacket, and a fedora hat atop
his wavy ebony hair caressing his unshaven face. When Sherlock was in
the middle of a case he rarely took time to attend to the niceties, the result
being that he had a bit of a wild, crazed look.

There was an uncontrolled intensity in the air, as always happened
when Sherlock was on the verge of something momentous.

"The police do have another eye witness. Longstaff." Dr. Watson
looked more than his twenty-nine years of age today as he removed the
white sheet, studying the body on the table. The good doctor, of course,
was impeccably dressed in a three-piece wool suit. Running along a train
track, dodging bullets, dissecting bodies, or dining at the *Clarence*, it
didn't matter, John Watson would be dressed superbly.

"Our esteemed butler has shed no light on the case." Sherlock
examined the instruments Mirabella had cleaned. "He said he never got
a good look at the scullery maid, other than stating that she was above
average height, sturdy, shy, and a brunette."

"What about Florence Fairclough?" Mirabella asked, handing
Sherlock the scalpel. "Has anyone questioned her? She had reason to hate
Lord Percival. It rather sounds like a description of her."

"I wouldn't call Florence 'sturdy'. Quite thin to my way of thinking." Dr. Watson put on his gloves, not generally done by doctors but something Mirabella had suggested after reading Robert Koch's publication on germ theory.

"The gentle sex is your department, Watson. I bow to your superior knowledge of female contours," Sherlock said. "Both Florence and Fairclough are each other's alibis, in a manner of speaking. Fairclough was in his study that evening, he said, while his daughter was in the laboratory behind the shop. She spends most of her time in the laboratory according to her father, who expressed a wish that she might socialize on occasion."

"So neither has an alibi," Dr. Watson concluded. "Fairclough believes his daughter was in the laboratory, and Florence believes her father was in his study."

"Correct," Sherlock agreed.

"And yet they didn't attempt to lie or to provide the other with an alibi," Mirabella considered.

"That is certainly noteworthy," Sherlock said.

"There is a murderer on the loose. We must do something." Mirabella protested their calm acceptance of the situation.

"There are many murderers in London," Sherlock examined the eyelids of the corpse.

This is cold-hearted, even for Sherlock Holmes.

He must have felt her disapproval, because he looked up momentarily, answering her thoughts as he was wont to do. "I have never cared so much about a case in my life."

His unexpected answer surprised her. "Why is that, Mr. Holmes?"

"Elementary. An unsuccessful resolution would destroy my career before it gets off the ground. My life's work. *My life.* And, of greater significance, because it impacts my brother. *His life.*"

"I see, Holmes. It's personal." John nodded without taking his eyes off the body."

"Exactly what a case should never be."

Mirabella could see the truth in this. Sherlock was a young detective with few cases under his belt. He was extremely gifted, but no one at the Yard liked working with him—probably for that very reason. Sherlock had, let us say, difficulty in social situations. If Mycroft were eliminated, there would be no reason for anyone to put up with the foreign secretary's younger brother.

"Caring about something does not insure failure." Mirabella lit several oil lamps that they might see better. "Do listen to yourself."

"I'm sure I never do anything else."

Mirabella placed the handkerchief over her mouth. "Honestly, Mr. Holmes. Your fear of emotional attachment is more likely to impede the resolution of the case."

Sherlock picked up the scissors. "I assure you that I fear nothing, my dear girl."

"Except the absence of work," she added softly. *And the entanglement of the heart.*

Dr. Watson chuckled. "Indeed, the absence of danger is far worse to you than the things most men fear, Holmes."

"To be sure."

Sherlock would rather be dead than to be bored.

"As long as the violence is directed at me alone," Sherlock added gravely.

"The clock is ticking." Mirabella shook her head, drying her hands. "Shouldn't we be searching instead of performing scientific experiments here?" *In this strange, dark, dingy room in Whitechapel.*

"Holmes is correct. It isn't our job to hunt down the murderer, merely to point the police in the right direction. Holmes is a detective, not an officer of the law."

"It rarely seems to work out that way," Sherlock said. He was new to detective work and still negotiating his relationship to the Yard, as evidenced by Sherlock's frustration with the case. He was not in a position where he could call the shots, though everyone might benefit from it if he were.

Sherlock handed Dr. Watson the razor who began cutting into the body. The young doctor was relatively new to his partnership with Sherlock as well, still learning the particulars of their alliance. John Watson had quickly concluded that his friend had a different perspective on, well, almost everything.

Sherlock's eyes followed Dr. Watson's razor. "Wiggins is on the case. Unfortunately, we cannot rush the resolution, though we might wish it. I am, even now, collecting data."

Mirabella moved the lantern higher above the body so all might see better. "Why are we here, Mr. Holmes? And where is this place?"

"I should think it would be evident why we are here, Miss Belle. I have rented this room in Whitechapel because you insisted I remove the cadaver from my rooms on Baker Street."

"Actually that was my Aunt Martha who insisted on the removal."

"Because you informed Mrs. Hudson the body was in my flat."

"No, the smell informed her. I had no need to say a word."

"Correct, there is never that need. And yet, you do, Miss Hudson."

"Holmes, I informed her myself," Dr. Watson looked up momentarily from his cutting.

"Oh, did you? And why is that, my friend?"

"Why do you think, Holmes? Because I found the living conditions unacceptable."

"I didn't know. I wish you might have said, Watson."

"I did."

Mirabella shivered while making every attempt to keep the lantern still. "Oh, this place is dreadful."

Right after torture and threats to her life, dissection and dealing with corpses was her least favorite part of the job. Although she believed in the afterlife, she could never get past the knowledge that someone had inhabited this body in the not too distant past.

I must remind myself that everything we do is to enact justice.

"There aren't many respectable places that allow one to rent a room for the purposes of dissection. Be thankful we have this opportunity and are able to arise out of the dark ages. There is nothing without knowledge."

"Yes, sir. You are right, of course." She glanced about to see the various tables, one with another body on it. "How many bodies do we need?"

"That is yet to be seen. If you would do the honors, Miss Hudson?"

Mirabella took the hand pump and began infusing the newly acquired body with alcohol, for the purposes of preservation, as Sherlock watched, coaching her.

"I've got it!" Sherlock exclaimed suddenly. Mirabella stopped abruptly to look at her employer, observing the light of revelation in his eyes. Mirabella sometimes thought Sherlock's enthusiasm upon discovery could illuminate all of London. She wondered that they needed the lamps any longer.

"What is it, Holmes?"

Sherlock took the device from her hands, studying it. "There was some type of hand pump utilized to drain the blood from Lord Percy's body. It's the only explanation which fits the facts."

"But why?" Mirabella asked.

"For the time being, let us address 'how'."

"Very well, what about the fangs in the neck?" She shuddered.

"That was a separate incident and had nothing to do with the draining of the blood," Sherlock said. "Recall the round prick inside the bite marks looking as if a dart had penetrated the skin. It might have been initiated by a needle and tube."

"I see. That was the venue through which the poison was administered," Dr. Watson considered. "And also through which the blood was drained. Ingenious."

"Indeed." Sherlock moved about the dark and dank room to the other body, even as Mirabella followed him with the lighting.

"Come here, Watson. What do you see?"

Dr. Watson set the razor down, calmly attempting the monumental task of transitioning his attention to match Sherlock's. John was remarkably patient, even as Sherlock's mind flitted from one thing to another.

John examined the neck of the second body. "Rope marks. It appears to be a hanging."

"Would you call it a suicide, Watson?"

"On the surface, yes. But since we are here, I have to suppose . . . Hmm . . ." Dr. Watson shook his head. "There are bruising marks—signs of a struggle, though very slight."

"I noted that. But could these marks have been inflicted after the death?"

"There are no marks or gashes on the head, only the slight bruising. Not the typical abuse to the body one would see in a murder."

"Perhaps the victim was poisoned first, as in the case of Lord Percy?"

"We would need to see the autopsy file, naturally."

"Ah, but the autopsy can lie."

Dr. Watson examined the corpse's fingernails. "Blood and skin underneath the nails, definitely a struggle. No, I would not deem this to be a suicide."

"There's something else, Watson. Look at the neck."

Dr. Watson let out a low whistle, shaking his head. "I'll be damned."

Mirabella attempted to peer over their shoulders without blocking the light. "There's another one of those small dart marks within the rope marks."

"Precisely," Sherlock exclaimed.

"It would certainly be easy to miss. Whose body is this?" Mirabella's suspicions were growing. *Please, dear God, don't let me be a part of an unholy endeavor.*

"Overton Bristow."

Mirabella's hopes were dashed as she almost dropped the lantern. "Oh my goodness. It wasn't a suicide."

"Precisely."

"We shouldn't be here." She gasped.

"It was your idea to investigate his death, you know."

"But I never meant that we should exhume his body . . ."

"Don't be absurd. We'll put it back."

"How long has he been dead?" Mirabella took a step back.

"Something over a month. As you can see the body has been embalmed," Dr. Watson said.

"Does the family know we have the body?"

"Certainly not. They never would have agreed," Sherlock said.

"This is very wrong." Mirabella felt her hands shaking. She hoped she didn't set the room on fire.

"Not at all. What is wrong is the murdering of innocent people," Sherlock stated.

"That is wrong also," Mirabella murmured.

"We shall find Bristow's murderer, and when we do, the family shall be grateful," Sherlock said.

"That is yet to be seen." Dr. Watson displayed a disturbing lack of confidence.

"At any rate, it is no concern of mine."

"It will be your concern if they put you in jail, Holmes."

"My objective is solving the case and protecting the innocent." Sherlock shrugged. "Besides, I would have you to keep me company, Watson."

"It does seem we have made a great deal of progress." Mirabella attempted to reconcile the benefits of their actions with her immanent descent into Hell.

"Without question, Miss Belle."

Mirabella added solemnly, "In addition to defaming the dead and disregarding the wishes of the grieving family."

"All progress has its cost." Sherlock's silver-grey eyes almost shone in the dark like moonlight.

"Now that we know both of these men involved in a love affair were murdered, it was unquestionably someone associated with Lord Percy and Overton Bristow who is behind these murders," Dr. Watson said.

"Percy, Overton, the Diogenes—and both friends of Mycroft's. All the connections strike me as strange," Sherlock considered. "Could it be a government conspiracy of some type? Mycroft is a powerful player."

"It is possible, but I'll be damned if I can come up with a motive." John Watson sighed heavily.

"And then there is the existence of Mrs. Kitchens. She holds the key to solving the puzzle. If it were an act of passion between two people, why do we have all these loose ends leading elsewhere?" Sherlock had a gleam in his eye which said he knew something he wasn't saying and which never failed to alarm her.

"Unless . . ." Mirabella considered. "Percival murdered Overton."

"It's unlikely Percival would be murdered with the same method he used to kill Overton."

"The tincture in the neck," Dr. Watson murmured.

"Correct. And there is no motive. I don't buy the 'our love affair is wrong' angle. That would be someone else's opinion, not Percy's," Sherlock said. "There's another consideration."

"Oh, and what is that, Holmes?"

"If this were truly only about Percy and Overton, the murderer would be finished, his revenge complete. And yet . . ."

Mirabella clenched her fists. "He isn't finished, is he?"

"No."

Sherlock shook his head. "Once one has a taste for murder, it gets worse. The relief the criminal expected never occurs—and yet he chooses to seek out the same remedy that didn't work the first time."

Chapter Twelve
The Madame's Apothecary

"After the first glass of absinthe you see things as you wish they were. After the second you see them as they are not. Finally you see things as they really are, and that is the most horrible thing in the world."

– Oscar Wilde

"How strange. There is none here," John Watson muttered, searching inside his doctor's bag.

"What are you looking for, Watson?"

"Laudanum. I have a patient who requires some for her nerves."

"I might have taken it," Sherlock said. "Laudanum is a helpful sleep aid."

"Dammit, Holmes! I only have on average twelve patients per week. Are you determined that I should lose them as well?" John knew that he owed Sherlock Holmes everything good in his life—as well as most of his aggravation.

"Ideally. That allows you more time for the essential work."

"Your cases, do you mean?"

"Precisely, Watson. You see? Your powers of deduction are already improving."

John slammed his bag shut. "It will be some comfort to me in my old age when I end my days alone and in poverty after you have been murdered by one of your many enemies."

"Do you truly expect to reach old age, Watson?" Holmes studied him with interest, never one to feign positivity.

"You're right. I can't possibly hope to stay alive if I continue keeping your company." To be sure, it was dangerous to be an associate of Sherlock Holmes, but that danger had taken John's mind off the memories which had been destroying him.

Better a quick death than a torturous existence.

Sherlock Holmes brought me back to life and gave me a reason to live. John Watson was half a man both mentally and physically when he came to Baker Street.

And I still am. Sometimes he feared he had lost his mind. Holmes had taught him—by example, no less—that one might be unhinged and a bloody disaster but still enjoy the heck out of life, living it to the fullest. Holmes had illustrated the co-existence of bliss and despair, advancement and destructiveness, service and encumbrance, genius and insanity.

His flat mate had no boundaries and less discipline.

"I have impressed upon you, Holmes, the necessity of giving up cocaine. Your body will always crave it, but the more you indulge, the worse it will be for you until you are a complete slave to the drug, with no control over your own existence."

"And I have given it up. I barely touch the stuff."

"So what are you taking? Laudanum. What do you think it's made of? Opium."

"At any rate, I can't agree with your assessment of my enemies, Watson. I can count my rivals on one hand." Sherlock appeared to consider John's words. "And I don't intend for any of them to get the better of me. Murdered by my enemies, why should you say so?"

"Or by your friends, as the case may be." The good doctor stared intently at his twenty-eight year-old flat-mate, extraordinary in so many ways and yet incorrigible in as many more. "And stop changing the subject, Holmes."

"If I am to die young anyway, I don't see what difference it makes: laudanum, cocaine, what have you. And as for poverty, I think not," Sherlock added, in general continuing the conversation in a one-sided fashion, as he was inclined to do. "I have invested your money well."

"And for that I thank you. Which has nothing to do with your drug habit, Holmes," John said stiffly. It was true. Certainly their weaknesses lay in entirely different areas. Holmes cared little for money and less for women or dalliance. He had a tender spot for Miss Mirabella, though the nature of that was difficult to discern. John had his suspicions.

As for money, it was ironic that Holmes always had plenty of blunt as well as an instinct for how to make it and how to invest it.

"And it may not be as bleak a picture as you paint," Holmes said consolingly. "Perhaps you will die with me in a victorious fight to the death over London's criminal element."

"Precisely the end I had hoped for, having survived Afghanistan."

Sherlock smiled in agreement. "An honorable end to a thrilling and meaningful life filled with excitement few can imagine."

"If we might put aside these rapturous imaginings for a moment." Dr. Watson raised one eyebrow at him disapprovingly. "You are not to remove anything else from my bag again, Holmes. Not only is it outside the bounds of friendship, but it is against the law. Do I make myself clear?"

Sherlock appeared surprised and somewhat affronted as his hands moved to straighten his cravat. "Certainly, if you wish, my dear fellow."

"I do wish."

"Only consider, though. You asked me to stop playing my violin at three in the morning which is the method I utilize to allow myself to sleep. It is at your door."

"And yet you have apparently both taken my laudanum and are still playing your violin at all hours of the night, Holmes."

"I only said you asked me to stop playing. I didn't say I complied."

Seeing that he was wasting his breath, Dr. Watson turned to Mirabella, now entering from the kitchen. "Could you, Miss Mirabella, go to the pharmacy?"

"Of course," Mirabella said.

"If it would not be too much trouble."

"It is no trouble at all," Mirabella smiled sweetly.

She was a dear girl. John held her in the utmost regard.

As a friend, he reminded himself as he appreciated her beauty. Miss Mirabella was too ambitious. Her conversation was primarily academic. She never tired of activity.

In short, she is too much like Holmes to be a romantic match.

John had yet to meet the woman who could hold his interest.

***

John's kind eyes met hers, and Mirabella found herself happy to do it. Studying the young doctor, so handsome with his athlete's physique and blond-streaked hair, Mirabella imagined that, even as an old man, John Watson's turquoise eyes would shine like the sun on the Mediterranean.

But now he seemed as if there were a storm raging on the waters.

John turned to look at Sherlock and those eyes turned glacial. "Except under extreme duress, laudanum should not be taken on a regular basis."

"I am under extreme duress," Sherlock objected. "The case is not yet solved."

"Perhaps I shall pick up some frankincense as well for Mr. Holmes," Mirabella suggested.

"Frankincense?" Dr. Watson inquired.

"If it was good enough for Jesus, I presume it should suffice for Mr. Sherlock Holmes. And," she added, "it aids in relaxation."

"Ah, your herbalist mother."

She caught the twinkle in Sherlock's eye before she headed for the door. For one who was so forthright and direct, he had a repertoire of subtle expressions one could miss if one were not observant.

Mirabella soon arrived at The Madame's Apothecary, almost a mile walk from the flat on Baker Street. At times a bit too far too walk, depending on the time of day and the packages one carried, but too short a distance for a cab. Many ladies would not think so, but she had no objection to exercise.

"Read all about it in the *Strand!*"

"Hello, Jeffrey." She smiled at the paper boy. She made a point to know everyone, following Sherlock's example. Though not social by nature, he emphasized the importance of contacts and was subsequently able to function in every social strata.

Quite remarkable actually. For someone who rubbed anyone in authority the wrong way because he did not hesitate to tell them when they were wrong, and for someone with few close friends, Sherlock had an astonishing number of acquaintances with whom he was on friendly terms.

Probably because Sherlock had charisma. He was memorable. Unforgettable. For someone so devoid of emotion, he touched everyone on an emotional level, engaging them.

Everyone either hated or loved him. *But they never forgot him.*

As she walked she heard the whistle of policemen, the ringing of a carriage bell, and the Westminster clock chiming. She found the *clippity-clop* of horses' hooves hitting the cobblestone pavement soothing, unlike the two cabbies yelling at each other from opposite sides of the street.

The *Madame's Apothecary* was owned by a Mr. Fairclough, who must surely be a wonderful man. She had heard it said the pharmacist had saved people from the workhouse—and that these paupers were even living on Mr. Fairclough's property. This was Jesus' work, surely.

She sighed happily as she approached the pharmacy door. For one interested in both science and medicine, the apothecary was a fascinating place to be. A doctor was unaffordable to most, so the sick sought medical advice from the pharmacist, who often was the local surgeon and dentist as well as the bloodletter.

The apothecary was a community center of sorts. Outside of the parish church, there was no place more central to the neighborhood.

Mirabella tilted her chin in greeting to one of the female workers inside, someone she had not seen before. There were two ladies stocking the shelves and a woman was even behind the counter handling the pharmaceuticals, herbs, and tonics. A woman could not be awarded a medical or law degree in Britain, but 'pharmacist' was one of the few professions open to women.

Which didn't mean anyone was required to hire them; Mirabella was under no delusions. It was Mr. Fairclough's shop and he was under no obligation to hire ladies, particularly since the vast majority of both men and women still trusted a male pharmacist over his female counterpart.

"Hello, I'm Mirabella Hudson." The wooden floor creaked under her steps as she headed towards the mahogany counter.

"Miss Hudson." A tall brunette with unusually dark eyes curtseyed, and she seemed troubled. She didn't take Mirabella's hint to introduce herself.

"And your name is?"

"Evie."

"Are you alright, Evie?"

"I'm fine, Miss. I must return to my work."

Goodness, the new lady was jumpy. It was obvious that keeping this job was paramount to Evie. She must be happy in her employment. This spoke well of Mr. Fairclough as a kind man.

And yet—was he? Fairclough had supplied Sherlock with his cocaine. It might be legal, but she nonetheless found it difficult to forgive the supplier.

Mirabella moved to the counter. "Hello, Mr. Fairclough."

"Miss Hudson. And how may I help you?"

"I need some laudanum for Dr. Watson." She forced herself to say it. "And valerian root and frankincense, please." Having a country mother well versed in herbal remedies, she was not without her own bag of tricks.

And she wasn't alone in that. Lining the shelves behind Mr. Fairclough was every manner of herbs, powders, tonics, drugs, candies, glass jars, ornamental labels, and colored liquids.

Some of the products were excellent—and some were not legitimate cures, she knew from her mother. She could see liver pills claiming to cure malaria, Holloway (gout and rheumatism), golden seal, scutellaria, and cactus grandiflorus green. "Dr. Batty's Asthma Cigarettes" were visible, claiming to treat asthma, hay fever, foul breath, all diseases of the throat, head colds, canker sores, and bronchial irritations. There was a disclaimer on Dr. Batty's that the cigarettes were not recommended for children under six.

Mr. Fairclough poured the contents from a large jar into a small brown bottle: a tincture of opium containing approximately 10 percent powdered opium by weight: the laudanum she requested.

"And will that be all, Miss Hudson?" Mr. Fairclough smiled at her, his grin a bit too toothy.

Mirabella glanced up to see Mrs. Winslow's Soothing Syrup, a medicine for children and infants that she knew to contain morphine. There were at least ten similar products used to quiet babies, the most popular being Godfrey's Cordial, consisting of opium, treacle, water, and spices.

"Nothing else, thank you." She bit her tongue but it did no good: her curiosity overcame her. "Do you sell much of Mrs. Winslow's Soothing Syrup and Godfrey's Cordial?"

"We do." He studied her inquisitively.

"I was raised in the country. Such things are rarely used."

"Probably because country folk can't afford them."

"I personally don't think opium and morphine are good for babies. Both are narcotics, and if infants are in a continual drugged state they will not be hungry—and could become malnourished." She held his gaze. "I see the same in Mr. Holmes, who has the smallest of appetites."

"You might very well have a point, Miss Hudson. I never use opium myself. But we do live in a country that values freedom for every citizen."

"Babies who are forced to take a narcotic are not given freedom," she said softly.

"If I don't carry it and other pharmacists do, I will go out of business."

"Perhaps. But everyone looks up to you. If you spoke out against it as unhealthy, no doubt many would listen to you."

He studied her with interest. "You are quite free with your opinions, Miss Hudson."

"So are many men, but that is not remarked upon."

His smile broadened, something she didn't think was possible. "I do like independent thinking in a woman. As a matter of fact, I didn't give any of those syrups to my daughter. I never wished her to be quiet—and yet she always was. Speaking of which, have you met my daughter, Florence?" Mr. Fairclough motioned to the lady assisting him behind the counter, a tall, thin brunette with an aloof manner.

"Only briefly. Hello, Miss Fairclough." Florence had dark hair and eyes, pale skin, and was not particularly pretty in appearance or manner, at least in a conventionally feminine way. Perhaps that came from her general demeanor and cold stare, however. She was rather long-faced with a square jaw matching her father's which added to the severity of her look. She did have lovely teeth, however.

"Good day, Miss Hudson," she said abruptly in a low, protected voice. And with that Florence spun round and returned to the back room.

Mirabella was taken aback, but perhaps Florence was shy rather than aloof. Sometimes the distinction was a difficult one.

Mr. Fairclough whispered, "I apologize for Florence. She recently lost her fiancé and it has been a trying time for her." He shook his head.

"I'm so sorry. And, yet, how wonderful that she has you—and employment. I envy all professional women."

"Florence is certainly devoted to her work. That's all she does." He frowned.

"And might I say I think it is wonderful you hire so many ladies here, Mr. Fairclough, in situations they would not otherwise have." Even were she able to earn a degree in science, it was unlikely she would be able to find employment in medicine unless she were able to open her own pharmacy or become a nurse.

The truth be told, under Sherlock Holmes' employ she had more interaction with bodies—albeit dead—than did most practicing surgeons. She had more interaction with corpses than did most zombie hunters. And, if she were honest with herself, she was more interested in research than in practicing medicine anyway.

"The ladies never give me any trouble. It is only the men who disappoint me." He looked down momentarily before his smile returned. "Do you enjoy your employment with Mr. Sherlock Holmes?"

"I do." She found herself responding to his friendly manner. And she wasn't the only one; she looked about at the women who were cleaning, dusting, and stocking the shelves. They were hard workers all. And they looked to appreciate their situation. Perhaps a bit too much in awe of Mr. Fairclough, but that was to be expected.

Something strikes me as odd, however.

"You and I have done business, Miss Hudson, but actually never spoken at any length," Mr. Fairclough said.

"I suppose that is true."

"Terrible thing about Lord Percival's murder."

"Oh, you heard about that?"

"Naturally. He was a client." He handed her the package. "Shall I put it on Mr. Holmes' account?"

"Yes, please."

Fairclough cleared his throat. "I do have a question which occurs to me now."

"Oh?"

"I heard Sherlock Holmes mention an older brother," Mr. Fairclough said perhaps a bit too nonchalantly. "I have recently learned that Mycroft Holmes is a person of note."

Mirabella couldn't imagine Sherlock making small talk with anyone, and certainly not mentioning his brother to someone who had no connection to him. "I suppose he is."

"Have you met him?" Mr. Fairclough asked, his lips suddenly pursed.

"We have crossed paths on occasion," she said. "In a professional capacity, you understand."

"And what is your opinion of the esteemed older brother?" The corners of Mr. Fairclough's lips turned down, as if he were disapproving.

She was a bit taken aback, but his manner was so cordial that she saw no reason not to reply. Naturally she would say nothing that wouldn't be generally known. "Gentlemanly, polite, delightful, intelligent—I should say wonderful on every level. The British government can't function without him, you know."

"Oh, I daresay it could. And do you hear much about the Diogenes Club, Miss Hudson?"

"What should I hear?" She really had no idea what he meant.

"I have a particular interest to join such an esteemed academic club. I understand the collection of periodicals is impressive."

"And what is your interest, sir?"

"Anything pertaining to science. Discoveries on the horizon are fascinating, are they not? Blood types are a particular interest of mine, most relevant to amputations and even dental work. And," he smiled, "There is a good deal of money to be had in it. No one knows why certain bloods are compatible—and others are not."

"It is a subject with enormous implications. As regards the periodicals, you would have to speak to Mr. Mycroft Holmes yourself on that matter."

"Have you done any reading on blood compatibility, Miss Hudson?"

"Yes, but there is not much to be read on the subject. No one knows."

"Some speculate compatibility is based on the purity of the soul."

"I find it unlikely that there is a match based on goodness. Otherwise, all good people would be healthy and all evil people ill. And you certainly know that not to be true."

He appeared to be considering her words, but it was a strange conversation to begin with.

"Besides," she added. "Who is to say whose soul is pure and whose is not?"

"There are certain reckonings."

What a strange choice of words.

Fairclough tapped his fingers on the counter. "The first blood transfusion was from a sheep into a fifteen-year-old boy who was thought to be mad. It was hypothesized that the blood of the gentle lamb might quiet the boy's agitation."

"And did it work?" she asked pointedly.

"I don't believe it cured the boy's madness. But it didn't kill him either."

"Returning the boy to the state he was in prior to the experiment cannot be deemed a success."

"Possibly not. Or perhaps such a small quantity of blood was utilized that the results cannot be deemed conclusive." He flashed that eerie smile at her again. "I understand that it can be difficult to obtain a private audience with Mr. Mycroft Holmes."

Not at all. He is remarkably approachable.

"I wouldn't be at all surprised, he is an influential man who travels in high circles." She replied matter-of-factly, but her manner was purposely stand-offish, feeling that the inquiries were intrusive.

"I meant no offense. All are aware of his . . . *influence*."

She nodded noncommittally.

"One hears of the intellectual clubs in London and might wish to be a member. That is the extent of my interest."

"I know nothing of membership, Mr. Fairclough, nor have I ever been, obviously, since the membership is all male." She took her package. "Thank you."

As she turned on her heel, she realized what had struck her as peculiar.

It was their teeth.

They all had beautiful teeth. How strange that all these ladies from the workhouse should have such lovely teeth. Either there was an incredible run of luck in the genetic pool, or these were all dentures. People who came from the workhouse could not afford dentures. She volunteered at *Lady Graham's* orphanage, so she knew how unusual it was for the poor and malnourished to have good teeth.

She turned to face him again and added softly, "It is so kind of you to give these ladies a position and a place to live."

He smiled. "Some take issue with it, but it is necessary to do what one can to improve the world."

"It is," she agreed. "And how nice that you have given all these ladies dentures. It must have been terribly expensive."

Fairclough appeared affronted, as if it was not information he wished generally known. He quickly grew resigned to it, however, as there was no use pretending Mirabella had imagined that which was apparent to anyone who looked. "It is training for Florence, so there is some personal benefit to it. If she is to someday take over the pharmacy, naturally she must be able to perform dentistry as well. Florence has a great heart for the ladies, you understand."

"But no dentures for the men?"

He frowned initially but instantly forced a smile. "If that is all then, Miss Hudson?" Suddenly he was the one in a hurry. He tapped his fingers on the counter a tiny bit louder than she felt was necessary.

She glanced in the corner to see Evie, a sturdy brunette, busying herself, as if she were uncomfortable with Mirabella's presence. "I've not seen that that young lady before. Is she new?"

"Yes, Evie just arrived from the workhouse. All her family lives on my property, including her children. She's had a terrible run of bad luck."

"That is most unfortunate." Mirabella pretended to recollect a conversation. "Could that be Evie Kitchens?" She was nothing if not bold. Or perhaps she had observed Sherlock one too many times.

Mirabella heard something drop and looked over to see Evie's hands shaking.

"Pick it up, Evie. Go in the back." Mr. Fairclough frowned, his eyebrows knitting together. He returned his gaze to Mirabella, correcting her. "Evie Travers."

But Mirabella was pretty certain she had hit the mark. Her words had clearly upset Evie. "Oh, yes, that is right."

His gaze fixated upon her, his expression suddenly dark. "'Kitchens' is nothing like 'Travers', Miss Hudson."

"Certainly not. I have no idea where I heard that name, I am much about town. Good day, Mr. Fairclough."

Chapter Thirteen
A Love Potion

"You can never be overdressed or overeducated" – Oscar Wilde

"Do you think it is safe to go out in public, Mr. Holmes?" Mirabella asked as Mycroft entered the flat.

"Because there is a vampire on the loose?" Mycroft's pale grey eyes added a softness to masculine features. A lock of black hair fell onto his forehead as he feigned a bow, acknowledging her even before turning to the gentlemen present. It was a rare gesture among Sherlock Holmes' guests—or society at large, for that matter.

It struck her once again how alike—and how different—the brothers were. Sherlock's resemblance to Mycroft was uncanny, but the elder brother was taller and more attentive to his appearance—unless it was a disguise and then Sherlock had the winning hand. Sherlock was more muscular, but one wouldn't know it from Mycroft's superb tailoring. And Mycroft had a more appealing manner: he was debonair and sophisticated, words unlikely to be attached to Sherlock Holmes.

Mycroft was—in a word—*exquisite*. He was always superbly groomed and dressed to dazzle. He had Sherlock's steel-grey eyes and piercing stare, hawk-like nose, and strong cheekbones. Whereas Sherlock's hair waved, Mycroft's was straight. His forehead was generally graced with a stray lock of dark hair. Somehow when you put it all together, it was a recipe for perfection.

"Because the vampire killed someone who was a member of your club." *Possibly two.* She felt a surge of anxiety. "Maybe there is a connection."

His mood grew suddenly somber, and yet he did not appear to be discouraged. "My dear girl, you're sounding like Constable Jones now. It is much safer to be amongst crowds than to be alone, to be sure. Believe me, I wouldn't meet privately with anyone I didn't know."

"What if the vampire is someone you know?" she asked softly.

"Someone I know? Don't be absurd. Even I keep better company than that. And the attack wasn't against me personally."

"That's a matter of opinion. I expect it was exceedingly personal," Sherlock muttered from his seat next to the fire. His resonating baritone voice made it almost impossible to miss anything he said.

Unfortunately. Sherlock has been particularly vexatious today, as he generally is until the case is resolved.

After which he is worse.

"And what will you be seeing at the opera, Mr. Holmes?" Mirabella asked, her eyes still on Mycroft.

He looked down at her through long dark eyelashes.

"The Elixir of Love," he said in that warm, open manner which was a bit disconcerting.

Oh my.

I am not man crazy, truly I am not. But neither am I blind. She knew very well there was not a woman in the world whose head would not be turned by Mycroft Holmes. Tall, handsome, sophisticated, *kind.*

Mirabella was also quite aware the debonair Mycroft Holmes meant to take no particular notice of her. It was mere amiability. Mycroft was congenial to everyone.

But no individual treated her with as much reverent politeness as did Mycroft Holmes. For a servant girl to be treated with chivalry and regard by a gentleman who associated with the Queen of England and the prime minister would make any girl's heart go a flutter. His charm was definitely not lost on her.

And she was nineteen years of age with no beaus in sight. *It is only natural for a girl to grasp at straws when she is doomed to the life of a spinster.*

There were worse fates—she would be a spinster scientist—but she was not without a young girl's dreams of romantic love, after all. She was not blind or without a pulse.

"An elixir?" She found she was somewhat breathless. "An elixir is medicine. How would anyone write an entire opera around that?"

"An elixir of love is a *love potion*, Miss Mirabella," Dr. Watson interjected, winking and smiling at her in his endearing way.

She looked at John for reassurance. He was the best of friends, someone she could count on to take up for her.

"Oh, yes. Of course." She blushed. No need for a love potion here.

Though perhaps a glass of ice water to the face is in order. She hated herself for not being more professional. She was such an ambitious and work-oriented person. Some handsome fellows show up and she was acting like a ninny-hammer.

"Miss Belle," Sherlock began, "I'm merely curious. Are you going to stand about gaping or do you have any intention of attending to your duties?"

"Holmes!" Dr. Watson protested. "Miss Mirabella works hard and does an excellent job around here. She deserves to be treated with some degree of courtesy and regard."

"And I deserve to see my paid employee working," Sherlock said matter-of-factly.

She glanced at Sherlock. Her eyes then moved to the knife in the wall holding his letters.

I wouldn't hurt him, honestly I wouldn't.

I merely wish to scare him into civility.

Why bother? There wasn't enough fright in the world to that purpose.

"Yes, my liege," she murmured with a slight bow of the head. Mirabella turned and headed towards the brandy decanter.

Sherlock's eyebrows shot up but he said nothing. At least that was something. Six months ago she would have been showered with a tirade of reprimand.

How I wish Sherlock might treat me as his brother does. As if he noticed all that she did, as if he appreciated it. Naturally her efforts were not merely for Sherlock—she liked her work and she wished to excel at whatever she did—but for some unknown reason she wished he might take notice of her.

Mirabella looked into his eyes and held his gaze, inviting him to pick up the torch. She, too, knew how to use the English language to her advantage, though she was confident he understood her meaning without the use of words.

For a moment, she thought he might. He shared his brother's grey eyes but Sherlock's were darker, like a thunderstorm. He was more muscular, less soft. His raven black curls were brushed away from his unshaven face. He looked particularly wild this evening, in contrast to Mycroft's pristine appearance.

"I believe you are jealous of the attention your older brother is receiving, Holmes," Dr. Watson suggested.

"I am immune to such emotions," Sherlock said.

There, he said it for her. He could never feel that way about her. "Mr. Sherlock Holmes is simply happiest when he is cross."

"I assure you, Miss Hudson, that I am not happy now." He stared pointedly at her.

"That is no reason to insure no one is." Mirabella wrinkled her brows as she handed Mycroft a brandy, thereafter moving towards the kitchen.

"Miss Hudson?" Mycroft called to her.

Oh my goodness, it is simply delightful being whipped about like the dirty laundry. How strange that there was always a reproachful word for her—and yet no one could get along without her.

On the other hand, Mycroft Holmes was saving her from an unpleasant exchange, whether he knew it or not.

"Yes, Mr. Holmes?" she curtseyed with feigned deference as she took care to keep her attention directed at the older Holmes brother. She was perfectly delighted to snub Sherlock after his earlier set down of her.

"Do you have anything to nibble on? Something light?" Mycroft continued.

"We do have some lovely grapes and apples," she replied, finding her voice. *Sprinkled with love potion, of course.* "I was to serve them with our dinner—"

"Perfect," proclaimed Mycroft, smiling. She began to move towards the small galley kitchen off the parlor when she heard his voice again. "I'm thinking . . . do you have any cakes to go with that? Nothing substantial. Merely to complement the fruit, to be sure."

"There is an assortment of lemon teacakes in the larder which I was going to save for our lunch tomorrow—"

"Oh, that would be divine." She resumed her course for the kitchen.

"Miss Hudson?" Mycroft called.

"Yes?" She peeked her head around the galley door.

"Do you happen to have any cheese? Just a slice or two. You know one can't go far on fruit alone."

"Naturally, a cheddar from Somerset." She smiled at him, unable to be annoyed. Mycroft might be tiresome, but he was always kind. "Is there anything else, Mr. Holmes?"

"What more could I possibly need?" he asked.

"You don't need any of it," Sherlock muttered. "What you need is a good row down the Thames."

"Unless you have some sausage," considered Mycroft.

"Miss Hudson, lay out the dinner as usual, and my esteemed brother can take what he will of our repast. Don't go to any special trouble on Mycroft's account."

"By all means. I wouldn't dream of being any trouble. I am only in search of a small snack, Shirley, and I shall be good as new," replied Mycroft so reasonably it was difficult to argue. "At any rate, I can't stay for dinner. I'll be dining with friends after the opera."

Honestly Sherlock's brother was so cordial, she would gladly pull a cart from one end of London to the other for him, while she found it difficult at times to cross the room at Sherlock's command.

"Pay attention, Mycroft," Sherlock commanded, as if he were the elder brother. "I have some news for you."

"Oh?"

"Overton Bristow was murdered."

Mirabella peered around the corner to see Mycroft suddenly as white as a sheet.

"How do you know?" Mycroft managed to utter.

"Never mind how I know. It is better for you if you don't know. Suffice it to say the body indicated foul play."

"So you've been to the graveyard." Mycroft nodded in contemplation. "I wonder how it wasn't caught initially."

"Very likely the coroner's obsession with the idea that the deceased was of immoral character caused him to overlook a few things, particularly since there was a suicide note. Some feel death to men of that orientation is well deserved. Suicide may have made perfect sense to the coroner."

"That is one explanation," Mycroft considered. "As is incompetence."

"Is it possible Percy was Overton's murderer?" Dr. Watson asked pointedly. Mirabella had no difficulty hearing the conversation as she worked in the kitchen a short distance from the conversation. It was a small flat.

"Oh, no. They got along splendidly. That's why it was such a great shock when Overton hung himself." Mycroft cleared his throat. "Or so it was assumed."

"So you see," Sherlock said, "There is cause for concern for your safety."

"I'm still perplexed as to what it has to do with Mycroft," Dr. Watson questioned. "Other than the fact that both were members of his club."

"Who knows what connections a demented killer makes in his own mind," Sherlock said. It was such a general statement that Mirabella knew he was hiding something: Sherlock never spoke in generalities. His was the most detailed mind she knew, and his conversation was specific.

To hide something from Watson was even stranger. Sherlock might be reserved with her, but never with John Watson. Even though their friendship was of a short duration, in some ways they were closer than Mycroft and Sherlock.

The fire now creating some warmth, not many minutes later Mirabella returned to the sitting room with hot tea, grapes, sliced apples, cheddar, salami and tomato sandwiches, spicy mustard, potato salad, and lemon teacakes, which she laid out on the table in front of the settee. It was roughly enough food to feed the British army—and all Her enemies. Thankfully the news of Overton's murder had not diminished Mycroft's appetite.

"Very good, Miss Belle." Sherlock motioned to the dining table next to the parlor furniture. "Please make a plate for yourself and sit at the kitchen table."

What does Sherlock mean by this? The invitation was quite a compliment to a female servant. Sherlock ran hot and cold; it was no wonder she never had any idea what he was about. One moment insults, the next honors. Sherlock Holmes was the most unpredictable man alive. But he certainly had his moments of generosity.

"Yes, Mr. Holmes." Sherlock was bestowing a great privilege in allowing her to eat in the vicinity of the gentlemen. If the truth be known, there was probably not another home in London where the female help was allowed to have meals with her employer.

Of course, as well as being the scullery maid and laboratory assistant, she was Sherlock's female operative on the rare occasion when he allowed her to be part of the team.

He's going to allow me to go undercover. This has to be it!

She attempted to hide her excitement. When she was on assignment, Mirabella chided herself that she must be as crazy as a loon to have allowed Sherlock to talk her into it. When she wasn't, she wished she were on the case.

I'm becoming as crazy as he is. Maybe I do have bats in the belfry. As does Sherlock Holmes. She was sometimes surprised at how much they had in common. A love of science, a desire to solve the puzzle, and now, insanity.

Mirabella moved to procure a plate for herself and to sit at the table. Her usual manner of obtaining information was to eaves drop—which was sufficiently effective—but this was certainly more comfortable.

"How delightful this is." Mycroft's mood had mellowed considerably since his arrival. "Wouldn't another brandy be perfect with this marvelous repast, Shirley?"

"Mycroft, let us get to the point." Sherlock sighed heavily. "Watson and I don't have all day to sit about eating. Frankly, I'm astonished you can eat anything after these murders. Miss Belle is past her appointed time of dismissal and is most assuredly tired from her day as well. Never mind the news I gave you; I have no doubt there is work to do or you wouldn't be here. What is the purpose of your visit?"

"It is very distressing." Mycroft popped a grape in his mouth. "But one has to eat."

"*Bloody hell*, Mycroft," Sherlock protested. "You might have been killed. It might have been *you*."

"Why do you think I am always in society, Shirley? This is a time to surround oneself with as many people as possible."

"Take care it's the right sort of people."

"You're one to talk, Shirley, always hanging about with criminals, convicts, and prostitutes."

"They tend to know what is going on, unlike the Yard."

There was a sudden knock on the door. Mirabella rose from her dinner to answer the door.

"Hello, Police Constable."

"And he doth appear," Sherlock murmured under his breath.

Athelney rushed passed Mirabella without acknowledging her, almost knocking her over.

"There's been another murder," he announced, standing in the middle of the room. Constable Jones' complexion was a pale, sickly color and his eyes were bulging. He looked like a man who was finally willing to to share the reins with someone else. Mirabella handed him a brandy, which he downed in one gulp.

"What I mean to say is there has been another murder associated with Lord Percival—but completely different."

"Another murder?" The color in Mycroft's face drained instantly. "You don't mean Mr. Denzil?"

"The cook," Watson muttered.

"That's it." Athelney's tone was both affronted and suspicious. "How did you know?"

"Do you mean to say that you didn't have a man trailing Denzil, Constable?" Sherlock demanded. "The only person who can identify your poisoner?"

"I didn't believe there was a poisoner. There wasn't any poison, after all."

"In theory Longstaff should be able to make a positive identification as well," Mycroft considered. "But I don't think he could identify his left foot from his right.."

"Speaking of which, isn't it interesting Longstaff was not killed—and Denzil was," Dr. Watson said.

"Most interesting, Watson." Sherlock stared pointedly at Athelney. "But he may be next with Constable Jones in charge of our suspects."

"Blasted nonsense! We've got no proof Mrs. Kitchens had anything to do with the murder. It was only one of your strange theories," Athelney huffed.

"A theory which appears to have been confirmed with Denzil's murder," Mycroft said.

"I must say that I overestimated your abilities, Jones," Sherlock said.

"I didn't think that was possible," Mycroft murmured.

"How did Denzil die?" Sherlock asked. "I presume the blood was not drained in this instance?"

"How did you know, 'Olmes?" Athelney looked at him in a startled fashion, his eyes wide.

"You said it yourself, that the murder wasn't the same," Sherlock said.

"This is very bad," Watson said. "This means the cook knew something. And that knowledge died with him."

"Precisely." Sherlock began to pace the room. "There will be one murder after another until we catch the killer. And now we've lost one of our two eye witnesses."

Constable Jones cleared his throat. "There's something else."

Sherlock turned on his heel to face Jones. "Longstaff is gone?"

"The saints preserve us, yes."

"You didn't have him in custody?"

"We did. But now we don't and Constable Cockburn has a lump on his head."

"An escape, eh? So you're out a cook, a scullery maid, and a butler," Dr. Watson considered.

"And a vampire," Mirabella said.

"It seems you've lost both eye witnesses and have no suspects," Sherlock said.

"I thank ye for pointing that out, Mr. 'Olmes," Athelney grumbled. He added somewhat sheepishly, "I do have a favor to ask of Dr. Watson."

"Of course." Dr. Watson was ever courteous. "However may I help?"

"It's just that our man is out sick—and Cockburn is laid up. Might you come and examine the body? Knowing your interest in the case and all."

Chapter fourteen
Killing Spree

"London, that great cesspool into which all the loungers and idlers of the Empire are irresistibly drained." – Sherlock Holmes, "A Study in Scarlet" by Sir Arthur Conan Doyle

Twilight. Mirabella walked towards Baker Street with her packages. It was becoming dark and she should have set out earlier. The gas street lights had not yet been lit, so illumination was at its worst point of the day: a fading sun without the benefit of gas lights. There was no Bobby in sight.

How could any street in London be so empty? It almost felt as if someone had been paid to disappear. What an absurd notion.

Granted there was an old man with a coal cart heading home. A fancy carriage heading north. A lady of the night who looked as if she were contemplating leaving for a location with more potential customers. That might have been an abandoned mine at this point. And a few children searching for a warm spot in the alley.

In other words, no one who would care about anyone in trouble.

London was not known for its empathy towards the destitute. There were so many unfortunates that one became hardened to it. In fact, it was now the fashion to go "slumming": a social night out at the slums observing those living in impoverished conditions as a source of entertainment. Mirabella shook her head in dismay. It was a depraved soul who, born into far better circumstances, laughed at the suffering and misfortunes of others.

She needed to make haste. Still, she couldn't ignore the children. They were shoeless, wearing rags with dirt smudges on too much visible skin, and thin.

"Hello there," she called to the children. "Don't be afraid. I have your dinner." She pulled a slice of bread and cheese out of her pocket, stored in the event she needed nourishment while on her errands. Once they saw the food, they moved forward. She could see the frenzied hunger in their eyes.

Mirabella tore the bread in half and gave a piece to each of the children, a boy and a girl, at arm's length. They immediately retreated but kept their eyes on her. She reached in her bag for a coin. She saved every tuppence for her dream of going to university, but the sight of these two, not more than six, broke her heart. "Here. Around the corner is a Salvation Army. This will buy you a coffin bed for the night which you can share."

The boy reached forward to take the coin and they both ran. She didn't know what they would use it for.

Survival, no doubt.

"The Reverend T.B. Stephenson on Bonner Road has a children's home for orphan and destitute children," she called after them.

They are too young to know how to care for themselves. But Mirabella knew she wouldn't be able to catch them—or to hold them if she could.

Probably the delay hadn't helped her. Mirabella resumed heading west on Marylebone Road and had not yet reached Baker Street when she heard footsteps behind her. She increased her pace. The steps picked up behind her.

While still moving, she glanced back to see a wide, muscular man, well-dressed, with pressed trousers, a flat cap, and a silk scarf around his neck. He certainly didn't look like a street thug. But there could be no question he was on her trail.

Why on earth am I being followed?

Being a modern woman and a one-time performer in the Parisian Circus—wearing tights and a form fitting skirt above her knees, no less— Mirabella sometimes dressed in a manner which would scandalize her curate father. For that which she had felt ashamed she now felt grateful.

Her Aunt Martha had said just this morning she looked like a dance hall girl. To be sure, there was a large white flounce at the bottom of her pale green dress. Completely inappropriate. But the most scandalous element of all was that the skirt was short—not quite reaching her ankles. Of course, her boots covered her ankles, but it was considered risqué to have one's skirt above the ankles regardless.

And thankful she was for those boots, allowing for movement. For heaven's sake, she was now officially a convert to the Sherlock Holmes' School of Fashion, something she never thought to say. Between corsets, form-fitting dresses, slippers, and floor length clothing, movement was in short supply among the ladies of her time.

In an instant, she was relieved of all guilt. Sometimes it was more important to stay alive than to be thought proper: she was able to move without tripping on her dress. She might be covered from head-to-ankle, but she did have freedom of movement, unlike her contemporaries of the female sex.

"Why are you following me?" she yelled back.

No answer.

"Answer me at once!" she demanded. But the assailant didn't respond; he only moved in her direction.

Mirabella's heartbeat was increasing. She knew she couldn't keep up this pace. Even if she broke out into a run, the man would be in a position of strength, coming up from behind her. She needed to face him rather than having her back to him. And her hands were full of packages, which put her at a disadvantage.

Mirabella saw an alley but didn't dare duck in there, completely out of sight. She might be country bred, but she had learned that city dwellers were accustomed to ignoring the plight of the poor and unfortunate—even victims of violence. She wouldn't give her pursuer the advantage of an alley or herself the disadvantage of being caged.

Turning to face him, she dropped her packages on a nearby bench. She moved behind the bench so at least a structure was between them.

But not far enough for a pistol or a blade to miss its mark.

Fear gripped her being, which she prayed might be exchanged for her anger. So far the fear was winning.

I may go to meet my Maker, but not without a fight. Quickly she reached inside her reticule for her Marlin.

The man moved towards her, but she had her pistol ready, a no. 32 Marlin pocket revolver. She gripped the ivory handle, which was smooth, in contrast to the silver embellishments on the barrel of the gun. "Why are you following me?"

"Na reason, miss." He moved forward, but she kept the bench between them. "Just keepin' an eye on you. A lady all alone shouldn't be out at night."

He reached up to the rim of his hat, a flat cap overshadowing his eyes, where his fingers pulled out a razor. "It 'ood be a shame if something were to cut that pretty face."

"Leave me at once!" she commanded, pointing her gun at him. "You're up to no good, and I've no need for an escort, as you can see."

"No need to throw a wobbly, is there?" His smile was even more terrifying than his stern frown. It was the smile of anticipation common to predators, to those who enjoyed overpowering a weaker prey. She might be relatively new to the underbelly of London, but she had learned to recognize evil during her one year in Sherlock's employ.

I had wished there might be more years to come.

"It's not safe on the streets after dark y'know. A lady might meet her death out 'ere." His voice was deep and bone chilling. He was mentally preparing her to be the victim. This she knew from Sherlock's training.

Not this girl. She shivered. *Not if I have anything to say to it.* Her heart was beating in terror even as her mind insisted she must not let this good-for-nothing put a period to her existence.

But no one was good-for-nothing. *No one.*

No, Father, not now. The voice of her curate papa came at the most inopportune times.

That was the problem. Because she loved God, she loved all His children, and she didn't see this man as irredeemable. She didn't see anyone that way.

Even as her would-be attacker with obvious ill intent cornered her around the bench she saw him as wounded and beaten down by life.

Everyone is born good. It is life that turns them dark.

He turned the razor in his hand, one angle and then the other. Life had done a pretty good job with this one.

Stop it, girl! Stop sympathizing with the beast or how will you save yourself?

"I told you to move on, sir," she repeated, mustering all the forcefulness she could. "What type of man are you to threaten a lady?"

"This type." He put the razor back in the rim of his cap and pulled an eight-inch blade from his pocket.

Heaven help me. I'll soon be the wounded one. At this time the voice of Sherlock Holmes would do her considerably more good than the compassionate voice of her upbringing. Sherlock had been working with her to insure that she had both the physical and emotional skills to protect herself and others. *To stay alive.*

But I hear nothing. Sherlock never ceased correcting her. Now that she could use his advice the air was empty.

Her attacker was only six feet from her—close enough to throw the blade and to hit her. Who would strike first, him or her? It was a game of Russian roulette.

The only time she was truly motivated to fight was when she was protecting someone *else*—and she was having difficulty summoning the necessary fury.

The moonlight hit the glistening blade and it suddenly became easier.

Play to win, girl! Do not allow the spread of evil or it will overtake all that is good. Finally, she heard Sherlock in her head, triggered by the weapon.

The blade of his knife was aimed towards her throat. This monster did not have a quick death in mind for her. He might have some redeemable feature in God's eyes, but that wouldn't stop him from murdering her in cold blood.

She felt her anger rising.

"Your time has run out sir." Her courage summoned, she clicked the revolver of her gun. "How dare you attack me in this manner. Why were you following me?" she repeated, pointing her gun at his heart. "Who sent you?"

He kept a close distance between them, the sharp blade glistening as it caught a flicker of the fading light. "I don't think you're goin' to kill me."

Mirabella kept the gun pointed at his heart, as Sherlock had taught her. Hopefully this indicated to the criminal she both had the skill to do damage and meant to do so.

At least the first is true.

"Tell me who sent you or I will kill you," she commanded.

Truly, I need to resolve this inner struggle in advance of a man coming at me with a knife. There is never time for hesitation or reflection in a battle.

"You shouldn't have gone nosing into what wasn't your business. Bloody wench."

"Nosing into *what*? I have no idea what you are talking about." She searched her memory, but only one event came to mind. She had done little else outside of housekeeping—with the occasional cadaver thrown in—for the past few weeks. "You don't mean The Madame's Apothecary?"

He moved forward, lifting his arm as if to throw the knife at her body. That was a fairly strong confirmation she had hit the mark. Let's hope he didn't hit his. He muttered, "I hate busybody females."

Heaven help me! I wish I had told Sherlock my suspicions about Evie. What with the commotion around Mr. Denzil's death and Sherlock being in such a foul mood, there hadn't been time. Now, if I die, no one will know.

Bang! She shot the Marlin.

As she shot the pistol, she was instantly transported back in time, reliving the moment she had killed another.

I know nothing of the family he left behind. Perhaps there were even children. She sobbed, the emotion of her present danger combining with her grief over murdering someone she didn't know committed to a cause she didn't understand.

I must not let the past interfere with my present functioning. Then, as now, the man will kill you if permitted. Then, as now, he is a murderer of innocents.

"Aeeee!" Her attacker wailed in pain, even as his knife dropped to the pavement.

He turned and ran, clutching his bloody hand.

He was right. She hadn't had any intention of killing him. At the last moment she had moved the pistol and only shot his hand.

Now this man is free to kill again. How many lives had he already taken? One? Two? Or more?

No matter what I do, I feel guilt. If she killed a man, she felt terrible. If she let a murderer go free, she felt terrible.

Her hand shaking, she reached down and carefully picked up the knife with her handkerchief in order to preserve the fingerprints, dropping the blade in with her packages.

I am horrible at this detective work.

Chapter Fifteen
Predictable Unpredictability

"Murder and torture must have a higher purpose"
- Moriarty, "Sherlock Holmes and the Chocolate Menace"

Still shaking, Mirabella arrived at the Baker Street flat in one piece, as surprised as she was grateful.

Stepping in the door, the scene before her was in stark contrast to her emotional state. Sherlock exemplified domestic tranquility sitting by the fire smoking his pipe. He was reading *The Illustrated London News*, a cup of tea on the marble end table beside him.

Mirabella made every effort to hide her turmoil, not wanting her inner landscape to become public, above all with Sherlock Holmes.

Sherlock glanced up at her, and in an instant his aloofness turned to alarm. And, it seemed to her, disapproval. "You've been assaulted, Miss Belle."

Apparently I have not suffered enough today.

Mirabella felt her hands trembling as she looked at him. When Sherlock's gaze met hers, she knew what was coming in spite of her efforts; she had witnessed it too many times to expect anything else.

I truly am not in the mood for Sherlock to see straight into my soul.

"It is utterly impossible that you should know this, Mr. Holmes."

"Clearly it isn't." Setting his pipe and newspaper down, almost knocking over his teacup with uncharacteristic clumsiness, he rose quickly from his chair and hurried towards her.

"I took care to be certain my hair was in place and my clothing smoothed so that you wouldn't notice any change."

"Attempting to fool me and succeeding at it are a world apart, it seems. But that is unimportant now." His voice was suddenly gentle.

Then Sherlock did the unprecedented: he assisted her with her packages before moving to procure a sherry for her. "Sit down and have a cordial while you regain your composure, Miss Hudson."

"I am quite composed, I assure you."

"Sit down." His actions were kind but his voice was firm, developing a hard edge. "Tell me who attacked you."

She bit her lip. As many times as she had seen Sherlock in action, she never got used to it. It was some small consolation that she was not alone in that.

"How did you know I had been attacked, Mr. Holmes? Was it my unsteady hands?" Although she was frustrated, she seated herself in Dr. Watson's chair, unable to keep her eyes from tearing up. She gladly took the sherry when it was offered.

"No. Although that observation supported my initial theory."

"Then how did you know?"

"Never mind how I know. There are more essential points to discuss. I can see you are still in one piece. Am I correct in assuming you are unharmed?" His demeanor was calm and resolute, but his pale grey eyes had turned smoky, fully focused on her.

"For the most part."

He seemed to breathe a sigh of relief as he returned to be seated in the fireside chair across from hers. "Then there is no need to enlighten me on that subject."

She shook her head in frustration at his blasé reaction to her near death. "I shall not waste your time then, Mr. Holmes, with a description of my terrifying attack."

"Not at this time."

"And what, pray tell, is the more important point?"

"I should say it is the unfortunate circumstance that your assailant is still alive and well. Give me a description of the blackguard without further delay, Miss Hudson."

Her jaw dropped. "How could you have ascertained . . ?" What she intended to be a sip of sherry was more like a gulp. "You can't possibly know that my pursuer is unscathed."

"I didn't say he was unscathed. I said he is alive." Sherlock's demeanor was emotionless. He always took everything for what it was, without emotion. And yet his tone was threatening. There was a dark side to Sherlock, a dangerous side. It was difficult to invoke Sherlock's wrath—he didn't care enough about anyone else's opinion to be concerned—but once he counted someone as his enemy, it was not a safe place to be.

"You can't know that either."

"And yet I do."

She stared at the half-empty sherry, wondering if it would be unladylike to refill the glass.

Of course it would. She rose and filled the glass to the rim. *It is a small glass after all.*

"Can you identify the person who attempted to harm you, Miss Belle?" Remarkably, he didn't comment on the sherry. Sherlock Holmes always offered an unsolicited editorial on everything no matter how minute or seemingly insignificant.

"No." She returned to her seat. "He was large. Wide, that is. Of average height. Not quite as tall as you, Mr. Holmes."

"How much shorter? Be specific."

"Only one to two inches."

"I wish you might be more specific, Miss Belle," Sherlock insisted impatiently.

"I do apologize. I didn't have a ruler with me." *Pardon me, could you put down your eight-inch blade while I take your measurements?*

"And what else?" Sherlock demanded.

She searched her memory, as uncomfortable as it was, even as she returned to her seat. "He wore a hat which covered some of his face. Except for his disturbing smile. He had rather large lips."

"Good." He nodded, as if he were committing her description to memory and drawing a composite in his brain. No doubt he was. "What type of hat?"

"It was a flat cap."

"And his clothing? Was he well dressed?"

"Yes." She gasped. "How did you? . . . Never mind." She grew weary of wondering how Sherlock knew the things he knew. Her head ached as it was. "That was the strange part about it. I hadn't really thought about it until now. He was exceptionally well dressed. His trousers were pressed and he even wore a *silk* scarf. He didn't look like a ruffian *at all*. But he was, the worst kind."

"Ah. And was he a Brummie?"

"From Birmingham? Oh, yes, I . . . I guess you are right, Mr. Holmes. He did speak with a Birmingham accent. Mr. Holmes, you're scaring me."

"Not as much as the Brummie did, I expect." Sherlock's expression was so hard it was rather frightening, exaggerated by his features: prominent chin, piercing stare, strong cheekbones, high forehead generally graced with dark curls, and a resonating voice perfect for reciting poetry or being on the English stage.

Sherlock's voice dropped, almost inaudible. "Did your attacker have a razor in his cap, Miss Belle?"

Her jaw dropped. "He did. How could you know this?"

"The vile beast is a Peaky Blinder."

"A *what?*"

"A member of the Peaky Blinder gang, so called because of the flat caps they wear, hiding razors, typically used to slash the faces of their victims." He rung his hands, something she had never seen him do before. "What sets them apart from numerous other street gangs is their dashing style of dress."

"Yes, quite fashionable to slash the faces of women."

"What was the color of his skin?"

"White. I mean, Caucasian. He was a bit tanned."

"Do you have a color for the eyes?"

She shook her head. "His hat covered them."

"Did you notice his shoes?"

"I'm sorry, no. I was more focused on the eight-inch blade in his hand."

He raised his eyebrows again, momentarily looking away. He seemed to be having some difficulty maintaining his composure, unusual for Sherlock. "Ah, and what type of knife was it?"

"I almost forgot. I have it!" She jumped out of the chair and ran to her packages. Gingerly she removed the knife, shuddering as she did so. In spite of her disturbance, she quickly dusted the knife and took a fingerprint. "Aha," she exclaimed. "I have one."

Feeling some pride in her achievement, she momentarily forgot her fear.

"Clearly the fiend expected to be successful in murdering you," Sherlock said gravely. "He took no precautions." He cleared his throat. "Excellent work in retrieving the knife, Miss Belle. Bring it here please."

She gingerly placed the knife in a handkerchief, handing it to Sherlock.

He studied the knife. "I am immensely gratified you were not injured, Miss Belle."

"As am I."

"Take a moment to consider this weapon. What do you see?"

"It. . . has a blade approximately eight inches in length," Mirabella said.

"I believe you'll find it is exactly eight," he corrected.

"Which is approximately eight."

He frowned. "I do not deal in approximations, Miss Belle."

Even if they are precisely correct. "Naturally you would not, Mr. Holmes. It would be a criminal offense. I stand corrected. The blade is *eight* inches." The idea made her heart stop. She swallowed hard. Somehow her usual banter with Sherlock helped keep the terror at bay.

He studied her intently but for some reason did not correct her insubordination. After a long pause he added softly, "And what else?"

"The knife has an edge on each side as well as a highly ornamented hilt."

"I am not interested in generalities but in specifics," he said tersely. "Your life may depend upon it, Miss Hudson."

Looking more closely, she observed, "The handle is a smooth material, possibly dyed and polished ivory. The hilt appears to be filigreed with . . . are those birds?"

His voice was even lower than his usual baritone timbre. "Bats."

"And on the pommel, a shield with a cross." She paused, a bit taken aback. "Bats and a Christian cross. What a strange combination."

"Not so strange." Sherlock was uncharacteristically silent for a long moment, his eyes fixed on the knife. "Bats. Vampires."

"But not vampires and Christianity," she objected, alarmed.

"In our villain's mind there is a connection." When he spoke again his voice was dark and dangerous. "Religion is among the most common reasons for murder. Do not let your beliefs blind you to this fact."

"I am well aware of that. Evil always finds a contorted reasoning to justify its acts of hatred."

"And your attacker's voice? What can you tell me about it, Miss Belle?"

"Baritone." She had learned this much in Sherlock's employ: to identify and classify.

"The same pitch as mine?"

"A little lower, definitely raspier, with an underlying sharpness."

"Good. If you only pay attention, there is much which can be discerned." From his chair, he glanced out the window onto Baker Street, as he often did when deep in reflection. "The overwhelming question is why were you attacked? I fail to comprehend the motive. There is no reason for someone to wish you injury. I have been wracking my brain attempting to answer this question and nothing presents itself."

She swallowed hard.

He reeled around to face her. "What have you done, Miss Hudson?"

"Why do you assume I have any part in this?" she asked sheepishly.

"You have obviously done something to get on the wrong side of someone. Unless I miss my guess, it has to do with this investigation. This macabre emblem on the knife is proof of that."

"Oh?" The implications were alarming.

"The design is likely part of an effort to present a supernatural element to the crime." His jaw was set in a hard line, his grey eyes dark and foreboding. "It would seem that you have done some private investigating on your own, Miss Hudson."

She leaned deeper into her chair. "I was only trying to help, Mr. Holmes. I had seen you do it so many times . . ."

"I repeat, Miss Hudson, what have you done?" His expression was a strange mix of relief and reprimand.

"I questioned Mr. Fairclough, and I must have hit a nerve."

"The pharmacist. When you went to the apothecary to get the laudanum." He seated himself in his chair.

"Yes. There was a new woman at The Madame's Apothecary: a Miss Evie. She had dark hair and dark eyes. I wondered if she could be Mrs. Kitchens."

"Wondering would not get you murdered. Surely you didn't . . . He slammed his fist into his other hand. "You voiced your thoughts? Of course you did, you always do. Miss Hudson, you absolutely must learn to control your tongue."

"I referred to her as 'Evie Kitchens' in order that I might watch Mr. Fairclough's reaction."

"Am I to understand that you goaded a possible murderer without first apprising me, Miss Hudson?" She rarely saw Sherlock display emotion, but she recognized contained fury.

And yet, she would place a wager he was impressed with her baiting Fairclough—at the same time he was clearly incensed.

"Why are you so angry, Mr. Holmes?" Generally his mood improved when the pieces of the puzzle began to fit together. No matter how horrible, the solution made Sherlock calmer. Even if he were to discover the end of the world was near, he would feel euphoria to have solved the riddle, despite the news of his ensuing demise.

"Why?" His eyes moved to the knife. "For one thing, you put yourself in danger, Miss Hudson."

"You put me in danger all the time, Mr. Holmes."

"Under my excellent supervision," he retorted.

"Irrelevant." Mirabella was surprised at how much she was sounding like him. Proof that she had been around Sherlock Holmes too long. "The work is always more essential than my safety."

His voice grew uncharacteristically soft. "Perhaps it has become a priority to me *both* to keep you safe and to solve the case."

"A recent development then."

"It is only logical. If you are alive you can solve more cases," he muttered.

"Your tender words are heart-warming, Mr. Holmes. You will make me giddy with sentimentality."

He rose from his chair and moved towards her, which somehow terrified her. In one fell swoop, he pulled her towards him. She could feel the taut muscles in his arms and even feel his breath upon her forehead. Her heart began to beat more quickly, she didn't know why.

"Is that what you desire from me, Miss Belle?" he asked softly. "Sentimentality?"

"No . . . no . . ." She gasped. "I don't know . . ." His dark hair fell into his intense grey eyes, impossible to ignore under his scrutiny. She felt completely out of her element.

He leaned towards her. She was so utterly astonished—this couldn't be what it seemed, after all. She opened her eyes wide in confusion.

For so long Sherlock had seemed larger than life to her, the most amazing, intelligent man of her acquaintance. She revered him even more than she did her own father, which was saying something. He was more like a magical entity than a human being to her.

It was inconceivable that Sherlock should view her in a romantic manner. Not only because of her reverence for him, but because his personality was almost mechanized. She didn't think he had those type of feelings for anyone.

I can't believe it. I don't believe it.

And yet, being held in his strong arms, her heartbeat quickened and she felt she was in the eye of the tornado.

And she was. Sherlock had enough charisma for all of the Shakespearean stage.

What would it be like? To be loved by Sherlock?

Madness. She would never be able to hold him. She was not his equal.

And he would break her heart.

Was she attracted to him? Of course she was. Everyone was. Even when people were repelled by Sherlock, it was because he had so thoroughly engaged them.

Even as she could not bear the thought of life without him, she could not bear the thought of being loved by him.

"What is it that you wish from me, Belle?" She felt his breath on her lips and wondered, for the first time, what it would feel like if Sherlock did kiss her.

I've just been through a terrible shock. I'm imagining things.

"Why do you criticize me when I have had a terrible scare?" *Why do I say such foolish things?*

He searched her eyes, his stormy grey eyes looking as if he might envelope her. She wished they might.

"Forgive me, Belle." Slowly he released her, stepping back.

"For reprimanding me? I merely wish you to care if I live or die. I don't wish to be corrected right now."

"It seems to me I'm the only one who does care about your life—you certainly aren't acting as if you care, Miss Belle," he blasted, returning to his usual form of communication, as if he were attempting to forget he had taken her in his arms.

I don't think I'll ever forget.

"That is what this entire conversation has been about. That and the fact that you are incorrigible, insubordinate, and wholly vexatious."

"Is this what not reprimanding me looks like?"

"You acted without my consent and that must cease immediately." He began to pace the room.

Mirabella would have been growing angry normally, but she still felt his breath on her lips and it was surprisingly pleasant.

Too pleasant. She did not wish to long for something that would break her heart in the end.

Something impossible. The last thing she wanted was to risk their friendship. His was the most meaningful relationship in her life.

There. I admit it. He is the world to me. His work. His life. His very being.

What an overwhelming day it was. The last thing she needed was an interchange with Sherlock. "So my almost losing my life is an affront to your authority? Is that your assertion, Mr. Holmes?"

It seemed easier to fall back into old patterns.

"You are entirely in the wrong here, Miss Belle," he exclaimed, clenching his fists. "Damnit, you could have been killed. You are in my employ. It is my job to discern which situations are safe and which are not, which are warranted and which are not. If you had spoken to me first, I would have scoped out Fairclough myself—and been prepared for him."

"As I thought, it's not really about my safety, you're angry because I compromised the case."

"I'm angry for precisely the reason I told you I was angry."

"Which is?"

"Because you jeopardized the case."

"As I thought. If I had died, you would have no idea why."

He glanced away momentarily, as if he were having difficulty containing himself. It surprised her.

"Sherlock?"

She had always called him "Mr. Holmes". It was strange how, over the last few weeks, his name had slipped out of her mouth. Even stranger that he had not corrected her.

He returned to his seat, his eyes intent upon her. "You would have died, Miss Belle. The criminal would have been alerted, subsequently threatening both the success of our investigation and my livelihood while placing the lives of other victims in danger. You're making as much a mess of this case as Athelney is—and that's saying something."

"Mr. Holmes, I realize now that I made a complete mess of things and for that I am sorry." She bit her lip. "But I've barely escaped with my life, if you could kindly go a little easier on me."

***

"If I believed that you ever learned from your mistakes, I would certainly do so, Miss Hudson. But, in fact, each mistake spurs you on to grander schemes and more pretentious disobedience."

Sherlock detested losing his temper. It was common. And uncivilized. *And no one can bring me to anger more quickly than Belle.* The idea of finding that sweet girl in a pale green dress of satin and white lace with splashes of blood on it, her features mutilated, was horrifying to him.

"I certainly meant to. But then the opportunity presented itself . . . I've seen you do this dozens of times . . . I thought I might smoke out our murderer."

"At that you certainly succeeded."

"Only we don't know who I smoked out."

"Precisely. Only observe where we now stand. All we have done is agitate the villain so that he is now prepared for us and plotting against us."

She looked as if she might cry. He hoped his words might cause her to reflect. And yet—she looked so young right now. So naïve. Belle was exceedingly youthful, at the same time she was a capable young woman.

A beautiful woman. *And I almost kissed her. Now, of all times, when she was looking to me for protection.* And she is so young, only nineteen.

It is not unheard of for a man of some ten years older to take a bride of nineteen.

A bride? Heaven forbid. Sherlock had no idea what had come over him. He was astonished himself.

He could not take advantage of Belle when she was in a state of terror. His own fear, his love for her had taken over.

Love? It could not be. . it must not be. *I do not wish to have emotions. I have a higher calling. I have work to do. I have a purpose.* But, whatever it was he felt it for Belle, a longing, a desire that she should always be in his world.

"You should have consulted with me, Miss Hudson, before initiating a plan. We would have found a way to take Miss Evie in for questioning and identification."

"If it had been before Athelney lost our only witness."

"Amateurs, all amateurs," Sherlock muttered under his breath. "Miss Hudson, this is important. Did anyone else overhear your conversation with Fairclough?"

"I'm fairly certain that Evie overheard it. Since I wanted her to."

Sherlock sighed heavily. "Anyone else?"

"I don't think so."

"Surely there must have been someone else in the apothecary?"

"There were at least two other ladies stocking the shelves, but they didn't appear to be attending."

"And Fairclough's daughter. Was she in the store?"

"Florence? She was behind the counter. I thought she had retreated to one of the back rooms. At least I couldn't see her from where I stood."

"I believe it is time for you to retire for the evening, Miss Belle. No doubt you are quite exhausted. And yet—I fear our villain may yet try again."

"Oh, no. You can't mean it?"

"I do." Worry overtook him. "If it was merely a warning, he might leave you be. If it was an act of revenge—he will attack again. You must be prepared at all times, Miss Belle. Frankly I lean towards the latter."

"And there is yet a third motive," Mirabella murmured.

"Indeed. If our would-be assassin still perceives you as a threat, believing you to know something he doesn't wish repeated."

Sherlock frowned. Ever since Watson—and now Belle—had come into his life, things were vastly more complicated.

And his life was richer. His use of cocaine had decreased, that must be an indicator of some improvement in his outlook. If Belle continued to play the musketeer, that trend would be reversed.

She must not.

"On the other hand, the scoundrel must surely think you have already told everyone you intend to by now. As well as knowing that you are not quite as easy a mark as he had thought."

"How did you know I had been attacked, Mr. Holmes? I believe my appearance is tolerably normal."

"Normal? I think not." *Exquisite? Perhaps.* She had on a satin gown of a lovely pale green accented with white lace and white flounces down her back, almost like a bustle, accenting her lovely hips and long legs. Not quite to the floor, displaying her ankles, risqué by some standards.

And delightful.

"How did you know?" she repeated.

"Hmm? . . . Oh, yes . . . I smelled the smoking gun when you walked in the door, of course. So you must have fired it."

"How does it follow that the knife thrower got away?"

"If you had killed your foe, you would have gone to the police, and they would have escorted you home. Hence, I concluded that you had been attacked, you fired your gun, and your pursuer is free."

"Oh, yes, I see." She pursed her lips in a sudden understanding.

"In addition, I know your aim to be excellent, Miss Belle, so it does leave me to wonder how you missed."

"I wonder that myself."

He closed his eyes momentarily. "It is possibly for the best. You would have had to justify shooting someone to the police, even though the brute was coming at you with a knife. That is the peculiar state of our justice system: you would have been the one on trial."

He studied her, so delicate and vulnerable—so exceptional in every way. *And so naïve.*

Complicating my life in all the ways I do not wish to have it complicated. Besides, Fantine was his perfect match: brains, beauty—and without any feeling or attachment. Outside of being his arch enemy's sister, it had been an ideal arrangement. Excitement and unpredictability without any connection.

Of all things, Sherlock hated attachments. They interfered with his work, compromising the integrity of his decisions and giving his enemies ammunition against him. Fantine had been too close to Moriarty—so he broke it off. It had been surprisingly easy to do.

Another thing he liked about her.

As for Irene Adler, Sherlock had always had the greatest admiration and respect for the actress—his ideal vision of womanhood—but he had never had the slightest emotional connection to her. Irene had led everyone to believe she was a loose woman blackmailing the King of Bavaria for money. She gave the impression of being a schemer and a contortionist. When, in fact, the King was the heel: he had used her and tossed her aside, desiring to keep the affair secret—or better yet, to sweep her under the rug for good. Irene held onto the only card available to her as insurance: the photograph.

Irene Adler outsmarted the great Sherlock Holmes, as well as the King of Bavaria and all his paid mercenaries. Every value of devotion, loyalty, and ethics Irene held dear; she had the brains to insure her own survival and that of her husband-to-be, Mr. Norton, while fooling all as to her true nature. Sherlock held Irene Adler in the highest regard. But that was where it ended.

All emotions, and romantic love in particular, were abhorrent to a mind which valued logic and reasoning above all else. Becoming entangled with a woman was like throwing grit into a well-oiled machine. A great distraction and a waste of time besides.

Sherlock glanced at Belle, still shaken, feeling something tug on his heartstrings. Precisely what he did not wish to feel. Belle had all of Irene's cleverness and drive, and all of Fantine's spontaneity and unpredictability.

She had something more too: empathy.

But romance? No. Belle was much too precious to complicate matters with that.

It was best if things went on as they had been.

Which would be remarkably easy since Belle felt nothing for him. Her newest infatuation was his brother Mycroft.

Damn it to hell! How have I gotten to this place from such an ordered existence? I will overcome it, I must. What mattered most was keeping Belle safe and having her in his life.

His life. Her life. They could not long be the same. Sherlock knew he should be relieved. When Belle entered university--all she ever talked about was going into university—she would no longer be his problem.

He wanted Belle to be his problem.

He was ashamed to admit it to himself, but Sherlock was not one to run from the truth: he would do almost anything to keep Belle out of university, the thing she wanted most in the world. She would be lost to him then.

There is a case to solve. What the devil does any of this matter?

She glanced at the knife, swallowing hard. "Do you think there is a correlation, Mr. Holmes?"

"Between what?"

"The attack on me and the vampire murder, of course."

"I do. The bats and the cross indicate a Christian correlation, at least in the mind of the one who commissioned the knife. The bats correspond to our vampire."

She gasped. "It is sacrilege. There is no such thing as a Christian vampire."

"There is in our murderer's world, which is the relevant point. As many have done before him, perverting the teachings of Christ as a vehicle for his private agenda and darker passions rather than as a vehicle for redemption."

"Who do you think is behind it, Mr. Holmes?"

"If the attack was instigated by our Mr. Fairclough, this means he has some connection to the murders of Percy and Denzil." His gaze was intense. "And possibly Bristow."

She swallowed hard. "But why would the vampire murderer be after me?"

"Because, Miss Belle, you have divined the connection."

Chapter Sixteen
It Gets Worse

"It is an old maxim of mine that when you have excluded
the impossible, whatever remains, however improbable,
must be the truth." - Sherlock Holmes
"The Beryl Coronet" by Sir Arthur Conan Doyle

"Was the blood drained from Mr. Denzil's body, Dr. Watson?" Mirabella asked the next morning.

"No." Dr. Watson was often brief when eating his breakfast.

"Were there fang marks on the neck?"

"No."

"So you concluded that it was not the vampire murderer responsible?" She poured him a hot cup of tea.

"Correct."

"To the contrary, I don't believe we can rule it out," Sherlock said.

"But the murder doesn't fit the pattern." Mirabella tapped her finger on her cheek in perplexity.

"What pattern, Miss Belle? If you start from the premise that the first murderer was not, in fact, a vampire, and the purpose of draining the blood is yet unknown to us, then any other murder might have been committed by the so-called Vampire Murderer."

"Possibly for showmanship or to enact fear," Dr. Watson suggested as he cracked his two-minute egg, leaving him with a thirty second interval in which to speak.

"Possibly. Without knowing the true motive, it's difficult to discern the 'pattern' as you say. The other issue is that our most recent murder was performed in public with other people about."

"True." Dr. Watson smothered raspberry jam on his toast. "The murderer couldn't very well suck the blood from his victim without identifying himself."

"Oh my goodness. Poor Mr. Denzil. How was he killed?" Mirabella asked.

"He was found dead at the Nag's Head. Apparently he had been drinking in the pub with a surly sort who appeared to have dropped arsenic into Denzil's drink," Dr. Watson explained.

"The poor man. No one deserves that."

"I call our murderer a reprehensible coward," Dr. Watson took his third piece of toast. "One who doesn't give his opponent a fighting chance and takes no risks himself."

"Do we have a description of the companion?" Sherlock asked.

"Tall, thin, dark. A middle-aged sailor with rotting teeth and his face well hidden by his hat and scarves."

"This is a terrible development for the case—one that might well have been prevented," Sherlock frowned. "Most notably by Constable Jones. I was not informed we had to keep an eye on all our key witnesses in addition to doing the actual detective work."

"And the autopsy report," John added.

Sherlock pushed his plate away, having only eaten one egg and a half piece of toast. "But I am not untrainable. Never again will I trust the word of others outside my own excellent team. Better to do all the work myself."

"There is the matter of stepping on others' toes," Mirabella considered. "You wouldn't wish the Yard to ban you from the scene, Mr. Holmes. You're not exactly *persona grata*."

"I don't exactly give a rat's ass," Sherlock said.

"You might not now. But you will if they ban you from the case," Mirabella suggested.

"Only consider, Miss Belle. While Constable Jones was losing all our witnesses, you were being attacked." Sherlock felt his jaw clenching.

"Miss Mirabella's attack does point to Fairclough, doesn't it?" Dr. Watson said.

"But he's such a kindly man." She shook her head. "Strangely sniveling and arrogant at the same time, but with so many good works. He does so much for so many."

"People are more complex than you would like to believe, Miss Belle. They are not always black and white." Sherlock's eyes were intent upon her. "Even the most reprehensible of persons are dear to someone."

"Particularly where there are wounds of the heart," she agreed, holding Sherlock's pale grey eyes for some time before he looked away.

***

The heart. She couldn't stop thinking about his holding her so close, his strength evident—and appealing. It had felt strangely . . . *right.* Of course, everything was topsy-turvy now, she didn't know how to think about anything. Having one's life threatened tended to shake one up a bit.

Sherlock cleared his throat. "Mr. Fairclough was to be Overton Bristow's father-in-law. Overton worked for him--and courted his daughter."

"The same Overton who had an affair with Lord Percival," Mirabella considered.

"The same."

"Overton was probably delivering a medicine of some sort from the pharmacy when he met Percival," Dr. Watson suggested. "They didn't travel in the same social circles."

Sherlock began placing tobacco in his pipe. "It is a shame you didn't confirm who sent your attacker, Miss Hudson."

"I invited him to tea, but he declined, being otherwise engaged." she demurred. *Attempting to kill me.*

"That brings up another point, Miss Belle." Sherlock grew even more deadly serious if that were possible. "You had your gun on your assailant. How were you unable to persuade him to tell you anything?"

"He wasn't afraid of me, I don't think."

"You had a pistol aimed at his heart, and he wasn't afraid of you? Explain that to me, Miss Hudson." A darkness crossed his expression.

"He didn't suppose I would actually kill him. He said as much." She poured a cup of tea for herself, adding a large dollop of cream. "I think he was actually surprised that I fired the gun at all."

"Really, Holmes, be fair," Dr. Watson interrupted. "Give the girl some credit. She managed to pull her gun on the beast and save herself, as well as wound a hardened criminal. I hate to say it, but some months ago, she might have ended up dead or wounded in the same situation."

She shivered. Being alive had to represent some improvement.

"This is precisely what worries me, Watson." Sherlock's grey eyes turned cloudy as he returned his gaze to her. "We have to work on your powers of intimidation, Miss Hudson. You must appear more fierce, more forceful."

She thought Sherlock had a point, but she wasn't about to say so. "And how do you propose I do that, Mr. Holmes?"

He raised an eyebrow. "It's in the eyes. The voice. And the sudden movements." His dark countenance turned softer, if no less serious. "It's in your intent."

"I'm so afraid of becoming a murderer."

"Your attacker knew that. With that fear, you allowed a killer to go free." His gaze refused to soften as he maintained his hard stare. "Strengthen your resolve, Miss Hudson. Your ability to frighten someone might save a person's life." He added somberly, "And that person may be you."

"I have to agree, Miss Mirabella." Dr. Watson wiped his mouth with his napkin after only four eggs, a large slice of ham, three pieces of bacon, and three pieces of toast. His breakfast left the room filled with a lovely sweet raspberry scent. "I would say, until the forcefulness is in your heart, Miss Mirabella, you must pretend that it is in your possession. At least in front of your attacker."

"Do you mean acting?"

"Precisely. Raise your voice, harden your words, make your movement deliberate. Try to make your attacker believe that you intend to kill him," Dr. Watson said.

"And be ready to kill him." Sherlock added, taking a puff on his pipe just lit.

"Do you now have a watch on the Madame's Apothecary, Mr. Holmes?" Mirabella asked.

"I do," Sherlock said.

"And yet you have never seen the vampire—or had any reports?" Sherlock shook his head. "No."

"Have you questioned Evie?" Mirabella asked.

"Naturally. She adamantly denies being our Mrs. Kitchens." He took a puff on his pipe.

"What do you believe, Mr. Holmes?"

"She's lying."

And yet, in spite of all we know, we have not caught the killer. Mirabella knew that Sherlock nursed the same frustration. *I must do something about that.*

Mirabella might be fearful in the face of self-preservation, but she had no fear when it came to saving others.

Chapter Seventeen
In the Devil's Lair

"It is stupidity rather than courage to refuse to
recognize danger when it is close upon you."
- Sherlock Holmes, "The Final Problem" by Sir Arthur Conan Doyle

Mirabella took a deep breath, running her fingers along the gold engraved sign on the large walnut door: "Professor James Moriarty, Chair, Department of Mathematics".

If no one else knows how to hunt a vampire, I know someone who does—and who lives where he lives, in the darkness. She hesitated but willed herself to knock on the door.

As yet, the Baker Street Irregulars had not found any clues to the vampire killer. She wouldn't be surprised if Sherlock knew who the murderer was. But he didn't have proof and Constable Jones continued to sabotage the investigation. In fact, Sherlock faced obstacles every step of the way. He was also convinced the vampire would strike again.

I will not stand by while Sherlock needs assistance and a murderer is on the loose. That's what she was paid to do after all. Sherlock might not know that he wanted her help, but she understood him: there was nothing in the world that was more satisfying to Sherlock Holmes than the resolution of a case.

She sighed heavily. Perhaps it was the only thing. And this case struck a personal chord with him, she would bet on it.

This was a sad state of affairs. Three people dead—Lord Percival, Overton Bristow, and Mr. Denzil—and they no closer to incarcerating the murderer or murderers.

"Come in."

She opened the door and walked in. "Hello, Professor." The smell of *La Intimidad* cigar smoke, old books, leather, chalk, wood, strong black tea, and cream permeated the air.

In spite of her fear, Mirabella never entered the University of London without feeling she was on hallowed ground. It was a place of learning and knowledge, creation and transformation, of dreams come true. A place where people left dramatically different than they entered.

Was that anything short of magic? Moriarty might be an evil criminal mastermind, but he was also a mathematical genius.

"I hope you came ready to work, Miss Hudson."

"I always do, sir."

"Does Holmes know you're here, Miss Hudson?" Expressionless, he moved to the blackboard. The professor's countenance might be serene, but she had learned to recognize the interest in his voice in spite of their short, though admittedly intense, acquaintance. It seemed she was destined to have strong personalities in her life.

"Of course not." She shook her head, gasping at the very thought. "Mr. Holmes wouldn't understand."

"Because he doesn't understand *you*, Miss Hudson," Moriarty said, a devious smile forming on his lips framed by a neatly trimmed beard. His auburn hair was cut short and oiled flat. He had the appearance of one who had a small, uninteresting personality and was entirely trustworthy—both impressions being completely untrue.

"And you do, sir?" She felt like laughing, but she dared not.

While being held at knifepoint by Moriarty, Mirabella had saved herself by impressing the professor with her understanding of the Poincare conjecture, a mathematical proof as yet unsolved. Unbeknownst to Sherlock, she now visited his arch enemy when the need arose.

Mirabella was aware of the danger when she looked at Moriarty, but she knew the path she must take. Everything in her being told her it was necessary and that she was the one to do it.

I must keep my eye on him. Certainly Sherlock Holmes did not have access to Moriarty's lab.

"Holmes doesn't appreciate your desire for an academic degree— which I do. He undervalues women and only tolerates them."

"I should think Sherlock Holmes' disapproval stems from the fact that you are his arch rival and sworn enemy, Professor."

"I assure you Holmes' desire to limit your advancement is stronger than his hatred of me." He fixed his eyes on her. "Holmes detests me—I grant you that, Miss Hudson—but his emotional connection to you is stronger, and the emotions never lie. Therein lies the solution to any question of motive."

"Emotions? Mr. Holmes? I'm not your green girl, sir." Despite Moriarty's dark gaze, she had the feeling very few people had the confidence to speak freely with him—and that he rather enjoyed it.

Still, one had to walk a fine line with Moriarty. He liked knowing others were afraid of him, and too much confidence ruffled his feathers.

Not a good thing when it comes to Moriarty.

"Ah, but you might be surprised, Miss Hudson, at the depth of emotion a man possesses." The glint in his eyes made her uncomfortable.

As for Sherlock undervaluing women, she would have said so at one time, but now she couldn't agree. Certainly all his mannerisms, pontificating, and reprimands gave one that impression. And yet, as in all things, the shallow exterior could be misleading.

Sherlock could be short with her, and he certainly demanded obedience, but he had taught her so much: the fighting arts, forensics, deductive reasoning, and disguises. Anyone who opened the door to knowledge so freely was allowing for equality and clearly not threatened by a woman's ability. True, Sherlock never expected anyone, man or woman, to be his equal—but he gave all the opportunity to try.

A true misogynist, a man who hated women, was, at his core, an insecure man threatened by the female sex. He didn't want women to succeed, he wanted to maintain his power over them, and his worst nightmare was for a woman to be superior in intellect and ability. His pride demanded that he would hate her on sight.

Such a man somehow felt that making women less made him more. In truth, it was the opposite.

Sherlock Holmes might be a man's man, he might not enjoy the company of women in general, he might have an aversion to emotion, but he had dedicated his life to helping those in need, many of them women whom society had abandoned. He had shown in his every expression and deed that he wished women to be stronger, more powerful, and to learn to think for themselves.

He disapproved of the Victorian ideal of womanhood: a helpless, non-thinking, pure, naive vessel of sighs and fainting fits. Mirabella had observed—as all women had—that it made men feel more manly to be in the presence of a woman who needed his care and protection.

Sherlock had no need for such fabrications: he never questioned his own manliness. And, if the truth be known, he could wrap women around his little finger if he so chose.

Sherlock's female ideal was Irene Adler, a stage actress and a master of disguise and deceit who had outsmarted him, taking matters into her own hands that she might secure her own future. Her duplicity and superiority had far from repelled him. It had quite the opposite effect, increasing his respect for Miss Adler.

Mirabella shook her head. No, she didn't think Sherlock disrespected women so much as he disrespected almost *everyone*. Outside of himself, that is. Besides, Sherlock disapproved of the woman created by a chauvinistic society. The woman who was the product of an equal society he did not—could not—know.

"I don't agree, Professor." Mirabella shook her head. "Mr. Holmes is decidedly unemotional—particularly where I am concerned. And he has always desired my success and education."

"You don't think Holmes wishes to suppress or control you, Miss Hudson?" He smirked, as if she were living in an illusionary world.

"Certainly not," she replied with all the indignation she could muster.

"How admirable that you should hold your employer in such high esteem. But I assure you, my dear, Sherlock Holmes feels intensely threatened by your success—and what it might mean for his relationship to you. Those in power always fear a change in the status quo."

You should know, Professor.

"Mr. Holmes has sound reasons for any opinion he holds," she replied indignantly. "He doesn't come to any conclusions lightly, and his distrust is well-founded—without any basis in emotion."

"It all begs the question, Miss Hudson. You are fully aware Holmes would disapprove of your being here." The smile he had subdued now expressed itself fully. "And yet, here you are."

"As you see." Everything was a competition for the professor. *Everything.*

And yet, even one's enemy's failings could be used to one's advantage. Sherlock had taught her that. She had every intention of using Moriarty's flaws against him.

"Do you not feel any guilt for being here, Miss Hudson?" he pressed, writing equations on the chalkboard as he spoke.

"Honestly, I don't." That, at least, was true. Whereas Sherlock would see her being here as a betrayal, she saw it as fulfilling her responsibility to him.

"Excellent. And why is that?"

"I don't see that my personal feelings have anything to do with mathematics." She motioned with her head to the blackboard. "I suggest we get to work. There are important matters at stake."

He chuckled. James Moriarty was not a person prone to smiles and laughter, but he was unusually jolly today.

Theirs was a strange alliance. And somehow with every encounter she felt less and less afraid in his company. Perhaps that should concern her.

"Indeed there are, Miss Hudson." His countenance was suddenly foreboding.

Keep your friends close and your enemies closer. If the truth be known, there was an element to the danger she loved. Otherwise, why would she work for Sherlock Holmes?

To be here was a drug to her desire for knowledge, her true passion. But she also saw it as her opportunity to keep an eye on Moriarty in the interest of one Sherlock Holmes. She wouldn't say she wished to impress Sherlock—that was a futile endeavor—but she did wish to do a good job for him. It was a strange fact that, in spite of his critical and demanding nature, the Great Detective inspired intense loyalty.

"Although I must say I feel more fear in your presence than I do guilt, sir."

"Tsk! tsk! And why is that?" He appeared pleased with her response.

"Probably because you once had me on the other end of a six-inch blade."

"Are you going to hold that one triviality against me forever, Miss Hudson?" He pulled on his neatly trimmed auburn beard. In an instant the amusement in his intelligent eyes turned dark and frightening despite their pale green, translucent color.

"Of course. I would be an idiot not to."

"You are, above all things, Miss Hudson, not an idiot. You are a true scientist," Moriarty curled his lip disdainfully. "Holmes is, essentially, not an academic but an investigator. Whereas he learns and catalogues every manner of cigar smoke as relates to the criminal, you wish to catalogue every manner of molecule, identifying the unseen and magnificent."

She knew very well Moriarty had a higher opinion of Sherlock Holmes' comparative intelligence than he disclosed, the main reason he had not attempted to murder his arch foe in her estimation. The professor would find the world lonely—and unbearable—without a worthy adversary.

The same reason she was now safe with Moriarty. As long as she had something to offer to his research, she was entirely safe. Initially he had wanted the Poincaré conjecture—and he still did—a solution that would bring him much fame. If she could solve it or appear to be making progress on solving it—many had spent a lifetime attempting to do so—she could buy herself time.

As much as Moriarty lived for crime, he wanted scientific notoriety and prestige. And, much like Sherlock, the professor wished to discover the unknown.

Moriarty was curious. But she feared his greed and addiction to power could potentially overcome his intellectual curiosity if allowed free reign.

"Mr. Holmes is simply more interested in practical matters than in academia," she said.

"Holmes is an imbecile. He can't even name the planets in the solar system."

"Because he has no need of them. They don't pertain to his cases." His work. *His life*.

"Then you must work for me, Miss Hudson. Imagine what two minds such as ours might do in collaboration."

A point in Moriarty's favor was that he held the key to her future dreams: a university degree. She wondered if this was how Jesus felt in the desert, being tempted by Satan.

A part of me longs to say 'yes'. To work with a mathematical genius would be pure bliss. The professor was almost as interested in mathematics as he was in his criminal empire. The workings of his own mind—and the pursuit of knowledge—was intoxicating to him.

As for myself, I sometimes wonder if I have more in common with Moriarty than I do with Sherlock Holmes. To be sure, the professor and she were simpatico. Except for the fact that Moriarty was an evil genius and she was a country girl from Dumfriesshire.

Except for that. Studying Moriarty in a three-piece plaid suit, she shuddered. Was she truly that boring?

In reality there was nothing conventional about Moriarty. He was brilliant, complex, devious, manipulative, and, well, as she'd already admitted, *wicked*, without a moral compass and without boundaries. He only knew one thing: how to please James Moriarty.

And yet, being a country curate's daughter, she believed everyone was redeemable. But strangely enough, it wasn't the Bible that she believed could save Moriarty.

Her father would be mortified to hear her thoughts. She was herself. *What has happened to me since I came to London?*

Sherlock Holmes that's what. She was now keeping company with prostitutes and sodomites, along with insane detectives and mad, vile scientists.

And now thinking there might be an answer other than the Bible?

They were all pathways to the same goal, she now believed. The Bible was not the prize at the end of the journey. God was. The Holy Spirit was. *A personal relationship with God.*

Telling the professor to read the holy book would be about as effective as telling him to sell everything he owned and give it to the poor. One had to start with a conduit that the recipient could receive.

What then had the power to save Moriarty? *Mathematics*. A venue he embraced. It gave him an interest in something outside himself.

Mathematics, for Moriarty, represented redemption.

For some the connecting pathway to the Divine was the Bible. For some it was nature. For still others, it was music. Or love. Public service. Whatever it was that opened the door to the Divine: the passageway which enabled one to touch one's Creator, to receive, to channel. Much like the painting on the ceiling of the Sistine Chapel in Italy.

Even the despicable Moriarty had the ability to channel the creative forces of the heavens—she had seen it. He simply channeled that ability for ill.

"Have you solved the formula I sent with you, Miss Hudson?" the professor asked.

"I have done some work on it." She retrieved a piece of paper from her reticule and handed it to him. The formula was the price of admission, but she was careful not to give Moriarty anything that could be used to hurt others. As long as it was research which would merely increase his stature in the scientific community, such as the Poincaré conjecture, collaboration was worth being able to keep an eye on him.

Though, granted, nothing was certain where Moriarty was concerned.

He looked at the piece of paper and frowned. "$X=V-E+F$ . . . where V is the vertices of the shape in question, E is the edges, and F is the number of faces in three dimensions." He looked up at her, his eyes holding danger. "You already solved this for me. You must have more to offer if you wish to return."

"I w-will do better," she stammered.

"Let us hope so." Moriarty turned towards a piece of equipment on his laboratory desk.

"I see you have a thermopile." She observed the device which converted thermal energy into electrical energy. It consisted of gas, a heat screen and a heat source. Or, more specifically, a brass tube, a vacuum pump, a galvanometer, and a manometer.

"Yes, but I believe the thermopile is underutilized."

"In what way?" She'd best be careful, or curiosity would kill more than the cat.

"What if, Miss Hudson, you could direct light to cut through steel?"

All the alarms went off in her head. At the same time she was almost dizzy with eagerness. "*Impossible*. It sounds like a miracle, not science."

"What are the components of light?" He glanced toward the window where the light streamed in, falling on his chalkboard covered with complex formulas.

She searched her memory. "Naturally the primary wavelengths are ultraviolet, visible, and infrared light."

"Ah, yes. And what about infrared light?"

"It is . . . much hotter than visible light." She knew where he was going with this line of reasoning, but it was utterly ridiculous. "But not hot enough for what you suggest—cutting metal, that is."

"So you say." A smile formed on his lips. "How would you make it hotter?"

"I don't . . . know."

"Come now Miss Hudson." His commanding frown inspired one to obey out of fear. She backed up a step.

"What if infrared light were concentrated and focused?" he asked, even as the idea had occurred to her, though she dare not say anything.

Oh my goodness. Could light then literally melt and evaporate *steel*?

"From your expression, I see you follow me, Miss Hudson." His eyes gleamed with the hope of unfathomable power.

"Not at all. I simply can't believe the temperatures you suggest could be attained."

She was torn between the intoxicating allure of the idea and her complete conviction that brainstorming with Moriarty on this matter was akin to introducing poison into the air.

This is not a technology Moriarty should have. Thankfully he didn't know how to concentrate the infrared light to the desired concentrations or he wouldn't be discussing it with her.

Moriarty was the master of manipulation. *Perhaps I am truly out of my league.*

"And how is the color of light determined?" He moved from the thermopile to the blackboard.

"By its wavelength. The shorter wavelengths are ultraviolet and the longer wavelengths are the infrared." She found that she was talking rather quickly. The longer wavelengths were here of particular interest.

"How is the smallest particle of light energy described?"

"As a photon."

"What is the formula for the energy of a photon?"

Easy. And harmless. Common knowledge. "It is equal to its frequency times Planck's constant. So, the higher the frequency, the higher the energy—and the shorter the wavelength."

"As you know, Miss Hudson, as an excited atom returns to a lower energy state, it emits photons," he continued, as if reading her mind.

"Well, yes, whenever a charged particle gives up energy, electromagnetic radiation is emitted," she said warily.

He stared at her for a long while, a gleam in his pale green eyes reminding her of a winter river frozen over.

"Fascinating. But that would mean . . . " She considered his words. "In the right circumstances, as light passes through a substance, it could stimulate the emission of more light." Mirabella knew he had already come to this conclusion himself, so there was no use in pretending, as much as she might wish to.

"Precisely." A sudden glow lit his eyes.

"How do you think it could be done, Miss Hudson? Finding the right type of atom that could set this into motion: essentially cutting steel with light?"

Nervous, she glanced out the window and caught her reflection. *Mirrors.*

She felt a mixture of thrills and dread. *If a cavity filled with photons of a particular wavelength were outfitted on both ends with mirrors, perhaps the reflection could initiate the desired reaction, causing the amplification of the wavelengths.*

"I have no idea."

"No ideas at all, Miss Hudson? I find that difficult to believe."

His demeanor was perfectly calm, but fury lay beneath the surface. He wanted something and she was refusing to give it to him.

"This is very advanced, Professor Moriarty. You can't expect me to solve a scientific mystery in a matter of seconds."

"You're lying." Moriarty frowned. "I can see by your expression that you do have an idea. I would advise you not to keep anything from me, Miss Hudson."

"My thoughts are my own. I don't owe you anything Professor."

"There, there. No need to become indignant."

"I will not allow you to abuse me, Professor. You have no claim on me."

"Not *yet.*" His voice grew very soft. "But I can open doors for you, Miss Hudson. Not only can I procure admission to university for you, but I can gain entrance into programs where women are not allowed. In the past, women were so persecuted by the male students, in any of the scientific fields in particular, that they withdrew."

"Women can't become doctors in Britain anyway."

"It would seem they can't attend the classes either."

"I would never let ill-mannered hooligans intimidate me."

"So you think. Particularly those women who scored higher than their male counterparts were resented—and pushed out." He smiled. "But I could make certain you are not bothered."

She released a deep breath as she envisioned the bodies of unruly male students turning up in the Thames.

Mirabella knew the professor spoke the truth. He could get her into fields of study no woman had yet been allowed entrance to.

And he could definitely protect her.

Is it worth it? Should she choose personal glory over the fate of the world?

I really have gone too far.

Studying the professor, she felt precisely the way she had felt when she entered the tigers' cage. "I will think about your equation. It is a complex problem requiring some thought."

"Let us be certain answers follow thought. Otherwise you are a waste of my time." His voice grew deadly soft. "I generally dispose of that which I do not need."

She feigned indifference though inside she was shaking. "If the chair of a university mathematics department with a doctorate degree doesn't know the solution, I don't know why you would expect me to know, Professor."

His pale green eyes somehow turned the color of steel. "I expect you to know, Miss Hudson, because that's why you are here. New . . . *blood . . . as it were.*" Now it was his voice which was frozen—and threatening.

"In the meantime, I have a question." She was anxious to change the subject, and if someone were up to no good, Moriarty would know about it. "Are you familiar with a Mr. Fairclough?"

"The pharmacist?" He suddenly became elusive. "And what is your interest in him?"

"Does he travel in your circles?"

"In academia?"

"No," she swallowed hard. "Is he involved in the criminal underworld?"

"Certainly not. As I am not." He smiled.

One distinct difference between Sherlock and Moriarty was that Sherlock never lied to her. And Moriarty rarely did anything else.

"However, Franklin Fairclough is a charismatic person," Moriarty reflected. "Those people he has pulled out of the workhouses, they are a particular type of person as well."

"And what type is that?"

"I have looked to Fairclough myself for some of my employees. I believe they would do anything for him. The depth of their gratitude is immense."

So Moriarty does have connections with Fairclough.

The professor continued, "More significantly, the fear of living without Fairclough's protection is far worse than anything he might ask them to do. He brings them to it slowly, of course."

There seemed to be an eerie similarity between the relationship he described and her own with Moriarty—or what it could become. She shivered.

"What would he ask them to do?"

"If you or I were commanded to do something we did not wish to do, we would laugh in the face of it, Miss Hudson." He studied her with what seemed to be admiration. "Much as you just did with me. But these are people who are weak."

"Or who have been beaten down by life."

"As I said."

"I see." She swallowed hard. "And do you know anything about their teeth, Professor?"

His expression was one of incredulity. She was not accustomed to seeing Moriarty surprised. "What on earth do you mean, Miss Hudson?"

"Those women who work in his pharmacy. They all have perfect teeth."

"Do they indeed?" A slow smile formed on his lips. "Very observant of you, Miss Hudson."

She bit her lip, almost afraid to ask the question. But she had to. "Do you know who is behind the vampire murders?"

"Which murder or murders do you refer to?" he said nonchalantly.

"Lord Percival, of course."

"Hmmm." He tapped his chin. "An interesting case."

"Do you know who is behind it?" she repeated.

"So you want to find a vampire?"

"I do."

"I might be able to help you. *For a price*."

"For the ability to cut steel," she murmured.

"Precisely."

"Even if it were possible, it seems to me the heat emission alone from such an experiment would make it too dangerous—and subsequently unworkable. And, if the infrared light worked, it could burn a hole in either metal or humans—and initiate fires and explosions." She attempted to appear resolute. "I don't believe it to be feasible."

"Ah, so you were thinking about my problem, Miss Hudson." He studied her with a fearsome intensity.

"I thought about it and concluded that it isn't possible." She shrugged nonchalantly, but she felt as if she were walking off a cliff. There was no doubt in her mind that Moriarty's intent for the infrared focuser was military in nature. The concentrated light beam, unlike other weapons, by definition moved at the speed of light. It would be more accurate and would not be affected by strong winds. And one might be able to be some distance from the target when firing.

"That is unfortunate." He frowned. "If you were to come up with a different conclusion, I might be able to produce your vampire."

Do I dare share my ideas with him? Could Moriarty use it to harm the world?

This was the problem with collaborating with a villain. One had to be too guarded.

Will I ever find the freedom of thought I am searching for?

Should I sell my soul for the right to learn?

It would be some time before any progress was made with this invention anyway. And the professor's involvement in the underworld—dividing his attentions as it were—dissipated his energy.

Maybe there would be no harm in sharing her ideas.

***

Moriarty had no idea who this vampire murderer was. It hadn't really interested him until now.

Clearly it behooved him to pretend he did, however.

James Moriarty watched Mirabella walk out the door. *She knows how to solve my equation. I'm sure of it.*

I must have that solution. An army which could cut steel could destroy any enemy.

This knowledge represented ultimate power.

And money. *I personally don't care who I sell it to, as long as they pay me.*

Everyone thought the flying machines would be the new weapon—but what if they could be knocked out of the sky?

And how much easier would it be to manufacture steel products? This technology would be worth a fortune.

His eyes fixated on the door. This young lady was the smartest scientist he had come across in a long time—possibly ever. Obviously brains could be equated with riches. And *power*.

But she lacked the key to the kingdom. *A key which I hold.*

He smiled, most pleased with his position.

Who has the power now?

Chapter Eighteen
The Vampire strikes again

*"What object is served by this circle of misery and
violence and fear?" - Sherlock Holmes in "The Cardboard Box"
by Sir Arthur Conan Doyle*

"Mr. Holmes, come quickly," the policeman said. "There's been a
murder at the Diogenes Club. Another *vampire* murder."

Sherlock felt his heart pounding out of his chest as terror gripped him.
He ran to the door, hat in hand. "Is it Mycroft?"

"I'm unable to say. Constable Jones just told me to send for you."

Sherlock dropped his hat and took the man by the shoulders, shaking
him. "Is it Mycroft? Tell me, man!"

"Calm down, Holmes! The man doesn't know," Dr. Watson objected,
pulling Sherlock off the officer, requiring no small amount of force.

"That's right, sir. I don't." The policeman caught his breath.

Sherlock took the stairs three at a time, the image of Mycroft lying on
the floor, drained of blood, terrorizing his very being. He rushed into the
street and hailed a cab.

Watson and Mirabella were fast on his heels, which was a fortunate
circumstance as he would brook no delays and would not have waited.
The three crammed into the horse-drawn coach and were soon riding at a
breakneck pace at his insistence.

"Hurry, man!" Sherlock yelled to the driver. "Faster, damn you!"

"Holmes," Watson said, "if we go any faster, we won't make the next
turn. Instead we'll be spilled into the street."

Sherlock knew that he was mad beyond reason. He had never known
what it was to be this terrified. Fear was something foreign to him: he did
not fear pain, nor his own death. He abhorred the absence of logic.

Sherlock had many acquaintances, but Mycroft had been his trusted
companion and only friend for most of his life—until he met Watson.
Mycroft was the eldest and the apple of his mother's eye; she had not
understood her younger son's rational, unexcitable approach to life. Their
excellent father, a country squire and local justice of the peace, had always
treated the two boys as adults, never looking upon them as children.

It was the childhood Sherlock would have chosen—living in an adult world observing the law unfold in local court sessions as well as access to private tutors—but it was not a childhood which lent itself to parental closeness. As for their other siblings, Honora, the oldest girl, was not the brightest bulb on the tree and had been almost exclusively concerned with her appearance and marriage prospects. The younger twins, Annabel and Rutherford, were fully ten years younger than Sherlock, and not of interest.

Mycroft, seven years older than Sherlock and with an intellect to match, had been both his parent and brother in childhood—his only real friend—as well as his schoolmate.

Sherlock did not know until this moment just how much Mycroft meant to him, as well as the great emptiness he would feel without him. Mycroft was unlike him in countless ways, and yet they shared a connection no one else could enter into.

They somehow arrived at the Diogenes Club without mishap and Sherlock rushed in.

On the floor was a large man, face down, with dark hair. Sherlock gasped. "*No!*"

Sherlock fell to his knees on the ground, his eyes watering and blocking his vision. Slowly he reached out to touch the sleeve of the superfine coat but couldn't bring himself to do so, terrified to see the face he loved in a grey pallor, the life drained out of it.

"No, Holmes, no!" Watson exclaimed. "Move away."

"But I must . . . I must see . . ."

Sherlock reached out again but Watson reached for his hand, adding softly, "Leave it to me."

"Ah, calm down, brother dear, I'm safe," Mycroft came around the corner, shaken and distressed but alive.

Sherlock jumped to his feet, embracing his brother, unable to hide his feelings of relief. He had never been so happy to be wrong in his life.

"*Blast it*, Mycroft," Sherlock seethed. His fear turned to anger in an instant. "Do you not see the danger you are in?"

Mycroft nodded solemnly. "Unfortunately I do."

"What has happened?" Sherlock demanded.

"It's Radcliffe. We found him in the same state as we found Percy. With the blood drained, the marks of the wolf fangs, and the same small prick in the neck."

Sherlock began to feel like himself again as his mind took over, assessing the situation. "I presume the body was found here, which appears to be one of the private rooms."

Mycroft nodded.

"Private rooms?" Athelney interjected, entering the room. "What would those be used for?"

"For dining and private conversation of course," Mycroft turned slowly towards Jones, an expression of disdain replacing his earlier torment. "There is no talking in the reading rooms or in the main library, as I'm sure you are quite aware, Constable."

"Watson, please examine the body at once," Sherlock directed.

Athelney muttered, "I don't know why you're still involved, 'Olmes. I can't see that you've made any progress in finding the vampire murderer—or Mrs. Kitchens."

"If you give me leave to do so, I will at once. I had understood that was your job, Constable Jones." *Believe me, if this were my case as opposed to yours I would have handled it very differently. In future I will not be such an agreeable fellow, career or not.* He had learned his lesson, to be sure. "And by the by, Constable, there is no vampire."

"Tell that to Radcliffe," Athelney muttered.

Staring at the body, Sherlock shook his head. "I do blame myself. I was attempting to follow protocol. I now perceive the error in my thinking."

"At any rate, Shirley is here at my request," Mycroft said.

Athelney turned his attention onto Mycroft. "It seems to me, sir, that you are a suspect."

"Me? A suspect in *murder* at the *Diogenes*?" Mycroft almost lost his balance, even as he began laughing. One of his assistants hurried forward and assisted the foreign secretary to the settee. "You must be joking, man."

***

Mirabella observed the conversation with interest. Sherlock and Mycroft knew more than they were revealing.

She held her tongue. She had learned to remain silent if she didn't wish to be excluded from accompanying Sherlock—an honor of recent development. Women were never allowed at crime scenes.

Glancing sideways at the constable, his surly expression revealed he was of the same opinion that something was being withheld.

"It's your club," he said. "One of the bodies was found here. *Both* were members of the Diogenes."

Smiling to herself, she noted that Sherlock didn't correct Jones to say 'three' bodies, if one counted Overton Bristow.

Athelney squinted, pursing his lips at the same time. "I still says there's something else going on here what you ain't sayin'."

Perhaps the constable was more astute than people gave him credit for. Still, there was no doubt that Athelney had a bee in his bonnet where Mycroft was concerned.

Glancing at the fury written across Sherlock's face, she wondered that the constable might get stung.

Despite his objections, the constable nodded to allow Watson access to the body. As the Foreign Office's Permanent Secretary, there could be no doubt Mycroft had both the rank and the clout to enforce his will.

For now.

Sherlock dropped to the ground alongside Dr. Watson, as Mirabella had seen him do before. "Fangs have bitten into this neck. There's the small mark in the center, as there was on Percy's."

Dr. Watson concurred. "Almost like a prick."

"Could it be from the fangs?" Athelney asked.

"No, much too small," Dr. Watson said. "It may have been where a needle was inserted."

"Ah, to remove the blood." Athelney nodded.

"This red circle is the result of some type of a suction machine," Sherlock said.

"It could be lips." Athelney's green eyes were shooting bullets. "I remember what you said at Percival's murder. You said, and I quote, 'I guarantee it relates to the murder of men of a certain persuasion.' And here we are again at the Diogenes Club."

Mycroft cleared his throat, never one to evade the issue. "What are you saying, precisely, Police Constable Jones?"

"I'm sayin' there is illegal activity goin' on here." He cleared his throat. "Between *sodomites*."

"Now see here, Constable." Mycroft rolled his eyes. "We are a club of intellectuals. Benjamin Disraeli, the former prime minister, was a member of my club up until his death. I have a finer collection of literature than the London library. All of my members are intellectuals and academics."

"That may be so, but I know what is going on."

"That is a most welcome development," Sherlock said. "I wish you would but apply it to the case and find our murderer."

"Here's the facts. Percival was a sodomite. So was Overton Bristow." Athelney glanced at the body. "Radcliffe looks a bit . . . er . . . *feminine* to me."

"Tsk! tsk!" Mycroft shook his head. "You are grasping at straws, Constable. Radcliffe was a man of fashion to be sure."

"Are you sayin' that Percival and Bristow were not sodomites?"

"Everyone knows they were. I'm sure that has nothing to do with me, they weren't at my request. Why are you interrogating me?"

"The constable's fury is merely a diversion for his ineptitude on this case," Sherlock muttered, not quite under his breath.

"By Jove!" Mycroft exclaimed, his expression suddenly alight. "I follow you now, Police Constable. Let me get this straight. You believe the murderer is targeting men of a certain persuasion?"

"Well, yes, I—"

"And your job is to protect them and to bring the murderer to justice?"

Athelney frowned. "That's not what I was sayin' precisely."

"What were you saying then, Constable?" Sherlock asked.

Mycroft shook his head in disapproval. "You did take an oath, Constable Jones. There was nothing in that oath to exclude any portion of the population."

"Well, no, but if there is criminal activity . . ."

"And now, Constable, I am quite fatigued. If you have no other questions, I believe I shall retire for the evening."

"You shall not, Mr. Holmes. Not until you've been dismissed. Where were you at the time of the murder?"

"For the past three hours I was in another of the private rooms with five other members having a brandy and discussing the Second Irish Land Act to abate rent arrears."

"For three hours?"

"It's a complex issue. There was a brief interlude in which we discussed the sale of Jumbo the elephant from the London Zoo to P.T. Barnum." He raised his eyebrows. "Would you like me to detail every conversation we had?"

"That won't be necessary."

Mycroft frowned. "Your obsession with the sex lives of the victims—and the Diogenes Club—appears to speak more to your personal biases than to the resolution of the case. How has it helped you to solve the crime? What have you discovered? What conclusions have you drawn from it? It appears to be nothing more than a way to divert yourself from the actual murderer or murderers. How many witnesses have you lost? Are you actually on the case? I wouldn't know it."

"Now see here, Mr. Mycroft Holmes. If the Diogenes is full of sodomites, it would mean that the Diogenes is a club full of criminals. The murderer must be housed in these four walls."

Sherlock began to pace the room. "This is a crime of passion, at least in part. In this you are correct, Constable. The murderer has a perverse hatred of sodomites—much like yourself. His hatred may have been initiated with an individual who harmed him, but now he has imagined that the entire group—people he does not know—have harmed him." He stopped in his tracks to study the constable with a certain intensity. "To be sure, you fit the profile of our murderer better than my brother does."

Mycroft laughed even as Athelney Jones puffed up, turning the full force of his gaze on Sherlock. "I did not murder anyone. Though I might like to. I am attempting to rid this city of crime—with no help from you two, I might add."

"Since you bring up Bristow and Lord Percival, that is a logical place to start," Sherlock said.

"You wish to revisit Mr. Overton Bristow who killed himself over Lord Percival?"

"Now you are using your brain, Constable. I do think there is a connection."

Athelney shook his head, his frustration evident. "Bristow was Percival's lover. Denzil was killed. And now Radcliffe is dead. This vampire is everywhere," Athelney said.

"And he must be caught," Mycroft said somberly.

"The vampire came to the Diogenes for a romantic liaison—" Athelney considered.

"—Excuse me, sir."

"Yes, Miss Belle?"

"Why do you assume the murderer was wearing a vampire costume?" she asked. "Did anyone see him?"

"N-no," Athelney sputtered. "Because of the way Radcliffe was killed, draining of the blood and all. How many murderers do that?"

"I can assure you, my dear constable," Mycroft said, "that no one in this club would have met privately—or publicly, for that matter—with a man dressed in a vampire costume after what happened to Percy. It's inconceivable."

"Then why did Radcliffe meet with his murderer?" Sherlock tapped his forefinger on his chin as he paced.

"And why do you presume that it was a romantic liaison, Constable?" Mirabella posed.

"Now see here, I won't be questioned by a female, and certainly not by your kitchen maid!"

"Excuse me?" Sherlock turned on his heel and moved closed to Athelney, his expression fierce. "Do not ever insult Miss Hudson again in my presence, again, Jones."

Athelney backed up. "I meant no offense."

Sherlock looked as if he might grab Athelney by the collar and throw him out the window, his career be damned. He asked through barred teeth, "Now as I think about it, why did you assume this meeting was a romantic liaison?"

"It stands to reason . . . The Diogenes . . ."

"What does the register say, Mycroft?" Sherlock asked.

"No name, just 'investment meeting'. Radcliffe was a bit of an investor," Mycroft continued, "and the meeting was to discuss a possible investment in medical research. He let in his guest through the private door."

"Look at this Holmes," Dr. Watson pointed to a wound on Radcliffe's head. "This is how he died. A blow to the head."

"But the same wolf bites and the same pin prick," Athelney objected.

"Yes, but there was no poison used in this instance, I'll wager," Sherlock said. "You'll have to confirm that in an autopsy, of course, Constable."

"But why was a different method used?" Athelney's frustration was palpable. Mirabella began to feel sorry for him. He did wish to solve the murder, whatever anyone might say.

"The murderer didn't wish to taint the blood," Sherlock said, realization suddenly alight in his eyes.

"And he did when he murdered Lord Percival?"

"Even vampires have a learning curve, Constable." Mycroft shook his head.

"Only recall how the men died, Constable," Sherlock said.

"How can I forget? What a holy show. Both Percival and Radcliffe have wolf bites on their necks, as well as a round pin prick. Mr. Denzil was killed in a less morbid way—that were a simple poisoning," Athleney considered.

"I doubt that Mr. Denzil would see it in that way," Sherlock said. "Who was, in fact, killed by the same person. Just because the method was different does not necessarily infer it was a different murderer. Our so-called vampire was in a public place and had to work with the mother of necessity."

"It's time for plain speakin' now, Mr 'Olmes. Your hypothesizing has no place here."

"A piece of advice, if you please, Constable. Instead of looking to the Diogenes Club, I would look to Overton Bristow's connections. You might be a practical man, Constable Jones, but in your obsession over sexual relations, you're looking on the wrong side of the fence."

"Indeed. My dear Constable," Mycroft moved to stand up. "Do get your mind out of the gutter and on the case."

Chapter Nineteen
The Baker Street Irregulars

"These youngsters go everywhere and hear everything. They are as sharp as needles, too. All they want is organization."
- Sherlock Holmes, "A Study in Scarlet" by Sir Arthur Conan Doyle

Sherlock and Watson were still with Constable Jones while Mirabella returned to Baker Street to straighten the flat before retiring to bed. It had been a long day and she couldn't wait for her head to hit the pillow. But working for Sherlock Holmes did not follow a schedule.

Glancing at the clock she saw it was ten o'clock. Just as she had finished her chores there was an infernal banging on the door. She opened the door to see twelve-year-old Wiggins looking disheveled and dirty, and certainly wild-eyed.

"We seen something!" Wiggins exclaimed. "Where is Mr. Sherlock 'Olmes?"

"He isn't here Mr. Wiggins," Mirabella said, catching his excitement. "What have you seen?"

The boy stared at her with distrust. "Mr. 'Olmes didn't say I could tell a bird."

Mirabella chided herself not to take offense. To his credit, Mr. Wiggins could be trusted to follow his orders and to keep his mouth shut with the enemy.

Unfortunately he seemed to think *she* was the enemy. Or, at least, all of womankind was. "You can tell me, Mr. Wiggins. I am his assistant."

"But you're just a gull. You can't be his assistant." Wiggins eyed her suspiciously. "Anyways, Dr. Watson is his assistant."

"Certainly not. Dr. Watson is his colleague. I am Mr. Holmes' assistant."

"Yes, I sees. An assistant is less important than a colleague, and you are a girl so you are less important. That makes sense."

"And yet an assistant is entitled to information."

Wiggins eyed her with suspicion. "Now you're trying to trick me."

"I certainly am not," she replied indignantly. "Mr. Holmes has more than one assistant, as well you should know. Aren't you his trusted assistant?"

"I am." Wiggins grinned proudly.

"Just so. And I am Mr. Holmes' female operative." She raised her chin. "The world's first lady detective. Didn't he tell you?" She had not been raised to toot her own horn, but it was a man's world, and sometimes it was the only way to wade through the mire and facilitate a solution.

Wiggins shook his head.

"I advise you to ask Mr. Holmes the next time you see him."

"I'd like to see him now!"

"He isn't here." She motioned about the flat. "You can see that for yourself."

Wiggins looked at her suspiciously, as if she might be hiding the great man. One who had committed the unforgivable sin of being born female was capable of any transgression, after all.

"As you see, Mr. Wiggins, you have no option but to relay the information to me. I will pass it on when Mr. Holmes arrives, I assure you, even if it be in the middle of the night."

"Naw. I ain't telling no one but Mr. 'Olmes."

"Very well, Mr. Wiggins." She saw it was useless: Wiggins' principles were incorruptible. "You had best wait here then."

Mirabella looked about, attempting to formulate a plan. Her eyes moved to the newly stoked fire burning in the fireplace, then onto the violin in the corner, the Persian slipper and calabash pipe next to Sherlock's wingback chair, and past the laboratory jars drying on the rack. She glanced past the beakers, chemicals, clamps, cylinders, microscope, and filtration systems to Dr. Watson's desk decidedly neater than Sherlock's, and finally to the chair in the bow window.

I am so tired I cannot think. Her mind drew a blank.

Her eyes perceived an apple in the fruit bowl, which had also caught Wiggins' eye, she noted. Sherlock had taught her to take in every detail, and this gave her an idea. "As long as you're waiting for Mr. Holmes, would you like a piece of bread and cheese? And perhaps a slice of roast beef?"

"I sure would!" He brushed his overlong brown hair out of his eyes. His clothes might be raggedy and too small, but his face was surprisingly clean. Suddenly his smile turned to a frown. "But I ain't tellin' you nothing, miss. Not wif'out Mr. 'Olmes."

"Absolutely not. I don't imagine for a moment that you would." She looked back over her shoulder at him as she headed to the galley kitchen. "Mr. Holmes would never forgive me if I didn't treat you like the valuable operative you are."

"Sure, that's right. You listen to the guv'nor!"

Mirabella quickly made a plate of bread, cheese, and cold roast beef which Wiggins ate with a gusto to rival the hogs on her family farm in Dumfriesshire. She had thought she could at least keep the boy here until Sherlock returned, but if Wiggins continued eating at this breakneck speed, she might run out of food first.

"Would you like a slice of apple pie, Mr. Wiggins?" She brought out a beautiful piece of apple pastry, its golden crust glistening in the candlelight.

"Indeed I would, Miss."

"And I'll give it to you if you convey the message to me."

"I said I won't."

"I'm so sorry, I forgot. I guess it shall have to be mine then." She picked up a fork and took a bite of the apple pastry, closing her eyes in blissful rapture. She moved her fork towards the pie again, indicating that she had no difficulty in not giving him a morsel, going so far as to take pleasure in torturing him. "It's the last piece you know."

"Wait! Stop!" This was apparently more than even this paragon of honor could endure. He swallowed hard, his eyes never wavering from the pie. "I suppose it wouldn't be no harm. As long as you promises to tell Mr. 'Olmes, miss."

"I most certainly do. I know my duty to my employer."

Wiggins glanced up at her with skepticism. Anyone who could be cruel to children, after all . . .

He snatched the pie out of her hand with the lightning fast responses of a pickpocket of admirable dexterity. Considering his speed, she was surprised he didn't break the Mandalay blue china dish holding the pie.

She was ready to fight for the pie unless he delivered, however. Thankfully Wiggins began speaking in between mouthfuls. "We saw a man in a black cape and a tall black hat leavin' the Diogenes Club only an hour ago."

"I'm sure there are many men who fit that description leaving the Diogenes."

"Yeah, but is they carrying a large container and in the company of one what looked to be Longstaff?"

"How do you know what Mr. Longstaff looks like?"

He shook his head in grave disapproval. "It's me job to know. I staked out the house right after Lord Percy's murder."

"Yes, of course," she nodded. "You saw him at nine o'clock?" *That would have been right after the murder.*

"Yep. That's right. I 'eard the chimes then: nine o'clock. I whistled for Tipton—I do a good nightingale, you know—we followed the two until they caught a carriage waitin' for 'em, but we ran and kept up wif' them. Then I came here."

"You kept up with a carriage the entire way?" she asked, disbelieving.

"It weren't far," he said, shoveling pie into his mouth. "And I have boots."

"Where did the man in the cape leave the Diogenes?"

"Through the side door. On the east side 'o the building."

Oh my goodness.

"How large was the package?" she asked, pouring him a glass of milk, which he happily took.

"Ah, it was a container, what so big." He stopped eating momentarily to make a motion with his hand. "It weren't small."

Approximately four liters. The blood. *He was carrying Radcliffe's blood.* She felt suddenly nauseous, placing her hand on her mouth.

I must control my impulses while Wiggins is talking.

"This is very important, Mr. Wiggins. Where did the carriage go?"

"The Madame's Apothecary."

She fell into the chair beside him, suddenly feeling she might faint.

"It was dark, and the caped man—I'm sure it was the vampire—went in a door in the back. You know, they'se can see in the dark, unlike us. They wouldn't be out in the light. And the only way to kill them is with a stake through the heart."

"I can see that you have studied the subject. How do you know the caped man was a vampire? Could you see his face?"

"No, it was mostly hidden by his hat, but I'm sure it was. He walked all creepy like."

"And the vampire—was it a man or a woman?"

"A man."

"Are you certain? You're not letting your assumptions make you see what you think you should see?"

"Phttt! He was a tall and skinny. But *powerful*, you know."

"But might the cape have hidden curves?"

He blushed momentarily. Wiggins might be a street urchin but he knew proper manners and what was expected of a gentleman. His lips formed an 'O'. "He had a long, angular nose and a square jaw."

"And did you see anyone meet the vampire at the door, Mr. Wiggins?"

"Nope. It was just Longstaff and the vampire."

"Did you hear their voices?"

"The vampire's voice was shrill; I thought he was mad."

"Did they leave the large container at the apothecary?"

"Nope."

"No?" *How strange.* "He took it with him?"

Wiggins' fork paused in mid-air, his face suddenly contorted as he pondered the question. "The carriage waitin' by the door took the container."

Mirabella tapped her finger on the table. Where could they be taking the blood?

"And did you follow the vampire into the apothecary?"

"No, too dangerous." He stared at her with surprise in his eyes. "He might suddenly decide to turn into a bat and reach out and bite us."

She appreciated the very real danger these young lads had been in—and their bravery. "He is a treacherous man. Mr. Holmes greatly appreciates your courage."

"We wuz' scared, and that's a fact."

"And neither Longstaff nor the vampire—they didn't see you?" She felt some fear for the child.

Wiggins shook his head vehemently. "I don't want to have fangs in my throat and me blood drained! We wuz careful."

"That is very wise, Mr. Wiggins." She procured two guineas for him and Tom. "You are irreplaceable and we would be most grieved to see anything happen to you."

"So would I." He took the last bite of pie and swallowed it with the same gusto he had employed on the first. Wiping his mouth with his sleeve, he added, "The funny thing was that Longstaff went with the vampire into the apothecary. I wouldn't do that, would you? And then there was a fight. We could hear it. Not smart to fight with a vampire in my opinion."

"Could you make out what they were saying?"

"Most definitely, miss. They was speakin' loud, and we moved closer to the window so as to hear."

She leaned forward. "And what did you hear?"

"The man who looked to be Longstaff said he wanted to quit. But the vampire wouldn't let him." He looked puzzled. "If Longstaff is a vampire too, isn't that like quitting being dead? I didn't know there was that much choice in the matter. Now a witch, she could quit, by not casting her spells. But a vampire, he's got to have blood—"

"And what did the vampire say to Longstaff's request, Mr. Wiggins?"

"He said they had to clean up the city, that the devil was loose. I sure hope there ain't a vampire *and* a devil loose."

"Are you sure that's what they said?" she asked anxiously. "That you're not embellishing the story?"

"I never do. Almost never. Mr. Sherlock 'Olmes says what I 'ave a photographic memory." He smiled proudly. "Like him."

"Go on."

"Then the vampire said, 'Give it time. You haven't killed enough.'" Wiggins shuddered. "And then Longstaff started sobbing. I didn't know vampires in training did that."

"And when did the vampire leave?"

Mr. Wiggins shook his head. "He didn't. But I figured I'd better come here and tell Mr. 'Olmes about it."

"Did Longstaff leave?" she asked anxiously.

"Not what we saw."

She jumped up out of her chair, reaching for a pencil and note pad. "Can you go with me, Mr. Wiggins? I need to return to the apothecary and I need protection."

Wiggins studied her for a long moment. "I can go wif' you, miss."

His estimation of her had obviously increased. At least a little. "Shall I get some o' the other boys?"

"There isn't time, Mr. Wiggins." Quickly she dashed off a note for Sherlock, leaving it in front of the brandy decanter, where he was sure to see it.

She headed for the door, grabbing her coat and the reticule that held her pistol, with her young protector close on her heels.

I hope we make it in time.

Or do I?

Chapter Twenty
On Their Own

"I began to smell a rat. You know the feeling, Mr. Sherlock Holmes, when you come upon the right scent—a kind of thrill in your nerves."
- Detective Tobias Gregson, "A Study in Scarlet"
by Sir Arthur Conan Doyle

Mirabella hailed a hansom cab. The cabbie frowned at the sight of Wiggins. The boy was grinning from ear to ear at the prospect of riding in a hired cab—probably the first time in his life he had ever done so—despite the fact he might be riding to his death.

Mirabella placed a sixpence in the cabbie's hand. Ordinarily one would not pay at the start of a journey, but she wished to show that a young lady and a street urchin were good for the fare.

"Wha' yew lookin' at, mister?" Wiggins demanded of the cabbie. "She paid ya'. And we're workin' for *Mr. Sherlock 'Olmes.*"

"Don' mean nothin' to me," the cabbie retorted.

"It will." Wiggins' expression was smug. "There'll be a day when everyone has heard his name."

"We must make haste, Mr. Wiggins." Mirabella shoo-ed Wiggins into the carriage, even though she agreed with his sentiment.

The boy let out an earsplitting whistle as he entered the cab, clearly delighted at his new found status.

"Let us keep our mind on the danger before us, Mr. Wiggins," Mirabella said as they sat down. Her heart was racing as she clutched the reticule containing her pistol, hoping against hope they would make it in time.

And hoping that they wouldn't.

"Ah, I'm used to it. There ain't a minute of the day I ain't in danger." He kept his eyes glued to the window as if the sight before him was completely new. And it was, from the perspective of a cushioned seat. Apparently Wiggins' expressed fear of vampires was experiencing a momentary hiatus as he luxuriated in the cab.

He laughed suddenly, revealing that one of his front teeth was missing. "Ain't we just a fine lord and lady, Miss Mirabella?"

Glancing at her companion, she fought the urge to hug him. She didn't wish to put an end to their new found camaraderie.

She wished with all her heart that Wiggins would make it to adulthood. If he did, he would be an outstanding member of society—if he didn't already have a police record—and one who would sincerely appreciate any good fortune that came his way. She felt her frustration rising. Of all the young people she'd ever met, Wiggins should have an education. He was such a bright young man.

"Indeed we are." She glanced at his feet. "Apparently your new shoes are comfortable, Mr. Wiggins?"

Wiggins nodded. "Yeah. And they is warmer, but they'se also a bit stiff."

"Do they not fit?"

"Oh, they fit a'right. I seem to be able to run a bit faster—if I don't fall that is. I've tripped and fell more than once." His expression grew somber. "That can be the difference between landing in the slammer or not, you know."

"Well at least you're not as likely to land in glass—or horse manure. I expect that you're simply not used to the boots, and anything new has an adjustment period, even if it's for the better."

He considered her words, never one to believe anything he had not evaluated for himself. "I guess you're right about that, miss."

This was a considerable compliment coming from Wiggins. She had observed that those who had abusive parents, or no parents at all, had a great distrust of all authority figures. They learned from an early age to trust only in themselves. It made for a capable person, but an unusually stubborn individual.

"No doubt you will run even faster in time." She patted his knee.

"Do you think so, miss?"

"I do. Are you wearing your new wool socks? It is getting cold."

"Gosh yes, I hates to be cold."

"And besides not exposing yourself to lacerations, wearing shoes is more sanitary."

"Sanitary?" He laughed. "What do I care about that?"

"You want to avoid cutting your feet as that can lead to infection. You'll care if you catch pneumonia and die of some bacteria-laden disease."

Wiggins grew strangely silent for a boy who rarely stopped talking.

"What's wrong?"

"Nuffin."

"Something is wrong. Please tell me."

"That's what me parents died of."

What an idiot I was to speak without thinking. When will I ever learn? Mirabella's heart fell in her chest. "Of pneumonia?"

"Yeah."

"I'm so sorry."

"Are you sayin' they might have lived if they had had shoes?"

"It's possible." What a startling realization that something so small might have stood between life and death. "But, of course, I can't know. Only the Almighty can know that."

He looked at his feet. "How much did these shoes cost?"

"About ten shillings." It was darkly disturbing that they had just put a price on the lives of this child's parents.

"Ten shillings!" he exclaimed. "I know a bricklayer who only makes six shillings per week." He said this as if it were a small fortune. And indeed it was to him. He whistled under his breath, "Only two weeks wages for a life."

Wiggins had a sudden change in his attitude towards his boots, admiring them as if they were a religious artifact—or a magical talisman. "I knows about starvation. But I never thought boots could save a man's life. Me own ma and pa." He added softly, "Those what matters most in the world to me."

"Though I won't downplay the value of shoes—and warmth—it's most likely the pneumonia germs were airborne and had very little to do with their shoes," she said. *Unless the cold added to the problem.*

Mirabella looked out the window to see an old woman hovering about a gas lamp, which gave off a small amount of heat as well as light.

London was indeed well lit. There were any number of other cabbies on the road. There always were in London, people going to the theatre, opera, men's clubs, lectures, or concerts—and their hansom cab moved easily in and out between the fancier carriages with a sturdy mare pulling them all. The sound of the wooden wheels hit the brick cobblestone street, the normally comforting cadence having turned to an ominous foreboding in her mind.

"What's air borne?" Wiggins asked after a few moments' reflection.

"Transmitted in the air," she said. "Or the bacteria could have been in the water. Germ theory is a new study, so not much is known about it."

"What do you have to be to know about bacterias and germies? A doctor?"

"That or a scientist."

"Whatever it was, they died because they didn't have money," he muttered.

"That's a very dangerous way to think," Mirabella said softly. "It allows a darkness into your heart."

"I'm not goin' to pretend somethin' true ain't true."

"Certainly not. Quite right." She paused to take care with her words, which Mirabella rarely did, but her words could dramatically shape the greatest wound this child would ever bear. "But it's a treacherous game to think 'if this happened, then this would happen.'"

"Why?"

"Because you can turn your soul black over something you can't possibly know or control. You have to continue doing what you think is right. The only thing you really have in the end is your soul."

He scoffed. "You mean there's a plan we don't know about. Where God wants the rich to live and the poor to die."

"You see, with that attitude you'll end up miserable and bitter, and possibly even in jail, Mr. Wiggins. But, yes, some people think it's all predetermined."

"You mean that we have no say?" His jaw was suddenly firm. "I don't believe it. I believe I makes me own fortune. And I 'ave eleven boys what depend on me."

"Of course you do. That's the attitude. You are a king among men Mr. Wiggins, and that's a fact. And glad I am for it, because I may need your help as well." She smiled at him, her admiration growing. She could see why the boys followed him; he was a natural leader. And a philosopher. "The essential thing you must reflect upon is the person you are—a young man who thinks for himself—and that your parents are very proud of you."

"Do you think so?"

"I'm sure of it. They are looking down on you."

The carriage turned left off Baker Street onto Marylebone Road. Shortly thereafter they passed Madame Tussaud's on their left.

"What do you want me to do, Miss Mirabella?"

"When we arrive at the scene, I'll look about, hoping to catch a glimpse of the person you saw. If he's still in the apothecary, that is."

"The vampire?"

"Yes, and the one talking to the vampire, to confirm it is Longstaff. Every bit as dangerous, in fact. Or more so."

"I've got it." Wiggins frowned, contemplating her words. "He was a werewolf—because, you know, they can change. Then he changed into a vampire."

"Mr. Sherlock Holmes believes he never was a vampire."

"He is one now. I saw him."

"Perhaps he is a man dressed as a vampire." She shook her head. "Even so, the man is every bit as treacherous as a vampire—remember, he has killed. So, if I am somehow threatened, you must promise to leave and go get help." She didn't want him to be in peril as well.

"I sees."

"It is quite significant that you have tied the vampire to The Madame's Apothecary, Mr. Wiggins; this will be of great interest to both Mr. Holmes and to the police." She sighed heavily. "Still we can't conclude anything without proof."

"I saw him leave the club with a large container. That's all I know."

"Yes, he could claim it was anything." She crossed her arms in front of her chest with indignation. "We need damning evidence."

"And the container is gone now anyway." Wiggins looked at her abruptly, surprised. "You cursed, miss."

"Only in context." She bit her lip. It was true, she wouldn't have dared use such a word in her father's house. *What has happened to me?*

Sherlock Holmes, that's what.

"Har! har! That's a porky pie." He grew suddenly somber. "Do you have a weapon, miss?"

"Naturally I do." She had learned the hard way not to be separated from her pistol.

Mirabella opened her reticule and took out the No. 32 Marlin Pocket Revolver and loaded it with a bullet. She always kept one in her hand purse.

"You need somethin' else." He reached inside his trousers leg and produced a knife, holding it out to her.

"That could certainly be useful. But I can't leave you without a weapon, Mr. Wiggins."

"Me without a weapon?" He grinned at the absurdity of the idea. "I 'ave at least five of these on me."

Apparently she could learn a thing or two from this child.

"Excellent. I knew I brought you for good reason." She placed the knife in a hidden pocket in her skirt.

They arrived at the apothecary, and Wiggins showed great delight at knocking on the overhead roof trap door to let the driver know they would like to depart.

Mirabella instructed the cabbie to wait for them, promising a large tip if he did so. His expression did not fill her with confidence. With more of a jerk than was necessary, he pulled a lever that released the doors, since they had already paid, and they alighted.

Mirabella fought the urge to turn around and get back in the cab.

Chapter Twenty-one
In the Lion's Den

*"Action may not always bring happiness; but there is
no happiness without action"*
– Benjamin Disraeli

Mirabella and Wiggins watched the back entry to The Madame's
Apothecary from behind a nearby shrub. The apothecary was dark inside.
"I fear we are too late."

"You stay here, Mr. Wiggins," she cautioned as she moved from
behind the bushes.

"What are you doin', miss?" he whispered loudly, fear and
admiration crossing his expression.

"I believe he has gone. I must study the ground for footprints and
other clues before the rain washes it away." The back of the apothecary
was naturally unpaved, and the usually wet English weather had made the
upper layer of soil slightly muddy. Perfect for foot prints.

"But it's too dangerous!"

"That's why I brought you, Mr. Wiggins. Stay out of sight and run for
help in the event I am captured. Do you understand?" *Although chances
are, I wouldn't be captured but murdered. Someone has already tried to
kill me. Most likely I'd be knifed and dumped in the Thames.*

I'd best not be caught.

"Yes, miss." She could hear him gulp loudly.

Aha! She found two sets of footprints near the door, seeming to
belong to the same person. Where were the footprints for the second
person?

It was an unfortunate location since it placed her both near the door
and the gas lighting. Still, as well as making her visible, it made the
footprints visible. She attempted to stay out of the light as best she could
while listening for anyone approaching.

Straight away she noticed a red thread in the footprint, which she
picked up and put in her reticule.

She took out her notebook and her ruler since she hadn't had time
to mix up plaster of paris. As she measured the footprint, taking notes,

she had the sense a monster was breathing down her neck. Not for the first time she thought of the massively bulky cameras she had seen, prohibitively expensive and heavy, in the hands of only the few. Even if she could afford one, she would have been unable to lift a camera without a tripod.

An observant mind is a disciplined mind. Sherlock, of course, thought there was no substitution for observation, and that such an acquisition would only make one mentally lazy, causing one to miss the significant details.

Hurriedly she noted the length and width of the footprint, as well as the shape of the shoe, an unusual square-shaped toe. She noticed that the right side imprint was deeper and heavily weighted. Probably the wearer of the shoe was right-handed and had been carrying the blood with that hand. She made a note to ask Wiggins for confirmation. The stride was shorter than expected, but that may have been due to the weight carried rather than being an indicator of his height.

Frantically she drew a replica of the footprint with the thought that a murderer might descend upon her at any moment. Wishing that the ground were soft enough for a rubbing, Mirabella outlined the print in ink—she did have a pen in her reticule—then carefully placed the paper atop it. She would fill in the details later from her notes.

Clang! She heard a noise inside.

Mirabella threw herself against the wall of the building, dropping her ruler in the process but holding tight to her drawing. Even in her terror her eyes returned to the outline of the shoes. These were not laborers' boots but the shoes of a gentleman or someone well-to-do.

Something is not right.

Her heart pounding, she heard the shuffle of feet inside moving to the door.

"Wait here," said a commanding voice. She couldn't make out who it was, being muffled from the inside. "I have something else to show you."

"*Tweet! Tweet!*" Wiggins whistled madly, indicating he had seen someone through the window. *Too little too late.*

Hurriedly she turned the corner, moving around to the side of the building but still only some eight feet from the door. If anyone turned the corner he would see her.

She heard voices. Was it Fairclough? She couldn't determine. Mirabella knew she should run but wanted to see if she could hear any of the conversation.

"*Tweet! Tweet!*" She motioned with her arm to stop.

"It may yet save a life," a shrill voice said.

"The blood?" the lower voice asked.

"Of course, you idiot."

Mirabella shuddered.

"But you had to kill someone to get it," the muffled lower voice said. Mirabella felt her hands trembling. She was unable to make out either of the voices.

"That was unfortunate, but it was the blood of a sinner."

"Can the blood be pure then?" It sounded as if he were pleading rather than discussing.

"We'll find out—if the experiment works. It is worth a try. The last woman would have died otherwise. Percival's blood saved her."

"But Percival died."

"That was no loss to the world."

Experiment? One moment it sounded like a scientist speaking and the next a monster. It was the strangest conversation she had ever heard, and being in Sherlock Holmes' employ she had heard her share.

"It is interesting," the shrill scientist said. "I mixed the blood from both men and the combined blood clumped."

"So they weren't compatible?" The lower voice was not the one in charge, Mirabella would stake her life on it. She hoped she didn't have to.

"No. And yet, both of the donors were sodomites. It's baffling. I was so sure . . ."

Mirabella bit her lip involuntarily at the horror of the actions being described. Were they admitting to the murder of both Radcliffe and Lord Percival? And here I am not eight feet from them. *I pray to God neither of them turns the corner and sees me.*

"Why then did the blood coagulate?" The 'scientist' seemed genuinely perplexed.

"Maybe one was sick."

Maybe you are.

"That has been the scientific belief, that bloods are not compatible if there is a pathology present. I had widened that belief to include a disease of the soul. . . And yet Percival's blood was compatible with the woman who was hemorrhaging after childbirth. It saved her life." It was ghastly how this heinous act was being discussed in such cool, logical terms. At least by the 'scientist'. The lower voice sounded on edge, as if he were on the verge of losing control.

As if on cue, the lower voice began shouting. "You poisoned the wine and injected the needle. I didn't have anything to do with killing Percival."

Heaven save us! Mirabella's heart began pounding out of her chest. Was he as much as saying that the scientist killed Percival?

"The kitchen cook set the stage. She was the real murderer, not you nor I."

The scientist had said 'she'. Mrs. Kitchens. There were times when finding the truth was painful. Mirabella's heart fell. She had never wanted it to be Evie, but had always had her suspicions. Was Evie Mrs. Kitchens? If so, did she know what she had done?

The lower voiced man started wailing. "I thought I could never feel worse than I did at the workhouse. But this is worse."

Who is the vampire? And what role did the vampire have in all this?

Mirabella heard footsteps moving towards her inside the building. She thought her heart might pound out of her chest. Still, she took a risk and looked inside the window.

She couldn't see anyone, hidden by the shelves.

At least one of the two had found a way in his mind to justify murder. For research. For *saving* lives. But it was not for man to decide the comparative worth of human beings. Or who might live and who might die. That was for God alone.

The gas light flickered and went out, as if to make a statement, leaving her in darkness.

The door opened suddenly and Mirabella almost jumped out of her skin.

"Come back here!" the shrill voice screamed.

Only one walked through the door, his back to her. He walked hurriedly, away from the building.

"I'll find you. I'll kill you."

"Why not? You've already destroyed my soul," the man yelled back, but he didn't turn. He kept his pace.

It could be Longstaff. Mirabella kept her eyes glued to his back but she couldn't make out any of the features of the departing man—and dare not make herself visible—but hoped Wiggins would make note of some of the details. Focusing on his back, she was lost in thought.

It grew silent inside the apothecary.

She felt a presence breathing down her neck. She whirled around to see a man facing her.

Chapter Twenty-two
Surprised

Mirabella dropped her equipment and reached for the pistol in her pocket, but she was too slow.

Her attacker knocked the gun out of her hand with his cane.

Quickly she moved into a *Jiu-jitsu* stance.

"Shhh! What are you doing Miss Mirabella? Shouldn't you be quieter out here?" he whispered.

"Dr. Watson! You scared the life out of me." She kept her voice low.

"And your pistol scared me as well." He began picking up her things. "Let's get out of here."

"I have to go inside. The vampire is in there."

"I'm glad I came." John sighed heavily. "So we're simply going to storm into the apothecary in the middle of the night. And accuse—who?"

"I'm not sure."

"Ah, so you haven't been able to identify the vampire?"

"I have his footprint. And I have learned a great deal."

"This may or may not be the vampire's footprint. And we can't accuse anyone until we know who we are accusing—and have proof."

"The man inside killed Lord Percival. He as much as said so."

"Did you see him?"

"No."

"Could you identify his voice if you heard it again?"

"No."

"So you have nothing."

"I know he is inside!"

"Unless he has already left through the front door." Dr. Watson tapped his cane on the ground. "Let us proceed to Baker Street and discuss with Holmes what should be done. He should have returned by now."

"We have to return to the Diogenes," Mirabella said once they were all three in the carriage.

"Now?" Dr. Watson questioned.

"It's important."

Outside the Diogenes, Dr. Watson struck a match that Mirabella might see.

She studied the footprints outside Radcliffe's room, holding her drawing beside it.

"It's a match."

An exact match to her drawing.

***

Back at Baker Street, Mirabella and Wiggins excitedly reported their findings to Sherlock with Dr. Watson in attendance.

"Miss Hudson, you took a great risk. You should never have pursued the criminal alone."

"I were with her, sir," Wiggins said. "And Dr. Watson."

"I commend you on writing the note at least, Miss Hudson." Sherlock tugged at his cravat. "This gave Watson the opportunity to talk you out of a foolhardy venture."

"I'm not so sure, Mr. Holmes. If I could have rushed the door and seen who was speaking, we would now know who killed Lord Percival."

"Not unless you returned alive, Miss Mirabella." Dr. Watson shook his head. "If it was the murderer, he would not hesitate to put a period to your existence."

"The speaker never admitted to killing Lord Percival," Sherlock objected. "In fact, he pinned the murder on Mrs. Kitchens."

"True, but he was lying."

"Did he admit to Radcliffe's murder as well?" Sherlock pressed.

"No, but I know he did it." Mirabella paced the room. "Remember the matching footprints."

"Indeed, excellent detective work. But we must proceed with wisdom; we do not want to act in haste and destroy our chances of convicting the murderer."

"I'm sure I would have thought of the wisdom of that course in time," she said.

"Everyone does in time. For some it is after they are dead." Sherlock shook his head, his expression dismal.

"I wouldn't 've let her die, sir. I was on watch," Wiggins added.

Sherlock muttered under his breath, as if speaking to an unknown presence, "At least Miss Belle has finally learned to keep a pistol with her—that in itself is a miracle—but she has never successfully used it."

"That was a bit below the belt, Mr. Holmes."

"In all honesty, I was in more danger from Miss Mirabella shooting me than she was from any attack, short of her storming the apothecary," Dr. Watson said.

"Miss Hudson, I forbid you from taking charge and doing things on your own initiative without my approval."

"Why? You allow Wiggins to do so."

"That is entirely different."

"Why?"

"In the first place, Wiggins doesn't take unnecessary risks. In the second place, he knows what he is doing." Sherlock cleared his throat. "And, in the third place, you are the most accident-prone person I have ever encountered, besides having a knack for courting trouble."

True. I accepted employment from you. "That isn't fair. I have survived several attacks on my life."

"You are also the luckiest person I know, right behind Watson." he murmured. "At any rate, it is out of the question."

"But think of all we discovered, Mr. Holmes," she protested. "It is most unkind of you to reprimand me when I have learned a great deal. We as much as know that Fairclough is somehow responsible for the deaths of Percival and Radcliffe."

"Not precisely. That is a bit of speculation on your part. But the connection is nonetheless of great interest," he agreed reluctantly.

"Fairclough has the vampire working for him," Wiggins said. "Who looks to be Longstaff."

"This we must determine. It is an excellent lead," Sherlock agreed. "Good job, Wiggins. This is information we can use."

Mirabella put her hands on her waist, staring at him expectantly.

"Holmes, just admit that Miss Mirabella did a commendable job. These are all exceptional findings," Dr. Watson's chin engaged in a half nod. "Even if her methods are somewhat foolhardy."

"I don't wish to encourage Miss Belle in rebellion and reckless insubordination. She is already an expert at these endeavors."

Mirabella reached for her reticule and pulled out the red thread. "Look! I almost forgot. I found this in the footprint."

Sherlock's eyes opened wide. "The red spats."

Mirabella gasped as realization hit. "Longstaff is the vampire, don't you think?"

"But the man I overheard was frightened. He weren't no vampire," Wiggins said.

"Think, Miss Belle. You have met Mr. Longstaff. Could the voice have been the same?"

"Possibly. The voice was so shaken and choppy. And I thought Longstaff couldn't be the vampire: they were seen together."

"You must not let your assumptions get in the way of the facts."

"Mrs. Gage saw both Longstaff and a man dressed as a vampire on the front porch of Lord Percival's home. She is a credible witness," Mirabella suggested.

"Then Longstaff couldn't a' been the vampire," Wiggins concluded.

"Unless there are two vampires," Dr. Watson said.

"Or unless Mrs. Gage was mistaken in Longstaff." Sherlock shook his head.

Wiggins slapped his hand over his mouth. "Why are they taking the blood?"

"It sounds like a scientific experiment, as disturbing as that is," Mirabella said.

"But then why transport the blood to a different location?" Sherlock posed. I had once suspected the blood might be for a religious ceremony of sorts—or simply to scare the public—but this development is of interest. I am particularly interested in your remark that Percy's blood saved the life of a woman in childbirth."

"And yet . . ." She sighed. "We must stop them."

"It is imperative that we do. But, as of yet, we have no proof. Only a simple red thread," Sherlock said, placing the tobacco in his pipe.

"Oh, I wish I knew where they had taken the blood," she exclaimed.

"And what will we do next, Mr. Holmes?" Wiggins asked.

"Certainly I have my contacts amongst the resurrection men and local hospitals. I believe some investigation is in order." He turned suddenly to face Mirabella. "*Not by you*, Miss Hudson."

Mirabella pursed her lips. "You need to decide if I am your lady investigator or if I am simply your scullery maid, Mr. Holmes. And, if it is the latter, I will go into university and leave your employ. It is your decision." She turned on her heel and left the flat.

Wiggins whistled. "That is some tough bird." He picked up an apple bit into it.

Chapter Twenty-three
The Ceremony

*"Love God, fear God if you wish, but question any doctrine which
enables you to play God. Not all sacred texts are sacred."*
Sherlock Holmes – "Sherlock Holmes and the Chocolate Menace"

"Father, this is the blood of thine enemy who embodies all that is
evil." The high priest, cloaked in a dark robe, bowed his head reverently.
He lifted the chalice above his head. A bit of the blood spilt onto the alter
from the chalice.

Candles were lit all about, hanging from the trees and positioned
on a stone altar. Only a sliver of moon was visible. The flickering lights
intermingled with the starlight and the shadows of the tree branches to
form shimmering shapes. The smell of pine from the European larch
filled the air, as well as the sweet honey of the balsam poplar and the
perfume of elder flowers, creating a magical ambiance to depraved
purpose.

"As your faithful servants we have removed this evil from the Earth,
that you might cast their wretched souls into Hell." A dozen or so people
stood about the priest, women and men, some enraptured, some looking
down, some looking away. "In Hebrews, you tell us, Holy Father, that
there can be no forgiveness without the shedding of blood."

We know from the Old Testament, Lord, the true works, that you
required animal sacrifices for the redemption of sins." Raising the goblet
higher, his voice rang through the grove. "This sacrifice, too, was from an
animal. A beast."

He moved the chalice close to his lips as if he were going to take a
sip of the blood. Some drew closer. Some gasped.

"I will drink the blood of those who harmed you. Help them on their
way to Hell for the evil they enacted upon others." The priest set down
the chalice and opened the book on the altar.

"Blood is the ultimate purifier. Under the law everything is purified
with blood, and without the shedding of blood there is no forgiveness of
sins. Hebrews 9:22."

"And Abel also brought of the firstborn of his flock and of their fat portions. And the Lord had regard for Abel's offering, but for Cain and his offering he had no regard," the High Priest continued. "Genesis 4:4-5."

The jagged stones of the altar matching his severely chiseled features, the priest bowed his head reverently. "God commanded the nation of Israel to make a sacrifice unto him. We have the blood here of men of unspeakable evils. Men who are so greedy they allow children to starve while they feast on wine and spirits. Men who play games of chance while others cannot afford heat and medicine. Men who attend frivolous entertainments while the poor who have served them lie in bed dying of consumption, having no money for a doctor." He raised his voice in a primal yell.

"And who are these evil doers? Men who have relations with other men."

A woman fell to the ground on her knees crying. "My own child, gone," she wailed.

"Remember Sodom and Gomorrah. Your child shall be avenged!"

Another man yelled, "My wife, she died of tuberculosis, starving and cold. We had no money for coal. I worked twelve hours every day, seven days a week."

"You who were good suffered while those who did not labor did nothing to help you—even engaging in unspeakable acts with other men, passing on diseases of the devil to their faithful wives."

Skillfully the robed leader channeled their grief into hatred. He lifted the chalice over his head. "Herein is their blood, their sacrifice. We must help them on their way to Hell for the evil they enacted on others."

"Do not be afraid. Pope Innocent VIII's physician himself bled three young men to death and fed their still warm blood to his holiness." And then the robed priest drank from the chalice of blood.

There were murmurs of confusion, approval, and horror in the crowd.

"There are others. Let us spread terror in the hearts of the wicked for their evil deeds. Let us end the evil in this city." He opened the book again. "Then the LORD rained down burning sulfur on Sodom and Gomorrah—from the LORD out of the heavens. Genesis 24."

"Friends, we are living here in Sodom and Gomorrah. This is the time of the reckoning. We will help the Lord our God to purify this city."

He placed the chalice in front of the cross.

"And we shall feast and our children shall live."

A gust of wind blew out the candle which had lit the cross on the altar.

Chapter Twenty-four
A Family Affair

"The Diogenes Club is the queerest club in London, and Mycroft one of the queerest men." – Sherlock Holmes
"The Greek Interpreter" by Arthur Conan Doyle

"The devil take it, Mycroft!" Sherlock greeted his brother with something less than cordiality, now arriving at the flat. "You might have been this madman's latest victim." He added under his breath, "You might still be."

Mirabella peered 'round the corner of the galley kitchen in time to hear Sherlock state under his breath, "Someone knows the purpose of the Diogenes Club."

The kitchen being situated only a few feet from the sitting area, she wondered what on earth Sherlock could mean. *The purpose.* The Diogenes was an academic club, naturally.

"Not necessarily," Mycroft said. "Radcliffe might have been the target. And the police merely happened to find him at the Diogenes Club."

"Well of course he was the target. He is now dead." Sherlock's impatience was evident. The Great Detective always looked more frightening when he was upset, and he was certainly upset, however deliberate his language.

"You seem distressed, brother dear." Mycroft stretched his legs out before him, his pale grey eyes adding a softness to his stark, masculine features. In contrast, Sherlock's grey eyes were darker, having much the look of a thunderstorm.

"Naturally I am distressed. I was called out in the middle of the night wondering if my brother was dead. That aside, there was a murder at your club, putting you in imminent danger."

"That alone is a great concern." Dr. Watson said. "But I find that my patriotism demands to be heard. We are all aware that you are critical to the functioning of the British government, Mycroft. I worry for the safety of the country if anything were to happen to you."

"To hell with the British government, Watson." Sherlock muttered. "I worry for the safety of *my brother*."

"Mr. Mycroft Holmes *is* the foreign secretary," Mirabella said as she presented the group with the tea service.

This is not like Sherlock: he always put work before personal feelings. This threat to Mycroft's safety obviously had the effect of removing several layers of Sherlock's emotional protection.

She found that she liked seeing there was something underneath the stony exterior. *I wonder if Sherlock knew it was there.*

"Yes, yes, we are all aware of that, Miss Hudson."

"Of course," she said apologetically. "But for some Mycroft is a difficult official to follow. He changes positions so frequently it is difficult to know his precise assignment at any given moment."

"No one knows what they are doing at any given moment in the government," Sherlock muttered.

"Precisely," Mycroft agreed. "There is no accountability. It is impossible to fail at that which is a mystery to all." He shrugged. "Still, it can be exhausting attempting to keep up with the pretense."

She handed their guest a sherry which he happily took, along with an offering of finger sandwiches of roast beef, cheese, watercress, and black bread which she had quickly assembled. The tangy, spicy flavor of the watercress enhanced the sandwich despite its low cost, making it a favorite of the working class. She had bought the watercress from a young boy pushing a vegetable cart for a pence per bundle. Many children were sent to school with watercress sandwiches in place of the meat.

Even Sherlock took a sandwich, to her relief. Outside of a slice of toast and a single egg, this was all he had eaten today. She had learned that she could manage to entice Sherlock to eat if she prepared it in small, bite-sized portions.

And if she added enough sweet mustard, which both Sherlock and John favored.

Mycroft sighed heavily. "I long for the days when I was a mid-level official."

"That was only a few months ago, Mycroft," Sherlock said.

"Yes, those were wonderful times." Mycroft's expression was wistful.

He was clean-shaven, unusual among men. The current style was for men to have facial hair, and most men did. Mycroft had always to be different—to stand out—and yet he somehow looked more fashionable than other men, even when he did not follow the fashion.

"But, if you didn't wish to be promoted, why didn't you simply refuse the position?" Dr. Watson asked.

"It is most tiresome," Mycroft said. "I intended to refuse the position but never got around to it. Before I could bat an eyelash I was swept off to my new office."

"Essentially Mycroft is so lazy he can't even run away from work," Sherlock said with characteristic simplicity.

"Not precisely true. It's a bloody maze at Whitehall," Mycroft argued, shaking his head derisively. "What the place wants is organization."

"The British government, you mean?" Dr. Watson asked. The good doctor sported a mustache and long sideburns. Unlike Mycroft and Sherlock, John always wished to follow the style of the day—to the letter. His elegance was in his adherence to the style. Mycroft's was in setting the style. Sherlock did neither; his only interest in fashion was his need for convincing disguises.

"Precisely. That place. Once one finds the correct person to speak to, in order to refuse one's promotion you understand, he is off and about somewhere at luncheon in a completely different building."

"Much like yourself," Sherlock said. "That is why you fit in so well in the government."

"One can't be expected to skip luncheon." Mycroft looked up with such woundedness that it was difficult not to have sympathy for him. "Besides, ordinarily people seek me out and I don't have to hop scotch all over the country attempting to find a person of absolutely no interest to me. They come to me, don't you see? Finally it was easier to just do the job."

To be sure, Mycroft had begun his career as a minor government official. Having an extraordinary gift for observation and analysis, as well as an excellent memory and the ability to interact socially with finesse and discretion, in no time at all everyone at the highest levels of government consulted with Mycroft—even the prime minister and the Queen. If there was a secret in the government, Mycroft knew about it.

"How can someone who is so indolent be promoted to the position of the *Foreign Secretary*?" Dr. Watson smiled, munching on a sandwich.

"I should say it is Mycroft's lack of ambition." The corners of Sherlock's lips fought a smile. "He has no political aspirations and the rare quality in a government official of knowing right from wrong."

"Thus everyone confides in him," Mirabella added.

"It is most tiresome." Mycroft took another finger sandwich. "I can't find a moment's peace."

"Your life is practically unbearable, brother dear."

"It has been of late, I can assure you. I don't dare be alone for a moment."

Mirabella wondered why Mycroft would be a target as she dusted the black marble mantelpiece. She glanced out the window to see the fog drifting, glowing yellow in the gas lights.

Definitely a pea-souper.

"At any rate, the foreign secretary is an influential and important position in the most powerful country in the world." Mirabella said. "Could these murders have anything to do with the government? Perhaps one of the countries unhappy with British rule?"

Sherlock raised his eyebrows at her, interest suddenly alight in his eyes.

Ordinarily she hated to see that look in the Great Detective's eyes.

"I had thought the murders to be personally motivated, but it is certainly something to consider." Mycroft turned to glance at Mirabella, pausing from his dining momentarily. "Will the lovely Miss Hudson be assisting you on the case, Shirley?"

"That would be a welcome development." Mirabella was suddenly hopeful.

Sherlock glanced her way with obvious disparity. "Unfortunately it may be necessary."

"Truly?" exclaimed Mirabella, finding that she was dusting more feverishly. "Will I be allowed to assist? Oh, that is wonderful. I promise, I—"

"Miss Hudson," interrupted Sherlock. "There will be some light investigative reporting necessary if and only if you can keep your tongue in your head. Unlike the episode when you gave our position over to the apothecary."

Her heart fell at the stinging remark.

Her feelings must have been evident because Mycroft said softly, "Be kind, Shirley. Miss Hudson does an exceptional job—at great personal danger to herself."

She felt her heart sing as quickly as it had fallen.

How could someone so handsome be so nice? Especially related to Sherlock Holmes?

"I have no quarrel with her job. It is her mouth which concerns me," Sherlock said.

"That is most unfair, Mr. Holmes."

"Is it? You were almost knifed to death after your last slip of the tongue."

She swallowed hard. It was difficult to argue with that one.

Sherlock turned in his chair to face her. "Miss Hudson, can you make investigative inquiries without revealing your position to our suspects?"

"Oh, yes. I will do much better. What do you want me to do? Go undercover in the workhouse?" she asked excitedly.

"Heaven forbid," Dr. Watson exclaimed, his concern evident.

"I second that sentiment," Sherlock said. "There are things to do of equal importance. Can you put aside your own preferences for once, Miss Hudson, and do what is needed for the good of the case and your employer?"

"I always do."

"It sounds like you are reprimanding Miss Hudson for doing precisely that—wanting to assist on the case," Mycroft drawled.

Why did Sherlock do that? Could he not stand to see her succeed? Maybe Moriarty was right about Sherlock.

His gaze was icy cold. "Going under cover at the workhouse is out of the question."

"There, there Miss Hudson," Mycroft said consolingly. "What my brother means to say is this is a very dangerous matter, as well as exceedingly delicate, and we must proceed accordingly. Are you able to both implement discretion and, shall we say, a certain worldliness?"

"I'm not certain I follow you . . . how am I to be both worldly and discreet?"

"Miss Hudson," exclaimed Sherlock. "If you would but listen to what Mycroft has to say, perhaps you will find out."

"But Mycroft asked me a question, Sherlock." She set down her duster and stood before them. "How can I answer his question and be quiet at the same time?" She was more convinced than ever that Sherlock expected the impossible from her.

"It is Mycroft's job to protect the security of the country," Sherlock explained. "If he has concerns, you cannot intimidate him into ignoring them. You must earn his respect. If you have not done so as yet, that is at your door and not at his."

"Yes, sir," she replied.

"It is true," acknowledged Mycroft. "This is a sensitive issue, which a young girl such as Miss Hudson might find morally objectionable. I must therefore understand if she is able to respect confidentiality under *all* circumstances."

"Indeed I can—and I will." Mirabella looked up in surprise. "It is my responsibility—my *commitment*—to let nothing that occurs in these four walls go beyond this room."

"And what if the case should involve scandal?" demanded Mycroft.

"*Scandal?*" she gulped.

"What if the case might involve something that does not agree with your personal high morals, Miss Hudson?" pressed Mycroft.

"I don't agree with murder, and that is what we face every day. Nothing could be worse than that."

"If a person, a *high ranking* person for example, were involved in something offensive to you, Miss Hudson, would you see it as your duty to make it known—or to keep quiet about the matter for the good of the country?" pressed Mycroft, clearly unconvinced. "If that were my determination?"

"Yes sir, I would keep quiet," she insisted.

"Oh, I should love to see it. If only for a moment," Sherlock murmured.

"I do have one question," she posed.

"You see, my wishes were in vain." Sherlock shook his head.

"Yes, Miss Hudson?" asked Mycroft.

"Shouldn't a person who is engaged in something morally objectionable be held accountable?"

"Oh, my dear girl." Mycroft laughed, though his eyes never lost their intensity, even when he was amused. "Morally objectionable *to whom*?"

"To decent people of course."

"Those are the worst type of people."

"I thought we were in the process of discovering truth and apprehending criminals." She was genuinely perplexed. "Or are you saying that doesn't apply to the rich and powerful? Or to those in high positions?"

"Truth is, at best, subjective," Mycroft said.

Sherlock placed his pipe on the end table beside him a bit too forcefully in her opinion.

She heard a bell ringing on a carriage outside, the whinnying of horses, and the newsies selling the paper.

"*Read all about it in the Strand.*"

Why did she suddenly feel that she had entered into a secret world, a world of subterfuge and deception?

"Let us cut to the chase. What we are trying to say, Miss Hudson, is that there may be something you will have to conceal from the police. Something *illegal*," Sherlock said.

In all my life, I never expected to hear those words come forth from the mouth of Sherlock Holmes.

Mirabella gasped, dropping her duster. "Conceal something from the police? Why would you wish me to conceal something that is illegal?"

Mycroft languidly patted his lips with a handkerchief. "My dear girl, not all things which are illegal are wrong."

Chapter Twenty-five
Undercover

*"Sherlock had twice now inferred that she was the
world's first female detective, but he very soon relapsed into
treating her like the scullery maid."*
— "Sherlock Holmes and the Chocolate Menace"

"You must permit me to go undercover in the workhouse," Mirabella
pleaded after Mycroft left. It appeared her answers had not convinced him
she was ready.

"It's far too dangerous." Sherlock's raven black curls framed his
unshaven face, causing him to look somewhat wilder than usual. His steel-
grey eyes were uncompromising. He wore a black brocade vest with silver
threads embroidered throughout, and a white cotton shirt with blousy
sleeves of the Lord Byron variety on his muscular frame, open at the
neckline.

"Precisely why I can be useful. I'll be near to the suspect."

"Near to a man who is murdering the unsuspecting and draining their
blood," Dr. Watson added solemnly.

"This is a cold-hearted killer, Miss Hudson. Or did you not
comprehend that from the four now dead?"

Overton, Percival, Denzil, and Radcliffe.

"Perhaps more," Dr. Watson added. "Not your garden variety
murderer, Miss Belle."

"This is the most dangerous case we've ever had," Sherlock said
solemnly. "A deranged murderer is on the loose."

"Strictly speaking, that is why I am needed. I thought the purpose
of our work was to stop the villain." Certainly she was afraid. Of all the
monsters they had dealt with, the vampire was the most macabre and
disturbing. *Someone has to do something, and I feel in my very being that I
am the one to do it.*

"And how do you propose to do that, Miss Hudson?"

"I'll be near to the suspect. I can obtain evidence to support what we
already know. And to find out what we don't."

"And what do you know, Miss Hudson?"

"Longstaff is the vampire and Fairclough is the brains behind it all."
She sighed heavily. "And Evie Travers was the cook."

"Ah. I see." Sherlock nodded. "And why are they doing this?"

"To run experiments on the blood to determine what makes blood
compatible. And because they are horrible people."

"It's an odd endeavor for horrible people," Sherlock considered. "To
seek a scientific discovery which will save tens of thousands of lives."

"They are abominable. And yet you want to fall in with them, Miss
Mirabella," Dr. Watson considered.

"I don't want to, but it is necessary. This is what we do. Has Evie been
arrested?" The idea saddened her, but she considered the mounting death
toll.

Sherlock shook his head. "Evie still works for Fairclough at the
apothecary. The constable doesn't wish us to spook either her or
Fairclough until they have proof of their involvement which would convict
them in court. I did pass on the results of your investigation, Miss Belle,
and Constable Jones was quite interested."

She smiled, pleased that she could make a contribution.

"The information did buy us the constable's continued good graces,
which will come in handy," Sherlock added.

"Have you found Longstaff?" Mirabella asked.

"After his jail break he disappeared." Sherlock took a puff on his pipe.
"Constable Jones asked Evie and Fairclough if they knew of Longstaff's
whereabouts and they claimed to have no knowledge of where he is."

Dr. Watson flapped his newspaper. "They were fairly convincing. Evie
Travers seemed frightened at best."

"She also denied being Mrs. Kitchens," Sherlock said. "But the fact
that Longstaff has gone missing . . ."

"They're all going into hiding," Mirabella said. "The man I overheard
wanted out."

"Maybe Fairclough gave him a permanent out," Dr. Watson muttered,
scanning the *Pall Mall Gazette*.

"Fairclough will need new recruits," Sherlock murmured to himself.

"And when he goes to Saint Pancras workhouse looking for fresh
faces, you'll have paid off the overseer, who will present me. Then I can
find out what Fairclough is up to—and find proof of his connection to the
vampire murders."

Dr. Watson looked up. "Listen to yourself, Miss Mirabella: this is work
for an experienced agent of the Yard. It's far too treacherous."

"Nothing we do is without danger." She placed her hands on her waist.

"And how am I to gain experience without working on a case? I don't see that much difference between ferocious tigers and a vampire." Honestly, it was strange how Sherlock had thrown her into every manner of danger on their first two cases, and was now so protective of her.

"You have not yet faced a vampire, Miss Hudson. And you will *never* on my watch." Sherlock's voice was soft but fiercely determined.

"Recall that I have now been in three knife fights. And yet here I stand before you."

"Let me point out that someone running towards you with a knife does not constitute 'being in a fight'. Particularly if a third party takes out a gun and shoots your attacker as he is heading towards you."

"I'll grant you that happened two of the three times. The third time I shot the assailant myself."

"And missed." Sherlock looked down at her condescendingly.

"I don't see how that is relevant." What was needed here was not armchair philosophical arguments but action.

"Neither do I. But you're the one who brought it up, Miss Hudson." Sherlock cleared his throat, picking up Watson's discarded *Pall Mall Gazette* and perusing it. It was obvious that he had dismissed her. "What I believe to be relevant is that, aside from the danger, Fairclough knows you. It would be a short time before realization hit. I would as sooner send Watson than you—and I'm certainly not sending Watson."

"You know very well that one of your disguises would fool him, Mr. Holmes."

"One of mine, yes. Not one of yours."

"I have not been your pupil for all this time to have learned nothing."

"That is an entirely different topic and equally exhaustive. At least we are both agreed that the workhouse subject is closed."

"I can improve, Mr. Holmes. I know disguises is an area where I need to learn, but you can teach me."

"I can teach you certainly, but it is less apparent if you can learn. At any rate, I forbid it. We are dealing with a deadly criminal, a heinous individual, and you cannot go unguarded into his clutches, Miss Belle. Not without a better and specific plan. It is out of the question. That is final."

"At any rate, that is for the police to accomplish; they have experienced agents for this purpose," Dr. Watson said. "Holmes has passed on the information, and it should not be long before they bring the murderer in."

"How many times have I heard that?" She sighed. "And who will protect your brother, Mr. Holmes?"

In an instant Sherlock assumed a dark countenance, causing her to step back. "You are venturing into unsafe territory, Miss Hudson."

She already knew that from his expression, there was no need to tell her. "But you are worried about your brother, Mr. Holmes, aren't you?"

***

Truer words were never spoken. Sherlock was exceedingly worried about Mycroft.

Belle's plan was his best chance at saving his brother. A sound plan, and the only logical course to take.

A detective knew the risks associated with the job. One must, at all times, pursue the criminal without regard to one's own safety.

That wasn't what he heard coming out of his mouth. "It is our job to point Constable Jones in the correct direction. It is not our job to bring in the killer."

Have I lost my mind? Why do I utter such things when there is a murderer on the loose? Sherlock was not accustomed to there being the slightest difference between his thoughts and his utterings.

Insincerity and deception are anathema to me. But he couldn't let Belle know his true thoughts.

Sherlock looked past the bay window to Baker street, which he could see comfortably from his chair beside the fireplace, opposite Watson.

He hated to admit it, but Belle's plan was a solid one: enter the workhouse, gain employment with Fairclough, and obtain the proof the law needed.

The stakes are too high to make a mistake. They were dealing with a nightmarish monster. A beast. Someone who would not hesitate to inflict a violent death on another. It was imperative they succeed in locking the demon up when they acted. It wasn't enough to be certain of the identity

Sherlock knew *who* they were dealing with, but not *what* they were dealing with. The behavior was utterly unpredictable.

They faced a new horror around every corner.

He looked up to see Belle's chestnut brown hair carelessly thrown atop her head, somehow all the more appealing in its disorder and disarray. Her glistening golden brown eyes were alight with the idea of running headfirst into danger.

In his mind's eye he saw that peach-toned ivory skin suddenly turn grey in pallor, surrounded in a pool of blood.

I have seen too much. His imagination tortured him. He shuddered, in the worst turmoil of his life, torn between protecting his brother and his precious Miss Belle.

Did I say precious?

Sherlock was never without the ability to act decisively. It was his trademark.

I must resolve this case. And quickly. He was conflicted. Cases never upset him; he merely solved them.

It made him wish for cocaine. Watson had been admonishing him to get off the drug altogether. Sherlock's thoughts went to cocaine when he experienced unwelcome emotions—which was to say, all emotions.

"Do you think he is up to it, Holmes?" Watson asked.

"Up to what?" Sherlock asked distractedly.

"Can Athelney solve the case?"

"We will have to see." *No, of course he cannot.*

"Athelney can't very well arrest Fairclough without proof," Watson said.

"No, no of course not." Sherlock rose from his chair. "That settles it then."

I shall be going undercover myself. Perhaps Fairclough needs a new vampire murderer. It quite sounded like his former vampire was losing his nerve.

Playing the part of a wounded man bent on revenge will not be so difficult a part to play. Sherlock smiled with a disturbed anticipation.

Miss Belle had been right all along: she had come up with an excellent plan. But it was for him to execute and not for her.

Images of the four bodies he had seen over the last few days filled the space before his eyes. It infuriated him when he did not bring a murderer to justice quickly. Reliving that first moment when he saw Mycroft still alive, his hands began to shake.

"Bloody Hell." Sherlock cursed under his breath. Fear was an unusual emotion for him; he was prepared to forfeit his own life in the pursuit of justice without the slightest hesitation.

"Mr. Holmes?"

"Yes?"

"What do you want me to do, Mr. Holmes?" she asked.

I want you to stay in this flat and remain safe. He knew very well that underneath that sweet exterior was a determined and intelligent young woman—a quick learner, willing to take on any challenge. Perhaps too willing.

"You are on the case, Miss Belle, and there is essential work to be done." He turned to face her, rising from his chair. "To begin with, take the drawing you made of the footprint outside of The Madame's Apothecary to James Taylor & Company and determine if Mr. Taylor made that shoe. It is unlikely, but he may have some idea who made it . .

." He added in an almost inaudible tone, "that was excellent work by the by."

"Excuse me?" She appeared surprised. It wasn't as if he was an ogre. He was merely concerned for her safety, receiving little help from her on that score.

The girl was a walking bullseye. She went out of her way to throw herself into harm's way.

"Miss Hudson, let me repeat, can you keep your tongue in your head?"

"Of course," she replied indignantly, placing her hand on her hip, accentuating her curves. Most becoming, at the same time she managed to look prim and proper in a tasteful silk beige day suit. Not many women could look smashing in beige or brown, but Miss Belle certainly did. To be sure, Sherlock liked her in every color—except, perhaps white. Not because it didn't become her but because she was accident prone.

He felt a pang in his heart at the thought.

"Have a care, Miss Hudson. No one must know, not your Aunt, *no one*. Most especially not the murderer. Let us try that tactic for a change."

"I will certainly do my best."

"That is what concerns me, Miss Hudson."

"I assure you that I don't wish to be murdered."

He frowned. "Murder is not a joking matter, Miss Hudson."

She swung around to stare at him. "I am not joking, sir. I remember when my safety was not so high a priority for you, Mr. Holmes."

"What the devil do you mean, Miss Belle?" Sherlock demanded, crossing the floor in a matter of seconds and taking her by the shoulders. "Never say that to me again."

She swallowed hard. "I've done what was required of me for my country, risking my life. And now you wish to treat me as if I am untried and a mere spectator?"

"No one would ever accuse you of being a spectator, Miss Belle, who would necessarily be silent." He dropped his arms as realization hit him. "What a bloody fool I've been!"

"What is it Mr. Holmes?"

"I assumed the rope burns on Longstaff's hands were from picking Oakum in the workhouse. There wasn't time for his hands to be burned to that degree."

"What was it then, Holmes?"

"The shipyards. Longstaff used to work in the shipyards." He punched the air. "By Jove! The red thread. Those spats belonged to someone else!"

Sherlock ran into his room and retrieved his overnight bag. *The workhouse will have to wait a few days.*

"Holmes, where are you going?" Watson asked. The good doctor always knew when he had hit upon a plan.

"I'll be gone a few days."

"And shall I accompany you?"

"Your company would be much appreciated, Watson. You must pack immediately. I'll be gone for a few hours on errands and then will return for you."

Watson jumped from his chair and moved to his room on the third floor. He always kept a bag packed as well, so it wouldn't be long.

"Shall I go, too?" Belle asked hopefully.

"No, Miss Hudson. You have a necessary errand to do here, as I have already explained."

He turned to look at Belle, the light streaming through the window onto her golden brown hair. "Never fear, Miss Belle. The sharp blade of the righteous shall soon be turned upon itself."

She dropped her duster onto the floor, her eyes opening wide. "What do you mean, Mr. Holmes? That sounds horrible."

"Believe me, it will be."

Chapter Twenty-six
In Pursuit of a Dream

"The greatest good you can do for another is not just to share your riches but to reveal to him his own."- Benjamin Disraeli

"What do you think, Prinnie? Is it to be London University or Bedford College?" Mirabella spread the papers out on the dining table, where she often did her work, seated in a small wooden chair. Sherlock maintained his messy desk in the chemistry lab next to the stairwell, while Dr. Watson's desk was on the opposite wall next to the bow window overlooking Baker Street. Neither gentleman was home at the moment, which suited her purposes.

"*Snort! Blubble! Blubble!*" Prinnie, lounging by the fire, had strong opinions on the subject of academics, as evidenced by the fact that he had allowed those opinions to interrupt his luxuriating, of supreme importance to the hound. The stout and lazy bulldog, so like his royal namesake the prince regent in both appearance and temperament, looked up from his nap just long enough to comment.

Looking at Prinnie's sweet, layered face, it was difficult to believe that an eighty pound dog would have the ability, audacity, and courage to toss a one-ton bull by corkscrewing its body around the bull's neck, throwing the bull off balance.

It had only been some fifty years since the baiting of bulls had been made illegal. The dog had used both the bull's weight and his center of gravity against the larger animal. Naturally, the bulldog had best be prepared to run after doing so, despite having been bred for aggression.

Sometimes one must put survival ahead of predisposition.

"I agree, Prinnie. Excellent choice. London University it is." She made it a policy never to disagree with Prinnie, in spite of her inherent love of the animal. A subject of Her Majesty's England knew the significance of breeding.

Mirabella picked up her pen and diligently set to filling out the application laid out before her. "I can't abide the segregation of the sexes anyway."

Bedford College was an excellent institution—providing classes in science as well as in the arts—but it was nonetheless a college exclusively for women. This did not diminish Bedford's credentials in her mind, but she wished to dispel the notion that women needed a different curriculum than men did, that they weren't up to the task. Mirabella might only be nineteen years of age, but she was definitely a woman up to the task.

The door to the flat suddenly opened, and Mirabella inadvertently covered the paperwork with her hands. Sherlock would *not* understand.

Actually, he did understand, and therein lay the problem. Her entry into college, taking away from her duties, was the last thing Sherlock wanted. He had made that quite clear.

"And when will you do my laboratory work? How will you be available to go undercover if you are in classes?" Sherlock had demanded of her.

And now he was refusing to let her go undercover. What was the point of destroying her dreams if she had nothing of interest to do and was going to be excluded from the spy work?

"Your work has never suffered, Mr. Holmes," she had retorted. *"It has always taken precedence over my dreams. And it always will. I will be attending night classes, and a light load, to insure you should never want for anything, nor have to fetch your own tea or slippers."*

"Do not make light of my work, Miss Hudson. Lives, as well as the safety of London, depend upon us." His exaggerated response did not fit the situation.

She hunched over her paperwork. She truly did not understand why people—even women—had an aversion to the improvement of a woman's mind. What was there to be offended by in an intelligent, successful woman? One would admire a man with those same qualities.

It had not been that long ago that Francis Power Cobbe had been the butt of jokes and universal ridicule after merely reading a paper entitled "Universal Degrees for Women" to the Social Science Association in London, as if the mere idea was absurd.

"Good morning, Miss Mirabella."

She breathed a sigh of relief. It was John. He had a habit of sneaking up on her lately.

"And how proceeds the fate of the world today?" Dr. Watson smiled. He brushed his blond-streaked hair out of his sea-green eyes, not the least of his fantasy-like qualities.

He glanced at the paperwork on the table. "Applying for college are you, Miss Mirabella? Does Holmes know?"

"What do you think, Dr. Watson?" She raised her eyebrows at him.

"I should think he does." His lips formed a half smile. "And that you haven't told him."

"You won't betray me, will you?"

"Since when does Holmes need to be told anything?" John chuckled, moving to the gasogene, where Mirabella had already placed the ginger, sugar, and water in the lower compartment. He placed a cup beneath the spout, adding tartaric acid and sodium bicarbonate to the upper compartment. The experiment begun, and the carbon dioxide forming produced a gas to push the liquid in the lower compartment through the spout in the form of a carbonated ginger beverage, which he eagerly brought to his lips. "Ah, refreshing."

She sighed heavily. "I certainly hope I can keep this from him."

"An ambitious endeavor, Miss Mirabella. Best of luck." He moved to his seat with the ginger beer, glancing over her shoulder as he walked. "I see you have selected my alma mater for your intended education. An excellent choice."

"The University of London is the only college in England bestowing degrees upon both men and women." She sighed. "The first time only two years ago."

He smiled at her. "The Bachelor of Arts might be more attainable. It is a Bachelor of Science degree you wish for if I'm not mistaken."

"You are correct, Doctor." Mirabella was determined to pursue mathematics, as well as chemistry and biology. "No doubt my strongest interest will emerge once I have the benefit of a formal education."

"I shouldn't say that your education has been so shabby, Miss Mirabella. Many a young man would envy it."

"Thus far, all of my learning has come from my father educating me at home in Dumfriesshire alongside my brothers—as well as a regimen of private reading, of course."

"How odd that you should forget your education from the world's finest private detective—as well as from myself."

"How could I forget? But I wish for the credentials as well, so there can be no question of my education's equivalence." Cambridge had already opened mathematics classes and examinations to women—but no degrees, even if they were earned. Mirabella had certainly availed herself of these night classes, but it was time to earn the accreditation as well.

"It is the knowledge that matters if that is what you seek."

"Could you hang your sign and open your door to patients without your license from the Royal College of Physicians?" she asked.

"Forgive my intrusion, Miss Mirabella, but I wonder that you should want more."

"I never thought to hear such words from you, Dr. Watson.

"You must agree, Miss Mirabella, that you are pursuing credentials when you are already receiving the knowledge."

"I am learning a great deal, true."

"Do not seek the approval of men. It is unlikely to be forthcoming." He took a sip of the ginger beer. "Pursue the knowledge and take your pleasure in that. No one can take it from you."

Mirabella glanced at a letter from her curate father on the table, feeling a sadness as she did so. Even her own father had begged her to be happy with her station in life and to pursue marriage and children, saying it was the natural order of things. He who had always encouraged her education.

Not so those clergy who condemned higher education for women as both un-Christian and 'dangerous', saying that female education posed a threat to the family, and hence to the very structure of society, by tempting women away from their natural and proper role. That of wife and mother.

Henry Hudson, a country curate, did not hold to the disturbing view that marriage would help 'tame' women; he liked to see his girls as independent thinkers and able to converse on any subject. He had surely gotten what he wished for in his eldest daughter. Even so, Hudson felt that the purpose of educating women was that they might be superior mothers to their children, not that they would seek accolades and honors for themselves. What was to be admired in men was vain and selfish in women

"I see," she said. But she didn't see. As long as she could remember she had wanted a formal education. An accredited education. "Honestly, if education is desirable for men, why isn't it desirable for women?"

"Indeed it is."

"Why did you say then that I should not wish for more, Dr. Watson?" she inquired.

"Not because I would wish you to limit your aspirations, Miss Mirabella. But because *you already have everything you want*."

"And what is it that I want?" she asked tersely.

"Education. Training. Knowledge." He shook his head. "It is a characteristic of the young not to know what they have. And, believe me, you *have it all*. The admiration of society will give you no pleasure. Do not lose what you have in seeking that which you cannot attain."

She glanced at Dr. Watson. A kinder man did not exist. And certainly he was progressive. He might be a flirt, he might enjoy the company of women, but he never wished to exert any power over women.

Except *charm*.

His turquoise eyes lit up in a way that had made many a woman swoon.

She lit the wood stove for tea and returned to the room. It would be some twenty minutes before tea was ready. She had an apple pie which she would re-heat as well.

Ding Dong! She heard the Westminster clock strike three o'clock. "Oh my goodness! I must make haste to the shoe shop."

She grabbed her application papers and hid them behind some of the laboratory books. She held her index finger to her lips in a sign of silence, receiving a smile from John in return. She then folded a piece of paper and placed it in her purse, checking to insure that she had cab fare.

"I almost forgot. The tea will be ready in twenty minutes. Can you please serve yourself? I mustn't miss the cobbler."

"Of course. I might have injured my leg in the war, but it still functions."

"Also take the pie out of the oven. Have a piece if you'd like."

"I certainly would like."

"I'll be back to make dinner."

"There is no need, Miss Mirabella. Holmes and I will have no doubt departed by then. We'll be out of town overnight."

She turned on her heel to face him. "I almost forgot. Where are you going?"

"Holmes didn't tell me."

"My goodness he has become secretive."

John laughed. "I don't believe this is a new development. I suspect he has always been so."

She bit her lip. *Two can play at that game.*

Chapter Twenty-seven
James Taylor & Company

"Nurture your minds with great thoughts.
To believe in the heroic makes heroes." - Benjamin Disraeli

"Dreadful."

Having arrived at James Taylor & Company, Mr. Taylor studied Mirabella's drawing of the shoe. Sherlock's cobbler shook his head disdainfully, his expression bearing a strange resemblance to the Great Detective's usual countenance.

Each was an artist in his chosen profession, and artists were known to be temperamental.

She didn't know how to interpret Mr. Taylor's disapproval. Her drawing was not good enough? He could make no deductions? He knew whose shoe this was, which disturbed him?

Please let it be the latter.

"I measured the footprint very carefully," she offered hesitantly. "I believe it is an accurate reproduction precisely to the size."

"No doubt it is," he muttered, his eyes fixated to the drawing.

"Is it one of your shoes?" she pressed.

Mr. Taylor looked up suddenly, obviously indignant. "Most certainly not."

"Oh, excuse m-me . . . I knew it was unlikely . . ." She apologized though she had no idea what she was apologizing for or why he would be offended by the question.

"Not unlikely. *Impossible.*"

"Forgive me. You are a cobbler after all. This is a shoe." She attempted not to give further offense.

Her words had the opposite effect.

"My shoes support the skeleton, the legs, the entire body. There is no other article of clothing which is so essential to overall well-being."

"In the cold a coat or scarf might very well prevent one from catching pneumonia."

He glared at her.

She swallowed hard. "To be sure, shoes are the most important."

"I am a master at my profession, I *care* about my work, Miss Hudson."

"I'm quite sure you do, or you would not be the shoemaker to Sherlock Holmes."

"Quite so." He tapped the drawing with his pencil.

She cleared her throat. "And how do you know this is not your shoe, Mr. Taylor?" This investigative work was more difficult than one might think. There was so much of human pride and individual character involved.

"The nails are too far apart. Very shoddy work. I wouldn't let such a shoe as this leave my shop."

"Quite Interesting." This was not what she expected to hear. Sherlock was right on this as he was on many things: it did pay to consult with the experts. "So the nails are far apart in order to save money with materials?"

"And time. That is the more relevant consideration."

"Time is money." She feigned agreement in an effort to build camaraderie.

Mr. Taylor raised his chin. "A true artisan does not resent the time it takes to attain perfection. There is joy in the process—and in the finished result."

It was apparent that her efforts had failed.

"So these must be inexpensive shoes?"

"My dear girl." He laughed. "Not necessarily."

My goodness, she was zero for two. "I'm sorry, Mr. Taylor, I don't comprehend your meaning."

"I'm sure you don't. Simply because they were cheaply made does not mean they were inexpensive. Many a ladies' fashionable shoe is made quickly by someone who has a *following*, shall we say." He frowned. "A fashion shoe is not made to last, as a working man's shoes must be."

"Hmm," she considered. "I see what you mean, sir. I realize it is asking a great deal, but can you tell from the drawing which it is?"

"Which it is what, miss?"

"Pauper's shoes or fashionable shoes, that is?"

"Of course I can tell. " He pulled at his vest. "I didn't start work yesterday. I'm a master cobbler."

"And your answer?"

"Without a doubt, fashionable shoes."

"How can you tell, sir, if I may ask?"

He chuckled. "You must attempt to keep up on the latest fashions, Miss Hudson. Because of the pointy toes, of course. The wearer is someone who is attempting to keep with the style. A pauper's shoes would not waste the leather when there is not even enough food on the table and his own children don't have shoes."

"I should have thought of that," she admonished herself. She must be more attentive to detail if she was ever going to succeed in detective work.

She looked up at him with a sincere admiration, impressed with all he had told her from a simple drawing. "Could you hazard a guess who made these shoes, Mr. Taylor?"

"Mr. Nugent's work comes to mind," he said disdainfully, taking out a pen and paper. "But I can't be certain of that. I could give you the names of several possibilities near to our area, assuming the shoes were made in London. I can almost guarantee they were, however, unless the wearer is a world traveler."

"I wouldn't expect the customer to be overly wealthy," she suggested. "Though he might pretend to be." A person who was wealthy had no need to go about killing people for recompense.

Unless he is killing for pleasure. She shuddered.

The vampire was obviously in cahoots with Fairclough, which indicated a symbiotic relationship, i.e. Fairclough was giving something to the vampire in exchange for the service.

"Why London and not the countryside?" she asked.

"Because the style would have not yet travelled to the country. The fashions originate in Paris, then move to London, and slowly move to the country. Unless we are speaking of the wealthy who can afford to change their wardrobes every year."

"I understand. Maids and servants would observe what their masters are wearing and begin to copy that as their pocketbooks allowed."

"And their station in life. Many would not wish to appear too pretentious by imitating their betters. Unless . . ."

"Yes?"

"Unless the master gave his clothing to his servant. This happens frequently when the master upgrades to the latest styles."

"I see." Her eyes scanned the list he had made. "I'll attend to this right away."

"And who are you looking for, Miss Hudson?"

"We don't know as yet. But I can tell you that he is not a nice man."

"I could have told you that from the shoe." He shrugged.

"Thank you so much. Mr. Holmes is indebted to you." She was as well but she didn't know that Mr. Taylor would be concerned with that.

He smiled graciously, raising his chin with an air of superiority. "I hope I have been of service."

Chapter Twenty-eight
The Shabbiest Shoe Shoppe

"Scotland Yard has no belief in such an extraordinary operation."
- Moriarty, "Sherlock Holmes and the Chocolate Menace"

Sherlock had told her to investigate the "shoes only". Had he meant for her to go to James Taylor & Co. only? Or to keep researching until she found the owner of the shoe?

It is difficult to say. In the absence of Sherlock's company, the interpretation of his orders would have to be up to her.

She hailed a cab with the intention of making inquiries at the ten names on Mr. Taylor's list. Her biggest worry at the moment was not disobeying Sherlock but that none of the cobblers would answer a female. And a young one at that.

Her questions would be considered both pretentious and impertinent. Mr. Taylor was the exception as he was familiar with her and assured of her relationship to the Great Detective, and thus able to overlook her offending femaleness.

This dilemma created an obstacle to solving the case. How to incite them to give her information? She ran Sherlock's methods round in her mind.

How can I make those methods work for me?

Sherlock might be arrogant, haughty, contemptuous, vexatious, and socially alienating, but he was, nonetheless, a man in a man's world, in addition to having a commanding and charismatic presence.

As she had neither, his methods would certainly not work for her, as well as the expectation of appropriate female behavior working against her. As much as she disliked the inequalities of society, she must adapt to the reality of her situation.

This was not a slight against men but against society and the difficulties she had as a female. There were many excellent men and some evil women of her acquaintance. In all of life, it was important to see people as individuals rather than assuming characteristics not in evidence. Mirabella had no tolerance for man-haters, or women-haters for that matter. This all ran round in her mind as she devised a plan.

But do I have to lie? She was repulsed at the idea. It went against everything her excellent mother and curate father had taught her.

Hello, I am looking for a vampire murderer, and I think perhaps the vampire was wearing your shoes. Could you please identify him for me?

She swallowed hard. *Yes, that is certain to inspire confidences.*

Even were she a man, this line of questioning would only result in closed lips. And possibly punched jaws and escorted exits.

How I wish Sherlock were here to help me. He would know what to do. He always did.

Mirabella reminded herself that they were after a monster who had killed at least three people—possibly more—and it was her duty to do everything in her power to stop him from killing again.

So she did the only thing left to her, something she had seen Sherlock do many times. She offered a coin for the information. If a discreet inquiry failed to solicit results, she utilized her purse.

For one who was remarkably unemotional and had little in common with the rest of the human race, Sherlock sized up people quickly, knowing where their motivation lay.

She went to six of the ten shops, observing the shopkeepers' responses carefully, attempting to emulate Sherlock's training. She met a dead end with Mr. Nugent. One cobbler said point blank it wasn't his shoe. A Mr. Upton took her bribe and then admitted he didn't recognize the style. She made a mental note to inform Sherlock. If she knew the Great Detective as well as she thought, he would be teaching Mr. Upton the error of his ways at a future date. Yet another cobbler was interested in the style, even asking to keep the drawing, which she of course declined, but it wasn't his.

Thankfully the shoe was a unique style—considered outlandishly fashionable by some. And yet it hadn't helped her to find the maker as yet.

"Excuse me, Mr. Hobbes." She decided to begin with the direct approach with cobbler number seven, pulling out the drawing she had made of the footprint. "I'm wondering if this is your shoe."

He looked at her suspiciously. "Why do you ask, Miss?"

Not the answer she had wished for. *But promising.*

"I'm working for Mr. Sherlock Holmes."

"You didn't answer my question."

"It is a matter of great importance. Lives are at stake." Mirabella found anything but the honest approach exceedingly difficult. "Obviously if Sherlock Holmes is involved."

She attempted to hand him a coin but he looked away.

"I won't be discussing my clients with you, miss."

Oh my goodness, it's his shoe. She would stake her life on it. Excitement welled up in her chest. *But how can I influence him to share what he knows?*

Why did the one she sought have to be the most honest man on the list?

She glanced to where Mr. Hobbes was working to see a hobbing foot, a piece of metal shaped like a shoe upon which a shoe was placed as the cobbler worked on it. As well as being a stand of sorts, the hobbing foot helped to mold the shoe to its eventual shape.

I must induce him to speak. Mirabella drew a blank, bringing up nothing.

Ring! Ring! The door opened and in walked a young girl, about nine years old, carrying a bag. She placed the bag on Mr. Hobbes' desk, and several of the shoes fell out. By the size of the bag, it appeared there were some half dozen pairs of shoes.

The child smiled up at him, and he smiled down at her: this was two days work for him and might feed him for a week if he practiced the economies.

He didn't hand the child a tuppence, which would have been the typical payment for this valuable service. Since a washer woman made about 30 cents per day for an 11-hour day, two pennies for an hour's work scouring the neighborhood might be considered a good return.

But the girl was given no currency. Instead, Mr. Hobbes kissed her on the head, murmuring "Good girl", which seemed to be all she required.

This child has a relationship to the older gentleman. She was more than a mere employee. Studying more closely, Mirabella saw that the girl bore a resemblance to him, her face not yet revealing the hardened lines of the difficult life he lead.

As if to sense Mirabella's gaze, Mr. Hobbes' eyes returned to hers, and his softened gaze hardened again. "We've got nothin' else to discuss, Miss."

"I don't ask for myself, sir, but for the safety of others," she pleaded. Without revealing the specifics of the case, and desperate to find something which would help him to understand, Mirabella looked to the back of the shop. She saw a small room with a fireplace through the door, apparently where the man and his family lived, perhaps only this girl, whom Mirabella thought to be a granddaughter.

She recalled an outside privy attached to the outer wall of the shop.

Upon entry she had also seen an upstairs to the shop, which either had additional bedrooms or was rented to another family for additional income, probably the latter from the clutter visible in the back room.

She knew something else. *This is a moral man. And a man who loves his granddaughter.* Sherlock had taught her to consider all the facts before her. *Surely there is something here I can use to my purpose.*

Mr. Hobbes' smile turned to a frown as his eyes returned to Mirabella's. "As I said, Miss, our business is finished."

She was learning to read expressions, and she knew that Mr. Hobbes knew something, besides being the maker of the shoe. Mirabella pulled out a guinea and laid it on the counter.

Very soon she saw that she had made a mistake. She should have known this from their earlier encounter.

"Go and lay out some bread and cheese, Lizzie," he said to the child. "I'll be there directly." Then he turned to Mirabella, not before his eyes lingered on the coin for some seconds, as if he were fighting with himself. "I told you to leave. I won't be bribed. I'm an honest man."

Even as Mirabella closed her reticule, leaving the coin on the counter, her eyes moving to where the child was. She had begun with telling the truth, so she had no choice but to see it to completion.

She pointed to the drawing and then to Lizzie, "Your child is not safe around the man to whom these shoes belong. Do not allow her to pick up shoes from him." She could say this with complete sincerity and conviction.

Mr. Hobbs looked at her with a startled expression. "He would hurt children?"

"The wearer of these shoes is a murderer—or he is working for a murderer. No one is safe in his vicinity." She repeated, "Do not allow anyone you care about to be alone with him."

Mr. Hobbs' mouth formed into a firm line and his eyes blazed a sudden anger.

"Longstaff," he said. "His name is Mr. Longstaff."

The old man handed her the coin. "You work for Sherlock 'Olmes?"

"Yes sir."

"I haven't heard of him."

"You will." Mirabella took one of Sherlock's cards out of her reticule and placed it on the counter.

"A private detective, is he?"

"Yes, sir. Mr. Holmes will not stand by while someone is being hurt. He is the best there is."

And she meant that too.

Mirabella moved towards the door, placing the coin on the tin box. "For Lizzie," she murmured, as she shut the door behind her.

Chapter Twenty-nine
An Alliance with the Devil

"Taking all of my secrets and knowledge into the realm of my
sworn enemy could be construed as a betrayal, could it not?"
- *"Sherlock Holmes and the Chocolate Menace"*

"I need your help, Professor."

Moriarty smirked. "You work for Sherlock Holmes. He has contacts in both high and low places. What access could I have that the illustrious Holmes does not have?"

"Quite a bit, I should think."

Suddenly his eyes twinkled with a light which tended to frighten. "Unless you don't wish him to know."

Mirabella sighed heavily. "That is correct."

"I must ask myself why you would be doing something of which Holmes would disapprove, Miss Hudson?" He glanced along his bookshelf, eventually pulling out a book after some deliberation. Her eyes followed his fingertips, longingly resting upon the row of books; she wished she might have such a library. It struck her that the professor's books were much less worn than Sherlock's.

"Miss Hudson?" Moriarty raised his eyebrows. He never had to yell, he was always exceedingly polite, and yet one quaked before him.

"Mr. Holmes wouldn't allow me to be in excessive danger of course." She attempted to sound as condescending as one might dare before the head of the London criminal underground.

"Ah, so it's risky." Moriarty placed the book on his desk. He pulled the vest of his three-piece wool plaid suit, his belly slightly protruding. In appearance, he was the least frightening person imaginable—until one came to know him. "I never knew Holmes to care one way or the other about the safety of his operatives. All must be sacrificed to the altar of his work."

He has a point. "It is difficult to know what he is thinking. All I know is he has forbidden me to go undercover, citing the hazards."

"Hmmm, a treacherous case. . ." Moriarty repeated, beginning to pace the floor. "It must be the vampire case. Two of the murdered men found with their blood drained." He smiled with appreciation. "Ingenious really."

It was odd how quickly they had come to be on familiar terms, she a country girl and he a criminal mastermind. It was as if they understood each other on some unnamed level—sharing something in common. And they did: they were both vexed to the extreme by Sherlock Holmes.

And both felt that life was somehow empty without him.

Still, that shared sentiment did not explain her camaraderie with the professor. Mirabella knew beyond a shadow of a doubt that Moriarty would kill her in an instant if he perceived her to be a threat to his objectives.

She felt her shoulders tense. "Are you behind it, professor?"

"Certainly not. Far too gruesome." He shook his head at her. "You disappoint me, Miss Hudson. Everything must have a purpose; I have no need for the macabre."

Looking like a monster is the last thing a monster wants. "True. Drawing attention to oneself is not to one's advantage."

"Most certainly. The greater the action, the greater the response. It is a law of physics. I am gratified we understand each other, Miss Hudson." A slow smile formed on his lips. The serpent in the Garden of Eden must have had the same expression.

Between the two—the vampire and Moriarty—she felt the vampire to be the greater danger at the moment. This could change in an instant, however. It never paid to give too much information to the professor.

"If not you . . ." She viewed him hopefully. ". . . Do you know who is behind the vampire murders, professor?"

He shook his head. "I do not."

Mirabella believed him to be telling the truth from the lines in his forehead and the glow in his eyes. His expression conveyed a certain irritation that he didn't know, coupled with veneration. Moriarty did not like to be out of any loop. "You must have some idea, professor."

"Perhaps. But that does not mean I am obligated to inform you, Miss Hudson." His lips tightened, as if he disapproved of her forwardness.

"Why does no one wish me to do or know anything?" she demanded, frustrated. "I am not a girl who wishes to watch everyone else have an active part in life while I sit in a drawing room absorbed in my embroidery."

"To be sure, you are not." Moriarty's frown turned to a smile in an instant. "And you do not think I have any objection to your being in danger, Miss Hudson?"

"Not in the least."

His voice grew soft. "You might be surprised."

The warmth in his countenance made her uneasy; it could only be misdirection. His specialty.

"Professor, please let us have none of your subterfuge and sophistry. This is urgent. The man I seek is a murderer of innocents."

"And why should that concern me?"

"True, no one you know would be affected."

He studied her momentarily, a slight smile forming on his lips. "Almost no one."

He seated himself at his large oak desk, everything neatly arranged and in its place, another contrast to Sherlock's desk. She observed a leather bound book next to an ink pen, probably where Moriarty had been taking notes for an upcoming book. His academic career single-handedly maintained his image of respectability.

"Perhaps I like the distraction while I go about my work. The case does interest me," Moriarty said.

"Because you would like this vampire to be working for you?"

"Very good, Miss Hudson."

She moved to stand beside the blackboard covered in formulas, studying it. "You wouldn't like this one, sir. I have seen his work." She shuddered.

"And why is that?"

She motioned to the blackboard as if to illustrate the contrast. "He is reckless and random. Without purpose and order."

Moriarty frowned, nodding slowly. "That does offend me."

I thought it might. "Of more significance, he is quickly escalating out of control." That was the strange thing about Moriarty: he might be cruel and without conscience, but the violent act was not the reward for him. There was always something he sought outside the brutality; he was not feeding off the assault. In fact, escalating emotion was repugnant to him.

A similarity Moriarty had with Sherlock.

"The vampire could not be part of your intricate web; he would tear its very fabric," she added.

Moriarty frowned at her effrontery, but he appeared interested. "Go on, Miss Hudson."

She moved towards him, leaning her hands on his desk not two inches from a House of Fabergé Imperial inkwell. Heaven only knew why no one questioned the possession of such a priceless item on a professor's salary. "And there is no purpose to his cruelty—no reward. Only vengeance."

"Most uncouth. A low life no doubt."

"I believe him to be an educated man," she considered.

"But a man who has no control of his emotions, who follows their every command." Moriarty shook his head in disapproval. Mirabella thought, not for the first time, how alike the professor and Sherlock were in temperament, intellect, and drive. Only an understanding of right and wrong kept Sherlock from being Moriarty.

And the absence of madness.

No, perhaps not even that.

"Uncivilized. And yet, most men are." Moriarty fixated his glance on her. "I might be able to assist, Miss Hudson. But you will have to tell me of what benefit my helping you is to me."

"This is very personal to Sherlock Holmes, professor." Her finger touched something, and she look down to see an ink pen adorned with the head of a serpent.

"Mycroft." Moriarty tapped his fingers on the desk.

"Perhaps." She shrugged. "But I speak of Sherlock. If this bedlamite succeeds, Mr. Holmes will lose his focus. He will not be a worthy adversary."

"Ha! ha! You will have to do better than that, Miss Hudson."

"You say that now, but you would be miserable without the challenge."

"I will have to take my chances I suppose." He leaned towards her, clearly unimpressed. "What else do you have, Miss Hudson?"

"This vampire's criminal empire is growing. He could be a threat to your position. Particularly as his attacks are random, fueled by his own generalized hatred."

"Vulgar and unrefined, to be sure, but no competition for me."

She swallowed hard. She hadn't wished to reveal anything of significance—but Moriarty left her no choice. "What if the vampire takes out someone of consequence to you? Someone who helps run your machine?"

"Then he would die, naturally."

"I'm quite sure there is a man of a different persuasion—someone brilliant—who could be targeted."

"Of a different persuasion?" He stood up from his seat. "So that's how it is, is it?"

"Someone important to you, Professor."

"That narrows the field, doesn't it?" He raised his eyebrows. "How important? Speak plainly, girl."

"A man critical to your financial empire." She could see from the sudden light in his eyes that he had an idea of whom she was speaking. She had given him two hints, after all.

Still, Moriarty would never give her the name. She would have to prove what she knew. Which would immediately put her in danger.

It never paid to know too much about Moriarty's operation.

"Give me the name, Miss Hudson," he demanded. His eyes said, *if you wish to leave here alive.*

Mirabella had been paying attention—to both Sherlock and Moriarty. "Mr. Gribbon is in danger while this vampire roams the streets."

"Gribbon is a financial genius." Moriarty frowned, murmuring, "What a great loss that would be."

Sherlock is right. Moriarty is connected to this Gribbon. Losing the banker would be a personal loss. "I assure you that is of no interest to our criminal."

"And why does our Mr. Holmes believe Mr. Gribbon might be a target?"

"He didn't say." That, at least was true.

Suddenly fury crossed his expression. "So Holmes told you about my relationship with Mr. Gribbon. And his *persuasion*?"

She feigned indignance. "I don't have to be told everything." The last thing she wanted to do was to implicate Sherlock. "Anyone might have deduced it. Mr. Gribbon is a high-ranking official at the Bank of England. You have been seen with him. He is no doubt your banker. Many men of wealth have financial advisors."

The gentleman in question was also a friend of Mycroft's—and, worse, a member of the Diogenes Club. She was new at this game, but there could be no doubt that any member of the Diogenes club was in danger. Moreover, both Overton Bristow and Radcliffe were exceptionally intelligent by all accounts. The bizarre notion had taken hold of her mind that the killer believed their blood to be superior—and wanted it.

Moriarty seemed to be reflecting upon her words. "What do you want from me, Miss Hudson?"

Mirabella took a deep breath. She held the winning hand, let's see if she knew how to play it.

Despite his nonchalance, she knew Moriarty well enough now to know that he considered Mr. Gribbon to be a matter of great consequence. "I want assistance getting into the workhouse. St. Pancras to be exact."

"You don't need my help for that. Just walk in the front door."

She cleared her throat. "I want to be one of the girls the overseer shows to Mr. Fairclough."

"Fairclough, is it?" He lowered his eyelids, as if understanding was dawning.

Moriarty stood and moved to the blackboard. "And what about my thermophile? What is the next step in developing it to cut steel?"

She frowned. "I thought securing Mr. Gribbon's safety was my part of the bargain."

"An elusive offer at best. You have merely pointed out that he is in danger in the hope that I would be sympathetic to your cause. You have no way of protecting Gribbon, do you Miss Hudson?"

"And are you sympathetic to my cause?"

"If you mean, do I care about Gribbon's safety, yes. But I will merely take matters into my own hands now."

"Do you not feel some gratitude to me, professor?"

"Indeed I do. But I am under no obligation to give you anything, Miss Hudson. You have nothing to offer. You have already given me the information."

She sighed heavily. Mentioning Mr. Gribbon—at potentially great personal cost—had gotten Moriarty's attention, but he would never help her until he would benefit from doing so. She bit her lip and bit the bullet. "I have an idea about the thermophile."

"I'm fully aware of that."

"And you will help me if I tell you?" she asked.

"Naturally." There was a sudden sparkle in his eyes.

"How do I know that you will fulfill your side of the bargain?" she demanded.

"If what you tell me proves to be useful, I will certainly want to keep you around to expand upon the idea. It is only logical." It seemed irrefutable when the professor said it that way.

"You can get me noticed by Mr. Fairclough?"

"I can and I will." And she knew he could. "So tell me what I wish to know. How do I cut steel with light? Do you have any ideas on how to begin research on answering this question?"

"I do."

"And what are they?"

She swallowed hard, remembering this man holding a six-inch bad in front of her neck. He would kill her without the slightest compunction if he felt it was to his benefit.

Which it was not at present.

"Miss Hudson? I am waiting."

"As soon as I get in with Fairclough I will tell you." *You see, I am not unteachable, and I thank you for today's valuable lesson, professor.*

Fury crossed his expression, but Moriarty quickly regained his composure. "How do I know you will?"

"Because, my dear professor, unlike you my word is good."

Chapter Thirty
On the Inside Looking Out

*"Data! data! data!" he cried impatiently. "I can't
make bricks without clay!" - Sherlock Holmes, "The Adventure of the
Copper Beeches" by Sir Arthur Conan Doyle*

There is no other way. Her hands were shaking as she inched forward. She wanted to turn and run the other direction, but she knew this was the only option left to her.

From their expressions of apprehension and fear, she was in line behind others who felt the same. The young woman directly in front of her was pregnant. As the workhouse was the last place anyone wanted to come, she was likely unmarried and cast out by her family. If the young mother had a husband—a wage earner—she wouldn't be here.

Mabel studied her reflection in the glass as she entered the Saint Pancras Workhouse. I am too young to look like an old lady. Blackened teeth, grey around her eyes, her hair long, stringy, and oily.

"Repent! Repent of your sins and turn to God!" There was yelling in the dining room of all places. Mabel looked around the corner to see one of the three clergy circling the floor, raising his voice so as to be heard above the other two. There was no difficulty in that. The workhouse inhabitants were relatively silent, occasionally murmuring to each other.

"Repent of your sins and turn to God!"

Of what sin was one to repent? Being poor? Sick? Poverty and sinfulness were apparently the same thing in the eyes of the clergy.

And in the eyes of the general population. To be a burden on the state, to require charity was a great sin.

Next to her was another girl about her age, who smiled at her, showing darkened teeth against her sallow skin. But there was a great deal of warmth in the girl's eyes, so she introduced herself. "Hello. I'm Mabel."

"I'm Denise."

"Hey, you! What's your name?" the lady guard demanded from a few yards ahead.

"Mabel Bernard."

"Keep your eyes forward, Mabel."

"I'm not bothering you, you old witch, and it's no sin being friendly to others—particularly on the Sabbath," Mabel said under her breath. She would be ashamed to say this as Mirabella, but it was necessary to becoming Mabel. Besides, no one would treat Mirabella the way they were treating Mabel. "What are they going to do, lock the gates of hell?" She glanced behind her. Another girl about her age giggled at her.

In the meantime, the guard was busy accosting the females ahead of them. No doubt their time would come.

"I'm Tilly," the girl behind her said, biting her lip. "You ought not to make the guard mad."

"From the looks 'o her she don't know no other way," Mabel said. "There's no law against looking about."

Tilly looked unconvinced. "Yer might be surprised."

"Why are you 'ere?" Mabel asked.

Tilly looked down, her shame apparent. "I had a job at the factory. A good job." She beamed momentarily, obviously proud of that job. "But I dropped on the floor of the factory—from being so tired, you see—and they sacked me."

"That's too bad, it is. It wasn't your bloomin' fault. Workin' twelve to fourteen hour days, seventy hours per week. We're only human, you and me. Those masters wouldn't treat their horses that way." For girls and women the wages were too low and the jobs too few. To be a factory girl was about all that was left.

Tilly nodded at Mabel's understanding, but there was fear in her eyes. "But we can't complain. It won't serve."

"Don't worry, I ain't here to make trouble for you." Mabel handed a piece of bread and cheese to each Denise and Tilly.

I'm here to make a name for myself.

Denise happily took it. As hungry as she obviously was, Tilly hesitated. "Are you sure? Don't you want it?"

"They'll 'ave it from us when they strip us. We'd best eat it now."

Tilly saw the wisdom in that—wasting food being akin to ungodliness in most households. She took the bread and hungrily devoured it, speaking while chewing. It seemed that whatever concerns Tilly had about befriending a troublemaker had dissolved instantly with the appearance of the fresh bread and cheese.

The pregnant girl ahead of Denise, also portraying an expression of shame and shyness, peered behind her just long enough to display an envious glance. Mabel tapped on the young mother's shoulder, handing her a piece of bread and cheese.

The girl hesitated.

"'Ave it! Oi!" Mabel commanded.

"I'm Clara, right," the girl said as she happily accepted the nourishment.

Mabel smiled. It seemed having food was the way to make friends here.

"I thought they only took away our clothes," Tilly whispered. "Why did you say they would 'ave your food?"

"Yes, they will strip us, to wash for varmints. They'll bathe us and give us uniforms, right? But they'll 'ave everything we own, only to be returned if we leave, if then." She snorted. "Naturally the bloody food would be disposed of."

Tilly nodded sadly. "That's the way of the world; to take everything from you and give nothing back."

"How do you know this, Mabel? 'ave you been in the workhouse before, eh?" Denise asked.

"No. And I plan to leave as soon as I can."

Clara's face fell. She would not be able to leave. Not with a baby.

Mabel pushed her way ahead of Clara so the young mother would have time to finish her food.

"Listen, here, Missy, if you give me any guff, I'll beat you—and like it." They had reached the guard by now, who, smiling with anticipation, pointed to a whip leaning against the wall.

"I meant no offense, Ma'am."

"That's what I thought."

Mabel reached inside her pocket and took out a beautiful velvet choker sporting a silver heart. "This is the only thing I have left, a gift from me mum. I'll give it to you if you'll watch out for me and me gals here."

"Ha! ha! I'm takin' it anyway." The old hag laughed, snatching the choker out of Mabel's hands.

"Consider it a present then. But, remember, right, a witch put a spell on it for me. If anything happens to me or me mates, it will be a sad day for you . . ." Mabel ran her hand across the air in front of her neck, to signify hanging.

"I don't want it, then. Blimey!" The guard threw the necklace on the table.

"It's too late. The spell 'as already been attached to you. Be a sweetheart then and nothing will 'appen to you." Mabel smiled with a certain all-knowing gleeful expression which showed the guard she had not the slightest fear of her.

"Empty your pockets," the guard woman commanded, her voice barely audible. Shaking, she warily continued with her usual lines. Mabel put a small jar on the table.

"Open it." the older woman commanded.

Inside was an ointment of a sickening grey color.

"Wossat, you evil girl? It smells horrible."

"It's an ointment the witch gave me. It protects the pure of heart and punishes the evil. Does it look grey when you look at it? It's pink when I look at it."

Tilly started to choke but kept her mouth shut.

"You can keep it! I don't want it any where near me!" the guard screamed.

Mabel shrugged, picking up the small jar.

"Who is the witch what put the spell on the necklace?" the guard demanded.

"*Me mother.*" Mabel smiled sweetly. "It's said I take after 'er."

Mabel walked inside, her head held high. She was ready to be stripped, scrubbed, and transformed into an inmate of the St. Pancras workhouse. She had called upon her angels to help her.

And indeed, they had.

***

Mirabella entered the dining room still in possession of her jar of grey make-up, necessary to her disguise. One needed such things to disguise good health.

It hadn't taken long to conclude that Sunday was not a pleasant day in the workhouse. Sunday started out well enough with an extra hour's sleep and the service, she learned, as well as some leisure during the day for the residents. Monday through Saturday were all working days.

But Sunday quickly began to feel like a working day; certainly it was not a day of relaxation. After supper, the howlers began in earnest: a troop of preachers yelling at the residents about their combined sin of poverty until bedtime. Sunday's goal appeared to be to make the inhabitants feel worse about themselves and their situation than they already did.

"Hello, Guv'nor," Mirabella said, moving to sit beside an older gentleman. Sunday was the only day when the ladies and the gents might congregate together.

Mirabella was waiting to be discovered by Mr. Fairclough, but, in the meantime, she sought to find out all she could about the people here and what drove them to enter. Even her father, as kind a person as she had ever known, seemed to hold those in the workhouse in some derision, however slight.

"Hello, miss. You must be new. And what is your name?"

"Mabel. And you, sir?"

"Mr. Kingsley, if you please."

"Woss a gentleman such as yourself doing 'ere, Mr. Kingsley?" Even from his few words and his accent, she could discern he was educated. He wore the workhouse men's uniform very well: trousers and a waistcoat, a striped cotton shirt, a stout woolen jacket of fearnought cloth, and a cloth cap.

"My you're a bold one, Miss Mabel." He chuckled, tipping his cap to her.

It was fine for him to think her a fearless girl, as this was the impression she wished to give. Sherlock had impressed upon her that it wasn't enough to look the part: one must also speak the part, move accordingly, and assume the correct personality. This might be her greatest test.

Speaking with Mr. Kingsley was her opportunity to practice.

She slouched in her uniform, though it was entirely unnecessary to making her appear formless. It was a waistless blue-and-white cotton shirt, utterly shapeless, covered with a smock. She wore a mop cap on her head. If the intent was to make the ladies as unattractive as possible, they had succeeded.

But that was for the best, it aided in her disguise.

Her undergarments consisted of a red flannel petticoat, thick black stockings, and black boots. At least she wasn't cold, to the contrary. This was better than living on the streets, that was certain.

The older ladies had a woolen shawl as well and wore bonnets. Thankfully they had done away with the practice of making the prostitutes wear yellow and the unmarried pregnant ladies wear red.

Still, everyone knew into what category everyone else fell. Much like the outside world, she supposed. Or, at least, they thought they knew.

"I was a gentleman," Mr. Kingsley continued.

"Blimey, then 'ow did you happen to end up 'ere, sir?"

"And what do you think, Miss?"

"Obviously you lost your brass somehow. What else could it be? You don't look like one who is inclined to Tiddley Win—and you ain't sick. That would leave a failed business, a poor investment, or you be a gambler, beggin' your pardon, sir."

His eyebrows raised, clearly surprised by his new friend. "You're right, Miss Mabel, I don't drink and I'm not sick—no more than any old man is. Of the three options, which do you think it is then?"

"I would not expect one who had succeeded at business to suddenly fail, right? And most who 'ave earned their brass do not gamble it away—as opposed to them what were born with silver spoons in their mouths." She shrugged. "So it seems to me it were a poor investment."

"Astonishing." He stared at her for a long while. "How did you come to be such a keen observer, Miss Mabel?"

"Believe me, you don't 'ave much choice where I come from."

Mr. Knightly chuckled before turning somber. "You are correct, Miss Mabel. I made a bad business deal and fell upon hard times. As you can see, I am older in years, and there is no other place for me."

The workhouse was indeed a place for the elderly, the sick, the insane, and the children—along with young women with child who had been turned out by their families—indeed anyone who was helpless. The able-bodied would not choose to be here.

"Turn to the Lord and forsake your evil ways!"

Mirabella shuddered. She could not imagine Henry Hudson, her curate father, behaving in this manner; he was such a compassionate soul. "Are they always this bloomin' loud?"

He chuckled. "Yes, and worse."

"Lawd above! And their manner is so . . . so . . ." She acted as if she struggled to find the right word. She knew from Sherlock that everything about her must match her station in life.

"Condemning? Self-righteous?"

"Yes, that is it. Struth!"

"Indeed the Sunday evenings in the workhouse are terrible. The howlers scream their religion at us." He studied her interestedly.

"I see some couples huddled together in corners. It's as if they can't hear the howlers. I wish I might not." Mirabella put her hands over her ears as a simple girl might.

"Sunday is the only day husbands and wives can see each other."

"I suspect what you was married but 'ave lost your wife."

"That's right."

"And you 'ad no children together?"

"How would you know that, Miss Mabel?" The old gentleman seemed quite astonished.

"Because you 'ave the manners of one who was once happily married—you know how to address the female half—and yet, if she were alive, right, she would be here with you after a week of separation. An' if you had children, you would be with them and not 'ere. Ain't that right, guv'nor?"

"I see. Also true." He studied her with interest. "You're a bright one, you are."

"It ain't no sin." She turned quickly to stare at a couple who seemed to be arguing, oblivious to all else. She motioned with her head. "Is that couple married?"

He nodded. "You would think it would be a lovely reunion, only seeing each other once a week, but there are often ill words between them, perhaps for the self-deprecation inflicted upon them by the workhouse."

There would, of course, be no conjugal visits. Upon arrival at the workhouse, husbands and wives were separated, and children removed from their parents, and even from their siblings if they were not the same sex.

I am beginning to understand. How a charlatan such as Mr. Fairclough could come along: it would be easy for him to offer something better than the workhouse. Being with one's own family was enough to make one agree to any proposal for a way out, all other things being equal, even hunger.

"The only thing to like about Sunday is, of course, the absence of work," Mr. Kingsley continued.

"Is the work hard for you, sir?" Concern filled her heart for the old man before her, distinguished in manner. It was a shame such a man had come to be disrespected in his old age.

"It's not bad. Separating the Oakum for eight hours a day."

"Old ropes?"

"Yes, Miss Mabel. We separate it out, which is in turn used in shipbuilding for caulking, in the joints, and in the deck planking." He shrugged. "It's rough on the hands, and I have an allotment." He smiled suddenly, leaning towards her as if telling a secret. "I never make it, but the younger ones pitch in and help me."

It was encouraging to learn that, even in misery, kindness occurred.

"In truth, the worst thing about this place is the food," he said as an after thought. "And, of course, the lack of privacy and complete disregard for personal freedom."

"And being separated from one's loved ones," she added.

"Life already did that for me."

Still, Mr. Knightly did not strike her as bitter, but as positive and full of hope.

As if to read her thoughts, he added, "Even then, I would be dead if not for the workhouse. For myself, I have no reason to complain, but I see unnecessary suffering for others. I've never been beaten or mistreated myself."

"I'm glad to hear it." She bit her lip. "It's a regular palace it is."

"It beats the cold and wet outdoors with no food."

She glanced around to see a child burying herself in her father's chest, her arms around his neck.

"It's touching, isn't it?" Mr. Kingsley asked. "They only have one visit per week. When they are told the children must return to their quarters, it is heart-wrenching to watch the fathers and their children tear themselves apart."

I must not tear up. Mirabella chastised herself. *I must be careful not to smear my makeup and invoke suspicion. I must learn to control my emotions.*

"But children . . . separated from their parents. Love is the thing these unfortunate children need most in the world." She swallowed. "And it is bein' withheld."

"Yes. It's as if the State wishes to demoralize these children during their formative years."

"That wee girl . . . where is her mother?"

"Mr. Aylesbury has lost his cherished wife. This is what has forced his children into the workhouse. He was not able to take care of the children— and to work as well."

"The Sabbath is a day to elevate one's mind and to live in communion with the Lord. I believe this keeping families apart makes a mockery of the Sabbath."

Mr. Kingsley studied her, interested. "Today is the Sabbath."

"Yeah, but to behave right only on the Sabbath is to disrespect God. Why ain't it being done every day?" She swallowed hard. Ordinarily it was not to her advantage to vent her feelings, but here it might be a good strategy for her to make a friend. Staying isolated would not help her discover the culprit.

"True. Such treatment makes the bad and lazy worse, and it breaks down the good. Of course, there are always those who will take advantage, but it is not most."

"AEEEE!" A blood curdling scream pierced through the howlers.

"What was that?" exclaimed Mirabella.

"The male insane ward. It also houses the imbeciles and the epileptics."

"The epileptics are put in with the insane?"

"The worst is the nursery room. It is a wretchedly damp and miserable room responsible for scores of preventable deaths of both mothers and children."

As she attempted to swallow the lump in her throat Mirabella's eyes moved to a book in his hand.

He laughed. "Not until the howlers stop. Then there will be a few stolen moments." He tapped the novel. "It's missing the beginning and the ending—but it gives me the opportunity to exercise my mind and to utilize my imagination. I console myself to make up the missing parts."

"But aren't there any newspapers here?"

"The newspapers are pure gold in here." A momentary expression of contentment crossed his face. "There are a few fortunate inmates who receive these regularly—perhaps from family members—and they are the kings of the establishment. They receive favoritism from all of the other inmates as well as extra bits of bread or tobacco in exchange for a half-hour's borrowing of the news."

"A lot of people think the poor don't wish to elevate their minds."

"I might have thought so myself." He looked down. "Before I became poor."

She made a mental note to drop off Sherlock's used newspapers for the inmates in the future. "And what's your news of choice, Mr. Kingsley?"

"*Reynold's* is my preferred, and after that, *The Dispatch* and *Lloyd's*."

"I know enough to know them are radical newspapers." She feigned shock. Naturally Sherlock had these papers, as well as *Punch* and the more conservative periodicals. It didn't much matter what side they played; the important thing was that the media kept the politicians accountable to the people.

Mr. Kingsley fingered his novel. "Can you read Miss Mabel?"

Her cheeks heated. She hoped he interpreted her blush to mean she was not a particularly good reader. "A wee bit."

He studied her suspiciously. "It doesn't seem like you belong here, Miss Mabel."

I am not fooling anyone. I am terrible at disguises. "I hope not. I don't wish to stay. But . . . Why do you say so, Mr. Kingsley?"

"You are able-bodied and smart. You should be able to find work."

"I have a bit of a mouth on me."

He chuckled. "I can see that."

"I can't abide stupidity."

"Ah, you don't suffer fools gladly? It's a failing, to be sure."

She motioned with her chin to another man, as if to indicate she wasn't the only one who didn't belong. "That gent seems able-bodied."

"There are some able-bodied in the workhouse who, for whatever reason, seem unable to find and keep employment. And naturally there are those of immoral character." His eyes moved to another man. "Stay away from him. However, there are mostly orphans, the elderly, women with children, the disabled, the mentally ill, and the sick. There are those, like myself, who lost everything through bad business dealings and poor management. And there are those who lost it through gambling or debt." He looked at her. "And those who never had it."

"How long 'ave you been here at St. Pancras, Mr. Kingsley?"

"About six months." He rubbed his chin. "I lived on the streets for a month. I was cold and hungry. My foot became swollen and infected, and I knew I had to enter. The first meal I received—though it was a tasteless gruel—was the first hot meal I had eaten in a month."

"Have you seen many blokes come and go?" She didn't know how to ask if he had seen anyone leave with the vampire she was searching for.

"The 'Ins and Outs' you mean, Miss Mabel?"

"I was thinking more of them what left and never came back. Are you saying then that anyone can come and go?"

"Naturally. A person can check himself in and out of the workhouse. It is not a jail and no one is required to be here. That would be debtor's prison. In fact, anyone who can get out, wants out, because of the separation of families, the food, and the desire to have one's jurisdiction back."

"It would seems to me that the residents would be out all the time looking for work instead of picking Oakum."

"Believe me, searching for a job is a job in itself. Leaving does require permission—if you intend to come back that night. And often one does not have appropriate clothing to face an employer, nor is the workhouse willing to provide the clothing. And there's a stigma attached to being in the workhouse from the employer's point of view. It's a difficult cycle to break. One can't just take off every day in search of work. One is supposed to be picking Oakum in return for a bed, food, and a roof. You can't get out to get a job, and you can't get a job if you can't get out."

"But what about the Ins and Outs. How do they do it?" She tried to be persistent without causing suspicion. But, as yet, she had found out nothing of use.

"The Ins and Outs are the type what get out, get a few bucks, spend it on booze and women, then end up back in the workhouse."

Mirabella was frustrated; it seemed she was getting nowhere. How to ask the right question to get the answer she sought without being too obvious? "And are there charities that come here to help people leave?"

"So you already want to leave, Miss Mabel?" He looked at her curiously. "You only just got here and all these questions about how to leave."

She smiled. "Do you blame me, sir?"

"I can see that a young girl would not like to be here. She would want to be out working—and to find a marriage partner."

She shrugged, feigning embarrassment. "I suppose if the right bloke were to come along . . . but I ain't holding me breath." She giggled. "For now, I just want my own room and a job of me own. Work is limited for young ladies with no skills."

"You've had education, Miss Mabel, I'd stake my life on it." He studied her shrewdly.

"Why do you say that, sir?" She had to fix whatever she was doing wrong.

"It's the questions you ask. The accent might be right, but the questions are wrong. You're a thinking girl, and that's a fact."

"Just because I'm uneducated, don't mean I'm stupid."

"There's nothing wrong with having a brain in your head."

"If you're a man. It's not always a good thing for a female. And I've had no formal education." True on all accounts. She had been schooled at home by her curate father. "I've been sacked from almost every job I've ever had. I doubt I could keep a job as the chamber pot maid." *Also true.*

"Too smart, I reckon."

"But you didn't answer my question. Are there those what come here to help people get . . . *out?*"

"Getting out and being free are two different things." He frowned.

"What do you mean, Mr. Kingsley?" He was an interesting man. A philosopher of sorts.

"There are those who come here and take people away. I wouldn't trust just anyone, Miss Mabel. Don't leave just because someone promises you a better life."

Now we are getting somewhere. "Oh? And why is that, sir?"

"Almost everyone wants something from you. They aren't just coming here out of the goodness of their hearts to improve your lot in life." His voice became low. "Ask yourself what they want."

"Who is not to be trusted?" Better to just put it bluntly.

"I'll tell you who you *can* trust. There are some Christian ladies who visit the wards, reading to the sick and infirm. Miss Louisa Twining in particular organized this, devoting years of her life to the workhouse sick."

"So I can trust Miss Twining?"

"Yes." He nodded agreement.

"But who can I *not* trust?"

"Nobody else." Mr. Kingsley seemed to clam up. She was so near to the truth—but sometimes being right outside the door at midnight was the same thing as being in the dark.

She looked about her, observing so much misery. "Please tell me, Mr. Kingsley."

"I have no proof of wrong doing."

"Who is it?" She attempted not to appear eager.

"There is a gentleman who comes. I've never trusted him."

"Why not?"

"Because he takes the ones with the most anger. The ones that no one would want. I can't figure it."

Oh, so he wants spirit, does he? That I can provide.

"I have to ask myself why he wants defiance in his servants," Mr. Kingsley continued reflectively. "I'd stay clear of him, Miss Mabel, if I were you."

"Who is he?" Mirabella asked.

"I don't know his name. But—he's a pharmacist."

Chapter Thirty-one
An Abrupt Departure

"He was on the brink of being termed brilliant—or insane.
The laughing stock of London."
- "Sherlock Holmes and the Case of the Sword Princess"

"*Blazes to Hell!* We have to get that ship!" Sherlock cursed as he, Watson, and their police escort dashed down the stairway to the Liverpool wharf, *the RMS City of Chester* departing Pier Head en route to America.

"You have reason to think a murderer is on the *Chester*, Mr. Holmes?" Sergeant Quinlan asked, panting as he spoke.

"Nathan Longstaff is on it alright. Let's make haste, man!" He and Watson had followed Longstaff's trail all the way from Scotland.

"I'm afraid it's out of range now, sir," Quinlan said, the *Chester* fading from view.

"Send a tug after it!" Sherlock ordered. He had already handed the sergeant the missive from both the Yard and Mycroft as authorization, but he would have assumed command regardless.

"Or signal with a flag semaphore," Watson suggested.

"The *Chester* won't see the semaphore at this point, and me tugs are all occupied."

"What about that one?" Watson pointed to a small coal-powered boat moored nearby. From the skipper's frantic movements, the tug was in no need of purpose.

"There's the last launch, on this very dock," Quinlan said.

"Stop!" Sherlock shouted as he ran towards the boat, with Watson and Quinlan close behind him. "We must have that boat."

The sailor manning the boat narrowed his eyes in defiance. "I'm headin' upriver. S'posed to be draggin' the river for a body."

"A murderer escaping has got precedence, mate. Follow that ship!" Quinlan yelled, close behind. Sherlock was gratified the sergeant had come round to his way of thinking, skirting the need to take the boat if cooperation had been lacking. The skipper was a rough sort, and sailors tended to have a way with knives, so this was a superior outcome for all concerned.

"What's your name sailor?" Watson asked in his polite fashion as they jumped onto the boat.

"Valentine," the sailor growled as he tossed some coal into the small furnace boiler, Sherlock and Watson casting off the lines. Quinlan took the tiller and they splashed out and down the River Mersey.

"The *Chester* has a pretty good lead," Watson said. "If this tub can't go any faster, it's going to take the entire eight miles to the ocean to catch her."

"She's a good little boat, and that's a fact. She ain't meant to be a racer," Valentine said indignantly. "That's a new ship there, lads. I knows for a fact that she can go quite a clip. I'd be frankly amazed if'n we caught her, even in crowded waters such as this."

"We damn well have to try," Sherlock's eyes were fixated on the *Chester*, already a good mile ahead of them. He dared not loose sight of it with all the other boats on the Mersey.

Sherlock heard the cry of a seagull in the background. If one could steer clear of cholera and crime, the Liverpool dock was a fine place to be with its sailing ships, steamships, clippers, and escaping criminals.

The next hour was spent dodging all manner of craft pushing to keep pace. While Watson manned the tiller, Quinlan was now in the process of using the flags in an attempt to get the *Chester*'s attention. With no success.

"Watson, let me take the tiller. Fire off a few rounds from your Webley. We've got to do something to stand out from the crowd. Once we reach the ocean, it's too late."

"Like a ladybug tryin' to get the attention of a elephant," Valentine grumbled, but he never stopped working, shoveling more coal while the other three tried everything they could think of to get the ship's attention.

As luck would have it, most of the crew was at the bow of the *Chester*, eyes forward, with the stern being overlooked. As for the passengers, the black smoke coming out the rear neither increased visibility nor made it the most pleasant place to be, moving the occupants forward as well.

"Look, Holmes!" Watson cried out, grinning with exuberance. "Second tier railing. There's someone watching us. No doubt he'll soon alert the crew."

Sherlock grabbed the seaman's binoculars to observe the man pointing and waving as a few people approached.

"It won't be long now," Watson said. "He's making quite a scene."

"Indeed he is," Sherlock murmured, a foreboding creeping into his consciousness.

"Keep at it!" Quinlan stopped for a moment, handing the flags to Valentine and grabbing the binoculars. "Bloody hell! He's pointing everywhere but here."

"Am I mistaken? Or--he looks to be diverting all the attention to the other ships," Watson said.

"Why the hell—?" Quinlan exclaimed.

"You're not mistaken, Watson, that blackguard has no intention of assisting in the capture of our fugitive." Sherlock was dripping wet with ocean spray, and his mood matched. "That's Longstaff."

"*Son of a gun.*"

"The black smoke ain't helpin' our cause either," Valentine muttered. "The fates are conspiring against us today, and that's a fact."

"Overload the coal box if you have to, man! They're crossing the breakwaters into the ocean," Sherlock insisted, his eyes glued to the horizon.

"The seas are too rough, laddie." Valentine said, shaking his head. "We go out there and we're takin' our lives into our hands."

Sherlock felt his blood might boil over. He couldn't tolerate giving up until there was no hope for success or death was knocking on his door.

In many cases, not even then.

A heavy wave hit the boat hard, almost turning it sideways. It was a mixture of luck and seamanship that allowed Valentine to both drop the flags and grab the detective before he was flung over the side.

"I thank you, my good man," Sherlock murmured. His pride had drowned along with his spirits.

"It's no use," Valentine yelled. "We'll broach if we don't turn back."

Watson, who had assumed control of the tiller again, turned the launch back toward the River Mersey without further comment.

The *Chester* sailed serenely out to sea.

***

Sergeant Quinlan narrowed his eyes. At the very least this adventure had caused him to recognize the Great Detective as one of his own, a man with stamina and fight.

"Never you worry, Mr. Holmes. We'll get Longstaff on the other side. I'll wire ahead and there will be men waiting for him at New York City."

"It's fortunate the ship is headed to New York instead of to Argentina," Dr. Watson said to a somewhat soggy detective and their attending officer, all three returning to the relative shelter of the stern.

"Yes, the New York constabulary is an advanced police force and favorable to us. They'll return him," Sergeant Quinlan agreed.

"Only because they don't want Nathan Longstaff in New York,"

Sherlock muttered. There was nothing he hated more than not apprehending a criminal.

Particularly one who had targeted his brother. "Vampire, henchman, and butler all wrapped into one disturbing package."

"Vampire?" The sergeant looked aghast.

"Longstaff is wanted as an accomplice in the murder of at least three persons," Sherlock explained. "Gruesome murders."

"The *Chester* will accommodate some fifteen hundred passengers, fully thirteen hundred in steerage and only one hundred and twenty five in first class," Quinlan considered. "A good place to hide."

Watson broke in, as much to distract his friend as to acquire information. "Which class do you think Longstaff is in, Holmes?"

"None. Except for that little display we just witnessed, I expect him to go into hiding, only coming out at night. Longstaff is a vampire, after all." Sherlock pulled a piece of folded paper out of his pocket, a detailed drawing of the *RMS City of Chester*, now soggy. He pointed to the map. "I expect he's hiding here."

"And what better place than on a ship he helped to build?" Watson posed.

"Longstaff knows all the nooks and crannies on the *Chester*." Sherlock smiled, water still dripping down his face. "Fortunately, so do I."

Their errand had taken a few more days than anticipated. They had first gone to the Caird & Company Ship Building Enterprises in Greenock, Scotland, a former place of employment for Longstaff, after locating the butler's family home. With Longstaff nowhere to be found, the obvious conclusion was that he had fled the British isles for a location where he might be invisible. Unfortunately for him and fortunately for justice, once again Longstaff's longing for the easy path and a more desirable location had led him astray. Australia or Argentina would have been a far better choice.

Finally, luck is on our side.

Frustrated and not feeling so lucky, Sherlock shook his head. He had not been on too many cases as yet, and could not accustom himself to the inefficiencies inherent in the work. "We've met failure at every turn. My only consolation is that, if the New York police don't find him, Longstaff will stay hidden on the boat and return to England—where I'll be waiting for him."

"Oh, we won't fail, sir, I guarantee it," Sergeant Quinlan said. "And you've showed us precisely where to look."

"Longstaff doesn't appear to be that hidden at the moment," Watson said. "Standing about on the deck waving his arms."

"As yet no one is looking for Longstaff or knows they are harboring a fugitive from the law. He'll go into hiding when the time comes."

"I have to agree with the sergeant, Holmes. We made enough progress that we scared Longstaff out of London." Watson pulled on the vest of his three-piece wool suit, looking quite out of place in the chugging tugboat, and remarkably dry. "And Miss Mirabella has no doubt advanced the case as well."

"Let us hope that Miss Hudson has managed to stay out of trouble while making said progress."

What am I thinking? It's Mirabella Hudson we're talking about.

Chapter Thirty-two
The Devil's Due

"She'll do fine," Fairclough said. "Please return her things to her. I'll be waiting outside with the carriage." Fairclough had chosen Mabel Bernard as his most recent recruit.

Moriarty was waiting in the wings.

"And the promised information?" he asked without further ado. "I have come to collect my debt."

"My goodness, couldn't this have waited?" Mirabella whispered, startled.

"You might not be around to tell me."

She shivered.

Moriarty frowned, his impatience showing. "Tell me, Miss Hudson, how shall I cut steel with light?"

Mirrors. Mirrors may multiply the effect of the light. The words circled round in her brain.

No! Don't say it! Giving Moriarty information was akin to the murder of people in the future.

"I'm waiting, Miss Hudson. Let me remind you that I can still undo this."

I'm so close to infiltrating this ring. Fairclough is waiting outside for me.

Someone will develop the weapon in time, it is just a matter of who and when. That was an insupportable justification to assist evil, and she knew it.

Moriarty motioned to his assistant some feet away to get Fairclough.

"No, wait!"

"Your time is up, Miss Hudson." His pale green eyes were the color of ice.

Her very being screamed at her not to say a word, but the words escaped from her mouth in spite of her every protest. "I will give you the idea, and that is where it stops. I will not assist you in hurting anyone.

"As you say."

Her eyes were glued to his insincere expression. He might as well have said 'so you say'.

I know this is a mistake. But she had to find out who was behind the vampire murders—and obtain proof. She had good faith in Sherlock's judgment, but she also had the conviction that this vampire must be stopped.

They had come up against a brick wall. Against every instinct, the words flowed from her mouth. "It seems to me we are talking about two things: stimulating electrons which, in turn emit photons, and something to stimulate the electrons."

"To be sure."

The dye is cast. "The atoms can be solid, liquid, or gas." *It is the gas which could cut through metal.*

"Of course."

"I suggest that you look at the solid state," she added.

"Hmm . . . I would have thought gas, but this is ingenious. How to stimulate the electrons?"

"A crystalline gem for example. Possibly a ruby."

"A ruby?" A slow smile formed on his lips.

"The gem would have to be enclosed and something would have to provide spurts of energy."

He was deep in thought when suddenly his eyes lit up. A slow smile formed on his lips. "Yes. Yes, I see."

There. She had done it. She had set him on a path which would appear to be successful, taking up many years of his time, but would eventually prove to be inefficient—and expensive.

"St. Pancras it is, then, Miss Hudson. Good work."

"Thank you, sir."

Mirrors. Mirrors may multiply the effect of the light.

***

I hate to see her die. Moriarty sighed as she walked out the door—presumably for the last time.

Strange, it was a rare occasion when someone's death bothered him.

He had the information he needed now, so it was no matter. Still, Mirabella Hudson was a great help: inspiring, insightful, and a force for change.

There were more inventions today than in all prior historical periods combined; she was a perfect person for her time—and for his.

How can I allow her to go, knowing how much danger she is in? The thought whirled round in his head, which he resented. It took his mind off more important matters. *The weapon.*

The only time Moriarty allowed his emotions full reign was when he had been betrayed. *Then he unleashed them and took his revenge.*

One of life's greatest satisfactions.

He had originally intended to kill Mirabella Hudson as retaliation against Holmes. But that could be re-visited at anytime. He had then discovered her to be useful.

Despite abhorring attachments of any kind, he felt a sadness he hated to admit to as the door closed shut.

Moriarty couldn't blame Holmes for taking a fancy to her, though he naturally did not stoop to such emotions. Completely without benefit or use.

I am superior to Sherlock Holmes.

And yet—the professor could not deny the evidence: he had grown rather fond of the girl. No doubt because he had seen her inventor's mind, something of which he wasn't certain Holmes was aware.

The detective had been blinded by his feelings. True, Holmes knew Mirabella Hudson was bright, but he didn't know where the girl's true talents lay. As she didn't.

She wasn't a great detective as Holmes was. She wasn't a doctor. She wasn't a pharmacist, a chemist, or a biologist. She wasn't even a researcher in the purest sense. Though she could be useful in all of those areas.

Mirabella Hudson is an inventor. A creator.

Just as he was a destroyer. That could potentially put them at odds.

But not now. Now they fed off each other.

It is no matter now. Mirabella Hudson wouldn't be around to realize what she could do.

But I will. Moriarty saw his chalkboard in his mind's eye, *his work.*

He frowned. His need to have Holmes in this world had become a thorn in his side as well.

Nothing should get in the way of my work.

His mind returned to the more pleasant Miss Hudson. He was indeed sorry to see her go.

I am also the fulfiller of dreams. In the truest sense he was a catalyst. He allowed the realization of a person's true nature.

"Ah, but the young will do what they will do." He had only facilitated what she had planned to do anyway. As he always did for everyone. It would have been better that she skip the workhouse altogether: it was not the place for a young girl—for anyone. But she would not be deterred.

He envisioned his thermopile.

And neither will I.

Chapter Thirty-three
Walking Into A Trap

"Damnation!" Upon their delayed return to Baker Street, Sherlock read Mirabella's brief note.

The thought of Belle in danger made his blood boil like nothing else could. "That girl has disobeyed me, as she always does. She has no respect for anything except her own intractable will."

"Are you speaking of Miss Mirabella?" Dr. Watson looked up from the *Illustrated London News* with an expression which said his suite-mate was over-reacting.

]]"So you immediately knew of whom I was speaking, Watson. Proof that my description was accurate."

"What has Miss Mirabella done to disobey you, Holmes?"

"What has she not done? For one thing, which should be quite obvious, she has vanished." Sherlock handed a piece of vellum splashed with inked calligraphy to Watson. "For another, she has omitted her whereabouts in the note."

"To the contrary," Watson said, reading Miss Belle's missive. "She says she is working on the case and will contact us when she has something."

"Communicating one's direction is not the same thing as announcing that one has disappeared, Watson." He slapped the note against his thigh. "Something we could have deduced for ourselves.

"She has lied to buy herself time."

"Presumably to work on the case, precisely as she says."

Sherlock frowned. "As incorrigible as she is, my frustration has to do with Miss Belle's safety."

"You were never so protective of Miss Mirabella before. She is invested in your interests, after all, as we all are. You've gotten strange about her, Holmes." Watson shook his head, letting his newspaper drop. "Are you in love with the girl?"

"In love?" Sherlock rose from his chair. "I am not now and have never been in love with anyone."

"I agree that you have never been before—although I shudder recalling when you and Fantine were an item, God forbid."

"Ah, I do miss Fantine at times."

"Yes, the countess might have been your dream girl, Holmes, except for a few minor personality quirks."

"Quite inconsequential, really," Sherlock agreed.

"Decidedly. If only Fantine weren't utterly self-centered, incapable of loving anyone else, and without the slightest degree of morality."

"And yet so nearly perfect." Sherlock sighed. "Most unfortunate."

"Did I mention her vicious streak?"

"I tend to be attracted to women who are, shall we say, *unladylike*."

"Fantine is a man-eater not a tomboy."

"Oh, I don't believe she shows any favoritism to one gender over the other."

"Stabbing you in the back if there is something in it for her is a bit more than being a hoyden," Watson muttered, finishing his thought.

"At any rate, I can't imagine why you ever thought I have the slightest romantic feeling for Miss Belle. She is much too conservative in her values—in her goodness."

"I would not consider goodness to be a fault. As to her conservatism, you might be surprised, Holmes."

Sherlock shot out of his chair. "I hope you are not speaking from first-hand knowledge, Watson."

Watson's eyes flew open. "Calm down, Holmes. I have no first-hand knowledge. I simply cannot think of one single thing to Fantine's credit or one quality which she has over Miss Mirabella."

Sherlock took a deep breath, returning to his chair. "Forgive me, Watson."

"Now that we have established that you are not in love and have no emotional connection to Miss Mirabella, explain why goodness is not an admirable quality in your mind."

"An admirable quality, but not a desirable one. A woman who is entirely good—as is Miss Belle—adheres to a code learned from society, lacking a certain spontaneity. My match—if I had one, which I don't, and which I don't wish—would have to be someone who feels no confines, no barriers, and no need to be anyone except who she is."

"I would say that is an apt description of Miss Mirabella Hudson. You do her no credit, Holmes, if you believe that her purity of heart and mind precludes her ability to grow as a person and to expand her horizons. I should say it enhances both."

"Expanding her horizons is precisely what I fear, Watson." Sherlock straightened his cravat. "We must go."

"Right you are, Holmes." Watson folded his newspaper and set it on the end table. "Do you have an idea where she is?"

"She is in grave danger. As well as jeopardizing the case." Sherlock stood again, reaching for his hat and cane.

"Most unforgivable."

"Precisely. This causes me to delay my own plans of infiltration in order to find the little miscreant first."

Watson put his pistol in his jacket. "Where do we start?"

"As I suspected, the red thread which Belle found was from the gaiters of the Royal Scots. Our trip to the Scottish highlands has confirmed this. If I'm not mistaken Fairclough served in that regiment."

"Finally we have some evidence the Yard can use." Watson paused to reflect. "So the thread wasn't from Longstaff's spats?"

"We've got to go, Watson! Before it's too late." Sherlock Sherlock reached for the doorknob. "Make haste!"

***

"Where is she?" Sherlock demanded, grabbing Moriarty by the neck, the professor's bowtie flying across the room.

Moriarty sputtered between gasping and speaking. "Have a care, Mr. Holmes. If something happens to me, you'll be the first to die."

"That is nothing compared to what will happen to you, Moriarty."

"Let him go, Holmes!" Watson commanded. "If we harm Moriarty, he won't be able to help us."

"Ah, that is the relevant point." Sherlock lowered Moriarty to the wooden floor but remained in his face. "Where is she? Damn your henchman!"

"Can't you keep up with your own employees, Holmes?" Moriarty narrowed his eyes.

Sherlock determined to play the game if it gave Moriarty some pleasure. In the end the professor would speak. "Apparently not."

In truth, it gave Sherlock no end of irritation that Miss Belle told Moriarty where she was going while failing to tell him. To find that she trusted his arch enemy, and the mastermind behind the London criminal underground, more than him was a distinct slap in the face.

And make no mistake, Moriarty knows where she is.

"Use those famous deductive powers of yours and take a stab at it."

"I already have, but I want to hear it from your lips, Moriarty."

"Time is of the essence!" Watson exclaimed.

"Ah, yes," Moriarty said. "Would that were all. She came to me because I could provide something which Holmes could not. Let's face it, my dear Dr. Watson, if Holmes were able to solve this murder, he would have already done so."

Sherlock bit his lip, refusing to rise to the bait. He was not accustomed to monitoring his responses, but there was too much at stake here. "True. Miss Belle desired a connection to the underground criminal world—and, being a clever girl, she knew where to look."

The professor puffed out his chest, even as he remained dangling in the air. "I commend you thus far."

"She sought out a criminal. That is nothing to feign superiority over." Dr. Watson objected.

"Never mind, Watson. Let Moriarty have his moment." Sherlock lowered the professor to the ground, retaining his hold on his shirt collar. *And I shall have mine.*

Moriarty nodded noncommittally. "I don't know why you brought along your sidekick, Holmes. We work very well together you and I." He appeared smug. "As do Miss Hudson and myself."

Sherlock felt his jaw clenching. "Indeed. Miss Hudson needed some insider knowledge on who might be gaining labor from the workhouse. She was able to disguise herself, making herself a desirable candidate, but, in order to do so, she needed to know what the villain was looking for."

"That's where you come in, Moriarty," Dr. Watson muttered. "You likely paid off the prison guard to present her."

"Correct. Once she can finger our culprit, she plans to return to me," Sherlock said. "This is where her plan fails, revealing her own naivety and inexperience."

"Indeed, it is a risk," Moriarty agreed, shrugging, as if accepting the inevitable.

"Damnit!" Dr. Watson exclaimed. "How could you let her go, knowing this?"

"The young will do what they will do. I don't see how you can blame your employee's insubordination on me."

You're a devil, Moriarty." Watson lifted his fist to punch Moriarty himself.

"Never mind that, Watson. There's no time and we've more important business." Sherlock returned his gaze to Moriarty. "Miss Hudson is in search of a vampire, a man who utilizes slave trafficking in order to do his bidding. Where will he find human slaves? Again, the answer is simple: in the workhouses."

"If you know so much, Holmes, I fail to see why you need me." The professor smirked.

"I could eventually come to the solution through my own means, but even twenty-four hours may be too long. There is no time to waste," Sherlock moved closer. "Tell me which workhouse, Moriarty."

"Oh, for God's sake, Moriarty, tell us where she is," Dr. Watson blared out. "Miss Mirabella's life is in your hands. Of what possible benefit could the death of that lovely girl be to you?"

"Miss Hudson's death is the last thing I desire. She is quite useful." There was a long silence in the room. Moriarty nodded his chin towards Dr. Watson. "As for your associate, that would be no great loss."

Sherlock lowered his voice, now deadly calm. "I've no more time to waste, Moriarty. Where is she?"

"My dear Holmes, all you had to do was ask. It pains me that you are forced to come crawling to me for the whereabouts of your own employee."

"And the answer?" Sherlock demanded.

"And what shall you do for me if I tell you?"

"I shall allow you to keep living, you blackguard." Sherlock tightened his hold, causing Moriarty to choke.

"Stop! This is very rude indeed."

"Rude or not, I guarantee if one hair on that girl's head is harmed, I shall hold you personally responsible." He added quietly. "I'll come for you."

Moriarty stared at him for a long moment. "I believe you mean it, Holmes."

"I've never been more serious about anything. And I'm *always* serious."

"We should go down together, you know."

"Very likely."

"Let me down." Sherlock released Moriarty and he gasped for air. "I don't believe the time is right for our final showdown. Have you tried the Saint Pancras Workhouse?"

Sherlock sighed heavily, relieved. He didn't think Moriarty was lying to him. It would soon become apparent, after all. "And who is behind the hiring? Are you associated with him?"

Moriarty appeared indignant. "I'm not behind everything."

"Aren't you?"

"This is penny ante stuff." Moriarty's straightened his collar, his eyes fixating on Sherlock. "Of course, to get rid of a thorn in my side is reason enough."

"And the name?"

"I've told you enough, Holmes. I don't want to ruin my reputation. I'll leave you to do some of the work. Good day."

Sherlock and Watson turned and headed for the door without further hesitation.

Chapter Thirty-four
Time is of the Essence

"There are moments when one has to choose between living one's own life, fully, entirely, completely—or dragging out some false, shallow, degrading existence that the world in its hypocrisy demands."
– Oscar Wilde, "Lady Windermere's Fan"

"For God's sake, man! Where did he take her?" Sherlock demanded of the overseer.

"Where is who?" Woodhead replied smugly, his lips forming into the self-serving smile of one who enjoyed having power over others.

He might soon realize his error.

"We told you quite clearly, Mr. Woodhead," Dr. Watson said. "We're looking for a young woman of five foot seven, having the appearance of being some twenty years old, with long brown hair and brown eyes, of muscular build."

"Lots of girls of that description come in here." Woodhead shrugged as he turned around. "Sorry I can't help you."

In a split second Sherlock twisted the Saint Pancras Workhouse overseer's arm behind his back. Woodhead was not a small man. In fact, he was at least sixty pounds heavier than Sherlock, who was of medium build and medium height. Anyone would have bet on Woodhead in a fight.

Which was why Sherlock had a plush banking account at the Bank of England. One of the reasons.

Sherlock whispered in his ear. "You'll tell us where she's gone, and you'll not waste any more of our time, do you understand?"

"Har! har!" Woodhead laughed between gasps. "You won't hurt me with all these people here."

"I wouldn't have the slightest difficulty in doing so." Sherlock tightened his hold. "You don't know how nice I am being right now, but you'll soon find out if you don't answer my question."

Woodhead managed to drop to the ground, loosening Sherlock's grip. The overseer attempted a punch to Sherlock's jaw, which was met with the empty air and a kick to the Woodhead's rib cage. Sherlock swiftly put his opponent's neck in a stranglehold.

The overseer had been correct in saying there were a good deal of people present. Being as they were in the men's ward where fights were not unknown, there was an unspoken acquiescence. All in attendance now circled the pair.

What Woodhead had not counted on, however, was a lack of assistance. No doubt he would beat them all at some point in the future— there could be no doubt in anyone's mind on that score—but apparently the future punishment was worth seeing their tormentor on the receiving end of humiliation today.

He was going to beat them anyway, whether they helped or not.

Still, one had to give Mr. Woodhead credit. Even being in a stranglehold with no assistance forthcoming, he did not offer the information.

"I know where she is." Mr. Kingsley stepped forward. He kept his eyes on Woodhead, as if he were envisioning his ensuing punishment. Fear crossed the older gentleman's expression, wondering if he would survive the abuse.

Sherlock did not loosen his grip, but he turned his head to view the old man.

"And where is that, sir?" Dr. Watson asked.

"The pharmacist took her—a Mr. Fairclough, I believe—as he has taken many of the young people here. They all live at the commune."

"Is that right, Woodhead?" Sherlock demanded, tightening his grip.

"It ain't none of your business," Woodhead boomed. He might be stupid, but he was certainly brave, Sherlock would have to give him that.

"It is now. As is your future employment. I guarantee you will not long be the overseer when Scotland Yard hears of your involvement in this crime ring."

"B-but I don't 'ave nothing to do wif it! I've helped these people gain employment to a respected member of the community. I don't 'ave nothin' to say to what the guv'nor does once he's got them." Woodhead had dropped his commanding persona and was now proclaiming his innocence. One thing he did not wish to lose was this job which allowed him to persecute others. "Wish I'd never seen the little bitch."

Sherlock released his hold, planting him a facer, which knocked Woodhead to the floor. "As do I, sir."

"We must be off, Watson."

Before the Great Detective left the room, he pulled a card from his pocket and handed it to his informant. "I thank you, sir. My card, in the event you ever require my services. And your name?"

"A Mr. Kingsley, if you please."

Sherlock nodded with his head to the ground. "Woodhead may be indisposed for some time."

"The cad," Watson muttered.

The old man nodded solemnly. "But he shall someday wake up. Still, I liked your girl, and could not bear to see harm come to her." Mr. Kingsley looked as if he expected to die himself as a consequence of his actions.

"I can assure you that your overseer will not long be in employment here," Sherlock said, as if to answer the unspoken thoughts. "Even so, if you wish to leave, I may have a small abode for you, sir."

"Oh?" There was definite interest in the old man's eyes.

"The Russian on the third floor of our Baker Street building is in need of a flat-mate to share the rent. To be honest, Mr. Uladimov may soon be seeking new living arrangements as my violin playing does not match his preferences. You, on the other hand, may not be as particular, having been accustomed to less luxurious arrangements."

"Certainly not. If I have an hour of peace a day, it's an extravagance." Mr. Kingsley's face fell. "But I don't have the funds to pay."

"That is of no moment. Tell Mrs. Hudson, my landlady, that I vouch for you and will front the rent."

Mr. Kingsley's expression washed with a sudden sadness, shaking his head. It was obvious that he wanted with all his being to take his new associate up on his offer. And it was no wonder. A private flat shared with one man as opposed to sixty coffin beds crammed together in a drafty room. "I can't take your charity, sir, though I thank you."

"Charity? Nothing of the sort, my good man. I am always on the winning end of these type of arrangements, you may ask the good doctor here."

Dr. Watson shook his head in weary agreement.

"I speak of employment, sir," Sherlock explained.

"You might find it more or less agreeable than your present circumstances, it is difficult to say," Dr. Watson added.

"Is Mr. Uladimov disagreeable then?"

"Only at three a.m.," Dr. Watson replied. "In general, he is most pleasant. And it is quite a nice set of rooms. Though I daresay you would not wish to climb three flights of stairs."

Mr. Kingsley chuckled. "I still get about quite well. The exercise is good for me. And certainly a better arrangement than picking Oakum for eight hours a day."

"That might be a vacation compared to what Holmes intends. His employment might not be agreeable to you," Dr. Watson explained.

"I expect it would be, I need more stimulation of mind. But what could I do for you, obviously a gentleman of some means? I'm an old man."

"I assure you, sir, that you are perfectly suited to what I have in mind," Sherlock said. "No one better. You have illustrated your skill to me on this very day. There would be a certain danger to it, however. Making inquiries and such—an operative, as it were. Who would suspect a kindly, elderly gentleman?"

A startled expression crossed Mr. Kingsley's countenance followed by one of some interest. He held the card with a tight grip even as Sherlock and Watson ran towards the door.

Woodhead still writhed in pain on the floor. Something the overseer had inflicted on all the men present at one time or another.

Suddenly it wasn't so much to his taste.

Chapter Thirty-five
Human Sacrifice

As if to bring a sadistic darkness into the light, the moon cast rays of foreboding upon a small group gathering in the center of Hampstead Heath, a massive, ancient park covering almost eight hundred acres.

It was a simple matter to find privacy, particularly in the heavily forested dark of the night. It was equally easy to forget that they were in the center of London, the Hampstead station not more than twenty minutes from Westminster by hired cab.

"Our God Almighty. . ." The high priest, cloaked in a black, woolen robe, lifted the chalice high into the night sky. The candlelight created a strange perspective, making it appear the chalice was resting on branches and treetops. "We have slaved to make these vultures rich with the sweat and blood of our own hands. We have worked sixteen hours a day, without shelter, without enough food for our children, that our enslavers might spend their days with drink, fornicating."

There were murmurs of outrage from the crowd, easily incited in these hard times of suffering and injustice.

"These evil serpents have persecuted everyone here: the hard-working poor whom you love, my Lord. Those who will inherit the earth, as Jesus told us."

The high priest quickly became more specific in who their persecutors were. "The rich *sodomites* embody everything you hate and loathe: the greed, corruption and cruelty of the wealthy upper classes and the lustful, unnatural desires of the perverted which is against the love of man and woman that you have decreed."

There's only one problem with that picture. It's a lie. And a forgery of logic. To love another human being is not exclusive to any gender. Neither is fornication and drink. Cloaked in a long, hooded robe himself, Sherlock concluded his opinion to be in the minority from the escalating sounds of agreement, having more to do with emotional release than logical assessment.

Ah, yes. Channeling one's suffering into hatred and revenge. To hate evil was one thing, to formulate a scapegoat was another.

"As the Christ taught us, without the shedding of blood there can be no forgiveness of sins." The priest's high-pitched voice gained an eerie vibrato even as the chalice caught the rays of the moonlight, glistening golden. "Because you have commanded it, we will now have a live sacrifice."

The priest motioned to some men in the clearing, who emerged from the darkness carrying . . .

Blazes to Hell, it's a body.

Carried by four men, Sherlock studied the form as best he could given all the people standing in front of him as well as the decreased visibility of the darkness and looking through a hooded cloak. He attempted to maneuver a better view but, despite the small group, everyone was packed closely together, making movement difficult.

The body was covered with a sheet and was perfectly still. Probably drugged. Probably still alive. A dead body would mean less drama and less theatrics, which would not be to the priest's taste.

Damn this devil has a taste for bodies.

Sherlock felt a fury engulfing his being. He had never missed Watson so much in his life.

I am outnumbered twenty-to-one here. He had dashed off a message to the good doctor prior to leaving the flat, instructing Watson to contact the police. Sherlock had no way of knowing if Watson would even see the message.

As luck would have it, Mrs. Hudson was visiting her sister in Portsmouth and thus was unable to contact the police for him. With Belle possibly among this mob he had no more time to spare.

Given my reputation with the police, they might not respond even if they receive the message. It was no secret that he and Athelney were not on the best of terms. And Sherlock had no proof of wrongdoing at the point of his departure from Baker street, only his hunch.

Belle was presumably here somewhere—everyone was cloaked—but even one more person against this irate mobocracy could not even the odds sufficiently. The cause of the oppressed was just, but it had become something unjust.

And terrifying. Not to mention that Belle very likely had no weapon; she seemed to have some difficulty keeping one on her. As well as using it if she had it.

Sherlock was not a praying man, but he prayed to God she was unharmed. Particularly considering the gruesome nature of this crowd, as evidenced by the nods and murmurs of support for the heinous act unfolding before them.

The message being spread here was creating monsters of execution. The murderer or murderers of Overton, Percy, Radcliffe, and Denzil—possibly more—was most certainly present, an accomplished and blood-thirsty killer.

The priest's voice grew louder. "Justice will be ours."

Justice and revenge. Not the same thing.

It was some consolation that the commune number was surely greater than this: the monster behind this had not been able to convert everyone.

Where is Belle?

In an instant, his eyes dashed to the figure now on the altar.

Fear gripped his very being. *No! Anything but that!*

His eyes returned to the priest. *I'll kill the monster—or die trying.* Probably the latter.

The priest's right hand held a knife over the body, briskly removing the sheet with the left, screaming, "You must help this evil creature on his way to hell for the evil he has enacted on others."

Sherlock fingered the Derringer hand gun in his pocket. He couldn't shoot through the crowd and he would very likely miss if he aimed over their heads. The best he could hope for was a distraction, and Belle would be killed anyway.

The sheet now removed, his horror was compounded.

Mycroft! It wasn't Belle, but his brother Mycroft.

Sherlock felt his hands shaking with the terror that gripped his body. Not terror for himself, but dismay at the improbability he could save Mycroft. He could only delay his brother's death.

Sherlock was prepared to run forward even though there were almost two dozen people present and he would no doubt be next on the altar.

As he was propelling himself forward a woman screamed.

"Stop!"

He turned to his left to see the hood fall back on one of the women present, revealing her face.

Oh, no! It is Belle! From her expression of anger, she was clearly prepared to show her cards.

It was bad enough to see Mycroft here, whom he wasn't able to protect. The thought of losing both of them was devastating.

Sherlock considered the hand gun in his pocket. Even taking into account that he wasn't as good a shot as Watson, who likewise had the military-issued Webley, he needed a clear line of sight to plant a bullet from this distance.

To be specific, two bullets before re-loading.

Let's hope it would be the right two. He certainly hadn't wished to replace one blood bath with another, nor was he assured of success, but he would do whatever he had to do to save Mycroft. And Belle.

Sherlock glanced at the altar. There was no movement. *Please, dear God, let Mycroft still be alive.*

"Miss Mabel, you are interrupting our Christian worship." The priest's grave expression was dark and threatening. "This will not be tolerated."

"This ain't a Christian ritual. This is a bloody Satanic ritual." Her defiant voice rang through the grove.

A collective gasp moved through the crowd.

The devil take it! What is she doing? Very likely speeding up our imminent slaughter. This is not a crowd to be reasoned with. Still, an attack always invoked an equivalent response. With only two bullets before re-load . . . Better to solicit cooperation as a stalling technique

Sherlock could not help but admire Belle's absolute resolution and bravery. She didn't appear to have the slightest uncertainty in her voice, nor fear the consequences of facing her enemies alone. Always one for method, he conceded it was not a bad tactic to maintain a speech pattern which made her "one of them".

Definitely their best hope with the odds stacked against them. They weren't good odds, but they were nonetheless odds.

Sherlock inched closer to the alter while the priest moved towards Belle.

"Blasphemy!" the priest shrilled. "We have a sinner who is an abomination to God."

"So you speak for God, do you? More like you think you *are* God! That makes you no different from the swells. Only God has the right to take a life. It says so in the Bible. It's one of the ten commandments from God hisself! Here you have the golden calf." She motioned with her hands to the altar. "And you have not even said who you 'ave here. It's to be a cold-blooded murder, is it? An how many others 'ave you killed while you made us all your patsies? Have you purposely cloffed this unfortunate geezer to hide your evil acts?"

Dash it all! Do not return the fiend's attention to the altar.

Belle turned to the crowd, her fury evident. "This is none other than Mycroft Holmes, right, the Secretary of the Foreign Department, an advisor to the Queen. Not only will you all hang, but right likely your children will be left to die."

Admittedly that was an excellent tactic. Sherlock nodded with appreciation.

She added, "I thought that was why you was here, for your children. But, no, it's because evil has entered your hearts. You know I speaks the truth."

But the priest had effective tactics as well. "God is angry with you all. This is why we continue to suffer. Read Leviticus. The high priest was to take two male goats for a sin offering.." He motioned to the men to remove Belle.

Sherlock was now some three feet from the altar, but he was a good twelve feet from Belle. If he shot the priest in the back, the men would no doubt turn on him for killing their protector.

He was ready to do it, though, if it might save Belle and Mycroft, but there was no guarantee of that. He expected they would all three die in the end. Mycroft was either heavily drugged—or dead. Sherlock shuddered.

His eyes returned to Belle. He didn't care about his own life, but he would like to be able to save one or both of them before he died.

As the men moved towards Belle she screamed, appearing to lose some of her newly found language skills, "You are not a priest! You are most certainly not a messenger from God. You are a pharmacist. Or did you forget? You do not have the right to conduct a religious ceremony." She raised her hands in front of her body as the men approached her. Mirabella lunged forward, pulling on the priest's robe to reveal . . .

Florence Fairclough.

As I knew. It explains why the crowd is relatively small: Fairclough is unaware of his daughter's exploits.

Sherlock glanced at Belle, who was astonished. Florence had an alto voice, but she had lowered it even further over the course of the ceremony.

Despite her obvious shock, Belle continued with resolve. "And the sacrifices are *only* in the Old Testament. Jesus brought a new order. If you don't heed the Christ, you aren't a Christian. You are workin' for the devil."

One of the men stepped back as if her words had struck home. Sherlock sighed heavily. Belle could handle one man. Sherlock had trained her well and she was an apt student. But six?

He glanced at the altar to see that Mycroft was still breathing, and he thought his heart would pound out of his chest, the degree of his relief so overwhelming.

"What this man has done is wrong," Florence screamed, waving to Mycroft.

"And what has he done?" Belle demanded.

"He is a sodomite," Florence exclaimed.

"Mycroft?" Belle gulped. "Mr. Mycroft Holmes?" she corrected herself, adding softly as she began to sway. "You're lying."

"Ha! ha!" Florence laughed, sounding like a madman. "You little fool! The Diogenes Club is a front for sodomites."

All eyes turned to Florence, and it was apparent the energy in the forest grove had tipped to her.

***

What if it is true? Mycroft a Marjery? Dismay and revulsion overcame her. Mirabella felt her legs grow weak; she was afraid she might stumble and fall.

She reminded herself that she knew Mycroft. She liked Mycroft. She had a little crush on Mycroft. He was so smart, so amusing, so charming. *So kind.*

No matter if he is marvelous or not—and he is—he doesn't deserve to die.

She glanced at Miss Fairclough. Suddenly everything clicked together. *Florence is telling the truth.* The large membership despite the strange rules one would expect to prevent any interest in membership. The ease with which members were kicked out. The quiet library in the front and the back rooms for private parties.

As if the library were a front.

And the way both Sherlock and Mycroft grew quiet when Constable Jones made his accusations. How bizarre that Athelney might have gotten something right.

And it is irrelevant. There was something so wrong about Florence. Her determination—and frequent success—in murdering someone who had never harmed her. Florence's expression of hatred was bone chilling, her eyes appearing almost red with fire.

This female vampire. *Who is the scourge upon society?* The one who preyed on those different from her? Or Mycroft, who had done so much to help so many? Invaluable to the government.

None of this matters. She glanced at the altar. All that mattered was saving Mycroft from this executioner. She could work through her own thoughts latter—if her own thoughts were of any importance. What did her opinion have to do with anyone else's life? Only God was judge.

She glanced at the altar and saw a hooded man moving close to the altar.

Could it be? He didn't move in the same way. But then, Sherlock Holmes was a genius at disguising his movements—as he was at all things.

Even though she had only been with Sherlock a little over a year, she could sometimes feel him enter a room, even if she didn't hear him or see him.

She didn't feel anything now; she was almost numb with fear and distress.

I must keep all attention away from the altar. She glanced at the three men drawing near. If she could distract them long enough to keep Mycroft alive, maybe help would come.

It was a long shot, but it was the only plan she had.

"Nothing, absolutely *nothing*, gives you the right to slay this man—or anyone." Mirabella planted her feet firmly on the ground. "Whatever he is, Jesus died for him, which leaves you nothing to say in the matter. You and everyone here. His soul is between hisself and God. If Jesus died for him, it is none of your business to interfere."

"It has everything to do with me." Looking about to observe the true discord amongst the group, Florence was furious. "I had my life ruined because of the sins of these evil men. My life is over. I am spoiled goods. Disgraced and humiliated."

"I am right sorry for you, but that has nothing to do with this man 'ere." Mirabella's voice grew soft. "And you didn't marry Overton Bristow. You can still marry someone else."

"I am spoiled goods. No man wants a woman rejected by a *sodomite*. There is no man now who would have me."

Very likely not. Quite scary you are.

"Your fiancé made his own choices. You have no right to inflict suffering on others because your man didn't want to be wif' you."

Florence threw the chalice on the altar and put both hands around the knife, raising it over her head. "No one has suffered enough. No one has suffered as I have. I have been destroyed."

No one can argue with that. For being insane, there is a surprising amount of truth to what you say.

"Stop! You have caused enough damage." Sherlock came from behind Florence and grabbed her wrist. "You have your own sins to atone for, Miss Fairclough. Explain to the group how you have been selling the blood for profit and personal gain unbeknownst to your father, their benefactor. I wonder if you cared at all about Overton. Your feigned outrage is its own front for your profitable illegal blood transfusions."

Mirabella gasped. Blood transfusions were widely frowned upon by the established medical community, but there were those who had made *millions* of dollars, a fortune beyond imagining. She knew that Dr. James Blundell had performed some ten blood transfusions, publishing the results.

Not all of Dr. Blundell's patients had lived. It was a highly risky business as no one knew what made a blood match. Even with these disturbing statistics, Blundell had still made something in the neighborhood of two million gold sovereigns.

Could Florence have been doing all this for *money*? Indeed, it was a great deal of money.

"My father told these people to assist me. I was within my rights." Florence clutched to her knife as she struggled.

"Because he thought you were running experiments to understand blood compatibility and to further science through legitimate channels. Not through murder. He had no idea you were killing people."

"The impure blood into the pure," Florence pronounced. "I sought to purify the world. When the diseased blood met the disease, they raged a battle, both being destroyed to bring about a new order, sometimes saving the recipient."

She is mad.

"Ridding the world of those you hated while risking the lives of those you pretended to heal," Sherlock said. "For the right price, and among the desperate. There are those who will pay anything in the hope, however slight, of saving their loved one."

Mirabella shuddered. It didn't make sense: killing people to save people.

"Some lived as a result of the blood transfusion," Florence proclaimed, as if to justify the murders.

"Ah, yes, but *all* died whom you killed."

"All *sinners*," Florence sputtered.

"You did it for money—and for hate. Lie to yourself but not to us." Sherlock looked about at the interested crowd. "You deal in death, Miss Fairclough, not in life. And you shall all hang for her if you do not denounce her now."

"My father gained his wealth through the opium trade. There is no difference. Those persons are shadows of their former selves."

"To be sure, while he fought in the Opium Wars he established the channels. I have been his customer for years. There is a vast difference between people choosing their own destiny and having no choice in the matter. And, as far as the law is concerned, it is not illegal to sell opium, while it is illegal to murder people in cold blood."

"Sodomy *is* illegal. Those people I killed don't deserve to live."

"A judge will very likely decide that *you* don't deserve to live, Miss Fairclough." Sherlock made the fatal mistake of letting himself be distracted with her sick words. She stomped on the inside of his ankle.

Chapter Thirty-six
Outlaw Justice

*"There are certain crimes which the law cannot touch, and which
therefore, to some extent, justify private revenge." - Sherlock Holmes,
"The Adventure of Charles Augustus Milverton" by Arthur Conan Doyle*

He might be the greatest detective in the British Empire, but he
still required the use both legs to move with any degree of efficiency.
The shooting pain in Sherlock's ankle threw him down the steps while
Florence made her way towards Mycroft.

She was a woman with a singular goal in mind. If she was going to
die, she intended to take as many with her as possible.

Sherlock righted himself, favoring his injured ankle, but he realized
he couldn't possibly hobble up the steps fast enough to stop this maniac
from murdering his brother. He drew his Derringer and prepared to shoot
her.

Hanging be damned!

"No you don't!" Two of the robed men grabbed Sherlock's arms
in an obvious attempt to drag their intruder to the ground. In spite of
his injury Sherlock was able to resist being thrown to the forest floor,
clubbing one assailant on the head with his Derringer, who immediately
fell unconscious.

Sherlock jabbed the other attacker in the gut with his elbow. The
miscreant managed to throw his muscled arm up, both blocking the attack
and knocking Sherlock's .41 caliber hand gun into the grass.

Damn the timing!

"Mycroft!" Sherlock yelled as Florence raised the dagger above her
head. "It's over Florence, there is no reason to kill anyone else. You won't
be able to sell the blood at this point."

"You have ruined everything Sherlock Holmes. And I will kill your
brother and enact my revenge upon you both." As Florence plunged the
dagger downward, Sherlock saw another body emerge from the shadows
and slam into the dark priestess.

Belle! He didn't think he had ever felt so relieved. Florence tumbled
down the stone steps herself, hitting her head against the rocks.

Mirabella moved to stand as a barrier between Mycroft and anyone
who might approach.

For the first time, Sherlock thought they had a fighting chance. A minuscule chance, but a chance. Mycroft must still be alive or Florence wouldn't have felt the need to plunge a dagger into his chest.

Mirabella's color was high as she appealed to the crowd. "You must leave this place at once. To stay here will endanger your futures and that of your families forever."

Good. It was only the group that gave Florence any power. Without her following this high priestess of evil had nothing. Getting them to disperse could potentially save everyone's life, including Florence's.

Clever indeed, appealing to self-interest rather than to morality.

Doubt began to cross the expressions of many, wondering if they had been lied to about the virtue of their mission of hatred. Just as the plight of the starving poor was a just cause leading to the French Revolution, it became a blood massacre of horror.

Sherlock was still under attack himself, but he could see several of the robed figures slipping away quietly.

The detective wished his newest assailant might have been among them, a particularly muscular ruffian attempting to wrestle Sherlock into a state of immobilization, and having some luck given his injured foot.

The pain was throbbing in Sherlock's ankle as well as his jaw, a bit of blood running from his mouth, but his mood was much inspired seeing Mirabella holding her own in protecting Mycroft with a combination of box kicks and Jiu-jitsu. Encouraged by her tenacity on behalf of his brother, Sherlock felt some hope that Mycroft and Belle might survive.

This was some consolation as he took a pounding. That was nothing new; he considered every fight a fight to the death.

There is some evidence to believe this one might actually be. But he wasn't ready to give up the ghost. *Yet.*

Though Belle was handling her opponents admirably, Sherlock's situation grew worse. While Belle guarded Mycroft admirably, fighting off advancers, an additional three men turned their attentions to Sherlock.

Four against one. Not great odds with an injury, but possible. Sherlock was quite ready to be done with them.

His right leg of not much use, Sherlock utilized both his shoulders and hips, thrusting his right arm down and forward, which caught the man on his right off guard, breaking the attacker's grip. As the man scrambled to regain his hold, Sherlock snapped the same arm he had only just freed, leaving his assailant screaming in pain.

Unfortunately a second man closed in on Sherlock with the opening left by the first. With lightning fast speed, Sherlock hit his attacker full in the face with his elbow. Ordinarily he would utilize a kick at this point, but Sherlock only had one good leg and he had to stand on it.

Most inconvenient.

Two punches to the face of his third foe sent the blackguard running for the trees.

All the while Sherlock had been hobbling over to a former position. Quickly he swooped up his revolver, holding it on his remaining attacker, who backed up before turning and running.

Oh, no! Florence has regained consciousness. The woman was as much machine as monster. Looking toward the altar, he saw Mirabella and Florence struggling. It shouldn't have been a contest: Belle was the far superior fighter. But Florence had gone into a frothing rage, and the blows Mirabella landed on the villain's face seemed to have no effect. In one insane thrust, Florence drove Belle off the altar platform down the steps.

Sherlock took aim just as Belle picked herself up and returned to the platform, directly in front of his line of fire. He wanted to shoot Florence, but he couldn't chance it. The pair were fighting so quickly and closely that he would risk hitting Belle.

In an instant Mirabella accessed her own rage. She lunged towards Florence, clearly determined to save Mycroft even at the cost of her own life. Florence knocked Mirabella to the ground, who rolled down the steps.

She isn't moving. Sherlock limped towards her.

"Belle!" Sherlock screamed. She didn't move. *My precious Belle.*

I'll kill that demon woman, I swear to God I will. He aimed the gun at Florence.

"I'm alright, Sherlock," Belle's eyes fluttered as the words barely came out of her mouth. "Save Mycroft!"

Sherlock limped quickly to the alter to intercept Florence, who now had her hands around Mycroft's throat.

Just as Sherlock took aim to shoot Fairclough, he heard Belle scream, a man beating her while she lay on the ground. Without a moment's thought, he turned and shot his pistol.

Misfire. The monster continued to beat and kick Belle.

Sherlock didn't hesitate, he shot again. The man fell back.

I'm almost to the altar. Damnit, I don't have time to reload the gun. A wave of anguish swept over him.

As Florence began choking Mycroft, Sherlock heard sounds coming from the his brother's lips. *Praise God, he's still alive.*

But not for long.

Sherlock raised the gun over his head, ready to bring it down on

Florence's skull when, in an instant, Mycroft's right arm flew up and hit Florence in the face, sending her backwards.

"Mycroft!" Sherlock exclaimed, his eyes watering as he reached him. "How did you possibly have the strength?"

Mycroft's eyes were barely open, but he was definitely coming to. "Oh, my dear boy, if there is anything I have it is a tolerance for drugs. Did you think you were the only one?" He smiled feebly. "I must always outdo my younger brother, don't you know?"

Sherlock was so relieved that every sensation of pain left his body when Florence stood up again—she was indefatigable, more demon than woman—but another robed figure interceded and grabbed Florence's arms, pulling her backwards.

Evie Travers had chosen a side. Unfortunately, her aid was short-lived as Florence backhanded Evie, sending her flailing down the same steps she'd sent Belle. As luck would have it Sherlock was in Evie's path whose momentum knocked him off his feet as well, sending a new stabbing pain through his leg.

Evie's intervention had actually hurt more than helped him. Stumbling to his feet, Sherlock once again moved to the alter as fast as his legs could carry him.

I will be too late. Sherlock knew it with a certainty.

But instead of focusing on Mycroft, Florence had turned towards Belle. His assistant's eyes were open, but she lay on the ground not moving. This terrified Sherlock so completely that he lost all concept of being limited by his body. He practically ran towards Belle. Florence raised the dagger above Belle's head . . .

Bang! Suddenly there was a shot out of nowhere and Florence fell to the ground. This sent most of the remaining group scurrying.

Watson? Could it be?

Sherlock looked about and saw no one in the direction of the shot.

Far in the distance Sherlock barely caught a glimpse of a dark figure atop Caen Wood Towers, the home of dye manufacturer Edward Brooke.

There was only one man in London who could have made that shot from this distance.

Colonel Sebastian Moran.

Moriarty's assassin.

Chapter Thirty-seven
A Close Call

"Belle! Miss Belle! Are you alright?" he cradled her head in his hands. She opened her eyes to look up at him. He felt a relief so great that he thought his heart might pound out of his chest.

"I think I am fine."

"Can you feel your legs?" he asked, even as the throbbing pain continued in his right ankle.

"Yes."

"Thank God."

"I'm a bit dizzy. I need to lie here a moment to regain my balance."

He saw his tear drop upon her cheek and knew she must have felt it. She looked into his eyes, surprised. Her characteristic bright curiosity instantly returned.

She is on the mend.

Sherlock started laughing. He wasn't one to feel embarrassed at what anyone else might think of him. His own opinion was the one that mattered most to him.

And his opinion was that he didn't want to be in this world without Belle. Staring into Belle's eyes, he realized that her companionship and peculiar antics had become dear to him.

Belle frowned. "Why are you laughing Sherlock? I have been injured you know."

He squeezed her hand in his relief. "My dear girl, in an instant I saw a look in your eyes that told me you would make it."

"Was that why there was a tear in your eye? You were relieved?"

"Naturally."

"You thought you might have to fetch your own tea?"

"Highly unlikely that should ever come to pass."

"What has happened here, Holmes?" Dr. Watson came running into the clearing.

"This is not your usual excellent timing, Watson," Sherlock said. "Even so, I have never been so glad to see anyone. Make haste, you must check Miss Belle and Mycroft."

"But Holmes, there are at least two bodies here. Shouldn't I see if they are still alive?"

"*Damn-it*, man! Attend to Belle and Mycroft first. The devil will attend to his own."

Gently Sherlock cradled Mirabella's head in his lap, looking about him. "Mrs. Travers, go and fetch the police. Immediately!"

"There's no need, Holmes, they are on the way." Watson followed the advice of his colleague. After some long minutes, he gave his report. "Miss Mirabella is bruised only, though she shall certainly be in some pain for a few days."

"My dear boy," Mycroft said, still lying on the altar. "Do you think you could fetch me a sherry? My head is positively throbbing."

"Mycroft is fine too," Sherlock muttered.

Watson had reached Mycroft by this time and was in the process of examining him. "Mycroft will no doubt be back at the opera tomorrow evening holding court."

"I believe Shirley has hurt his ankle. I suppose you must attend to that before you fetch my sherry."

"It appears to be a clean break," Sherlock said.

"Perhaps a brandy would be better," Mycroft added.

Watson looked up from his examination of Mycroft, alarmed. "We must get that bound, Holmes."

Sherlock searched Belle's eyes for any recognition of the realization he had seen there only to observe apprehension and confusion crossing her expression.

"Thank goodness Mycroft is safe," she murmured, looking away.

And the tender moment was gone.

It cut him to the quick, but it was not unexpected. She was a beautiful young woman and he was nothing if not strange.

I don't give a damn. I have never felt so blessed.

Both Mycroft and Belle were alive and well. That was all that mattered.

Chapter Thirty-eight
Sherlock Reveals All

His mood might be unpredictable, his personality both disturbing and intense, but he was a rock in his own way. Everyone looked to Sherlock to make things right. And he always did.
– "Sherlock Holmes and the Chocolate Menace"

"When did you first suspect Florence Fairclough was the mastermind behind this vile plot, Holmes?" Dr. Watson asked.

"I can put it quite clearly at the moment when Miss Belle told me about the pharmacy ladies' dentures. I knew from that instant." Sherlock limped to his chair while leaning on his cane. His foot was set but it still throbbed when he moved too much.

"Their teeth?" Constable Athelney Jones repeated. "What the devil …"

"Their dentures, Constable," Mycroft corrected. "Quite the opposite from their teeth."

The party gathered round the fireplace at the Baker Street flat, experiencing a rare camaraderie with the Yard, celebrating with buttered rum and shortbread cookies. Sherlock was feeling a marked relief in bringing the case to a conclusion as well as in the safety of Mycroft and Belle. Watson he didn't worry about, who seemed to have the devil's own luck, making the good doctor a perfect companion.

So satisfied was Sherlock in the outcome that he momentarily set aside the disturbing revelation that Moriarty had a great deal to do with Belle's rescue. It was a bitter pill to swallow that Belle wouldn't be alive were it not for his arch enemy. Not only did he resent having to feel gratitude to Moriarty, but Sherlock could not like that the professor had an obvious attachment to Belle, although it must be preferable to the alternative.

"Blast it all! How did dentures lead you to any conclusions?" Athelney exclaimed, emptying his cup of buttered rum. He feigned annoyance, but Sherlock knew very well the constable was in high spirits today.

Explaining that he was working under cover on that particular day, Athelney wore an off-duty plaid hat atop his street clothes, a complement to his red hair and green eyes. He couldn't have brought any more color and joviality into the room if he had tried.

"Once you know who the dentist is, you always know who the villain is," Sherlock said.

Athelney laughed with considerable merriment. He was seated on the settee next to Mycroft, while Sherlock and Watson faced each other in their usual wingback chairs before the fireplace.

"An axiom of timeless truth," Dr. Watson agreed.

"You might be surprised, Dr. Watson. Dentistry may advance in the same fashion as medicine," Mycroft suggested.

"You don't say." Dr. Watson appeared unconvinced.

"Stop twattling on," Athelney interjected, waving a shortbread cookie about in the air. "Explain yourself."

Belle offered the constable another mug of rum, which improved his congeniality of manner instantly, if any improvement was indeed needed.

"Do you think it wise to indulge, Constable?" Mycroft asked, amusement crossing his expression. "While on duty, that is?"

Athelney was not one to refuse libations, on duty or not. And neither was Mycroft, if the truth be told.

"It's for the good of the case. A bit of fraternity puts them I am interviewing at ease." Athelney looked to Sherlock as if to prove his point.

"Most considerate of you, sir," Sherlock said.

Athelney nodded. "I knows how to work the crowd. Go on, Mr.'Olmes."

"The relevant point is, once I knew who was making the teeth for the ladies," Sherlock explained, "I knew who was behind the plot."

"Dentures for the poor was suspicious in and of itself." Mycroft nodded.

"It struck me the same. There was no reason to do so, these ladies were non-paying customers. They were already being fed, housed, and clothed. It was well beyond charity." Mirabella stood behind the settee with a pitcher in her hand. She looked quite mature, professional, and more than her nineteen years today in a lavender silk suit, a lovely compliment to her coloring. Her coiffure was elegant, an abundance of glossy chestnut curls piled high upon her head. Her finest feature, her golden brown eyes shown with interest and curiosity, as they generally did. A simple pearl necklace was her only jewelry.

"Precisely," Sherlock said, tearing his eyes away from Belle. "Florence was using the working poor for her own purposes, it was never about charity for her."

"Mr. Fairclough said the gift of the dentures was for practice," Mirabella said.

"Indeed it was. But Florence was already sufficiently skilled. She wished to take her skills to a new level."

"A new and disturbing level," Dr. Watson added.

"Indeed, Watson. She practiced on the ladies to perfect her craft—and to recruit. I expect we will find that she got some addicted to the arsenal of drugs she had available to her."

"And the fang marks on the victims' necks?" Mirabella grimaced, setting the pitcher down and pouring herself a cup of tea.

"The wolf marks on Percy's and Radcliffe's necks? Yes, Florence fitted herself with a special pair of dentures. She made dentures which fit into her human mouth, inserting wolf's teeth instead of human teeth," Sherlock explained. "It became an easy matter once Florence had made one pair of regular dentures to fit her mouth."

"So sinister." Mirabella shivered.

"But wait a minute! Who was the vampire? Are you saying it was Florence? It couldn't 'ave been. Percival wouldn't 'ave met with a woman dressed as a vampire? Wasn't the vampire Longstaff?" Athelney stroked his handlebar mustache distractedly. "We found the dentures with the wolf's teeth among Florence's things, but I didn't think they fit *her* mouth . . ."

"By all means, you must verify our claim, Jones," Sherlock said.

"Nah, it couldn't be. Then how did Percival and Radcliffe not know the vampire was a woman?" Jones asked, befuddled. He added with arrogance, "If there was a woman dressed as a man, *I* would *know* she weren't no man."

"Eventually you would, Constable," Mycroft murmured.

"Recall that Florence was tall, thin, and straight, with masculine features, almost androgynous in appearance. She had a low voice and wore make-up. No doubt she wore a cape and a codpiece."

"In Lord Percival's case she drugged him," Mirabella said.

"Generally helpful in altering one's perceptions," Sherlock said.

"Certainly you would know, Holmes." Dr. Watson stretched his legs out before him.

"I always thought Florence would have made a beautiful man," Mirabella considered.

"Apparently she did," Mycroft said. "She intended to make men desire her whom she couldn't entice as a woman."

"And then kill them," Mirabella added.

Athelney cleared his throat. "Sickening. Not my cup of tea."

"I don't believe it was Percy's or Radcliffe's either," Mycroft said.

"You had best expand the human experience in your mind, Constable, if you mean to be successful in police work," Sherlock suggested. "The human race is not homogenous."

"'Tis a shame."

All eyes turned to stare at the ruddy face showing off bright sea-green eyes and topped with carrot-red hair.

"And I'll 'ave you know I am successful," Athelney boasted, wiping the milk atop his lip with his sleeve. "I've been made sergeant over this."

"Have you now?" Mycroft smiled. "Congratulations my good man, Sergeant Jones. I was fairly certain you'd received a promotion for stopping a murderer of Florence's magnitude. Lord knows the entire city of London is relieved."

Athelney beamed, turning to Sherlock with a sudden alertness. "But if you knew who the culprit was, why didn't you tell us, Mr. 'Olmes?"

Sherlock smirked. "And have you tell me I was wasting your time with my imagination and flights of fancy?" He shook his head. "I think not, Jones. Even if you had believed me—an idea which is a fantasy unto itself—you know very well one is helpless to do anything without proof. One must catch the villain in the act."

Athelney muttered his agreement.

"Perhaps you shall take my brother more seriously on the next case, Jones?" Mycroft suggested.

"That might smooth things along," Sherlock agreed.

"I hope there might never be another," Athelney grumbled.

"There's appreciation for you, *Sergeant*." Sherlock wondered if resolving the case for others would ever win the admiration of the Yard. He desperately needed their cooperation to continue working. It wasn't about income—he received a mere pittance, if anything, unless he had a private case, which was often less interesting. Work was far more important than money.

Work is life.

"And yet, Florence can't have pulled her own teeth," Dr. Watson suggested.

"No, her father did at her request. But she made the dentures," Sherlock countered. "This was the part which required practice."

"Certainly. One wouldn't wish to be biting into another's neck and having one's teeth fall out. It rather takes away from the magic of the moment," Watson muttered.

Mirabella moved to sit in her basket chair. "And Mr. Fairclough wouldn't have thought anything of it."

"Precisely," Sherlock agreed.

"A unique invention, to be sure," Dr. Watson agreed. "The pharmacist's duties reach into both medicine and dentistry, and Florence was no fool. She became an expert at making dentures."

"Unique and disturbing." Athelney tapped his fingers on the couch. The truth be known, he appeared to take a strange delight in the more macabre elements of the case.

"But why was Mr. Fairclough secretive about the dentures? I could have sworn he was distinctly uncomfortable discussing it with me," Mirabella said. "Florence had already removed Evie's teeth and given her dentures. Many young ladies consider this a great luxury to have."

"Fairclough probably didn't want us to delve too deeply into Florence's activities. He knew she was experimenting with blood types, which is frowned upon in the scientific community."

"So Fairclough was innocent all along?" Mirabella was disbelieving.

"Define 'innocent'. He was well meaning and genuinely wished to help the poor—as well as his daughter," Mycroft said.

"He's also a dealer of addictions," Mirabella said.

"Miss Hudson, you surprise me," Mycroft said. "People are complex, like crystals, with both good and bad qualities. They might be savior to one, and heel to another."

She took a sip of her tea. "I suppose this case is proof of that."

Sherlock studied Mycroft. His color had returned, and he was his usual debonair self, though certainly subdued as a result of the loss of his friends and colleagues, and understandably so.

As one who was not prone to sentiment and feeling, Sherlock hated to see Mycroft any less than enchanted and pleased with life; it was one of his brother's gifts, to thoroughly enjoy his existence. It was a crime to steal this from one of the few who reveled in delight.

"Just what was Nathan Longstaff's involvement?" Athelney insisted.

"Longstaff was Percy's butler. He had to be an accessory; Florence couldn't do it all herself. He helped transport the blood—doing whatever was needed. He drove the carriage and helped to collect the blood."

"But it wasn't his idea and he probably didn't approve," Mirabella said.

"No doubt, but the fact remains that Florence couldn't have done it without him," Sherlock countered.

"Florence administered the wolfsbane in the tincture in Percival's neck, but Longstaff would have had to hold his lordship down," Dr. Watson suggested.

Mirabella trembled. "So Florence couldn't have killed Lord Percival without Longstaff's assistance."

"I'm afraid not," Mycroft said. "Dressed as the vampire, Florence would have claimed to have been sent by 'the agency' or as a 'gift' from friends, it wouldn't have been difficult to gain entry. But it helped a great deal to have someone on the inside."

"I thought it was the butler's night off," Mirabella asked.

Sergeant Jones shook his head. "No one could corroborate that Longstaff was at the theatre."

"Precisely," Sherlock said. "Florence dined with Percy, and when his lordship was getting sleepy she called Longstaff for assistance. Together they administered the wolfsbane."

"Even drugged, Percy would have fought back." Mycroft frowned, his grey eyes as dark as thunderclouds as he recalled the death of his two friends and associates.

"Then Longstaff was to change clothes and act like he was the butler returning from the theatre," Sherlock said.

"TThey hadn't quite finished when one of the neighbors contacted the Yard, having seen a vampire entering the mansion," Athelney added. "We beat 'im to it, as we often do."

"When did you first suspect Mr. Longstaff was not actually a butler?" Mirabella asked, taking a shortbread cookie and dipping it in her tea.

"From the moment I laid eyes on him, naturally," Mycroft balked, as it the question itself were preposterous. "Of course, it was confirmed when he opened his mouth."

"Because of his northern brogue?" Mirabella asked.

"Not at all. The man was unsure of the scullery maid's name," Mycroft frowned. "The butler would know the names of all of the household staff, without question. It is unthinkable he would not."

"But Evie was really Mrs. Kitchens, the scullery maid who assisted Denzil in the kitchen," Mirabella said.

"Your question is also your explanation, Miss Hudson," said Mycroft.

"Precisely. For a diabolical plan to be successful, all the details must be attended to," Sherlock said. "In a normal household, regardless of its size, the butler would know every employee's name. The fact that he had not bothered to learn her name—alias or not—implicated Longstaff."

"He did it for money, then?"

"Probably quite a bit of it," Mycroft said.

"How did you know he had built ships, Mr. Holmes?" Mirabella asked.

"You'll recall he used the term 'galley' when referring to the kitchen, a sailor's term. He had an injury, explaining his slight limp, and ended up in the workhouse. Working on the docks is hard work for low pay. When I first saw the rope burns on his hands, I thought it was from picking Oakum in the workhouse, but then I realized those burns originated in his ship building days," Sherlock said.

"Fairclough picked Longstaff up at the workhouse. Florence zoomed in on him, seeing that Percy needed a butler," Mycroft said.

"I expect Longstaff didn't know what he was getting into," Mirabella said. "Until the poisoning started taking effect. Probably the horror of seeing Florence's plan unwind was a bit of a shock."

"We could see that when we arrived; the man was completely out of his element," Mycroft agreed. "As it turned out, good looks weren't enough to play the role."

"The man I heard at the pharmacy was mortified with what he had done," Mirabella said.

"As well he should have been," Mycroft said.

"He wanted out," Mirabella added.

"So you're saying . . . Longstaff ain't . . . a fairy?" Athelney asked.

"Unlikely. And no way of knowing," Sherlock said. "It's irrelevant to the crime."

"Being a fairy is never irrelevant," Athelney grumbled.

"And what of the red thread? Was it from Mr. Longstaff's spats?" Mirabella asked.

"Yes and no." Sherlock took a sip of rum. "It was Fairclough's military plaid gaiters from his regiment which Florence had loaned to Longstaff."

"The Royal Scots," Dr. Watson added.

"Yes. Which we verified on our trip to the Scottish Highlands."

"The honor due to a military man," Dr. Watson said.

"But why?" Mirabella asked. "Why did Florence give her father's gaiters to Nathan Longstaff?"

"It was symbolic, a hateful act. As well as planting the evidence on her father. She wished to implicate him if it got to that point. Recall that Longstaff had to assist Florence and might well have gotten blood on himself." Sherlock said. "Upon returning the spats to her father, blood was unlikely to be visible. However, if the police thought to test the spats for blood, Fairclough would appear to be the guilty party."

Mirabella shuddered. "Why did Florence hate her father so much?"

"Was there anyone Florence liked?" Mycroft picked up a small cucumber sandwich from a tray Mirabella had placed on coffee table in front of them, alongside the shortbread cookies.

"Indeed, she channeled her hatred in many directions," Sherlock added.

"Perhaps it was because her mother was not attached to her and her father was absent for the most part when she was growing up," Mycroft added. "She was somewhat parent-less until she became an adult. She must have felt abandoned and unloved her entire childhood, which was re-ignited with her broken engagement."

"No doubt she did. And yet look at Wiggins," Sherlock said. "Who has had far fewer advantages and is primarily concerned with the welfare of his men."

"Did Florence kill Overton Bristow?" Mirabella asked.

"Beyond a doubt," Sherlock said.

"No! You don't mean it!" Athelney's jaw dropped.

"When she killed Lord Percival her revenge was complete," Mycroft said. "It was her plan from the beginning."

"Then why did she kill Radcliffe?" Mirabella asked. "For the money?"

"Yes, at this point she saw all the money to be had in her endeavors," Sherlock explained.

"She found that murder was a profitable business," Watson said.

"As many have done before her," Mycroft added. "Spreading hatred is one of the oldest money-makers there is."

"If Radcliffe refused her proposition, she may have felt he knew too much," Watson suggested.

"Perhaps she became addicted to murder, the very thing which was supposed to end all her suffering," Mirabella considered. "Using another murder to momentarily make her forget the horrible things she had done."

"Oh, I don't think she was much distressed over her actions," Mycroft suggested.

"So then . . . who killed Denzil?" Athelney asked.

"Why don't you work that one out for yourself, sergeant?" Sherlock suggested.

"Alright then. Longstaff." Athelney said.

"Incorrect," Sherlock said.

"I would have thought it was Longstaff. Denzil wasn't killed like the others," Mirabella agreed.

"There were no marks on his neck, and no blood was drained. It couldn't have been the vampire," Atheleny said.

"Florence couldn't very well mutilate a body in a public place without calling attention to herself," Sherlock said.

Mycroft swirled his buttered rum. "Recall that Florence had a gift for disguises—and as dressing as a man. Perhaps she liked the idea of being a man in a man's world. She was disguised as a sailor on leave. She and Denzil were having drinks in a public place."

"But Denzil had to have helped Florence, and been part of the plot," Athelney said.

"Perhaps not," Sherlock said. "Florence got Evie the job for the one night only and Denzil was focused on his dinner preparations. Women do tend to be covered from head to toe, particularly servants." He glanced at Mirabella.

"However the conversation went, Florence decided Denzil knew something or was onto something," Mycroft said. "And Florence hated men. Not just men of a certain persuasion. All men, I believe."

"So sad," Mirabella murmured. "Florence might have done so much good—she was in the position to do good. How fortunate she was to be a professional woman when there are so few professions available to women."

"And Radcliffe? We didn't find any poison in the wine," Athelney said. "Perplexing."

"Florence was at close range with Radcliffe. She could have killed him easily any number of ways. And yet she chose the less elegant way of knocking him over the head," Sherlock said. "By this time Florence's confidence would have been increasing, as well as her audacity."

"Yes, working in an apothecary, Florence would be familiar with all the herbs and any number of poisons," Mycroft said. "But it had finally occurred to her that she shouldn't taint the blood, which would increase her chances of compatibility and success. She did want to continue selling the blood, and she was a chemist and a scientist."

"So, if Florence was dressed as the vampire, why did Radcliffe give her admittance?" Athelney asked.

"Because she wasn't dressed as a vampire. She was disguised as a man," Watson suggested.

"At the *Diogenes*," Athelney said slowly. "A liaison between men."

"We've already been through this, sergeant. Why do you assume the meeting was of a romantic nature?" Sherlock asked. "Even if you presume that it was two men meeting?"

"Well, it had to be . . . It was at the Diogenes . . ."

"You are starting with your hypothesis and turning it into the conclusion," Sherlock objected. "A circular argument. And why do you presume that Radcliffe favored men? As Radcliffe noted in the log, this might have been a business meeting not a romantic liaison."

"Well he would. He wouldn't write 'hanky-panky' in the log."

"There is another possibility," Mycroft added. "Certainly in Percy's case Florence was dressed as a man—a vampire. In Denzil's case she was dressed as a man--a sailor. But in Radcliffe's case, she may have been dressed as Florence."

"You mean, as a woman?" Mirabella asked.

"Yes, as herself. Everyone was on watch for someone dressed in a vampire's costume, after all. She may have suggested to Radcliffe that he invest in the research of blood compatibility and blood transfusions." Mycroft sighed. "Radcliffe would not have discriminated. He did not attribute brains to his gender only."

"Only cruelty," Sherlock said.

"And what was Evie's involvement?" Mirabella asked anxiously. Despite the horror of the subject, it obviously warmed Belle's heart that she was able to ask questions and to be involved; this would ordinarily be absolutely taboo for the help, particularly the female help.

"She knew up from down, no doubt," Athelney said.

"Evie had a much smaller role," Sherlock said. "She was the scullery maid, assisting in the kitchen."

"So Evie didn't administer the poison?" Mirabella asked with a sigh of relief.

"In a manner of speaking, she did. She cooked the mushrooms which Florence had brought, but technically they didn't contain any poison. It was combining the foods that created the poison. Evie didn't know she was doing anything more than cooking," Sherlock said.

"Though she had some awareness of the sale of the blood," Mycroft said. "She must have pieced some of it together."

"Still, Florence couldn't have done it without Mrs. Travers. She was a party to the crime," Athelney said.

"It's important to note what she believed at the time of the murder," Dr. Watson suggested. "Mrs. Travers can't be held culpable if she truly didn't know. Particularly since there was no actual poison in the food."

"For all the body knew," Athelney said.

"Once she did know, she didn't assist with Radcliffe," Dr. Watson argued.

"Or maybe she wasn't asked to assist with that murder," Mycroft mused. "The more the merrier doesn't always apply."

"Evie didn't plan the murder and she certainly couldn't have approved." Mirabella sighed heavily. "It was wrong. I just mean I can understand now how a good person—a *hungry* person—can do something immoral. Or look the other way."

"I never thought to hear you say such a thing, Miss Belle," Sherlock remarked with interest. "You're always so black and white about these matters."

"I am never an advocate of the end justifying the means. I always believe if you choose the Godly path, a solution will be present itself." Mirabella sighed heavily. "But that is my standard. I am not a mother and I have some compassion for Evie after having seen the workhouse for myself."

"Quite so," Dr. Watson nodded. "Florence no doubt threatened to throw Evie and her children out of the commune if she didn't assist. Evie didn't care for herself, but she would have done anything for her children—and to keep her family together."

"I wish we might apply some of that compassion and sense of justice to Percy. He was the one with wolf bites in his neck." Mycroft said.

"Wrong is wrong and right is right is what I say," Athelney stated.

Mycroft turned to the Sergeant. "I am gratified to learn your empathy has grown to encase all victims of violent crimes, Jones."

The Sergeant twirled his handlebar mustache and grumbled.

"Recall that Evie has seen much horror in life," Mirabella said solemnly. "And possibly Longstaff. I have no way of knowing."

"Our esteemed butler will have his opportunity to give his account before the court," Sherlock said. "He has been apprehended in New York."

"What was Mrs. Travers' explanation when you asked her, Sergeant? I presume you have interviewed her?" Dr. Watson asked.

"O' course! We are not newbies at the Yard."

"And her response?"

"She had no idea what she was getting into. She thought she was only cooking at Lord Percival's."

"Makes sense. Florence wouldn't have told her," Dr. Watson said.

"Later Mrs. Travers knew about Florence's experiments with blood. Evie was told it would save mothers in childbirth. She didn't realize there would be an actual murder at the Percival residence until she heard about it later from people talking in the pharmacy. Naturally she didn't think she had anything to do with it. She wasn't allowed on the main floor," Sherlock said.

"Obviously, Longstaff had to know something was up when he went to the Diogenes," Mycroft said. "And yet he went."

"Likely after Florence killed Radcliffe. Longstaff showed up after death ensued," Sherlock said. "Florence drained the blood and then returned to the pharmacy ahead of Longstaff, leaving him to transport the blood. This was why he wanted out, when he realized Florence was grooming him to be part of an army of vampires."

"And what was the first clue?" Mycroft posed. "A bit slow on the uptake I should say."

"It is difficult to know if it was the body writhing in pain, the fangs in the neck, or the container of blood," Sherlock considered.

"Why did Florence wish to kill Radcliffe?" Mirabella asked.

"She had no objection to killing anyone," Sherlock said. "But it's difficult to say whether her greed or her hatred was greater: at this point her revenge was complete. It was the blood she wanted."

"It's importune to recall in instances such as this that, no matter how villainous an individual, she could have done nothing without her followers," Mycroft said.

"If it was for greed, why did Florence leave *The Roses of Heliogabalus* behind?" Mirabella asked.

"Simple." Mycroft smiled. "She didn't have an artist's heart. She didn't recognize its value."

"Understandable," Athelney said sympathetically.

"It was critical to her plan to present a certain picture to the public—and her victims," Sherlock said. "All of her actions had to fit the pattern for her scheme to work."

"What about the attack on Miss Mirabella after she spoke to Fairclough in the pharmacy?" Dr. Watson asked.

"Florence, who was behind the counter, overheard the conversation, of course, and sent one of her goons after Miss Belle."

"I see," Mirabella shook her head. "When I mentioned 'Mrs. Kitchens', Florence must have suspected I was on to her."

"Naturally. As you intended, Miss Belle."

"But the attack only confirmed Florence's guilt."

"Clearly it didn't. Everyone suspected Mr. Fairclough." Sherlock lit his pipe.

"All the better: Fairclough would hang, and Florence would receive the shop, getting the independence she so desired," Dr. Watson said.

"Her own father?" Mirabella said, aghast. "I thought she desired revenge."

"You credit the criminal mind with too much logic," Sherlock said. "Florence, in spite of her many blessings, was a disturbed person."

Dr. Watson sputtered. "There's an understatement of vast proportions, Holmes."

"I am a master of restraint."

Chapter Thirty-nine
Suspicions

"I never travel without my diary. One should always have something sensational to read on the train." – Oscar Wilde

"So everyone is back home and safe—your brother Mycroft and your assistant Miss Hudson." Athelney appeared uneasy despite having concluded a shocking case. "Florence is dead from the gunshot . . ."

"It's a shame." Mirabella poured another round of hot buttered rum for the gentlemen and tea for herself, exposure to the ghastly side of humankind being no excuse for a respite in the employ of one Sherlock Holmes. "Florence might have been running the pharmacy in time. A *lady* pharmacist in London."

Dr. Watson shook his head in disagreement. "She didn't have the temperament or bedside manner for it. That whole killing people and draining their blood while they were still alive was rather off-putting."

"I hate to ask—"Athelney hesitated, a rare demeanor for the confident police detective. "—as you've helped me solve the case, and it's no small matter with me superiors, I can tell you—"

"—*Helped* you?" Sherlock repeated, but a smile formed on the corners of his mouth. He was not one to hold a grudge. He either resolved the problem or didn't think it worth his notice.

"I might have said we did one better than that," Dr. Watson said.

"You did a fine job, and that's a fact," Athelney allowed. "Beginner's luck, one might say. Though I might be willing to work with you again, Holmes, if the situation was right. Now as I reflect upon it, you're a young man, and you'll become more prudent with experience."

"Very good of you, Jones," Sherlock said with a rare humility. "You're a giant among men."

"At least his ego is," Watson added under his breath.

"Yes, yes, but there is still an unanswered question." Athelney narrowed his eyes at Sherlock. One could say what one would, but Athelney was a policeman until the end.

"You, a sergeant, would wish to ask me, a beginner?"

"I would."

"What is it then?"

"Who killed Miss Fairclough? Who fired that shot?"

Mirabella almost dropped her teacup in recalling the shot that saved her life. It was the strangest thing to realize that a minuscule interval of time and a single act made the difference between life and death.

"Ah, so that's your worry, is it?" There was a fire in Dr. Watson's eyes as he downed his rum. "You can put your mind at ease, it was none of us. Though I certainly would have fired that shot, and been proud to claim it, had I arrived in time. I wouldn't have let that monster kill Miss Mirabella." He leaned forward. "And I hope I might count on you as well, Jones."

"You know very well from the lack of gunpowder present the shot was fired from a great distance, Athelney," Sherlock said. "It was therefore no one in our party."

"Quite true. Since we were all in the midst of the danger in hand-on-hand battle where the police should have been," Mycroft added. "Doing your undercover work for you."

"Oh, yes, I see." Athelney nodded distractedly. "It is odd. Do you have your suspicions as to who fired the shot?"

"More than suspicions," Sherlock said definitively. "It could only have been one man."

Athelney fixated his eyes on him. "And who is that?"

"Dr. Sebastian Moran."

"Quite impossible," Athelney sputtered. "Dr. Moran is the son of Sir Augustus Moran, Minister to Persia. He was educated at Eton and Oxford before embarking upon his military career in the 1st Bangalore Pioneers."

"The very one," Sherlock said. "Professor Moriarty's top man. And a skilled shot. Rumor has it he once pursued a wounded man-eating tiger in closed quarters."

"Don't start with the professor nonsense again. And even if it were true, why would Moran help you out? The way you tell it, Moriarty is your sworn enemy."

"I wondered that myself." Sherlock glanced at Mirabella, the tone of his voice suddenly foreboding. "Obviously he feels a debt to someone."

"But what will happen to those in the commune?" Mirabella asked.

"Most were not involved," Sherlock said.

"How can you say that? There were at least twenty people there."

"Some were Florence's hired ruffians and disenchanted hoodlums from the streets," Sherlock explained. "Florence used the numbers and the crowds to validate her purposes with the members of the commune.

She needed to insure they didn't turn against her and believed her to have her father's support while she sought recruits."

"Those from the commune that were involved are awaiting trial as well. I expect it will become evident they did not have an understanding of what they were doing, essentially following Florence's orders," Mycroft said.

"They knew what they were doing when Florence held a knife over your chest, brother," Sherlock objected. "And yet no one attempted to stop her."

"Difficult to prove since there was no actual murder," Athelney said.

"No thanks to anyone there except Evie," Sherlock said.

"I feel sorry for Evie," Mirabella said. "I really believe her love for her children was her only motivation."

"She may yet survive—and thrive," Mycroft said.

"I wonder that desperation drove her to something short of madness." Mirabella added sadly, "Losing her baby was the final blow."

"One thing still puzzles me," Athelney considered.

"This would be the second 'one thing' in the space of five minutes," Sherlock corrected.

"The Diogenes Club."

The amusement left Sherlock's countenance. Few would have observed it, but Mirabella had watched him long enough to know the signs. The slight lowering of his eyelids, the sudden darkness in his slate-grey eyes, and the tightening of his fingers around the neck of his pipe told her he did not wish to pursue the subject.

Sherlock Holmes is being secretive.

This in itself was so rare, and against his straight-forward nature. If Sherlock said something, one never doubted that he meant it. There was nothing Sherlock was more devoted to than justice and the law.

"Did you wish to become a member, Sergeant Jones?" Sherlock asked, not missing a beat. "I wouldn't have thought it. The Diogenes is an academic club, you know."

Athelney's eyes narrowed. "Why aren't you a member then, Mr. Holmes?"

"I am an honorary member."

"You're not much there, are you?"

"And you're not much at Scotland Yard, are you, Sergeant?"

"Pffft!" Athelney Jones sputtered. "Too busy working."

Sherlock shrugged. "There you have it. Our reasons are the same."

"Now you listen here, Mr. 'Olmes," Athelney put his glass down and leaned in closer to Sherlock. "Three of those what died—Overton

Bristow, Lord Percival and Radcliffe—were members of the Diogenes Club. There has to be a connection."

"Certainly there is. They were all intelligent men. Simply because a butterfly flaps its wings in Okinawa and there is a tornado in the East Indies several weeks later does not mean the two events are related," Sherlock said.

"Beyond a doubt, they would be," Mycroft considered. "A better example might be because there is an influx of immigrants and the typewriter is invented, it doesn't not necessarily mean the two events are related."

"It depends," Dr. Watson considered. "Was the inventor an immigrant?"

"Now you listen here, I won't be bamboozled by the likes of you."

"A grave disappointment," Sherlock murmured.

"The commonality is Florence, Sergeant," Mycroft said. "She had it in for her fiancé and his lover, both of whom happened to be members of the Diogenes."

"True. We know for a fact Florence had it in for Marjeries—she hated them—because Overton had broken her heart and ruined her reputation."

"As well as his own," Mycroft added. "Overton Bristow wasn't able to find employment anywhere after the broken engagement."

Athelney wagged his finger in reprimand. "But the question is, why were there fairies in the Diogenes? Bristow wasn't a member until he fell in with Lord Percival."

"Florence was mad," Mycroft said without hesitation. "Many a woman has been devastated in a similar matter and doesn't go about killing everyone in sight and draining their blood."

"And pulling their teeth," Dr. Watson added.

"She still managed to have a good head for finance throughout it all," Athelney posed.

"True. She saw an opportunity to enrich herself—with the blood—and ran with it." Mycroft tilted his head in perplexity. "Are you saying she wasn't mad? Being a greedy swine capable of profiting at the expense of others isn't an argument for sanity."

"It is a strangely held common belief that being good at making money is a testimony to sound judgment," Sherlock said.

"Be that as it may, at least two of the murdered men had recently had sexual relations with other men."

"And your point, Sergeant?" The amusement left Mycroft's expression.

"Why did Florence target the Diogenes Club?"

"She didn't," Mycroft reiterated. "She targeted men who happened to be members."

"Because she hated men? And the Diogenes is a men's club?" Mirabella considered.

"I say because the Diogenes is a front for fairies."

"Oh, for goodness sake, Florence hated her own father," Mirabella objected. "Who, by the way, told me *he* would like to be a member of the Diogenes."

"He'll never get in," Athelney muttered.

"The criminal here was Florence Fairclough—going about killing innocent people unrelated to her personal heartbreak. I do wish this was not such a difficult concept for you, Athelney." Sherlock's impatience was beginning to show.

"You haven't answered my question, Holmes."

Mycroft, who was generally so pleasant, suddenly had the appearance of one who was taking charge of the situation. "What do you propose to do, Sergeant? Arrest all the members of the Diogenes Club? Its members are among the most respected and prestigious families in Britain. I assure you that you can kiss your job at Scotland Yard good-bye if you proceed." He added softly, "You shall not be 'Sergeant', you shall not be 'Police Constable', you shall be unemployed."

There was a quiet stillness in the room.

"Particularly in the wake of the suffering imposed upon the families of the dearly departed." Mycroft continued. "And I doubt very seriously if you will be able to prove anything, Jones. As I have already alluded to, these are prestigious and intelligent people with whom you are dealing."

"So you don't deny it?"

"That you would lose your position? Certainly I do not deny it." Mycroft smiled sweetly. "I'm not without my connections either, as you may have surmised."

Sherlock cleared his throat, adding softly, "Not to mention that at least one of the dead at Hampstead Heath was a Peaky Blinder, which you personally took credit for, Sergeant, if I'm not mistaken. I don't believe you would wish it to hit the papers that it was a group of private citizens who disbanded these criminals, with no help whatsoever from the force."

"I meant to ask you about that body." Athelney stood to leave. "I'm keeping an eye on you two." He glanced at Dr. Watson. "And anyone associated with you."

"You're welcome, Athelney. We are most pleased to have ended your murderer's reign of terror." Sherlock turned to Mirabella. "Could you please get the sergeant his hat and coat, Miss Belle?"

"I'd be delighted to," she said, rising.

Chapter Forty
The Butterfly and the Bat

"Always forgive your enemies; nothing annoys them so much." –
Oscar Wilde

After the door had closed, Mirabella turned to the men present, frowning.

"What is it Miss Belle? You seem dismayed."

"It was a dismaying case," Dr. Watson said.

"Will Evie hang?" she asked.

"Not a chance of it," Mycroft said.

"How can you possibly know that, Mr. Holmes?" Mirabella asked. "She and Longstaff are the only ones left to be punished for all that has happened. They will want to punish someone, they always do."

"Evie was able to identify some of Florence's more zealous followers," Mycroft said.

"So because she cooperated, the law will be more lenient?" Mirabella asked.

Mycroft tilted his chin in agreement. "That and the fact that Mrs. Travers has escaped custody and is even now on a boat to Australia."

"She escaped jail?" Mirabella exclaimed. "How? And how do you know where she went?"

"She was advised to avoid the mistakes of destination choice made by Mr. Longstaff," Mycroft explained matter-of-factly.

"Australia is a forward-thinking country and a good place for women," Dr. Watson nodded his approval. "Very right."

"That and they are not much concerned with escaped convicts," Sherlock added. "If I'm not mistaken, the Lord Mayor of Sydney is an escape convict."

"Actually he's a potter." Mycroft said.

"Ah, yes. A Robert Fowler."

"I believe you're thinking of one of the provinces in Queensland, Shirley."

"Quite so."

"Evie *escaped*? But how? . . ." Mirabella turned to Sherlock. "*You* . . . did you arrange this, Sherlock?"

"Certainly not. I don't have those kind of connections." There was a gleam in Sherlock's eye. "That should be obvious by now."

Suddenly comprehension dawned. "But Mycroft does."

"Very good, Miss Belle."

". . . But Evie . . . What she did was against *the law* . . ." Mirabella considered. "You always uphold the law."

"Not all laws are just," Mycroft said simply. "Or fit the crime."

The terrifying image of Mycroft on the altar flashed before her eyes. "But after what they did, I can't believe you would help her . . ."

A quivering smile formed on Mycroft's lips. "Do you mean what she did to *my own kind*, Miss Hudson? I am first and foremost a member of the human race." He stretched his legs out before him. "I take your point, though. I didn't help Longstaff—he had to have known what was up after Percy's murder. But I actually believe Evie was in the dark. She didn't—*wouldn't*—assist with the second murder, children or no."

"Exceptionally kind hearted of you, Mycroft, considering . . ."

"Some of us have empathy for others. Not everyone feels hurting others will prove one's superiority," Mycroft said. "Entirely illogical. Besides being no way to live."

"Certainly. When one knows oneself to be superior, there is no need to prove it," Sherlock said.

"Moreover, an act of kindness is more likely to enlighten than an act of vengeance," Mycroft added.

"Decidedly," Dr. Watson agreed. "Evie Travers will never forget you."

Mycroft took another sandwich but his expression remained imperturbable. "Mrs. Travers has been betrayed by almost everyone who ever pretended to help her. I couldn't bear that she should have her trust destroyed once and for all."

"I have never in my life witnessed such an act of forgiveness," Mirabella whispered.

"It's all in a day's work." Mycroft popped the finger sandwich into his mouth.

"And what of Evie's children and husband?" Mirabella asked. "I expect they couldn't go to Australia with her."

"True, the family would make her too identifiable at the present time. Her children and husband will have to follow, slipping away at intervals. But they will. When things have calmed down."

She stared at him, stunned.

"What is it, Miss Hudson?"

"Longstaff. You knew he was involved almost from the beginning."

"True."

"Because you knew he hadn't long been a butler? That couldn't have told you. Everyone has to start their career sometime," she said uneasily.

"Indeed. From the beginning both Longstaff and Denzil implied— quite effectively—that there was a constant stream of orgies going on at Percy's mansion."

"Naturally, Athelney latched onto that like a dog on a bone," Sherlock muttered. "The age-old trick of diverting attention from oneself by defaming another."

"It wasn't true?"

"Not at all. There was only the occasional orgy." Mycroft's expression was indignant.

"Quality over quantity I always say," Sherlock murmured.

Mirabella bit her lip.

"I've other news." Mycroft sighed heavily, fanning himself.

"Do tell, brother dear," Sherlock said.

"Just as Athelney has been promoted as a result of this case, I have been demoted."

"Oh, no," Mirabella exclaimed jumping out of her chair.. "That is *not fair*."

"Life is not fair, my dear." Mycroft lowered his eyes in humility.

Sherlock burst into laughter, a rare sight.

Mirabella turned on her heel to face her employer. "How can you be so insensitive, Mr. Holmes? This is your own brother who has been treated shamefully by the government."

"Many people have been so. Let us look instead for someone who has been treated well by our governing body."

Mirabella shook her head in dismay. "Your own brother."

"Unless I miss my guess, this was a voluntary demotion," Sherlock said, taking a puff on his pipe.

"Quite so." Mycroft nodded. "I've resigned from my position as Foreign Secretary. In point of fact, I was begged to stay."

It was Dr. Watson's turn to burst into laughter. "I'm not surprised."

"The Queen herself called me to Buckingham Palace and made a plea. Most tiresome."

"You refused Queen Victoria?" Mirabella's jaw dropped. "I don't understand . . ."

"It was only a matter of time until Mycroft quit." Sherlock expressed feigned sympathy. "Has the stress of all this been too much?"

"Most assuredly. But that is not the reason I resigned."

"It has nothing to do with this case?" Mirabella asked suspiciously.

"Perhaps a little. But it was inevitable regardless."

"Let me guess. The office of the Foreign Secretary was too much work," Sherlock said.

"Precisely. I barely have a moment to myself."

"To the contrary, that's all you have, brother," Sherlock said under his breath.

Dr. Watson chuckled. "The government doesn't run itself. It does require a modicum of work."

"An extraordinary amount." Mycroft shook his head. "And the number of meetings I was required to attend. Preposterous! Those briefings greatly interfered with my keeping abreast of what was going on."

"But what will the country—what will *we* do without you?" Mirabella asked. "And are you now without an occupation?"

"Would that it were so, I would get more done. But, no, I'm a sort of attaché in the foreign office. Wining and dining foreign dignitaries and such."

"I expect you will accomplish much more in that capacity," Sherlock said. "You'll keep abreast of everyone who is coming and going—and what they are up to. I expect those at the top will be seeking your advice more than ever."

Mycroft sighed heavily. "It's so tedious being consulted on every matter, no matter how mundane."

"You must increase your leisure hours, Mr. Holmes," Mirabella suggested.

"I shall certainly endeavor to do so."

"I should like to see you move from no work to less work, brother dear," Sherlock said. "That will be your greatest accomplishment yet."

"I hope the effort does not vex me too much. At any rate, I am much relieved to return to the life of a mid-level government employee." Mycroft sighed. "I expect to accomplish a great deal more. Nothing gets done at the top."

"But your entourage of assistants will be greatly reduced." Mycroft required attendants. She couldn't imagine this would be to his taste.

"*Au contraire.* I negotiated an increase in my staff." As he stood, Mycroft glanced out the window onto Baker Street. "In fact, my carriage awaits. I must be off. I don't wish to be late for opening night at the opera."

"Oh, and what are you seeing, Mr. Holmes?" Mirabella asked.

"Die Fledermaus."

"Ah. *The Revenge of the Bat*." Sherlock nodded with appreciation. "Sometimes art *does* imitate life."

***

"Is it true, Mr. Holmes?" she asked after Mycroft had left. "Is the Diogenes Club a front for sodomites?"

"I've told you how I feel about that term, Miss Belle. Please do not use it again in my presence."

"I apologize, sir. But Mycroft . . . he's so handsome. So polite." Why did she always like the wrong type of man?

"What does that have to say to anything?"

"I mean, men . . . and men. It's just not right."

"It's not right for you, Miss Belle." A slow smile formed on his lips. "I'm glad to know it."

"Mycroft is so . . . so . . . *wonderful*."

"Indeed he is. It's all rather different when you love someone, isn't it Miss Belle? He becomes a real person instead of a label or a category." Sherlock added softly, "with a heart and soul just like yours."

"I can't believe it."

His eyes met hers. "Miss Belle, life is hard. Do not deny anyone what love they can find in this life." His silver grey eyes looked like clouds in sky. "They would never wish the same for you."

She thought of how Mycroft had treated Evie, and knew it to be true.

Chapter forty-one
An Organization in Crisis

"As if anyone would choose to be poor. What people wanted was work."–"Sherlock Holmes and the Chocolate Menace"

Sherlock looked behind the bars to see a child seated among the men. It sickened him. "Wiggins, I thought we had an agreement."

"We did, sir. I wouldn't steal anything, and you would keep me employed."

"And I fulfilled my part of the bargain, didn't I?"

"You did, Mr. 'Olmes."

"And what were you doing when we met, Wiggins?"

"I was a chimney sweep for a' while, but the twelve hour days and barely any food was makin' me sick, so I were in search of a new occupation."

"I wouldn't call thievery an occupation," Sherlock said.

"It paid well, sir."

"The pay has lured you back into the life of crime?"

"Oh no, sir, no! It ain't nothin' to do with the pay."

"By your actions I conclude that you wish to go to the workhouse or the Foundling Hospital. Is that correct, Wiggins?"

"Oh no, guv'nor. I'd rather stay 'ere." Wiggins looked appalled at the idea. "To be in jail is respectable."

"And to be sent to the workhouse is the ultimate shame?"

"Yessir."

"Then answer me, Wiggins. Why did you steal when you had employment? Above all, I must have loyalty from my employees. And to steal a bowler's hat of all things. Of what possible use could you have for such a frippery?"

"It makes me look like a gent."

"I had no idea you wished to join the ranks of 'gentleman', Mr. Wiggins." Sherlock eyed him suspiciously.

The child stubbed his toe into the dirt, still wearing his new shoes. "Miss Mirabella told me bein' poor is what killed me parents."

"Oh, she did, did she?" Sherlock frowned.

"Yep, maybe the disease killed 'em. Which maybe happened because they couldn't have medicine or shoes or sane-sation."

"Sanitation?"

Wiggins nodded agreement.

"That still doesn't answer my question, Mr. Wiggins. You have an income. You have enough to eat. You have a far smaller income in jail, so it wasn't about the money."

"I don't always have a place to sleep."

"I had understood that you boys were sleeping in an abandoned warehouse. Don't tell me my sources have failed me there as well?"

"Yeah. That's right. But it ain't a home."

"It has four walls and a roof. Why is it not a home?"

"We're never going to advance—or get a home—without an education."

"Miss Hudson, again?"

"Now don't blame her, Mr. 'Olmes. She's a nice lady. She just made me say what I was already thinkin'."

"Yes, she has that effect." Sherlock, for once, could not offer an argument.

"And we don't always eat as fine as I would like. Sometimes all we have is bread."

"I haven't heard you complain before. And I guarantee you'll receive a great deal less to eat at the workhouse—where you'll be sent next due to your age—and a lot less blunt for your labor." Sherlock grew impatient. "Enough of this foolishness and deceit. Answer me now. Why did you steal when you have the skill, the brains, and the wherewithal to earn your own income?"

"I dunno' guv'nor. It was like somethin' came over me. I got sad thinking about me parents, and, well, I just did it."

"Do you plan to 'just do it' again, Mr. Wiggins? I need to know what to report back to your men. They are without leadership, you know. Tom is attempting to take over as the head of the organization."

"The Baker Street Irregulars?" Wiggins exclaimed, standing up suddenly.

"How many organizations are you running?" Sherlock wasn't certain he wanted the answer to that question.

"Tom?" Wiggins shook his head, disbelieving. "He couldn't do it."

"I agree. But if you don't return, they'll take what they can get. A vacuum will not long stay empty."

"Alright," Wiggins agreed, resolution crossing his expression. "I'm ready to go." And indeed he did look ready. Sherlock had never before seen the young hoodlum looking so clean, like a shiny new sixpence.

"It's not that easy. I would have to pull some strings with the constabulary. Which I won't do if I don't have your solemn vow you'll never pull this stunt again."

Wiggins looked down at the ground, his enthusiasm waning. "What do you think killed my parents then, Mr. Holmes? Was it not having enough blunt?"

"It's never quite that simple, Mr. Wiggins. It's always best to go forward. The point is your parents would want you to make something of yourself and to live a good life—and to right some of those wrongs. Perhaps you'll end up in the London sanitation department, what would you think of that?" Sherlock had never known Wiggins to take a particular interest in sanitation before, but facts change, and he was not one to ignore the facts.

"You mean a real job, Mr. Holmes? Wearing a suit and a top hat to work?"

"Hats again, is it? Why didn't you tell me you had such a particular interest in hats, Wiggins? I would have procured one for you."

"No sir, it ain't the hat. It's havin' an important job."

"I see. Being a policeman or detective—which you already are—is as important as a sanitation officer. Either way you're cleaning up the city."

"I hadn't thought of it that way, Mr. 'Olmes."

"That is apparent. But I have no objection to any profession you choose to pursue and I pledge my allegiance to assist you—provided it is a legal occupation. You'll have to decide."

Wiggins placed his finger on his chin, seeming to consider Sherlock's words. "I guess you couldn't very well assist me in bein' a criminal, no matter how good I was."

"No, indeed. Personally, I would like to see you taking over my business someday, Mr. Wiggins."

"*Me*? Take over your business?" A tenderness filled his eyes, as if this was beyond anything he'd ever hoped for. "Like I was your son?"

"I couldn't hope for a better son," Sherlock said softly.

"But me, I ain't educated or well born."

"That isn't the measure of a man. For my part, I look to bravery, brains, leadership, and the fight for justice."

"But what if you was to have a son of your own, Mr. Holmes?"

"A remote possibility as I'm unmarried and unlikely to become so."

"What about Miss Mirabella?"

"What about her?" Sherlock felt his posture stiffen.

"You could marry her," Wiggins said unselfishly, in spite of paving the way to lose his future inheritance with the suggestion..

Sherlock chuckled. "Whatever put such a foolish idea into your head, Wiggins?"

"She's awfully pretty. And smart too. You wouldn't wanna' have dumb kids."

"To be sure."

"Then why don't you? Marry her?"

"She wouldn't have me, I assure you," Sherlock said softly, surprised at the disappointment in his own voice.

"Hmmm," Wiggins considered. "You might be right."

Sherlock frowned. "Thank you for the vote of confidence, Wiggins."

"I calls it as I sees it." Wiggins was pensive for a moment. "So you could train me? Someday, that is.."

"That remains to be seen. And only on the condition that you stay out of jail. I'll not hand my business over to a common criminal."

The boy stood up. "I'll do my best to make you proud, Mr. Holmes. And me parents."

"Good boy." Sherlock considered the young man before him, little more than a child. "There's something else, isn't there, Wiggins?"

The boy looked away momentarily. "You'll think I ain't manly if I tell you."

"I certainly will not. You're worth ten of the average man on the street." In an instant realization hit. "For God's sake, Wiggins, what a fool I've been! Don't tell me you got yourself locked up in order to get a bath?"

"Keep your voice down, guv'nor! Those are the kind o' words what can make me the laughing stock o' the place." Wiggins blushed, looking frantically about him. "How did you know, Mr. 'Olmes?"

"Quite simple, actually. I should have seen it before. In the first place, you're too smart to end up in this jail cell unless you wanted to be here. That is what has perplexed me since I arrived: why would you want to end up in jail? I don't see anyone in this cell you would wish to question, which would be my primary objective were I in your shoes."

"Oh, yeah. I've seen meaner types in the Bank of England."

"Then I observed the red marks on your ankles from the vermin," Sherlock added.

"The itch was something awful, Mr. 'Olmes."

"It would be. And you couldn't use any of your blunt to purchase a night in a decent lodging house: you're too honorable to take away anything from the other boys. You knew you wouldn't be admitted into the jail without a bath, so you waited until a Bobby was watching—and then did something to put you here."

Wiggins lowered his head sheepishly. "There weren't no other way."

Sherlock cleared his throat. "The workhouse might have achieved the same end, however. Then you could have escaped at the earliest opportunity."

"The workhouse?" Wiggins exclaimed. "There's no honor in that!"

"Whereas there is in the jail?"

Wiggins shook his head adamantly. "Anybody can walk into the workhouse. I had to do something to earn me place here." He beamed with pride.

"Not to mention the jail leaves you with a record."

"It's the price 'o honor."

"I might ask why you didn't steal the Persian powder instead of the hat," Sherlock posed. It was a well known fact that even fashionable guests took Persian powder with them to hotels and boarding houses, sprinkling the sheets and the pillows with the powder in the event of unwanted visitors.

Wiggins' face fell. "I didn't think of that, sir."

"Perhaps you might consult with me before resorting to desperate measures, Wiggins. We might be able to come up with a solution satisfactory to us both."

"I take pride in solving me own problems, Mr. 'Olmes." Wiggins raised his chin.

"And I take pride in having an unblemished work force," Sherlock retorted without compromise.

"Yes, sir. I'm telling you, though, where we is at the warehouse, sometimes the vermin is so thick they fall from the ceiling on our heads."

"I can see why you needed the hat." Sherlock cleared his throat. "I didn't realize your accommodations were not acceptable to you, Mr. Wiggins."

"I said you'd think me a sissy." Wiggins bowed his head with shame.

"Not at all. Watson and I are frequent customers of the Turkish baths." Sherlock raised an eyebrow. "And though I don't approve of the outcome, your method was most ingenious. I would have expected nothing less, Wiggins. You had a problem and you solved it. And yet, we now have a bigger problem. How to get you out of here and keep you out of the workhouse."

"Simple. I'll run away."

"And you'd be in hiding for the rest of your life now that you're on the books. No, that will never do."

"What then?"

"The sergeant owes me a favor." Sherlock tipped his hat to Wiggins. "I do hope I can resolve this issue before Tom runs the Baker Street Irregulars into the ground."

Chapter forty-two
A Good Deed Borne in Tragedy

"Suffering has been stronger than all other teaching, and has taught me to understand what your heart used to be. I have been bent and broken, but, I hope, into a better shape."
– Charles Dickens, "Great Expectations"

"I hope you don't mind my coming, Mr. Fairclough," Mirabella said. He looked like a man who had been crying for days. "I must be a terrible reminder of Florence's death. I'm so sorry. I never wished it to end that way."

"The only person I blame is myself."

"You mustn't, Mr. Fairclough. No matter how good a parent is, sometimes a child is bent and determined to follow a wrong path. At the same time there are those children who don't have anyone and are ever so grateful for the slightest attentions."

"I would have done anything for Florence." He stifled a sob. "I loved her."

"You were an exemplary father, sir." Mirabella added wistfully, "She might have been a lady pharmacist—in London, no less. To be perfectly honest, I envy the life you offered her."

"Her heart had turned so black. She lost all ambition."

Oh, she had plenty of ambition, believe me.

"You do so much good, sir. You mustn't dwell on it." She added softly, "Ultimately we are only responsible for our own actions." Mirabella felt a bit hypocritical, tending to assume responsibility for the deeds of others herself.

"Perhaps this is a bad time, Mr. Fairclough, but I wonder if I might ask a favor?" She swallowed hard. "I mean, not for myself, but for someone else in need."

"And who might that be?"

"I believe one of your cottages has opened up?"

"Several," he said sadly. "I was betrayed on more than one level."

"I know some very good people—hard workers too—who need a home."

"Good people?" He looked disbelieving.

"I assure you they are. I speak of a band of orphan boys who have been dealt every misfortune by life. Mr. Holmes can vouch for them, as can I."

Disapproval crossed Fairclough's expression.

"Before you say 'no', they are very good boys. They will keep the grounds clean in exchange."

"Oh, I don't think so, Miss Hudson, those cottages are for families."

"These boys are definitely a family of sorts. And they're accustomed to sleeping in an abandoned warehouse—with one of them awake and on guard—that they would very likely all sleep together in the same room."

"They're currently sleeping in a warehouse?"

"Yes. It's not a good place for children at all." She swallowed hard. "Or anyone for that matter."

"That can't be safe."

"Not at all. And the place is . . . filthy."

Fairclough's expression softened, for an instant forgetting his broken heart. "How many are there?"

She swallowed hard. "Twelve."

"Oh my goodness." He knit his eyebrows. "How old are they?"

"Between the ages of six and thirteen. They are all smart. And ambitious as well."

A glimmer of approval crossed his expression. "They would have to attend school."

She smiled. "Yes, sir. Of that they are well aware—and most anxious to comply." *It is the price of a good night's sleep.*

Chapter forty-three
Promises were meant to be Broken

"A very little key will open a very heavy door." – Charles Dickens

"That must be Mr. Kingsley." Mirabella heard footsteps in the hallway heading to the third floor flat.

"He seems to be settling in. I believe Kingsley will be quite useful." Satisfaction crossed Sherlock's expression.

"And he gets along famously with Mr. Uladimov, who frightens everyone else. Mr. Kingsley calls the Russian 'Uli', who doesn't appear to take the slightest offense." She giggled.

"Kingsley has a conversational manner which is agreeable to people, so they confide in him. He appears to be perfectly harmless, being an older gentleman." Sherlock's lips formed a quivering smile, indicating intellectual amusement. "Quite misleading."

"But he is genuinely kind."

Sherlock's grey eyes turned cloudy as he focused them on her. "One shouldn't confide in everyone. One's secrets have a way of surfacing in the most unexpected places."

She felt a sudden alarm. *He knows something.* Or, more likely, *everything.*

"I want you to stop seeing Moriarty, Miss Hudson."

Sherlock was not one to mince words so it was common for an element of shock to accompany them. But this gave her true cause for alarm. "Oh. How did you find out about that, Mr. Holmes?"

"Perhaps my first clue was that you are not dead."

"So you forgive me?"

"It skirts the issue." His gaze looked like it might swallow her whole. "You should no longer be in my employ, you know. Confiding my business to my arch enemy."

She did know. Please, please, anything but that. "It is all work-related, I assure you, Mr. Holmes." The fear that he would kick her out on her ear took hold of her. Six months ago, he would not have hesitated.

He laughed a dark, sinister laugh to rival the professor's. "Secretly meeting with my adversary and the head of the criminal underground? Explain that to me, Miss Hudson."

When you put it that way . . . She stumbled for words. "The professor is a useful contact. You have always said to keep your friends close and your enemies closer."

"Moriarty is the exception. He is far too dangerous. He is pulling you into his web, or did that fact escape you?"

She shook her head. "No. It didn't."

"It is never advisable to enter into an arrangement with someone depraved who then has expectations of you. If you disappoint them, which you invariably will when you follow your conscience, they enact their revenge. Better to never be part of their schemes."

Though she knew Sherlock's words to be true, she felt reluctant to break the connection with Moriarty. Aside from the benefit to knowing what one's enemy was up to, she hated to admit that she enjoyed Moriarty's company.

No doubt the same way Sherlock enjoyed his cocaine.

"The last time I went to see the professor, it was to gain entrance into the workhouse for your case, Mr. Holmes."

"Where you almost died and I was injured."

"We did solve the case. Please don't dismiss me from my position, Mr. Holmes."

"But the case isn't the only reason you see Moriarty, is it, Miss Hudson?"

"I don't suppose so." She shook her head.

"There are other ways to learn science, Miss Belle."

How does Sherlock always know everything?

"I am quite serious. This association is a threat to me." His expression had a severity which made her wish to sit down. "And to you."

She swallowed hard. "To you more so than to me."

"Unless he kills you."

"There is that."

"Why do you wish to hold onto this liaison, Miss Belle?" he asked softly.

"I'm not sure I know the entire answer to that question," she said truthfully. "I suppose the most important aspect is the intellectual stimulation."

***

He frowned. "And are you so lacking in intellectual stimulation in my company?"

There were many areas where Sherlock did not feel up to the task of providing satisfaction, but the intellect had never been one of those arenas.

She suppressed a giggle, and it was quite becoming, as displeased as he was. "Of course not. I suppose I am greedy." She grew serious. "But, honestly, Mr. Holmes, I believed I was assisting you and your work."

Sherlock gave up attempting to command her. That had gotten nowhere. "What would it take to receive your assurance you will stay away from Moriarty, Miss Belle?"

"Do I still have a position?"

"Answer my question, please."

Her lips quivered. "Perhaps if you stayed away from cocaine?"

"Of course."

"And laudanum."

He chuckled.

"Why do you laugh?"

In truth, he was astonished at her effrontery. She had thought of every angle and then been forward enough to propose it, even at the threat of her dismissal. "I am not an addict. I merely use drugs when I am bored—or waiting for a case."

"You are an addict. Merely a high functioning addict."

"I shall take that as a compliment."

"It wasn't intended as one."

He studied her. "So you will stop seeing Moriarty if I stop using cocaine?"

"Correct. And laudanum. And all related drugs."

"I didn't know you cared, Miss Hudson."

"Certainly I do. Who is more intertwined with my life than you, Sherlock?"

He was startled by her words as well as her form of address. Belle was a significant part of his life, but he hadn't expected her to reciprocate the sentiment.

"What do you say, Mr. Holmes?" she pressed.

Sherlock was already practically weaned from the drug. Watson had seen to that, pronouncing his habit to be "always present, but asleep."

There was no need to pass that information on to Belle, particularly since it gave him the leverage to keep her out of Moriarty's path.

"Agreed."

"We have a deal then?" she asked hopefully.

"We do."

She sighed heavily.

"What is the matter, Miss Belle?"

"It's just that I will miss my conversations with the professor. About mathematics, that is."

Sherlock placed an envelope on her desk. "Open it, Belle."

Chapter forty-four
A Dream Come True

"Never apologize for showing feeling.
When you do so, you apologize for the truth."
– Benjamin Disraeli

The return address read "The University of London."
What on earth could it be?
She opened the letter frantically and began to read. *We are pleased to accept your entrance into the University of London.*

Her hands began to shake and she almost dropped the letter. "But I never applied. My application is still here." Quickly she sprang to her desk in search of the application. "I can't find it."

"It might have been misplaced." He stood up, moving to pour them each a sherry. "And I took the liberty of pulling some strings. I believe a celebration is in order."

"Oh, Sherlock." She rushed to hug him. With her arms around him, feeling his strong muscles under her hands, she felt a strange sensation. An excitement. A longing. He felt so solid, as if he were a person she could always depend upon.

His expression was stern as he looked down at her. "You shall have to work your classes around my schedule, you understand."

"Of course." She looked up to meet his eyes. "I have my duties here."

"And you must be rested when you come to work in the morning. I shall not allow sloppy work."

"Naturally you would not." There was a sadness in his delivery, in great contrast to the happiness she felt. "Why did you change your mind?"

He released her, poured his sherry, and downed it in one gulp. He served himself another and handed a glass to her. "I didn't.."

She studied him suspiciously as he returned to his seat. "Was it a ploy to remove me from the professor?"

"That I had already accomplished with my bargain. I had no need to give you the letter."

"True. But it is better arranged according to your terms." It was very wrong of her to tease him when he had been so kind. She was simply elated and baffled at the same time, and she had a tendency to babble on at the best of times.

He stared at her with a stern expression, but his eyes were laughing. "So you can give me no credit for any good deed, Miss Hudson?"

"I can't imagine you would do anything unless it suited one of your purposes, Mr. Holmes."

His voice grew soft. "In that, you would be wrong, Belle. And I wish you would call me by my name."

"Honestly, Sherlock," she said softly. "It is the nicest thing anyone has every done for me."

***

I did it because . . . because . . .

"I'm so grateful to you. It was very kind of you, *Sherlock*." She returned to her seat with the glass of sherry.

"I expect it was. And a grand waste of time. You can learn everything you need to from books, from me, and in being out in the world. That path would be more honorable—and faster—than any degree. I don't have a university degree. I merely pursued a course of study, and you must agree I am the most intelligent person you know."

"Outside of Mycroft." She giggled.

He felt a smile tugging on his lips. "Agreed."

"At any rate, ladies have to work harder to prove themselves. Men are given respect from the outset, ladies have to earn it."

"Do you honestly believe that a university degree will cause people to take you seriously, Miss Hudson?"

"It would certainly help."

"I fear you delude yourself. You must pursue this course for the knowledge it will bestow and for no other reason." Sherlock had many misgivings about Belle going to university. But it was what she wanted, and he had come to care about her wishes. Even so, it would be a difficult path. "You must be aware, Miss Belle, there will be those throughout life who don't want you to succeed. You will need to be prepared for that."

"How can I possibly do that?"

"Contacts. Always necessary to success."

"I have you. And Dr. Watson."

"Naturally you'd wish to start with the best. But you may need encouragement from another woman, someone who understands your difficulties. I've arranged a meeting with Elizabeth Garrett Anderson."

"Dr. Garrett?" she exclaimed. "The only female doctor in Britain?"

"Indeed, Garrett found a loophole in the charter of the Society of Apothecaries by which they could not legally exclude her."

"I told you the pharmacists are the most progressive medical group in England." Mirabella raised her chin.

"In that one instance. They have since committed to excluding women from practicing as doctors," Sherlock countered. "The Society of Apothecaries immediately amended its regulations to prevent other women from obtaining a license. Garrett was literally the only woman who slipped through. So why bother pursuing that course of study?"

"If Dr. Garrett had taken that attitude, she wouldn't be a practicing doctor."

"In order to take the test to obtain the license, Garrett had to hire private tutors in anatomy and physiology because the male students had forced her out of the dissecting room and chemistry lectures. This is the welcome you too will receive, Belle."

"Dr. Garrett will help me. As will you, I am sure."

"Very likely," he said softly.

"Moriarty said you didn't want me to succeed, Sherlock. That you were afraid of losing me," she said, her eyes alight with curiosity.

In that, he is correct. "Moriarty has a poison tongue and is a master manipulator."

"And those are his good points," she agreed.

"Speaking of Moriarty, his henchman saved your life. Does that not strike you as odd, Miss Hudson?"

She dreaded where this was going. Lord knows she had run this question round in her mind hundreds of times.

"I have no doubt one day Colonel Moran will attempt to put a bullet in my head. And yet he saved your life." Sherlock pressed. "What have you done for Moriarty in return, Miss Hudson?"

"Well . . . I . . . I didn't know what else to do. There were lives at stake. As it turned out, your brother Mycroft."

"I repeat, what have you done?"

"It was a mere scientific idea."

"An idea? Not a specific formula?"

"No." She shook her head.

"Is it an idea which represents great power?"

"Of course." She bit her lip. "But I sent him down a convoluted path which should take years to unravel."

"Let us hope he does not punish you for the diversion." Sherlock shook his head in disapproval. "When will you learn not to fight fire with fire?"

"I shall follow your example, Sherlock." She smirked.

He sighed. Once Belle got into university, there was no telling where it would take her. No doubt far from him. "As for university, I cannot control what you shall do with your newfound knowledge. I expect you will pursue an academic career."

She shook her head in disagreement. "I can't imagine ever leaving detective work. It is too exciting."

He felt his mood lift. "Excellent news."

"Just as I can't imagine ever tiring of science."

"It is our lot in life, is it not?" It was sometimes shocking how much alike they were.

But what of me, Belle? Will you ever tire of me? I expect you'll meet some young man at this university of yours. My brain is strong, often to the exclusion of all else. There are those who believe my heart is stone, but, indeed I am a man and I do have one.

It is the most fearful thing I have ever encountered—more terrifying than the thought of losing my life.

But I find I love you, Belle.

"It is an exciting time in life for a young person," he added.

"You're not so very old, Sherlock."

"I recall when you said quite the opposite."

"You manage to get about, don't you? Quite agile, actually." She blushed. "You have a habit of growing on people, Sherlock."

Chapter forty-five
Partners

"I loved her against reason, against promise, against peace, against hope, against happiness, against all discouragement that could be." – Charles Dickens, "Great Expectations"

"Do I?" He felt a strange hope rise in his chest. "In what way?"

She leaned in close, seated across from each other as they were. He could smell lavender and roses in her hair. "You know, for the longest time, I thought you were insufferable, Sherlock."

"Is this your expression of gratitude for my gaining your entrance into university, Miss Belle? Or your apology for cavorting with my arch foe? I confess that I am not always enlightened on the sweet and sensitive ways of the fair sex."

"You're funning me, Sherlock."

"Am I?"

"Naturally I respected you and appreciated the opportunity to learn from you. But you have always been difficult."

"I see. I might say the same for you, Miss Belle, if I were less civilized, as you appear to be."

She giggled. "I'm sure you would. But now I feel completely different towards you." She took his hand, and he didn't attempt to remove it.

"Which is?"

"Sherlock, you're . . ." her voice grew soft. "You're my best friend."

The hope that had been in his chest dashed even as he felt a surge through his arm with her touch. He made no attempt to smile, which could only have appeared false, as it was not felt.

Your friend. *And yet you fall in love with every other man who comes into your vicinity.*

Much to his chagrin, she continued. "Everything good I have in my life has been from you, Sherlock."

"I certainly haven't done anything with that intent," he said stiffly.

"Oh I know, it was all for your cases. And yet you have introduced me to every manner of person I would have considered derelict before I met you. Now I see them as human."

"And you have seen some not so human individuals." It felt strangely natural to be sitting here and touching hands as they spoke. The hurling of insults aside.

Her golden brown eyes shone as she looked at him, and he suddenly found he didn't care. She was . . . *his Belle.*

"Those as well. And people who are different from me whom I judged—who didn't become real until I met them as individuals."

"As in Mycroft?"

"Yes. A person with a heart and soul just like mine." She sighed, withdrawing her hand and placing it on her cheek. "Though perhaps I am not as kind as some."

Assuredly not.

"And you are pleased with this change, Miss Belle?"

"Naturally I am. I was blind before. I thought I knew everything—and, with you, I have learned I knew *nothing.*"

"Many have said the same." He studied her. "And your religious views? How have you reconciled them to your revelations?"

"Jesus didn't come that I might cease having a brain—but that I might gain a heart."

"And the Bible?"

"The Bible speaks of the coming of the Holy Spirit, that we might have an ongoing relationship with God—who is not so frozen in time as we might imagine." She sighed. "The purpose of religion is not to feel superior and protect the authorities in power. Jesus *never* protected the authorities."

"No doubt the Christ would be repulsed by many of the organizations bearing his name." He shook his head disdainfully.

As if in response, she added, "You cannot blame this on God but on man. And I cannot be expected to toss out everything dear and meaningful to me."

"Ah yes, family and church. I have observed young girls especially fear being outcast by either."

"I am sorry the approval of your family has no meaning to you, Sherlock."

"To the contrary. I am well aware what I owe my family. How could I not be? But not to the exclusion of logic."

There was a long moment between them as they held each other's gaze. *Dash it all!* How could he have so much trouble knowing—and understanding—the thoughts of someone who was so transparent?

"I only wish . . . I wish . . ."

"Yes, Miss Belle?" It seemed wishes were rampant on this day.

"I wish you wouldn't be so critical of me. I do try my very best."

"I have to be critical in order to keep you alive, Belle." *Because it would break my heart if something were to happen to you. Before I met you I was quite happy without a heart.* He added softly, "None of us are invincible."

"I never thought to hear you say that, Sherlock. Instead of your always bossing and criticizing me," she smiled up at him, "I wish we could be *partners.*"

In an instant he rose from his chair and pulled her abruptly from hers.

Before he could change his mind he took her in his arms and kissed her, kissed her with all the attraction he had felt for her from the moment of meeting her, an electrical charge he had fought with every ounce of his being, channeling into anger and distancing.

"So do I, Miss Belle," he whispered in a gruff voice.

There was no distance now. He expected her to push against his muscular arms, but instead she looked into his eyes, her expression one of bewilderment.

Her eyes opened wide, disbelieving, and he felt like a fool. Above all, Sherlock hated to feel stupid.

The added rejection was gut-wrenching.

I've made a terrible mistake, forcing myself on Belle in an unwanted embrace.

What an idiot I am. How could I?

Because he had loved Belle almost from the moment of meeting her. He had watched her fall for every man but him.

Never in his life had he displayed the slightest inhibitions in anything, and, at almost thirty years of age he had found it suddenly necessary to hide his feelings, his inclinations, his very reactions from Belle.

And himself.

Kissing her was against his nature as well. *I never let my emotions control me.*

"Belle, I'm sorry, I wasn't thinking . . ."

"I know, Sherlock. For a moment you weren't thinking. I've never seen you throw logic to the wind before."

That was a low blow. He didn't think it was possible to feel any more disconcerted than he already did. Another state he detested: that of being out of control.

A slight smile formed on her lips. "I heartily approve."

His heart soared, but he quickly chided himself. *I mustn't take it to mean more than it did.* Belle was kind-hearted and forgiving, and she didn't wish to hurt or reprimand him, though she must.

Sherlock had to be certain what she meant. He abhorred assumptions in all things. This was not the way of the scientist.

Data, I must have data.

"You what? You liked it but you're sorry I kissed you, or you liked it but I should never have—"

As quickly as he had kissed her, she took his lapels in both her hands and pulled him to her— no small feat with a middle-weight boxing champion—planting her lips on his.

Very interesting. She used no words and yet conveyed her meaning clearly.

This is excellent data of undeniable legitimacy.

He kissed her thoroughly this time, claiming her mouth, caressing her soft lips with his own, pressing her body to his while attempting not to crush her.

After a long, glorious moment she pulled away again, gasping for air.

I've gone too far again.

But there was no mistaking her response. Even in her most passionate state, Fantine had not responded with that level of enthusiasm.

"But Watson. And then Mycroft. You seemed to admire every man but me. I understand, of course, I'm no catch, incorrigible, difficult—"

"Sherlock, I . . . I've always loved you, admired you, *hated you . . .*" she giggled. "But I never imagined you could love me back, I'm so inferior to you. So I cast my attentions everywhere else."

"No, Belle, you're superior in every way. And . . . you're *my heart.* My brain has always been my strength." He kissed her forehead. "And now, *my heart has come alive.*"

There was a sudden banging on the door.

"*Bloody Hell*, is there never a moment's peace?"

"I've never known you to want one before, Sherlock." Belle appeared dazed. "Oh, I suppose I should get the door. I forgot my duties for a moment."

"Never mind, my dear, I shall get it." He sprang to open the door.

Chapter forty-six
An Unwanted Education

"You have a child trailing the world's most powerful criminal?"
- Mirabella, "Sherlock Holmes and the Chocolate Menace"

"I quit, Mr. 'Olmes. Nothing is worth having to go to school for!"
Wiggins stood before Sherlock. Far from appreciating his new situation, he
was both angry and agitated.

"What is the problem now, Wiggins? Are you not receiving caviar with
your dinner? Or does your valet require a night off?"

"I've no complaint about the cottages. Them is sweet," Wiggins said
sadly, clearly not wishing to part with his new home though he deemed it
necessary.

"Good. I wish you might stop interrupting my work with your constant
demands. You're worse than a whining debutante and her lazy, socialite
mother."

Wiggins puckered his lips at the insult to his manliness. "I ain't no
wimp, Mr. 'Olmes! You can beat me, you can torture me, you can throw
me in jail—but don't expect me to go to school every day."

"This is not negotiable, Wiggins. School is a condition of staying
at the Fairclough cottages," Sherlock said simply. "And how are the
accommodations?"

The boy suddenly appeared wistful. "They'se very nice. Clean. No
vermin."

"And you're keeping the cottages pristine and the grounds neat and
pruned?" Sherlock asked.

"Oh, yes, sir. But we can't stay there. Not if we have to go to school."

"Perhaps you are unaware, Mr. Wiggins, going to school is the law,"
Mirabella said. "Since 1880, school is compulsory for children."

Sherlock stifled a smile. The girl wanted to make certain everyone in
her vicinity was educated.

He felt his heart soar for an instant as he glanced at her. *His love*. He
hoped she might remain so, but the nature of their business was fraught
with uncertainty. And change was Mirabella Hudson's nature.

"For those what are five to ten years old." Wiggins interrupted his
thoughts. I am almost thirteen."

"So you wish to be out-smarted by a five-year-old?" she asked.

"I ain't stupid!" he protested.

"Not that I have the slightest interest in your complaints, but what precisely is your objection to school, Mr. Wiggins?" Sherlock asked.

"The schoolmaster, he beats the boys with a cane if they so much as misspell a word. There's no talking—ever. And we have to sit in those chairs for four hours at a time. If anyone misses anythin' the schoolmaster makes 'em wear a dunce cap in the corner."

"So you don't like wearing a dunce cap, is that it, Wiggins?"

"For meself, I can take it, but I can't have me men treated that way. And the ragged schools is no better. That's why I never went afore."

Mirabella wiped her eyes with her handkerchief. "There is nothing I want more in the world than an education, Mr. Wiggins, and here you are throwing it back in our faces. I never met such an ungrateful person in my life."

Sherlock stifled a chuckle. She gave a performance worthy of the stage.

"We don't want book learnin', we want to learn something useful."

Sherlock could certainly sympathize with that viewpoint. "I can understand your feeling, Mr. Wiggins, having dropped out of university once I had learned everything I needed." Sherlock stared pointedly at Mirabella. "I have no degree, nor do I have any need of one."

Belle bit her lip, and he found himself curious to know what her unspoken retort was. He turned his attention to Wiggins, adding sternly, "That said, you'll learn to read, and you'll learn your figures, and after that, it's up to you."

"Were you ever in the schoolroom, Mr. 'Olmes?" Wiggins asked. "As a boy, I mean?"

"No, my father was the local justice of the peace, and I was educated by him, as was my brother Mycroft. Naturally we had a private tutor, but the majority of our education was experiencing the criminal justice system and the law from a young age."

"In a manner which was close to the people," Mirabella added. "If I recall correctly, court was often held in the local pub."

"It was the stuff of a great childhood: drunkenness, profane swearing, highway robbery, and rioting." Sherlock closed his eyes momentarily in sweet remembrance. "Smuggling, assault, and burglary. Pure bliss."

"That sounds like a bit 'o heaven," Wiggins said. "Then why must I go to school?"

"Because your father is not the J.P. and life is not fair," Sherlock opened one eye. "I had thought you were well acquainted with this fact, Mr. Wiggins."

"I think it might be too late for us, Mr. 'Olmes . . ." Wiggins said quietly.

"I see. So you believe you are unable to learn at this point?" Sherlock nodded gravely with understanding. He moved to his chair and began loading his pipe with tobacco. "I fear the same."

"Nothing of the sort," Mirabella objected, her indignation re-directed. "How dare that horrid schoolmaster make you feel that way."

Sherlock glanced up at her with interest before turning to the child. "So you don't have any objection to learning, Mr. Wiggins, only to the treatment of your men?"

"And the hours. We 'ave work to do. I can't work for you and be in school all the day."

"There are many children who go to school in the morning, work all day—even in the textile mills—and then do their lessons at night," Mirabella offered.

"Yeah, and I've seen 'em come out without arms and legs from being so tired," Wiggins protested. "Besides, the nighttime is our busiest part 'o the day."

"Very well," Sherlock said. "I'll obtain a private tutor for you, four hours per day, but you had better do me proud and show a return to my investment."

"Yes, sir."

"Are you quite through with your tantrum, Wiggins? Or is there anything else?"

"No, sir."

"The older boys can teach the younger. But sooner or later you're going to lose some of these boys to trade apprenticeships as you give them the tools to advance, you understand this, don't you, Wiggins?"

"Yep." Sadness crossed the boy's expression, but only for an instant.

"Believe me, I understand the inevitability of losing someone to ambition." Sherlock felt a sudden melancholy.

"It's a better life for them," Belle said. "It isn't right to hold anyone back from their true calling."

Sherlock raised his eyebrow at her even as her expression softened his mood.

Belle was young. He knew he could not hold her. But, in the meantime, his heart soared to think that she reciprocated his feeling in some small measure.

At least in this moment of time.

Wiggins shook his head in disagreement. "We have a job, now we 'ave a home, we work for the world's best private detective. There ain't no better life."

Belle caught Sherlock's eyes, sharing a stolen glance. Softly she added, "I have to agree, Mr. Wiggins."

"I daresay no one has ever had a more interesting life with more captivating company." A wicked smile formed on Sherlock's lips. "The company becomes more enchanting every day."

The Beginning
Of a Formidable Partnership

Thank you for reading this book

Thank you for reading this book. If you enjoyed it, this alone means the world to an author. We love to hear from our fans. Personal notes are always appreciated! Certainly I wish to correct any errors as well as hearing from my readers. http://suzettehollingsworth.com/contact/.

If you enjoyed this book, please consider writing a review. Reviews are the magical amulet of authors today and readers have a great power today. Without reviews, our books have no visibility on Amazon – and readers do not find them. If you like a book, the surest way to insure that an author can continue writing for a living is to write a review.

Thanks again to the excellent beta readers for this book who made such a positive difference: Renee Arthur, Lisa Millett, Susan Cambra, and Heather Chargualaf.

If you, as a reader, want to receive ARC (advance reader copies, kindle or word format) and become a beta reader, please email me through the contact form on my website, http://suzettehollingsworth.com/. Be advised that this is not be the finished book: the beta reader is an editor who helps create the finished product. I do not write a clean first draft.

If you want to write an honest review just as the book is going live, use the same form. This is very helpful in boosting the book's visibility. I will provide a free mobi or print book for this purpose.

Visit Suzette's website at www.suzettehollingsworth.com. You can contact her http://suzettehollingsworth.com/contact/. Like her on facebook "Suzette Hollingsworth".

Author's Notes
Sherlock Holmes and the Vampire Invasion

This is a work of historical fiction, meaning that some of the settings and characters are based on actual historical fact and that some of the characters and settings, as well as the plot, are fictional but possible given the right set of circumstances. In the best of worlds one wishes to time travel through books.

The PBS series "Victorian Slum House" is absolutely mesmerizing, and helps us to understand what it was like to be poor in Victorian times, as many people were. The middle class is a relatively new development. This show is eye-opening, life-changing, and fascinating. http://www.pbs.org/program/victorian-slum-house/

The workhouse:
The references in this book were modeled after the Andover workhouse, which was in Hampshire, not London. I used the name of the Saint Pancras Workhouse, which was in Middlesex, London just northwest of Whitechapel. St. Pancras was no European holiday or model of reform, but I don't believe it was anything in the league of Andover. I apologize here to St. Pancras; the use of the name was all about geography.

I read of an Andover account where a woman was separated from her 2-year-old baby and, because the woman begged to be able to care for her sick child, was beaten and forced to eat her own excrement. I was so disgusted that I didn't note the reference. It's hard to believe that someone could be so deliberately cruel to another person.

Inmates were allowed to come and go in the workhouse (unlike debtor's prison, which was literally a jail). Many people did leave and the workhouse primarily consisted of orphans, the elderly, and the sick: obviously it was so horrible that, if people had the wherewithal to get a job and to leave, they did. But it was also difficult to get a job, both in reality and because of confidence issues. And there were limited times inmates could leave if they choose to stay in the workhouse: they had jobs to do in the workhouse to pay for their food and shelter.

London is rainy and wet, and those on the street often slept sitting up because sleeping on the ground was a sign to the police that they were homeless; the police moved them along.

Fascinating first-hand account of the workhouse: "Indoor Paupers: Life Inside a London Workhouse", compiled by Peter Higginbotham. There are very few first-hand accounts in existence.
http://www.workhouses.org.uk/memories/
https://smile.amazon.com/dp/B00B4GUNAG

"The newspapers are pure gold in here. There are a few fortunate inmates who receive these regularly—perhaps from family members—and they are the kings of the establishment. They receive favoritism from all of the other inmates as well as extra bits of bread or tobacco in exchange for a half-hours borrowing of the news." – direct quote from workhouse inmate

"Children might also be abandoned by their families. Sometimes, when there were a large number of children in a family, a few of the children might be sent to the workhouse to ease the burden on the parents.

On arrival at the workhouse, children were separated from their parents, and even from their siblings if they were not the same sex."
From "Life in the Victorian & Edwardian Workhouse" by Michelle Higgs

"It is a lamentable fact if, in the midst of our civilization, and at the close of the nineteenth century, the workhouse is all that can be offered to the industrious laborer at the end of a long and honorable life. I do not enter into the question now in detail. I do not say it is an easy one; I do not say that it will be solved in a moment; but I do say this, that until society is able to offer to the industrious laborer at the end of a long and blameless life something better than the workhouse, society will not have discharged its duties to its poorer members." The Times (12 December 1891), p. 7., William Gladstone, Prime Minister

Drinking blood, it's not for everyone:
I do not personally drink blood and am not a proponent of drinking blood, but was astonished to learn that there are people who do so.

Is It Safe to Drink Blood? - Live Science
https://www.livescience.com › Strange News

"Jun 6, 2016 - You, however, are not a vampire bat. Because humans did not evolve such an iron-extracting mechanism, drinking blood can kill us. If you're thinking of sampling human blood, make sure there's a doctor handy — for you, not your victim."

"It was not always this way; across history, we can find cases where human blood was considered a bona-fide medical cure. At the end of the 15th Century, for instance, Pope Innocent VIII's physician allegedly bled three young men to death and fed their blood (still warm) to his dying master, with the hope that it might pass on their youthful vitality."

BBC - Future - The people who drink human blood
www.bbc.com/future/story/20151021-the-people-who-drink-human-blood
"Oct 21, 2015 - In many cities around the world, thousands of average people – nurses, bar staff, secretaries – are drinking human blood on a regular basis."

Blood Transfusions:

The first blood transfusion from animal to human was administered by Dr. Jean-Baptiste Denys, eminent physician to King Louis XIV of France, on June 15, 1667.[57] He transfused the blood of a sheep into a 15-year-old boy, who survived the transfusion.[58] Denys performed another transfusion into a labourer, who also survived. Both instances were likely due to the small amount of blood that was actually transfused into these people. This allowed them to withstand the allergic reaction.

"In the early 19th century, British obstetrician Dr. James Blundell made efforts to treat hemorrhage by transfusion of human blood using a syringe. In 1818 following experiments with animals, he performed the first successful transfusion of human blood to treat postpartum hemorrhage. Blundell used the patient's husband as a donor, and extracted four ounces of blood from his arm to transfuse into his wife. During the years 1825 and 1830, Blundell performed 10 transfusions, five of which were beneficial, and published his results. He also invented a number of instruments for the transfusion of blood. He made a substantial amount of money from this endeavour, roughly $2 million ($50 million real dollars).

In 1840, at St George's Hospital Medical School in London, Samuel Armstrong Lane, aided by Dr. Blundell, performed the first successful whole blood transfusion to treat haemophilia.

However, early transfusions were risky and many resulted in the death of the patient. By the late 19th century, blood transfusion was regarded as a risky and dubious procedure, and was largely shunned by the medical establishment.

Work to emulate James Blundell continued in Edinburgh. In 1845 the Edinburgh Journal described the successful transfusion of blood to a woman with severe uterine bleeding. Subsequent transfusions were successful with patients of Professor James Young Simpson after whom the Simpson Memorial Hospital in Edinburgh was named.

The largest series of early successful transfusions took place at the Edinburgh Royal Infirmary between 1885 and 1892. Edinburgh later became the home of the first blood donation and blood transfusion services.

It was not until 1901, when the Austrian Karl Landsteiner discovered three human blood groups (O, A, and B), that blood transfusion was put onto a scientific basis and became safer."
https://en.wikipedia.org/wiki/Blood_transfusion

footprints:

"Holmes's best use of footprints occurs in The Boscombe Valley Mystery, the sixth story, which he solved almost entirely on footprint evidence. After examining the ground around the site of the murder, Holmes tells Inspector Lestrade, "The murderer is a tall man, left-handed, limps with the right leg, wears thick soled shooting boots, and a gray cloak, smokes Indian cigars, uses a cigar holder, and carries a blunt pen-knife in his pocket." Despite Holmes's clue, Lestrade fails to apprehend Mr. Turner. Readers, however, are not surprised by the amount of detail in Holmes's description of the culprit. We have known since the second story, The Sign of the Four, that Holmes is an expert in footprints. There we learned that he had already penned a monograph entitled, "The Tracing of Footsteps with Some Remarks on the Uses of Plaster of Paris as a Preserver of Impresses". Indeed, throughout the Holmesian Canon our hero must deal with footprints on a wide variety of surfaces: clay soil, mud, snow, carpet, ashes, and blood."
https://en.wikisource.org/wiki/The_Boscombe_Valley_Mystery

Science:

Tyndall invented the thermopile in the late 1850's.

"It was actually Einstein who first came up with the idea of "stimulated emission".
First, Einstein proposed that an excited atom in isolation can return to a lower energy state by emitting photons, a process he dubbed spontaneous emission."
https://www.aps.org/publications/apsnews/200508/history.cfm

Cost of living, Victorian times:

http://www.victorianweb.org/economics/wages4.html

The Metropolitan Police 1829 ⚡ 1900:

"Between 1829 and 1830, 17 local divisions each with its own police station were established, each lettered A to V, allocating each London borough with a designated letter. These divisions were: A (Westminster); B (Chelsea); C (Mayfair and Soho); D (Marylebone); E (Holborn); F (Kensington); G (Kings Cross); H (Stepney); K (West Ham); L (Lambeth); M (Southwark); N (Islington); P (Peckham); R (Greenwich); S (Hampstead); T (Hammersmith) and V (Wandsworth). In 1865 three more divisions were created, W (Clapham); X (Willesden) and Y (Tottenham); J Division (Bethnal Green) was added in 1886."
https://en.wikipedia.org/wiki/History_of_the_Metropolitan_Police_Service

Victorian money:

http://www.victorianlondon.org/finance/money.htm
£1 (also shown as 1l.) was 20 shillings.
1 shilling (1s.), was 12 pence. Also often known as a 'bob', as in "I paid six bob for this",
Thus there were 240 pence (20 x 12) to every pound.
Other Victorian words to do with currency:-
1 guinea was £1 1s. (or 21 shillings) - ie. a pound with an additional shilling.
1 crown was five shillings. (and half-crown two and a half shillings, of course)
A half-sovereign ten shillings.
1 farthing was a ¼ penny.

ßow mucß ðið peopfe earn?

A matchbook-maker made about 18 pennies/day

https://outrunchange.com/2012/06/14/typical-wages-in-1860-through-1890/
This appears to be 30 cents/hour (for a man), machinist, etc. (or $2-$4/day)

In summary, skilled labor (men), 30 cents/hour; unskilled men, 10 cents/
hour, unskilled women, 30 cents/day.

The premise of the interesting PBS special "How Sherlock Changed the
World" is that, in Victorian times, there was no forensic investigation
of the crime scene, and that, these actually developed because of Arthur
Conan Doyle's creation. Prior to the introduction of Sherlock, according
to the show, the only methods utilized were interviewing and torturing
suspects.
http://www.pbs.org/show/how-sherlock-changed-world/

Women anð Ðentistry:

"People were amazed when they learned that a young girl had so far
forgotten her womanhood as to want to study dentistry" (Lucy Beaman
Hobbs, 1884)

"The practice of the woman dentist of the near future will be confined to
dealing with patients of her own sex and children."- 1914

Lilian Lindsay becoming the first woman to qualify as a dentist in the UK
in 1895. Further female members were slow to follow as English dental
schools were not accepting women applicants at this point. That would do
it.
https://bda.org/library/history/womenindentistry

"The first woman to establish herself in a regular dental practice in the
United States was Emeline Roberts Jones of Connecticut. In 1854, at age
17, she married a dentist, Daniel Albion Jones, and became "intensely
interested" in his work. After watching her husband work, she began filling
extracted teeth. She filled a two-quart jar with her work and then showed
her husband what she had done. Reluctantly, in May 1855, he agreed to allow her to practice with him in his Danielsonville office. Finally, in 1859,
he took her in as his partner. She enjoyed a reputation as "a skillful den-

tist"...she was the first woman to open her own office independently and offer her services to the public "as a competent dentist."
(Hyson Jr, JM. Women dentists: the origins. CDA Journal 2002; 30 (6): 444-54)

"People were amazed when they learned that a young girl had so far forgotten her womanhood as to want to study dentistry" (Lucy Beaman Hobbs, 1884)

Women and Education

Women could not be certified as doctors in Britain in this era. Women couldn't even get a bachelor of science degree until 1880 from the University of London (you will agree that the study of science and math is necessary to medicine).

There was one practicing female doctor in England, Elizabeth Garrett Anderson, from 1865 when she set up her own private practice because she was not allowed to take up a medical post in any hospital. The cholera epidemic in Britain made people more willing to receive assistance, even from a woman.

Garrett was a licentiate of the Society of Apothecaries; as a condition of their charter, they could not legally exclude her. After Garrett obtained her license to practice medicine The Society of Apothecaries immediately amended its regulations to prevent other women obtaining a licence. In order to take the test to obtain the license, Garrett had to hire private tutors in anatomy and physiology. She had been allowed previously into the dissecting room and chemistry lectures—and the male students forced her out, presenting a memorial to the school against her attendance as a fellow student.

America was way ahead; the first female doctor in America was Elizabeth Blackwell in 1849.
https://en.wikipedia.org/wiki/Elizabeth_Garrett_Anderson

There is a wonderful account of Philippa Fawcett (4 April 1868 – 10 June 1948), daughter of the prominent Suffragist Millicent Fawcett, and niece of Elizabeth Garrett Anderson, achieving the highest marks in the Cambridge Mathematical Tripos exams (1890).
"There was a great and prolonged cheering; many of the men turned

towards Philippa, who was sitting in the Cambridge Senate gallery with
Miss Clough, and waved their hats.... She was, of course, tremendously
delighted."

Fawcett received a much more positive response from her male counterparts than is described in other accounts of women competing with men,
so I wonder what the difference was. I would be very interested to know.
For men to raise their hats and cheer is a fairly strong response of support.
I'm not a big fan of man-bashing anyway, as there were good and wonderful men through-out history and today, as well as some horrible women.

Even though Philippa's score was 13% higher than the second highest
score, she was not named "Senior Wrangler", the accolade going to the
highest-scoring male student. Nor could she even claim to have a degree,
only to have the passed the degree examinations. (Kenyon 74-75).
Kenyon, Olga, ed. 800 Years of Women's Letters. Stroud: Sutton, 1994.

"Coming amidst the women's suffrage movement, Fawcett's feat gathered
worldwide media coverage, spurring much discussion about women's
capacities and rights."
https://en.wikipedia.org/wiki/Philippa_Fawcett

"In Cambridge the question of awarding degrees to women caused bitter
controversy. The question arose (again) in 1897 and was overwhelmingly
defeated, provoking near riots in Cambridge by university men opposing
the move. Women did not become full members of the university in Oxford until 1919 and in Cambridge until 1948.

The University of London is usually credited as the first institution to open
its degrees to both sexes on an equal basis (except for medicine) in 1878,
but the pattern of women's admission is complex and much depends on
definitions. In 1907 University College London (a segregated woman's
college which in 1878 offered degrees in the Sciences, Arts and Laws to
women) ceased to have a separate existence and was incorporated into the
University of London."
http://www.london.ac.uk/history.html

Mathematics ⸱ too hard for women?
"We ought to recognize that the average girl has a natural disability for
Mathematics. One cause may be that she has less vital energy to spare"

Herbert Spencer believed that female evolution, meaning intellectual evolution, had stopped at a stage before man's in order to preserve vital organs for childbirth. If a woman undertook rigorous 'brain work' such as mathematics, energy could be diverted from her reproductive system, threatening fertility and general wellbeing." – Herbert Spencer, 1912, 22 years after Phillipa Fawcett took top honors Cambridge Mathematical Tripos exams (1890).

In line with Arthur Conan Doyle's depiction of Sherlock Holmes and John Watson:
January 6, 1854: Sherlock Holmes' birthday. Mycroft 7 years older
John H. Watson's birthday on July 7, 1852   1.5 years older than Holmes
Mirabella's birthday: Nov. 7, 1863

Many of the characteristics depicted in this book were introduced by Arthur Conan Doyle, e.g., the description of John Watson's campaign in Afghanistan and resultant insomnia, the description of Mycroft as a lazy but brilliant mid-level bureaucrat, the description of 221B Baker street, and the statement of Sherlock's parents as being country squires. Although not explained by Arthur Conan Doyle, it is a fact that a country squire might live on the largest manor, and would very likely be the local Justice of the Peace. All the explanations surrounding this is consistent with the history of the day. The location of Sussex as the family home is my own invention, but is in line with Doyle saying that Sherlock retired to Sussex. Arthur Conan Doyle made very little mention of Sherlock's family, parents, home, and no mention of siblings outside of Mycroft. These additions were in line with the framework established by Arthur Conan Doyle and were written with the idea of "making sense" within that framework. Mirabella Hudson is my own creation.

It does seem very likely that Sherlock Holmes would need a female operative, doesn't it? He cannot play every role. Some readers who are avid fans of Arthur Conan Doyle do not want a feminine presence in any books containing Sherlock Holmes as a character. There cannot be giggling or emotions, and the feeling must be somber and intellectual because, naturally, there were no women in Victorian times.

I have attempted to write a book true to the original characters and the Victorian ambiance. I understand that some readers want to read a book which was written exactly as Doyle would write it, but those works are still all here. This is a pastiche. Nothing can diminish Doyle's genius. That is why the Jane Austen and zombie books do not take away from or diminish Jane Austen: she was a literary master and nothing can detract.

from her talent and the enjoyment of her works.

Author Bio

Suzette Hollingsworth grew up in Wyoming and Texas, went to school in Tennessee (Sewanee), lived in Europe two summers, and now resides in beautiful Washington State with her cartoonist/author husband Clint, Barney D. Barncat, George Cloney (who looks just like Casanova Coffee Cat) and StingRay the miniature poodle. It is her dream to be a snowbird and to head south in the winter.

Suzette's writing style combines wit with elegance and has been described as "Sherlock in Mr. Darcy mode" by a reader.

She is also re-publishing her historical romance series ("Daughters of the Empire"), previously published by Bookstrand: The Paradox, The Serenade, and The Conspiracy.

Suzette's goal in writing historical fiction is that you, the reader, will engage in a magical journey and time travel through her books. She is very excited about her current Sherlock Holmes series in which Mrs. Hudson's niece is a potential love interest amidst these Victorian mysteries. Sherlock Holmes is a great, fun hero to write because he is liked from the get-go despite being pompous and insufferable (or perhaps because of it!), something which might result in an unsympathetic hero in another narrative. The series draws on the imagery surrounding the beloved Sherlock Holmes and Dr. Watson (Robert Downey Jr. and Jude Law, in particular, though the author is a fan of all versions, including Jeremy Brett and Basil Rathbone), incorporates the witty banter into the relationship between Sherlock and Mirabella, and lends itself well to Steam punk, blending the "Age of Invention" with something old-fashioned, elegant, and slower-paced.

Enjoy. *The game is afoot.*

Also by Suzette Hollingsworth

"The Great Detective in Love" mystery series:
Sherlock Holmes and the Case of the Sword Princess
Sherlock Holmes and the Dance of the Tiger
Sherlock Holmes and the Chocolate Menace
Sherlock Holmes and the Vampire Invasion

"Daughters of the Empire" historical romance series:
THE PARADOX: The Soldier and the Mystic
THE SERENADE: The Prince and the Siren
THE CONSPIRACY: The Cartoonist and the Contessa

Coming in 2018:
"Sherlock Holmes and the Confirmed Bachelor"